MEDICAL

Life and love in the world of modern medicine.

Vet To Heal His Heart
Caroline Anderson

Flirting With The Florida Heart Doctor
Janice Lynn

MILLS & BOON

A VET TO HEAL HIS HEART
© 2024 by Caroline Anderson
Philippine Copyright 2024
Australian Copyright 2024
New Zealand Copyright 2024

First Published 2024
First Australian Paperback Edition 2024
ISBN 978 1 038 93895 4

FLIRTING WITH THE FLORIDA HEART DOCTOR
© 2024 by Janice Lynn
Philippine Copyright 2024
Australian Copyright 2024
New Zealand Copyright 2024

First Published 2024
First Australian Paperback Edition 2024
ISBN 978 1 038 93895 4

MIX
Paper | Supporting
responsible forestry
FSC® C001695
www.fsc.org

Published by
Harlequin Mills & Boon
An imprint of Harlequin Enterprises (Australia) Pty Limited
(ABN 47 001 180 918), a subsidiary of HarperCollins
Publishers Australia Pty Limited
(ABN 36 009 913 517)
Level 19, 201 Elizabeth Street
SYDNEY NSW 2000 AUSTRALIA

Cover art used by arrangement with Harlequin Books S.A.. All rights reserved.

Printed and bound in Australia by McPherson's Printing Group

A Vet To Heal His Heart

Caroline Anderson

MILLS & BOON

Caroline Anderson is a matriarch, writer, armchair gardener, unofficial tearoom researcher and eater of lovely cakes. Not necessarily in that order! What Caroline loves: her family. Her friends. Reading. Writing contemporary love stories. Hearing from readers. Walks by the sea with coffee/ice cream/cake thrown in! Torrential rain. Sunshine in spring/autumn. What Caroline hates: losing her pets. Fighting with her family. Cold weather. Hot weather. Computers. Clothes shopping. Caroline's plans: keep smiling and writing!

Huge thanks to SarahRossi@TamingTwins
for the Marry Me Chicken recipe,
the missing ingredient in the story
without which this book would not be the same!

And, as ever, to my long-suffering and apparently
endlessly patient editor Sheila Hodgson, whose
guiding hand has hauled me back from the brink on
countless occasions over the past almost twenty-five
years. Thank you from the bottom of my heart.

CHAPTER ONE

FINALLY!

Ellie turned onto the drive with a sigh of relief and stared at her little house for a long moment.

She'd saved hard for a deposit and since she'd bought it three years ago as an investment she'd let it to tenants to cover the mortgage. She'd never lived in it herself because she hadn't needed to, but she did now, so thank goodness it was available.

It shouldn't have been. Wouldn't have been, if it hadn't been for her tenant doing a midnight flit a few weeks ago. She'd been furious at the time, but now she was grateful that it was empty, even if, in the words of the agent, it needed 'a little attention'. But that was fine. Thanks to Craig she had time on her hands now, if nothing else. Certainly no job security, that was gone and the rent-free flat that went with it...

No. She wasn't going down that rabbit hole again. Time to find out what 'a little attention' actually meant.

She sucked in a deep breath, then turned to look at Lola in the back seat. After six horrendous hours in heavy traffic, it wasn't just Ellie who was more than ready to get out of the car. Her little black Lab was sitting up now, her face expectant, tail wagging, and Ellie dredged up a smile.

'This is our new home, Lola. It's going to be great!'

Maybe her voice had been more convincing than she

thought, or maybe the dog was just as relieved as she was, but she jumped up, and Ellie got stiffly out of the car, let her out and led her to the front door.

The paint was a little chipped and faded now, but that was hardly a major issue. She slipped her key in the lock, turned it and stepped inside.

And stopped.

A little attention? It smelt stale and unpleasant, and she wouldn't feel happy until she'd scrubbed it from top to bottom and cleaned all the carpets. Lola was busy sniffing, and she led her through the sitting room to the kitchen at the back and peered out of the window.

The light was fading, but she could see the once-tidy garden was a mess and heaven knows when the grass was last cut. Well, her agent had warned her, and it wouldn't take long to get it in order. Like the house, it was only tiny and easily manageable. She let Lola out for a wee and a sniff and left the door open while she went to check out the rest of the house.

She'd furnished it sparsely when she'd bought it three years ago, but everything was tired and dirty now, the mattress grubby, the bathroom filthy, and her optimism hit a brick wall. She came back down and sat with a plonk on the bottom step, her usually relentless optimism crushed.

What had she been thinking? Yes, she owned the house, but she knew nobody in Yoxburgh, and her rose-tinted family holidays here seemed worlds away. And the house was awful now. Beyond awful, really. 'A little attention' didn't even scratch the surface.

She sat up straight. No. She just needed to clean it, get the paintbrush out and—

The loud yelp made her turn her head sharply, and she ran out through the kitchen and found Lola limping towards the door. Even in the fading light she could see the thin spurt of blood from her right hind leg, and her heart went into overdrive.

'Lola! Oh, sweetheart...'

She needed a vet fast, but how to get her there before she bled out? She laid Lola down on her side, pressed her thumb firmly over the femoral artery high up in her groin above the wound to stop the bleeding, and studied it carefully. Whatever Lola had slashed herself on, she was pretty sure it wasn't glass. The cut wasn't clean enough for that, more a jagged tear, and it was just above her knee on the inside of her thigh, so she could get a pressure pad on it. If she had one...

She held her fingers on the artery while Lola whined and struggled to get free, stripping off her sweater and thin vest-top, swapping thumbs, then she balled the top up into as firm a wad as she could manage one-handed and wrapped her scarf tightly around it to hold it in place over the wound.

Lola did her best to resist, and at one point she put her teeth on Ellie's hand, not hard, just a gentle protest, but Ellie knew it must be very painful for her.

'Good girl, it's OK, I've got you, sweetheart, it's going to be all right,' she murmured, but she wasn't sure if it was. Tying it tight enough to stop the bleeding was next to impossible, and Lola wasn't helping, but it was as tight as she could get it and at least it had slowed the blood flow down.

So now what?

Back to the car and head to the nearest vet. She'd been scoping out the practices online this morning with the intention of visiting them to ask about locum work, and the closest by miles was just three streets away in a big old Victorian house. She'd driven past it on the way here, and they had excellent reviews. She tugged her sweater back on hurriedly, carried Lola to the car and set off, praying that the makeshift tourniquet would stay put until she'd got there.

Please be open, please be open, please be open...

There! Yoxburgh Veterinary Practice. She swung through the open gates into the empty car park in front of the building, jumped out and ran to the door. She could see lights on at the back, but the entrance was in darkness, and her heart sank. She rang the bell and pounded on the heavy old door.

Please be open...

Nothing. She fumbled for her phone and rang the practice, and was automatically transferred to the night service. It was miles away, but she'd been watching the wound as she'd phoned, and she could see the blood slowly seeping through the wadded-up top and her scarf every time she took her hand off the pad.

If she didn't get help soon, Lola was going to die.

She felt a sob rise in her throat as she hung up and pressed hard on the pad, and Lola whined and licked her hand.

'Oh, baby. I can't lose you, not like this, not now after everything else...'

She fought down the sobs, kneeling on the edge of the back seat and stroking her sweet, gentle dog with her other hand while she tried to work out what she could do. Move her to the front seat so she could reach to press on the pad as she drove? No, the front seat and footwell were packed to window height and it would take too long.

So—leave her in the back and drive fast? She couldn't, not that fast. If she took the pressure off she'd bleed out in minutes, and the tourniquet, such as it was, had already been on nearly ten minutes.

Five more minutes and the leg would be compromised...

Stay there all night pressing on it until the surgery opened again, and resign herself to Lola losing her leg?

Or just pray for a miracle?

So much for their new start. If only she'd stayed put—but she couldn't have, not after what had happened, and now everything was falling apart and Lola was going to die. She'd never felt so helpless in her life.

She went back to the door and pounded on it again.

'Where *are* you?' she wailed. 'Why won't you open the door?'

But they didn't. Whoever was in there was ignoring her, and she went back to Lola, leant on the pressure pad again and stroked her head gently with a hand that shook with grief and guilt and horror.

'I'm sorry, sweetheart. I'm so, so sorry...'

The pounding on the door seemed frantic, and Hugo hesitated another few seconds and gave in.

He went out through the staff entrance, Rufus at his heels, and saw a car in the car park, the back door hanging open. A woman was half in, half out of it, giving him a distractingly tempting view of a gently rounded bottom in snug jeans.

He ignored the inappropriate urge and was gearing up to explain that the practice was closed when he heard a wrenching sob that made his heart sink. So much for his quiet Friday evening walk with Rufus...

He peered in at her. 'Can I help you?'

She turned her head, her face streaked with blood and tears, a strand of dark hair clinging damply to her cheek. He didn't wait for a reply, just told Rufus to stay and ran round to the other side of the car and opened the door.

A dog, a black Labrador by the look of it, still alive but

bloodied and whimpering, and the woman was leaning on some kind of makeshift bandage on her hind leg.

'What happened?'

'No idea. I let Lola out into the garden and heard a yelp and she was hosing blood—'

'OK, let's get her inside. I'm Hugo, by the way. And you are?'

'Ellie.' Her eyes held his and he could see hope in them. 'You're the vet?'

'Yes.'

Another wrenching sob made her whole body convulse, and he took over, lifting the injured dog into his arms and carrying her swiftly round to the side door. He opened it with his elbow and went inside, Rufus beside him, and he sent him to his bed and headed straight through to the prep room, putting the dog down on the table.

'It's OK, Lola, I've got you, sweetheart,' he said gently, and the dog licked his hand and gave a quiet whimper. A trembling, bloodied hand reached out and stroked the dog's head, and he leant on the makeshift pressure pad and looked up and met Ellie's distraught eyes.

'Right, tell me everything you know.'

Her voice had a tremor, but her words were calm and concise. 'It's her femoral artery. No idea what she tore it on, I'd just let her out for a wee, but it's a jagged cut, so most likely not glass. I did what I could to contain it, but she's probably lost two hundred mils, maybe more?'

He gave an inward eyeroll. She'd probably spent her life watching vet programmes. 'That's a wild guess,' he said, but she cut that off with her next words.

'It's an educated wild guess. I'm a vet.'

He met her eyes again. 'Seriously?'

She rolled her eyes, echoing his thoughts, which under normal circumstances he would have found funny, but this wasn't exactly normal. But if she really was a vet...

'Do I look as if I'm joking? My dog is bleeding out, and that pressure has been on for about twelve minutes now! Can you please just give her a GA and clamp the artery before she bleeds to death or you have to amputate her leg?' Her voice cracked on that, and he frowned.

'I'll call my nurse—'

'You don't need a nurse, Hugo, I'm a vet! I've got all my paperwork in the car, or you could call my old boss James Harkness, but we don't have time for that now. Please—before it's too late?'

His mouth opened, but then he clamped it shut and held her eyes.

Come on, come on...

'You know Jim?'

'Yes. He owned my old practice. I worked with him for eight years.'

Another pause, then, 'OK,' he said at last, and her shoulders sagged with relief. 'Right,' he went on, stepping up a gear. 'You hold this while I get everything ready, and once I've got her under I can clamp that artery and get a proper look at it. Meanwhile tell me a bit more about her, please.'

She watched him, heart pounding, itching to do it herself, hoping he'd do things the way she would, and while he prepped at lightning speed, she filled him in.

'She's got no pre-existing conditions that I know of, no contra-indications, she weighs twenty kg. I gave her a general anaesthetic to drain an abscess at the back of her mouth three and a half weeks ago, she was fine for that and it's healed well. She hasn't eaten since this morning, she had a drink about three hours ago.'

'Good.' He was moving briskly and efficiently, doing what she would have done. Warming a bag of Hartmann's in hot water because Lola would need the compound sodium lactate solution to replace her lost blood volume, pulling up the induction agent, checking the anaesthetic gas in the vaporiser, selecting an ET tube, and she began to think they might after all be able to save Lola and her leg.

He clipped the hair on the front leg that hadn't been recently cannulated, asked her to hold it while he slid the needle in, and moments later Lola was asleep, intubated and out of pain. 'OK, let's move her into Theatre,' he said, and they carried her through and he connected her up to the gas. He was setting up fluids, injecting pain relief and antibiotics, checking Lola's stats, moving reassuringly swiftly. Then he looked up and met her eyes again.

'Right, we're good to go,' he said, then added, 'Which end do you want?' which surprised her.

The leg, because she wanted to know exactly what was going on in there, but she didn't know where anything was in his theatre, and anyway, her hands were shaking too much and vascular surgery needed steady hands. And she realised she trusted him.

Not that she had a choice…

'You do the leg, I'll monitor her.'

To her relief, he did exactly what she would have done.

Keeping his thumb on the artery, he removed the makeshift pressure pad, then released the pressure carefully.

Blood welled in the wound, but at least it didn't spurt.

'It might have closed up a bit,' she said hopefully, but as

soon as she said that it started again, a thin stream streaking out across the room, and he shook his head and clamped the artery.

'OK, let's clean this up and get a better look. Up the fluids, please. We need to boost her circulation now.'

She'd already done it as soon as the artery forceps were on, and she watched as he filled the wound with sterile gel to protect it from the clipped hair, ran the clippers over the inside of Lola's thigh, scrubbed the skin with chlorhexidine, sucked out the gel and irrigated the wound thoroughly.

Just what she would have done. She heaved an inward sigh of relief.

'How's she doing?' he asked without looking up.

'She's fine. All good.'

He nodded, laid out all the instruments he'd need, then while he scrubbed she opened the outer packets ready for him.

'OK, let's get a good look at this.'

He laid a sterile drape over the leg, blotted the wound with a swab, and she leaned over and studied it with him. The artery was punctured, but it was also grazed, not extensively but enough that it would need a skilled vascular surgeon to fix it.

'That's a nasty graze. Can you repair it?' she asked without any real hope, but he shook his head.

'No. If it was just the tiny hole, I'd give it a go, but the graze has damaged the vessel wall and I don't have the equipment or skills for fine vascular surgery. It needs a graft.'

'So what do we do?'

'Tie it off and hope? The artery's been clamped for a few minutes but her foot's still warm, she has good perfusion of the tissues, so I reckon she's got a good enough supply from the other vessels. She should be fine, but realistically, we have no other options.' He looked up and met her eyes. 'Unless you want her to go to a specialist? We can probably get her stable enough. Up to you.'

She shook her head. 'No. I've tied it off in a similar case, and frankly, if she's got enough of a blood supply to that leg for it to survive the journey, it's probably fine anyway.'

He nodded, and his gloved fingers explored the wound carefully.

'Nothing in there that I can feel. You've got no idea at all what she cut it on?'

'No, none. I'd literally just got the keys off the rental agent and walked in, and I'd got no idea what's in the garden, so I should have been more careful.'

He raised an eyebrow. 'X-ray?'

She nodded. 'Might be an idea, as I haven't got a clue what it was. She was probably racing round like a mad thing. She'd been in the car for six hours.'

He winced, and she pulled a face.

'Yeah. Long story. I'll tell you later.'

He wondered what the story was, but it would keep.

He X-rayed the leg, studied the images closely and tried not to think about the scent of something delicate and delicious drifting from her hair as she leant close to look at the screen.

'I can't see anything,' she said.

'No, nor can I.' He straightened up and told himself to focus. 'OK, let's close it.'

He tidied up the wound, debriding the edges so they'd come together in a clean line, tied off the artery and then hesitated.

'Does it need a drain in the dead space so she doesn't get a seroma?' she asked, echoing his thoughts, and he nodded.

'I'd rather put it in and take it out if it's not needed than have to do it later. Negative pressure drain?'

'I would.'

He made a tiny hole through the skin to the centre of the wound, slid in the fine flexible tube and taped the drain in place, then repaired the muscle damage before he drew the edges of the wound together and closed it with a continuous soluble suture. Then he squeezed the empty drain bottle and attached it to create suction in the wound and watched as a thin trickle of pink-tinted serum filled the fine tube. He gave a satisfied nod and looked up. 'How's she doing?'

'Fine. Stable.'

'Good. I'll get some local into that so it's not too sore when she wakes up, and then let's bring her round and see how she is.'

He stepped away from the table, pulled off his gloves and gown and binned them while she monitored Lola.

She was slowly coming to, but still sleeping, her breathing slow but steady, and together they put her into a mesh vest, tucked the suction bottle into it up against her tummy and then Hugo carefully moved her into a kennel and covered her with a warm blanket.

Ellie sat down onto the floor beside the kennel, her legs suddenly too weak to hold her. Lola was alive, her foot was warm, and she wasn't going to die. She realised she was shaking uncontrollably, and she felt a gentle hand on her shoulder.

'Hey, it's OK. She's going to be all right.'

Hugo hunkered down beside her, his hand still on her

shoulder, warm and reassuring, and she turned her head and met his eyes. They were the kindest eyes she'd ever seen, and she couldn't hold that gentle, understanding gaze. She turned her head away again and blinked back tears.

'Have you had anything to eat or drink recently?'

Recently? Hardly. She shook her head. 'Not since this morning. I had a bit of water when I stopped to let Lola out, but—no, not really.'

'I'll knock something up. You OK with pasta and pesto?'

'Um—yes, fine. Sounds lovely. Thank you.'

'Good. I might even have some parmesan.'

She dredged up a smile, suddenly realising how hungry she was. 'Even better.'

He went through a door into what she assumed was a staff room. She could hear him talking to his dog, the sound of a food bowl being chased around the floor, and he came back a couple of minutes later with a large mug full of steaming tea.

'It's got sugar in it—and don't argue, just drink it,' he said over his shoulder as he walked away again.

She didn't argue. She was beyond arguing, and his kindness suddenly overwhelmed her. She put the tea down, buried her face in her hands and gave in to the tears.

She was crying. He could hear her as he ran back downstairs from his flat with the ingredients from his fridge, the quiet sobs tugging at his overused heartstrings.

He wondered again what the 'long story' was. Something that had taken her alone on a six-hour journey, ending up in a rental place with a garden that was clearly unsuitable for a young, energetic dog like Lola. Or any dog, really, by the sound of it.

He dumped the fresh pasta into boiling water, drained

it, stirred a hefty dollop of pesto into it, grated the parmesan generously over their brimming bowls and carried them through.

'Here you go,' he said, and sat down cross-legged beside her.

She'd stopped crying now, and he could see why. Rufus was curled up in her lap, and she was stroking him with one hand and nursing her mug with the other. He called the dog over to his side, and he lay down between them, sharing the love. She got the head end, he noted wryly.

He handed her a bowl, and she put the tea down and took it with a smile and a hand that was still shaking. Low blood sugar? Shock? Exhaustion?

All of the above, probably.

They ate in silence.

She was glad of that. She was too tired, stressed and hungry to engage in polite conversation, and it seemed he was, too.

But then it was done, her bowl scraped clean, and she put it down and met his eyes. They were slate blue, and she thought they could see to the bottom of her soul, but that kindness was still there in them and she felt oddly safe. 'Thank you. That was amazing. I really needed it.'

'Yeah, me, too.' He smiled, his mouth tipping up a little on one side. 'You'll feel better soon.'

'I do already,' she told him honestly. 'I can't believe how kind you've been. It's restored my faith in human nature.'

'I haven't billed you yet,' he reminded her with a wry smile, and she gave a fractured little laugh.

'No, you haven't, but I'm sure you will.'

He chuckled, then held out his hand. 'It's probably time

we introduced ourselves properly,' he said. 'I'm Hugo Alexander, and this is my practice.'

She knew that already from her research last night, but she took his hand—the warm, strong and yet gentle hand that had squeezed her shoulder and reduced her to tears, that had saved Lola's life and leg with quiet competence—and she smiled at him.

'Eleanor Radcliffe. Ellie to my friends,' she added, and he cocked his head on one side, a smile playing around his lips.

'So, *Ellie*,' he said with quiet emphasis, 'this long story…'

She looked away from those kind yet piercing eyes that would see too much and gave a little shrug. 'Oh. That. I'm sure you've heard it before. I was working in Jim's practice in the Cotswolds. He was a brilliant boss, but he was getting on and he wanted to retire, so he stepped back and made me senior vet, which was great for a while, but things had moved on, some of the equipment needed upgrading, and he didn't want to invest any more in it, so he decided to sell it to a corporate.'

'Was that a problem?'

'Not initially. The building needed investment, and it was going to get it, which had to be a good thing. And then within a year the corporate sent in a new senior vet over me.'

'Ah…'

She threw him a wry smile. 'It's not what you think. He was an ex from uni days. We'd had a brief relationship, I'd dumped him when I realised he was a lying, cheating snake, then he'd said stuff about me that wasn't true that caused a rift with my best friend—and then he reappeared in my life and got his revenge.'

'How?'

'Oh, picking fault here and there, snide remarks, trying to

undermine me with my colleagues—it went on for months, then we had a row over Lola, and I lost it.'

He frowned. 'What kind of a row?'

She sighed and looked over her shoulder at Lola. 'Her owner brought her in. She'd been off her food for a day or so, could barely open her mouth and her eye was being pushed out of the socket by something—a tumour, an abscess—I didn't know and I couldn't see without an anaesthetic, but her owner said she couldn't afford it, didn't have insurance because it was too expensive—she was heartbroken.

'She loved Lola to bits but she wasn't well herself, she was struggling to look after her properly, and she was utterly distraught. She'd tried every rescue place she could find without success, and now, with this issue, she thought it would be better for Lola if she was dead than facing an uncertain future, so she asked me to put her to sleep. And she's three. There was nothing wrong with her apart from whatever was going on in her mouth, she's a beautiful dog and she didn't deserve to die. I couldn't let that happen.'

'So you treated her for nothing?'

She shook her head. 'No, because that wouldn't have solved the problem going forward, but I said I'd take her on, keep her myself, give her a home for life and she signed her over to me on the spot. It turned out to be a massive abscess at the back of her jaw. She'd yelped when she'd been chewing a stick in the woods a few days before, her owner had said, so it was probably blackthorn or hawthorn, but I drained the abscess and flushed it, it healed up really quickly, and I paid the bill.'

'So what was his problem?'

She sucked in a breath. 'I'd used my staff discount for her treatment, and then Craig refused to give it to me, billed me in full for the initial consult, the op, the drugs, the dispensing fee, the kennel time, the overnight care, even though I'd done all that myself while I was off duty... He said it was company policy, which was a crock of nonsense. A staff discount was in my contract and he knew it, but he said the dog hadn't been mine at the time of the first consultation, so technically it was down to the previous owner, and if I didn't pay up he'd bill her.'

He frowned. 'That's horrendous. So what did you do?'

'I paid it, because I didn't want her being hassled and I don't want a bad credit rating, so I told him exactly what I thought of him, finished my shift, wrote a stinking letter to the company, went up to my flat over the practice, packed up all my stuff, put it in the car and drove away with Lola. I spent last night in a dog-friendly motel, got up this morning, spoke to the rental agent and drove here.'

His eyes widened. 'So this was only yesterday? You were lucky to find a house to rent so quickly.'

'Oh, no, I didn't, it's mine. I've been letting it, but a few weeks ago the tenant did a flit and left it in a bit of a state, so I thought—well, I don't know what I thought, really, but maybe I'd been naïve imagining I could just drive up here and move in, but I can't live in it, not like it is. Maybe I should have been less impulsive and stayed, but I just—I couldn't even look at Craig any more I was so angry.'

'I can see that. So when was her op?'

'Three and a half weeks ago. The Monday.'

'And he's only just now decided to bill you?'

'Yes. He didn't know anything about it. He started a three-week holiday the day Lola came in, so he didn't know. Then someone said something about Lola, and he looked at the accounts yesterday afternoon, and it all hit the fan.'

* * *

Hugo leant back against the wall, taking it all in.

'Wow. That's quite a twenty-four hours you've had.'

She laughed, but it ended on a tiny sob. 'Tell me about it. And now my poor little house turns out to be lethal, filthy and—I can't take her back there, not with a wound, and I have nowhere else to go.'

'No family?'

'No, my mother's in Spain.'

No mention of a father. He wondered why. 'No boyfriend, partner, significant other?' he asked, realising as he'd said it that he was blatantly fishing.

'No other at all. Just me and Lola.'

She shot him a smile, but it didn't look convincing. 'So there you are. I'm jobless and unemployable, I have a broken dog, and my house is bordering on uninhabitable.'

He frowned again. 'Why?'

She stared at him. 'I just told you why. The tenant—'

'No, I mean why are you unemployable?'

'Are you serious?' She gave a tiny huff of laughter without a trace of humour. 'You didn't see my letter! And I'm in breach of contract because I didn't give three months' notice, so who's going to employ me with a record like that? And I didn't hold back when I talked to him, so I wouldn't fancy his reference,' she added with a wry smile.

He grunted. 'Yeah, I can imagine.' He studied her face. It was still streaked with blood, her sweater was on inside out, her tired green eyes were red-rimmed and exhausted, but she still had fight in her. Impressive.

He took a deep breath, let it out again, and said, 'I have an idea. Feel free to say no, if you want to, but I'm short-staffed tomorrow.' He rolled his eyes. 'That's nothing new,

I'm permanently short-staffed, but the locum who was doing tomorrow morning is sick. If you can show me all the appropriate certification, how do you fancy covering the shift?'

'But what about Lola?' she asked without missing a beat, and he smiled. He wasn't in the slightest bit surprised that the dog was her first thought.

'Lola needs to stay in overnight, probably for at least two nights, and we have a bed in the office that the night vets used before the staffing situation got ridiculous. You're welcome to stay and look after her tonight, do the shift tomorrow, and when that finishes we can go over to your house and blitz it together.'

She stared at him. 'You'd do all that for me? For a perfect stranger you know nothing about?'

Her eyes were welling with tears, and he had to stifle the urge to wrap his arms around her and kiss the tears away. He gave himself a mental kick and stuck to the facts.

'I know quite a lot about you. I know you're a competent vet, I know your dog comes first, I know you did exactly what I would have done under the circumstances, and I'm not being entirely altruistic. I do need a vet for tomorrow. I need another vet, full stop, so you could look on it as an interview, if you like?'

'An *interview*?'

'That's what I said.'

She looked away, then looked back at him, her face awash with a whole raft of conflicting emotions, and he held his breath.

Ellie, please say yes...

CHAPTER TWO

ELLIE STARED AT HIM, trying and failing to read his expression.

Could it really be so simple?

She blinked away the tears and felt one slide down her cheek. She swiped it away crossly with her hand, and it came away tinged with blood.

She tried to laugh, but it cracked in the middle. 'Gosh, I'm such a mess. How can you even consider employing me?'

'How?' he asked, sounding incredulous. 'Because I need a vet? Because you clearly know what you're doing, and you're passionate about your job?'

'How on earth do you know that?'

'Because you took Lola on and treated her because it was the right thing to do, and today you stood your ground and made me help you. So that's twice she would have died if you hadn't stepped in to help her. You saved her life today under really tricky conditions—'

'No. *You* saved her life.'

'No. You did, by getting that tourniquet on, getting her here and making damn sure I helped you fix her.'

She felt her cheeks colour. 'Sorry, I'm not normally that pushy.'

'It's fine, you were fighting for Lola, and if it helps, I would have done exactly the same thing.'

She stared down at herself and laughed in despair. 'Look at me! My sweater's on inside out! How on earth did I do that?'

His mouth twitched, and he gave a soft chuckle that resonated inside her in a weirdly unsettling way.

'Er—one-handed, while you wrestled with a dog that I'm guessing wasn't being too cooperative? It's not rocket science and I imagine you had bigger things to think about.'

A vivid image of Lola struggling as she tied the scarf around her leg flashed into her mind, and she shuddered.

'I guess I did.'

Behind her, Lola gave a little whine, and she reached out and laid a hand on her head, stroking it gently. 'It's all right, Lola. I'm still here. It's OK, there's a good girl.'

Her tail thumped gently, and a wet tongue came out and licked Ellie's hand. She struggled up onto her elbows and looked around, clocking Hugo, and her tail thumped again.

'What a sweetheart,' he murmured, shifting in beside Ellie, so close that she felt the breath jam in her throat as he held out his hand for Lola to sniff.

She licked it, then looked round at her leg.

'Leave it, Lola,' he said, easing her head back down gently and stroking her to distract her, and she sighed and settled again.

Then he sat back on his heels, and Ellie breathed again.

'She's going to need the cone of shame,' she said, trying to focus on Lola and not the lingering masculine scent of his body, and he nodded ruefully.

'Yes, she is, otherwise she'll have that drain out in a minute.' He cocked his head on one side. 'So—what's your answer?'

She turned her head and looked at him, just inches away,

and the breath jammed in her throat again. Those slate-dark eyes, so kind, so mesmerising, so intense...

'Did you mean it?'

'What, that I need a vet? Absolutely.'

She laughed softly. 'No, I believe that. I meant about helping me clean the house.'

He frowned. 'Of course I meant it. Lola needs to rest, anyway, and the first thing we need to do is find out what she cut herself on and deal with it. So—locum tomorrow?'

'On one condition. I do the shift for free in exchange for your help.'

'That's ridiculous.'

'You haven't seen the house yet,' she pointed out, and then added, 'I don't want your charity, Hugo. Take it or leave it.'

She held her breath, and then he gave a soft huff of laughter that echoed through her again as he gave in.

'OK, I'll take it—but only if you do the shift in exchange for Lola's treatment.'

'What? No! Absolutely not.' Ellie shook her head firmly. 'Anyway there's no need. She's insured.'

That expressive eyebrow quirked at her. 'Is she? Even though you've had her less than a month?'

She had. Damn. 'I can pay you,' she said, wondering exactly how she was going to do that, but his mouth twitched, drawing her attention again to those firm, sculpted and oh-so expressive lips.

'Lord, you are stubborn.'

'I am,' she retorted, dragging her eyes and her mind off his mouth. 'So what's it to be?'

He let the smile out then, and her heart quickened. 'I'll take it.'

She smiled back, relief flooding her, her pride restored.

'Good. My paperwork's all buried in the car somewhere but I could call Jim?'

His smile was warm and it made her heart hitch. 'Yeah, do that. I did a practice rotation with him when I was training. He's a great guy. Be good to talk to him again.'

She pulled her phone out of her back pocket, glanced at the time to see if it was too late and decided that nine fifteen would be OK. She rang him, and he answered immediately.

'Jim, it's Ellie. I have an odd request. I'm with Hugo Alexander, and—'

'Hugo? Really? How is he?'

She laughed. 'Stressed and overworked, I think. He's looking for a locum. Could you vouch for me, please?'

'Of course I can. Put him on.'

She handed the phone over, and watched Hugo's face as Jim spoke. At length. Hugo looked across at her, his eyes alight, that expressive mouth twitching. 'So you rate her, then, Jim?' he asked, and Jim started again.

'I'll take that as a yes. Thank you.' He was silent for a moment, then added, 'Ah. You'd better ask her that,' and he handed the phone back. 'He wants to know how come you're here.'

Jim's voice was concerned. 'Ellie? What's happened?'

'Yeah, I had a bit of an issue with the new senior vet. We have previously, and I—er—I walked out. Long story, I'll tell you another time, but it's not your fault. This was strictly personal and a bit of a vendetta on his part.'

'Oh, Ellie, I'm so sorry,' Jim said heavily.

'Don't be. It's not your fault, Jim, you did what was right for you and right for the practice. You had no control over who they hired, and neither did I.'

'No, apparently not, but it sounds like you're well out of

it. You'll be all right with Hugo, though. He's a good lad. You can trust him.'

She hoped so, because right then she was all out of options. She said goodbye, hung up, met his eyes and raised a brow. 'Well?'

'According to Jim, you're the best vet he's ever had. I reckon that'll do me.'

He unfolded his legs and stood up, picked up their empty bowls and held out a hand, pulling her to her feet and sending tingles all the way down her arm.

'Why don't you get some fresh clothes from your car and see if you can find that paperwork, and I'll get the buster collar for Lola and keep an eye on her. There's a shower out the back, I'll find you a towel. And leave your clothes outside the shower, I'll throw them in the washing machine to get the blood off.'

She emerged from the shower feeling infinitely more civilised, to find he'd taken her clothes away. He'd also changed, so she guessed his scrubs were in the wash, too. And he'd put a pile of bedding in the office for her.

'I thought you might want to sleep next to Lola. You know, so you can hear the second she moves?'

She felt her shoulders drop as yet another worry fell away from her. 'That would be amazing. I was contemplating setting an alarm to check on her every half hour.'

He frowned. 'You can't do that. You need your sleep. You've got another long day tomorrow. I've topped up her pain relief, but she'll need to go out before you go to bed.'

She nodded. 'Where can I take her?'

'I'll show you, I've got to take Rufus out anyway now. I normally set the burglar alarm when I knock off, but I'll

show you how it works so you can set it and unset it in the
night if you need to take her out again.'

He led her out through the kitchen at the back, and into
a garden. She wasn't expecting that, somehow, but as the
light came on automatically she could see a large square of
lawn with shrubs and trees around the sides against the old
red brick walls, and an area of paving with some seating.

Rufus trotted off and started sniffing around, and Lola
followed, limping a little unsteadily down the gentle ramp,
then making her way onto the grass. She didn't bother to
sniff, just bopped down awkwardly.

'Good girl,' Ellie said softly when she was done, and the
dog turned and made her way back inside to her kennel without a fuss, lying down and letting out a big sigh.

'She's doing well.'

'She is. I'm so grateful to you—'

He rolled his eyes. 'You're like a stuck record. Wait till
tomorrow, I'll get my own back.'

She somehow didn't think so. Nothing she did could ever
make up for his care and kindness, but doing that shift for
him might go some small way to redress the balance.

'I found my paperwork,' she told him. 'It's on the desk
in the office.'

'Great. I'll take a look in the morning. Right, let's get
this cone on Lola so she can't rip the drain out while you're
asleep, and then I'll move your bed.'

They had to shoo Rufus off the folding bed before they
moved it out beside Lola's kennel, and he showed her where
the light switches were, put on a dim nightlight so she could
see Lola, and showed her how to set and unset the alarm,
a necessary evil because the drugs on the premises were a
prime target.

CAROLINE ANDERSON   31

Then he handed her a slip of paper. 'My mobile number. Call me if you're worried about her and I'll come down. I live over the practice.'

That didn't surprise her, she'd done it herself until last night, and lots of vets with small practices did the same. It was the 'I', not 'we', that struck her, but it might not be significant. And anyway, it was none of her business.

'Thank you. I'm sure she'll be fine. Will my car be OK outside? It's just it's got my whole life in it right now.'

'It should be if you've locked it. I'm about to close the gates and there's CCTV on the drive.'

She felt another layer of stress peel away and smiled at him. 'That's great. Thank you.'

He went out through the side door and she watched him go, her mind whirling as she made up the bed.

He needed a vet. He wanted her to 'interview' for the post by doing the shift tomorrow. Was he serious? And would she contemplate it, so soon after the fall-out of the last one? But Jim had called him a 'good lad' and said she could trust him, and he'd been nothing but kindness...

He came back in then, cutting off her tumbling thoughts. 'Right, that's me done. Help yourself to anything you want in the kitchen, and shout if you need me. I'll be down here by seven. Sleep tight.'

Not a chance. She had far too much to think about. She dredged up a tired smile. 'You, too. And thank you, Hugo. For everything.'

His eyes creased into an answering smile that did something strange to her midsection. 'You're welcome. Rufus, come on, you're not sleeping there,' he said, and Rufus hopped down off her bed and trotted after him.

They went through a doorway, and she heard his footsteps

recede as they made their way up, leaving her alone with Lola and her thoughts.

Did she want to work here? Maybe—and maybe not, or not long term. But—locum? At least that way she'd have an income while she decided.

She lay down fully dressed, with her head close to Lola's kennel so she could see her just by turning her head. She'd settled down, and after a moment Ellie heard a gentle snore.

Poor Lola. What a start to their new life together, but at least they wouldn't starve, so maybe it wasn't going to be so bad after all…

She slept surprisingly well, and so, to her relief, did Lola.

She picked up her phone and looked at the time.

Six forty-three. He'd said he'd be down by seven, so she threw off the covers and got up, turned off the burglar alarm and checked on Lola.

She wagged her tail but didn't move. Not surprising, really. Her leg would be sore this morning, now the pain relief had worn off, but she hadn't complained once in the night and she'd accepted the cone without argument.

She put the fold-up bed away in the office, coaxed Lola out of her kennel, took her out for a sniff and a wee, then put her back in her kennel, had a quick wash and was heading for the kitchen when she heard the light patter of little feet running down the stairs, followed by a heavier tread, and Hugo and Rufus came through the door.

'Morning,' he said cheerfully, all freshly showered and smelling delicious. He handed her a neatly folded pile of yesterday's clothes.

'Gosh, that was quick! Thank you.'

'Pleasure. How are you both today? Did you sleep?'

'Better than expected,' she said with a wry laugh, trying not to think about how good he smelt. 'That bed is seriously comfy and Lola slept all night.'

'Good. I'll have a look in a minute. Ready for the fray?'

'I will be when I've eaten something. Can I make some toast?'

'Sure. Stick a couple of bits in for me while I have a look at Lola. Has she been out?'

'Yes. She seems fine, but a bit sore, I think.'

'I'm sure. I'll give her another shot. I just want to check her leg for the circulation, make sure it's not cold or swelling—'

'It isn't. It feels fine, which is a relief. I just wish I knew what she'd cut it on.'

'Well, we'll find out later, won't we? How about the drain?'

'The bottle had a little in. I left it for you to see.'

'Have you fed her?'

'No, not yet. Her food's somewhere in the car, but it's buried. I'll get it.'

'Is she a fussy eater?'

She laughed. 'She's a Labrador. What do you think?'

His mouth twitched. 'I'll give her something bland, then, see how she gets on with it. She may not want much.'

'Tea or coffee?'

'Coffee. White, no sugar. There's a machine in the corner and pods on the side.'

To his relief, Lola's foot was warm and not swollen and the drain was doing its job. She greeted him with a wag of her tail and a lick, and didn't even flinch when he gave her the painkilling injection, just inhaled her breakfast and lay down again. She was very lame, but that was to be expected, and she'd accepted the plastic cone around her head without too much fuss.

She seemed an utter sweetheart, and he could absolutely see why Ellie had refused to put her to sleep. He would have done the same under the circumstances. *Had* done the same, hence Rufus, and he hadn't regretted it for a moment.

He sorted out the suction drain, then went back to the kitchen, drawn by the smell of toast and coffee. They took it through to the office and after he'd looked through her paperwork they went through the morning's appointments together.

'OK, I've switched things around a bit, given you all the routine stuff, but we've got Kerry in, she's our head nurse, and she'll be able to give you a hand if you can't find anything. Oh, and I've found you some scrubs to wear.'

He showed her how the computer system worked, then swivelled round and met her eyes. 'Any questions?'

Too many.

She was still reeling with the shock of the last forty-eight hours, and she was glad he'd given her the simple consults, but there would still be much she didn't know about the practice.

'Can you give me a quick guided tour?'

'Sure.'

He got up and led her through a door to the reception desk in a corner of the waiting room. It was a lovely room, with a bay window to the front, high ceilings and ornate plaster cornicing. There was a screened waiting area for cats, and across the hall, past the lobby with the beautiful old front door she'd pounded on last night, was the main waiting room and doors to the two consulting rooms. They had doors at the back leading via a corridor to the stock room and pharmacy, the X-ray room and the areas she'd already seen. These areas, unlike the waiting rooms and entrance at the front, were modern, crisp and clinical. Pretty standard fare, really, and nothing she hadn't seen before, but spotlessly clean and very well equipped.

'Happy?'

She nodded, feeling a flicker of nerves, the word 'interview' hovering in the back of her mind. Actually, make that front…

'I'm fine.'

Her list of consults had been, as he'd promised, simple and straightforward, and Kerry had been a huge help. She'd also kept an eye on Lola, and said she was doing fine.

One less thing to worry about.

She saw her last client of the morning and was just filling in the details on the computer when there was a tap on the door and Hugo stuck his head round.

'Are you done?'

'Pretty much. I'm just writing the last one up.'

He closed the door and propped himself against it, somehow sucking all the air out of the room. 'How did you get on? Was everything OK?'

Was it? She'd thought so, but maybe Kerry had raised some concerns?

'I think so.'

'Kerry thinks so, too. She basically told me if I don't offer you the job she's going to walk.' He shrugged away from the door and shot her a grin that turned her heart inside out. 'Fancy a quick sandwich before we go and tackle the house?'

'Um—yes, please, that would be great. I'll just finish up here.'

He nodded and walked out, and she stared after him.

Had he just offered her a job?

Maybe… And maybe she was reading too much into it. She closed the file, shut down the computer and followed him out.

While Ellie took Lola out to the garden for a moment, he loaded his car with milk, teabags and a packet of biscuits, the carpet shampooer and cleaning stuff and some gardening tools, then once Lola was settled he put Rufus in his crate in the office and followed Ellie to her house.

It was small, modern, unprepossessing but innocuous—until you got inside.

'Hmm,' he grunted, and Ellie looked over her shoulder and gave him a wonky little smile.

'See what I mean?'

His answering smile felt every bit as crooked. 'Well, you didn't lie, let's put it like that.'

He followed her through the tired and grubby living room into the kitchen. 'This looks OK. I think you can rescue it with a bit of elbow grease.'

'I can, it just needs a good scrub. The rest is harder—especially the garden.'

He nodded, a glance through the window enough to make his heart sink. Then she opened the back door, and the full story of last night's horror with Lola was revealed.

'Wow,' he murmured, staring at the stains all over the paving. 'She really was hosing blood.'

'She was. It's a miracle I managed to slow it enough to

get her to you. Goodness knows what's lurking in the grass to tear her to shreds.'

Whatever it was, he couldn't see it. It was well and truly hidden by the overgrown grass and the tangle of weeds. No wonder she'd felt so defeated last night. Time to sort it out.

'Right,' he said briskly, 'I'll find out what tried to kill her in the garden while you tackle the kitchen, then we can have a cup of tea and work out a plan for the rest of the house.'

Ten minutes later she was on her knees scrubbing the kitchen floor when he propped himself up in the open doorway.

'I think I've found the culprit. There's a coil of barbed wire with a loose end hanging out into the grass, and there's blood and hair on one of the barbs. I'm guessing that's what she caught her leg on. Come and see.'

She followed him out and studied the wire thoughtfully. 'I think you're right. It's the right height, and it looks vicious enough. Poor Lola.'

He shot her a sympathetic smile. 'Absolutely. And poor you, too. Did you say you had a letting agent?'

She suppressed a sigh. 'Yes.'

'Well, I have to say I don't think they earned their commission, not by the look of it. I would have thought at the least they'd have had it cleaned up.'

'I told them not to bother. He said it needed a little attention, so I'd already booked a week's leave to come up here to clean it. I just ended up coming a day early, but I think he might have been a tad frugal with the truth.'

The snort said it all, and she smiled wryly. 'Yeah. My thoughts entirely. Shall we drag the wire out of the grass so you can mow it and find out what else lurks beneath?'

'I've got a better idea. You go back in and finish cleaning up the kitchen, and I'll sort this out.'

It wasn't just the barbed wire—not that that wasn't bad enough, but he ended up going over the mercifully small lawn with a fine-tooth comb and pulling out all sorts of stuff that had just been dumped. Plastic bottles, nappies, broken crockery, a bamboo cane from some long-dead house plant, the occasional brick...

And until it was all out, he couldn't cut the grass.

He tipped the last lot of rubbish into the bin and headed for the kitchen door, just as she opened it.

'I've made some tea. Are you finished?'

He laughed at that. 'Not exactly. I've got the worst of it, so I might run the strimmer over it next and then rake it all off.'

'After you drink tea and have a biscuit,' she said, handing him a mug. 'Sorry about the chip, the crockery seems to have suffered along the way.'

'Yeah, I found some in the grass, along with everything else.'

'I'm not surprised. Come in and sit down. You should be safe, I washed the chairs.'

Two hours later they were back at the practice, tired but satisfied with their progress. The kitchen was clean, the sitting room was almost respectable, and she felt much more positive.

And grateful, because Hugo had been a Trojan in the garden, and it looked worlds better—which was just as well, as Lola was going to have to start using it very soon.

Immediately, if it hadn't been for Hugo's insistence that Lola couldn't be moved yet, and she couldn't argue with that.

'I should be able to stay there tomorrow night,' she said, for the umpteenth time, but he just leant back in his chair, Rufus curled up on his lap, and raised an eyebrow, his eyes sceptical.

'What, on that mattress? You need to wash it first at the very least—or replace it. And anyway, there's Lola to think of. At least here it's reasonably sterile and she can stay as long as she needs to.'

She sighed. 'I suppose you're right, and she's fine in the kennel while she recovers, but I'll go back there tomorrow and carry on until I've finished, then we should be able to stay there.'

He gave her another of those looks. 'On a wet mattress.'

'Or a new one.' Although she couldn't really afford it…

'Or you could just stay here?'

'What, sleeping by her kennel?'

He hesitated for a moment, as if he was about to say something else, then shrugged. 'Or in the office. It makes sense, at least as long as she's got the suction drain. She looks wiped, and after you took her out when we got back she went straight back into her kennel and went to sleep again. She needs more time, Ellie, you know that. There's no rush, and if you're with her you can keep a better eye on her, and reassure her.'

He was right. Of course he was right, but she felt like she was imposing on him, taking advantage of his good nature, and he'd already done enough. More than enough. Starting with saving Lola's life…

'OK. Just until Monday, though. That should give me time to get a replacement mattress from somewhere, and get everything clean.'

'We should be able to make some decent progress on it

tomorrow,' he said then, taking her completely by surprise, and she stared at him.

'We?'

He frowned. 'Well—yes. I said I'd help.'

'You said you'd help *today*. I can't ask you to do that—'

'You didn't ask. I offered. And anyway,' he added with a grin, 'I'm trying to convince you I'm a decent human being so you'll take the job.'

She stared at him blankly. 'What job?'

Hugo did a mild double-take. 'The one I offered you this morning?'

Her heart thudded against her ribs. 'That was a serious job offer?'

'What did you think it was?'

She blinked and looked away. 'Uh—I don't know. I didn't realise you meant it.' And then she looked back and met his eyes, sincere and oddly intent. 'You seriously want me?'

Her words hit him like an express train, and he realised they were true—in every sense.

His heart thudded against his ribs, and he swallowed the sudden lump in his throat. 'Yes, I want you,' he said honestly. 'I need you.' And as he added that, he realised it, too, was true in every sense.

He ignored the thrashing of his pulse as he forced himself to hold her searching eyes. 'I desperately need another vet,' he said, to himself as much as to her. 'I think last night and this morning were a pretty good interview, Jim Harkness couldn't pile enough praise on your head—what else is there to think about?'

Apart from the fact that every time he caught the waft of scent from her body his gut tightened, every time she smiled or frowned or scraped that unruly tendril of dark hair back out of her incredible green eyes he wanted to kiss her—

He looked away, unable to hold that steady gaze for another second, not knowing what she might read in his eyes. He'd been told more than once that he'd be a lousy poker player.

'Can I think about it? I'm not sure I'm ready to commit to anything permanent yet. It's all been a bit sudden.'

He made himself meet her eyes again. 'Sure. I don't suppose you want to locum while you think?'

He held his breath while she hesitated, and then she nodded slowly. 'OK. Just for a while, until I decide what I'm doing with my life, and Lola's a bit better.'

That sounded a hugely sensible idea, and it meant neither of them would be committed to what already felt like a complicated relationship, at least on his side. And that was the last thing he needed. Thank goodness he hadn't offered her the flat. He'd been so close to it just now. He allowed himself to breathe again and hauled out a smile.

'Excellent. I think that calls for a celebration. How about a takeaway? I'll let you choose.'

By the end of the next day the upstairs was cleaned, the mattress included, and the bathroom had been scrubbed within an inch of its life, and with the windows open and a lovely fresh breeze blowing through the house everything was drying nicely.

'Better?'

She smiled at him and laughed. 'Much better. So, so much better. I don't know how to thank you, Hugo. You've been amazing.'

He chuckled softly and turned away before he did something stupid like haul her into his arms and kiss that smiling mouth.

'I had to do something to keep you on board,' he said lightly, and then picked up the carpet shampooer. 'I'll put this lot in the car while you shut the windows, and then we need to get back to the dogs. I think Lola's drain's probably ready to come out now, but I want to have a proper look at her first.'

'If she's OK and you've got a crate I can borrow, she and I can stay here tonight now.'

He frowned. 'Really? You've got no food, the mattress is still damp—what's the rush? And anyway, Lola isn't out of the woods yet, she'll need cage rest for another two weeks and you're working tomorrow, so you might as well be there or you'll have to move her backwards and forwards, which won't be comfortable for her. Besides, I've got a lasagne thawing and I can't eat it all.'

His logic was unassailable, but she still felt as if she was taking advantage. Plus, she was worried about the bill for Lola's in-patient treatment. All of it, really, because she'd taken out insurance for her after her abscess, and that wasn't yet a month. And anything in the first month was excluded, as he'd pointed out.

She thought about that all the way back, and as soon as they were in and the dogs were fed, she tackled him about it.

'You need to bill me for Lola's treatment and her care,' she said, and he raised an eyebrow and smiled.

'I think we've gone a little past that now, don't you?'

She frowned. 'But—'

'No buts. We'll be horrendously busy tomorrow morning with all the people who've hung on over the weekend so they didn't have to pay the out-of-hours rate, on top of an already full clinic, so I'll well and truly be getting my own back. And anyway, you're doing most of the caring, and we're hardly short of kennel space.'

He wasn't going to budge, she could tell that just from the look he gave her, but there was still room to negotiate.

'On one condition,' she said firmly. 'I don't want the standard locum rate, I want you to work out what you'd pay for a full-time vet, divide it by the number of hours they'd work, and pay me that pro-rata. And I'll pay her bill. You can give me a staff discount if it makes you feel better.'

One eyebrow quirked up. 'You're cheating yourself.'

'No, I'm just not cheating *you*. I don't need to rip you off, I just need to earn enough to live on. Take it or leave it.'

'And if I say no?'

'Then you're a vet down tomorrow.'

He held her eyes, then a slow smile tipped his mouth at one side, and he nodded, and she felt the tension seep out of her. 'You're a very stubborn person, do you know that?' he said mildly, and then with a little shake of his head and a tiny huff of laughter, he looked down at Lola, resting in her kennel and watching them.

'We need to check that drain,' he said, and closed the subject.

CHAPTER THREE

THERE WAS NO 'easing in gently' or giving her the simple stuff on Monday morning. After an early start to sort Lola out, she was straight in with a dog spay, a cat castrate and then a cruciate repair on a terrier who'd snapped a ligament in his knee joint.

Kerry must have given him a heads up on that, she realised, as he stuck his head out of his consulting room.

'I think he probably needs a lateral suture. Are you happy to do that?'

'Sure. I've done it before—I've got an ortho certificate.'

He nodded. 'Good. Kerry'll give you a hand, help you find what you need and assist. Shout if you run into any issues.'

'Will do.'

She didn't, to her relief, and after she'd finished the operation and they'd X-rayed him and Ellie was confident the joint was going to be stable, she and Kerry put him into a small kennel cage in the area where Lola was lying, looking bored.

At least her drain was out and her leg was healing nicely. It would still take a good while, but she'd be left with a fine, neat scar and a functional leg, thanks to Hugo.

She was relieved by that. Poor Lola had had enough to deal with. 'Hello, sweetie,' she said, giving her dog a little tickle through the bars, but there wasn't time for more, even though Lola was pleading and pawing at the door.

'I'll take her out for a wee,' Kerry said, and Ellie left them to it and went to see if there were any more consults she could help with.

She was on the last one, a little spaniel puppy called Mr Wiggles in for his second vaccinations, when the door at the back opened and Hugo stuck his head round.

'I hear there's a puppy,' he said with a grin, and he came in and gave the wiggly little pup a cuddle while she drew up his vaccinations.

He obviously knew the owner, and they chatted while she gave him the injection.

'Oh, you're such a good boy,' Ellie said, ruffling his long floppy ears, and he wiggled and licked her.

'They're so forgiving,' his owner said with a laugh, and carried the puppy out, leaving her alone with Hugo.

'So how's it been?'

'Busy? Good? Let me fill this in and we can talk about it.'

'Tell me over lunch, I'll make you a coffee,' he said, and she glanced up at the clock. Half past one, and consults started again at two.

'Thanks,' she said, and he left her to it. By the time she emerged three minutes later there was a coffee and a sandwich waiting for her in the kitchen, and she took it into the office and sat down with him.

'So, tell me all about your morning. How did you get on?'

'All right, I think. The spay and castrate were routine, and the cruciate repair seems stable.'

'Yeah, I had a look. Nice tidy job.'

It had been and she didn't really need his praise, but nevertheless it was good to hear, and she felt a silly little glow of pride. What a contrast to Craig, still bitter because she'd dumped him ten years ago.

Hugo, on the other hand, seemed like a genuinely decent human being. To date he'd been nothing but generous towards her, and she owed it to him to do her best in return.

'What are you doing tonight?' he asked, and she swallowed her bite of sandwich and shrugged.

'Moving my stuff into the house, I guess. Taking Lola home with me, settling her in, buying some food—is it OK if I borrow a crate for a while?'

Hugo frowned. 'Ellie, you're welcome to a crate, but I don't think she's ready yet. She can't jump into the car, she can't do steps, she has to be on cage rest—I've been thinking, why don't you keep her in the kennel here and move into the flat upstairs till she's better?'

She stared at him. 'Hugo, you—I can't just move into your flat, it's ridiculous!'

'Not *my* flat,' he said hastily. 'There's another one, at the top. I'll show you later. I'm assuming you'd bring Lola to work every day anyway, wouldn't you?'

'Well, yes, if that's OK, but—'

'That's fine, then. She can lie here in the crate in the day for a change of scenery, and she can go back in the kennel at night. She'll have plenty of company, lots going on, you'll be able to keep an eye on her, and it won't stress the wound.'

She stared at him, slightly stunned. 'But—I thought you'd want us out of the way?'

'You're not in the way. And she's a sweetheart, she's no trouble. The flat's fully equipped, so you'll only need clothes and anything else you might want, so after we shut up shop I'll give you a hand to empty your car, and you can sort out what you want up there and put the rest in the store room, if you like?'

Did she like? She wasn't sure. He'd done so much for her,

and being independent was hard-wired into her DNA, but nevertheless it seemed churlish to refuse his help after he'd already been so generous. And then there was the question of the rent, but she had no choice really while Lola was so immobile, she knew that. She just hoped she could afford it.

'Thanks for the offer, but I've got plenty of room for my things at the house, if you don't mind me leaving Lola here while I go and dump them?' she said, and he got to his feet.

'Sure. We can sort out the details later,' he said, drained the last of his coffee and headed out, and then Kerry came in, followed by Jean, the practice manager.

'Ah, Ellie, I need your bank details and all the other HR stuff for the records,' Jean said to her as she stood up to follow Hugo out. 'Not urgently, but when you can?'

'Sure. I've got to empty my car later, it's all in there. I'll give it to you tomorrow if that's OK?'

'That's fine. It's good to have you here, by the way,' she added. 'Hugo's been struggling for too long, and with our only other full-time vet off on maternity leave it's been ridiculous, so we're all really relieved that you turned up when you did.'

'I'm only locuming,' she said, feeling the net of commitment tightening around her, and Jean smiled knowingly.

'So he tells me, but you're still very welcome.'

And now she felt guilty for refusing to consider a permanent job.

Although the door to that was also still ajar...

As soon as she'd finished for the day she fed Lola and let her out, then put her away again and headed for the house.

It was the first time she'd been in it alone since Lola's accident, and she stood for a moment, listening to the silence.

Would it ever feel like home?

Weird thought. She'd never lived in a home that she owned, but it still felt like someone else's. Moving in might help, but Hugo of course had had a view about that and the moment Lola's leg was healed enough she'd be here like a shot.

She ferried all her belongings into the house, dumped them on the floor and stared at the pathetically small pile. It was everything she owned, but now she had a permanent base—

Did she want it to be that? Not necessarily. It didn't need to be, although apparently it could be, if Hugo had his way.

Did she want to take the job he'd offered, live here in Yoxburgh, start to put down new roots in a place she'd always loved but never really known?

A bit of her—the bit she didn't trust, because it had shown pretty lousy judgement in the past—said yes. The rest, the bit that had told Craig exactly where to stick his job, said no.

She didn't know enough about Hugo.

Yes, he'd been kind, yes, he'd been highly spoken of by her old boss, but what would he be like to work with? Fair, definitely, she was sure of that, but it all seemed too easy, and she didn't trust 'easy'. Not now, after all that had happened. And another job going wrong, if it did, would firmly put the kibosh on her CV. No. She'd locum for him, but that was it. She really, really wasn't ready to commit herself again so soon, and especially not to someone as charming as Hugo. She couldn't trust it. Couldn't trust *him,* whatever Jim had said.

She went through the pile of bags, pulled out the things she might need, stacked the rest under the stairs and then headed back to the practice with—not dread, exactly, but reluctance.

She knew it made sense, she knew Lola couldn't easily be moved backwards and forwards yet, but right now she felt so dislocated that she was desperate for a home of her own.

And she was going to be living in Hugo's flat. Well, not *his* exactly, but as good as. Was that a good idea? It didn't sound like it, but he was frankly too kind for his own good and she owed him so much already that she didn't really want to put on him any more. But she felt stressed and a bit cornered, and if it hadn't been for Lola…

If it hadn't been for Lola she'd still be working with the odious Craig, but she wasn't, and Lola had to come first.

She drove into the car park just as Hugo was parking his car, and he got out and waved a shopping bag at her.

'Supper,' he said, and she felt another wave of guilt to add to the stress.

'Hugo, you should have sent me a shopping list! I didn't even think about food, but I can't keep sponging off you.'

'Don't be ridiculous.'

He closed the gates and locked them, and she followed him in through the staff entrance, bags in hand.

'Right, I'll just get Rufus and we'll take all this up and go and eat.'

'What about Lola?'

'She's fine, I checked on her before I went out. She's sleeping and there's a camera so we can keep an eye on her on my phone. Let's get this food cooked. I'm starving.'

He let Rufus out of his crate and she followed them up what must once have been the wide main stairs of the house, past a glorious stained glass window and onto a large, open landing with a high ceiling and ornate cornicing. The flat was much bigger than she'd imagined, certainly bigger than the one she'd recently vacated, thanks to Craig, and significantly nicer. Much bigger than her house, too, but that wasn't difficult.

His bedroom door was open just enough to see a large sleigh bed, the duvet neatly turned back to air. She dragged her eyes and imagination off it and followed him into the kitchen, light and bright and spotlessly clean, with a range of integrated appliances and a table by the window.

'Right, food,' he said, and unloaded the shopping. 'Are you OK with fish pie?'

Her stomach rumbled, and he chuckled. 'I'll take that as a yes.' He put the oven on to heat, and she leant against the worktop and tried not to watch him as he removed the film from the top of the ready meal and put it in the oven.

'This is a lovely flat,' she said, and he smiled.

'It is, isn't it? I've redecorated it and refitted the kitchen and bathroom, but I don't spend nearly enough time in it. I'll show you the other one now while the food heats, if you like?'

'Sure.'

They went through a door off his hallway, onto the landing of what must have been the old back stairs. She followed him up into a much smaller but equally well-presented space, with a double bedroom, a shower room, a small but well-equipped kitchen and a welcoming living room, all with sloping ceilings at the sides making it seem cosy and intimate. And homely.

She stood in the dormer window of the sitting room looking down into the garden and felt him move to stand behind her.

'You can see the sea from here,' he murmured, pointing towards the gap between the houses. 'Look along my finger.'

She did, leaning altogether too close to him to look and

feeling the brush of the soft hairs on his forearm teasing her cheek and making it tingle.

'Found it? It's only a glimpse.'

She had, the line of the horizon peeping through the rooftops, but it wasn't nearly as fascinating as the scent drifting off his body, an intoxicating combination of citrus and the rich, warm note of musk from his skin, and her cheek was still tingling.

'Yes, I can see it,' she murmured, and he dropped his arm so she could breathe again.

'So what do you think?'

She thought he smelt more delicious than a man had any right to smell, but she put the thought firmly out of her mind. She inched away from him and sucked in a quiet breath.

'It's lovely. Perfect,' she added, and felt some of the stress drain away.

'Tell me if you think it would be any kind of incentive to a new vet. I was thinking of putting it in the advert.'

Her eyes widened. 'Goodness, yes, I would have thought anyone would be tempted by it, especially as you live here, too, so it means they don't have all the responsibility for the practice at night. I found that quite challenging, sometimes, and I was always the first person to any emergency, of course.'

He laughed and moved away. 'Yes, I know how that works,' he said, and headed towards the door. 'Come on, let's go and have our meal, then you can settle in.'

'We need to talk about rent,' she said, and he turned back to her with a frown.

'Rent? What rent?'

'For the flat.'

He gave a soft huff of laughter and shook his head slowly.

'There is no rent, Ellie. If it goes with the job, it goes with the job. And right now, you're doing the job. End of.'

Feeling slightly stunned and a lot relieved, Ellie followed him back down.

The fish pie was delicious, and after they'd eaten it he made them coffee and picked the mugs up.

'Let's go and sit down somewhere comfortable,' he said, and led her to the sitting room, with a beautiful marble fireplace and the same original plaster cornicing. It must have been a very grand house in its day.

Not that it wasn't grand now, but in a more relaxed way—especially since Rufus had made himself at home on the sofa.

'This is a beautiful room,' she said, and he smiled.

'It is, isn't it? I really should spend more time in here.'

She settled herself into what had to be the comfiest sofa in the world and cradled the mug in her hands.

'So how come you're a vet?' she asked, partly out of curiosity and partly to fill the silence, and he gave a soft grunt.

'Oh—long story.'

'I've got time. And you've had to put up with mine.'

She looked at him and he smiled, but it didn't reach his eyes and he looked away before she did.

'Well, you asked, so here goes.' He hesitated for a moment, then started to speak, his voice flat and matter-of-fact.

'My father was a consultant surgeon at Addenbrooke's in Cambridge, my mother was a GP until I came along, then she stayed at home and looked after me and did all the admin for his private work. They got a dog, because I nagged, and every time she needed the vet I went along, and I was interested. I told my father I wanted to be a vet like my godfather Peter, and he said no. Be a doctor. If you're a vet, you'll spend all your time killing things. If you're a doctor, you'll be saving lives.'

Ellie stared at him, stunned. 'We save lives. We save lives every single day!'

'I know. That's what I told him, and I told him lots of people die, doctors or no doctors, but looking back I think he didn't want me to be a vet because he regarded it as inferior. And then our dog got sick, and our vet couldn't save her, and she was put to sleep—which just proved his point.'

'So why *aren't* you a doctor?'

'Because I've never wanted to be. Peter's influence, probably, and because I've always loved animals. This was his practice, and I used to love it when we stayed here and I could spend time with his menagerie. And then when I was ten, Mum was diagnosed with cancer, and Dad had a heart attack. They inserted a stent, put him on all the drugs, and he was fine and she was responding well to the chemo, but then two years later she was told it had spread and it was terminal, and a week later he had another massive heart attack and died.'

She sucked in a breath, her heart aching for the boy he'd been. 'Oh, Hugo. I'm so sorry. How old were you?'

'Twelve. But in a way it proved me right, because the doctors couldn't save him, any more than they could save my mother. She died two years after him, when I was fourteen, and I spent a lot of time here with Peter and Sally during her last few months. Mum had made Peter my legal guardian when she knew she was dying, and they took me in and welcomed me with open arms. They'd never had children, and Peter would have been a brilliant father. He *was* a brilliant father, and Sally was a wonderful mother figure, so kind, so understanding. And after Mum died, I was horrible to them.'

'Horrible?'

He gave a tiny huff of laughter. 'Yeah. I was fourteen, and I was an orphan. That's all I could hear, that word, and nothing could take it away. I was utterly broken with grief and anger, but they understood why, and they gave me the little flat. I still ate with them, lived with them, really, but it became my bolt-hole, my sanctuary, and it saved my sanity because I had a private space to grieve in and to come to terms with what was now my life.'

Her eyes welled over and she blinked to clear them. 'That must have been so hard.'

'It was, but I left my old school and went to one in Woodbridge, and I never told anyone there that my parents were dead, so I didn't have to deal with their sympathy, which made it easier. Peter took me under his wing, gave me his time unstintingly, and when I'd got over the initial trauma, he showed me everything he could. He had me doing stuff in the practice every holiday, and when that got boring he fixed me up with some farmers so I could learn about sheep and cattle, then he sent me off to a stable yard where I spent a glorious summer mucking out the horses and learning how to handle them, and all the time he was keeping me on target in school, making sure I got the grades I needed.'

He threw her a wry smile. 'Not that he had to push me, I was all the way there myself, but then they supported me through uni until I got my first job in a mixed practice, then he took me on himself when I decided I wanted to specialise in companion animals. He mentored me, taught me everything he knew, and when he retired eight years ago at sixty I bought him out. I'd moved back into the little flat when I started work here, and I lived in it until Peter and Sally moved out, and then I renovated this one, moved into it and did up the little one.'

'So it really is home to you,' she said, and he nodded.

'Oh, yes, absolutely. This place has been a lifesaver, one way or another, and it's been my home and sanctuary for the last twenty-five years.'

So he was thirty-nine, and he'd been a year younger than she was when he'd bought the practice. There was no way she could even dream of doing that.

'It feels like it wraps itself round you,' she said softly.

'It always did. I think it was their love that did that. I owe them everything, him and Sally, and my parents. They left their estate in trust for me until I was twenty-five, which meant I was able to buy the practice, but—yeah, everything I am today, I owe to Peter. He literally saved my life and gave me a reason to go on, and I owe him more than I can ever say.'

'He sounds pretty special,' she said softly after a long pause. 'You were lucky to have him as a father figure.'

'I was. I've been so, so lucky to have them both in my life, and without them there's no way I'd be here doing the job I love.'

'And Jim? How did you end up there?'

'Rotation via college. Peter knew him, though, so maybe that was another string he pulled, but he never said so. It wouldn't surprise me. They've stuck by me through thick and thin, and some of it's been pretty tough.'

He drew in a long, slow breath and turned to look at her, and she knew from the shield that had come down over his eyes that there was something else that he wasn't telling her.

'So that's me,' he said, done with the confessions. 'How about you? Why are you a vet?'

* * *

She held his eyes for a long moment, then gave him a strange little smile and looked away.

'Good question. I don't really know the answer. It just sort of…evolved. I wasn't sure it was what I wanted, but there was nothing else that was ever on my radar, and I had to do something.'

'Had to?' he asked, probing a little.

'Well—yes. I had to earn a living, but I needed a career that would give me job satisfaction, I was bright, I loved animals—it just seemed a bit obvious really.'

'But?'

She shrugged. 'But I was never really sure. I found it all a bit intimidating, but my mother was very keen that I should make the best of myself and take whatever opportunities were presented to me.'

My mother?

'What did your father think?' he asked, probing a little.

She gave a hollow little laugh that spoke volumes. 'I have no idea. He left my mother when I was little and I haven't seen him since, so I've never had a father figure.'

That shocked him. 'You've never seen him?'

'No, and there's never been any father figure in my life. You don't know how lucky you are.'

'Oh, I do. Believe me, I do. So how did your mum cope?'

'I don't know. It must have been tough. She had to work hard to support and house us on her own. There were times when it was really hard, and after all she put into it, I couldn't let her down.'

'And if she hadn't been like that?'

'Then maybe I would have found something else to do, something less challenging, less complicated, less—difficult.'

That was odd. 'Difficult?'

She looked at him, then away again, a slightly twisted smile on her lips. 'Difficult. Yes, we save lives, but as your father said, we also take them, and we have to break a lot of bad news. I always find that hard. It breaks their hearts, and—I don't know, sometimes there just seem to be days when you have to do it over and over, and it drains you.'

'But not as much as watching animals suffer because the owners, often for good reason, can't bear to let them go. I watched my mother die of cancer, and I wouldn't wish that on anyone, human or animal.'

She nodded slowly. 'Yes, I get that, and I absolutely agree. It's a privilege to be able to spare them that, but—then you get a dog like Lola, otherwise fit and healthy, who can easily be saved with a simple operation and some antibiotics, and you have to put it to sleep, because you can't just take them all in or you'd end up running an animal shelter.'

'But you took Lola.'

She looked down at Rufus between them, and he watched a tear slide down her cheek as she stroked him gently.

'Yes, I did, and I'd do it again, but look where it got us both. And what if it happens again? What if there's another Lola? When do you stop?'

He reached out and put his hand over hers and gave her fingers a little squeeze, then left it there, his thumb absently stroking the back of her hand.

'There'll always be another Lola. That's how I got Rufus. Elderly owner, unaffordable bill, energetic pup she couldn't cope with. Her kids had bought him for her to cheer her up after her husband died, but she wasn't ready for it and she couldn't cope with a puppy. And her family weren't able to take him on, because they all worked full-time, and they

couldn't pay the bill either, so I did what you did, I took
him on.'

She looked up and met his eyes, her lips tilting in a sad
little smile that made something inside him ache to comfort her.

'We're a right pair, aren't we?' she said, and he chuckled.

'You could say that,' he said, and gave her fingers another
quick squeeze and retrieved his hand before it got too used
to holding hers. 'And talking of dogs, we need to take them
both out, and then you need to settle in.'

She followed him down the stairs, and while he took Rufus
in the garden she went into the kennel area and found Lola
fast asleep.

'Lola? Wake up, sweetie,' she murmured.

She opened the kennel door, and Lola lifted her head and
stared at her, and she took the cone off and stroked her gently.
'Come on, poppet, let's take you out in the garden and then
put you back to bed. We've got another busy day tomorrow
and I need some sleep.'

They went out, and after Rufus had sniffed Lola and she'd
returned the favour, she bopped down for her wee and then
led Ellie back inside and went straight into her kennel and
lay down.

He's right, Ellie thought. *She's not ready for anything
other than rest right now.* She sat with her for a while until
Hugo came in, and he crouched down beside her, the tantalising waft of warm male body drifting over her again as he
gave Lola a gentle stroke.

'She's a good girl,' he murmured, and she swallowed hard.

'She is—and you were absolutely right, she's not ready for

anything other than lying here and recovering. Thank you for letting me use the flat while that happens.'

'You're welcome. Shout if you need anything, you know where I am.' His mouth tilted in a slight smile, and after a second he straightened up. 'I'll take your bags up for you. See you tomorrow. Sleep well.'

'You, too—and thank you.'

His mouth tipped again into that smile she was getting all too fond of, and he went upstairs with Rufus, taking his warmth away but leaving the faint lingering trace of his scent that teased her senses and made her think things she really, really shouldn't. Not if she wanted to keep her sanity.

She put the cone back on Lola, changed her water and settled her for the night before heading up the back stairs, past the door that led to his flat, on up the second flight to her temporary home.

At least the bed was made, presumably in readiness for a guest, and she was more than ready to crawl into it and find some oblivion. He'd put her bags on the chest of drawers, and she found her wash things and cleaned her teeth, then lay down in the welcoming, comfy bed, desperate for sleep and yet wide awake, her thoughts tumbling.

Yet again, Hugo had come riding to the rescue. Yes, sure, he needed a vet and if she'd taken Lola home, she could only have worked restricted hours for a while, so he might have had a vested interest, and of course there was the permanent job he kept dangling in front of her like a nice juicy carrot.

But she knew enough about Hugo now to realise that his offer might simply have been an act of kindness. Did he really need another vet? Jean had said someone was on maternity leave. Did he know that she wasn't coming back? Or coming back part-time? Or was it just Hugo being Hugo...?

She rolled onto her side with a little growl of frustration, tugged the pillow into the crook of her neck and shut her eyes firmly.

One day at a time. Starting with tomorrow.

CHAPTER FOUR

ANY DOUBTS SHE might have had about Hugo's motivation vanished the next morning. By the time she'd dealt with Lola and was ready to start it was a quarter to eight, but there were already three cars in the car park, and she could hear Hugo's voice rattling off instructions in the background.

She followed the sound and found him surrounded by nurses, all working furiously on a puppy. Her little spaniel puppy of yesterday, Mr Wiggles.

'Anything I can do?' she asked, and he shook his head.

'No, short of teaching puppies not to eat stuff they shouldn't. Right, let's open him up and find out what's going on. Ellie, could you pick up the consults, please? I'm going to be tied up for a bit.'

'Sure.'

She left them to it, and for the next half hour she did mostly routine things—until it all hit the fan with Chester, a two-year-old Dalmatian that had eaten chewing gum.

His owner was distraught. 'I wasn't sure if it mattered, but I looked it up on the Internet and I thought I ought to bring him in. He hadn't wanted to go for his walk, and then he seemed floppy and started to vomit, and a bit of gum came up, and then I saw the pot lying on the floor. He must have got it off the worktop—'

'How much was in the pot?'

'About a third? I don't know. I brought it to show you.'

She pulled out a small pot, her hands shaking, and Ellie's heart sank. Sugar-free gum with xylitol—and a third of the pot?

'OK, I'm going to have to admit him and get him on a glucose drip fast because his body thinks he's had a lot of sugar and will be pumping out insulin. Get Reception to give you a consent form to sign, and I'll get the drip in now, but don't worry, I think we've got him in time.'

She scooped the floppy dog up and carried him quickly out to the prep room. 'Can anyone help me, please? I've got a dog who's ingested xylitol.'

Kerry detached herself from the puppy group and came over. 'I'll warm the dextrose. Can you get a line in?'

'Sure.' She shaved his front leg, slid in the cannula, withdrew bloods for analysis and flushed the line, and by the time she'd done that and given him a bolus of dextrose to kickstart his blood sugar recovery, the bag of dextrose was warmed and she hung the drip up and checked the blood results as soon as they came up, with Kerry monitoring him constantly.

His glucose levels had been at rock bottom, but he was slowly starting to wake up, to her relief.

Then Hugo arrived at her side, a brush of warmth against her arm, sending distracting tingles through her body.

'How's he doing?'

Focus!

'OK, I think. We might just have caught it in time. Do you have any hepatoprotectant, in case his liver's affected?'

'Yes, I'll get you some. Kerry, what does he weigh?'

'He was twenty-six point four kg last time he was

weighed,' Kerry said promptly, and Hugo nodded and disappeared, coming back a minute later with the drug.

'So how's Mr Wiggles?' she asked as they worked, and he rolled his eyes.

'Better without a rubber toy in his gut.'

'What? How on earth did he swallow that?'

'No idea. It's a special skill dogs have. Do you want me to update Chester's owner on how he's doing?'

'Sure, if you've got time. I'm just going to check his bloods again, but I think he needs hospitalising. He's not out of the woods yet. He's going to need his glucose and liver enzymes monitored hourly for seventy-two hours.'

He gave her a wry smile. 'I'll go and break the news. I'm sure Mrs Grey will be delighted.'

Mrs Grey *was* delighted. Not by the fact that she'd have to drive him to the specialist centre, but because he was still alive and they'd hopefully managed to start his treatment in time.

She sat and waited for an hour until they were sure he was stable, then Hugo carried him out to the car for her.

'Thank you, Hugo. And please thank Ellie for me,' she said. 'She was so lovely to me, so quick and efficient and yet she still found time to be kind. I'm so, so grateful to you all.'

'I'll pass it on,' he said, and he went back inside. She was in consults again, and he checked on Mr Wiggles before he started his next op, a routine spay that had already been delayed two hours.

Thank God for Ellie. If he hadn't been sure of her before, he was now. He needed her in his practice. He just wasn't sure how to persuade her. Maybe Mrs Grey's message would do the trick…

* * *

The rest of the day didn't get any better.

Apart from a snatched biscuit, Ellie hadn't eaten since breakfast and by six she was running on adrenaline alone.

She said goodbye to her last client with a sigh of relief, and went out to Reception.

'Right, that's me done for the day, unless you've got anything else that's come in?' she said to Jean.

'No, we're done. Hugo's last client didn't turn up, so he's in the office and I'm going to lock the door.'

'Thank goodness for that,' she said. 'I can't believe it's still Tuesday.'

But before Jean could get to the door, a woman burst in.

'Where's Hugo? Nell's had a dreadful accident—'

'Find him, I'll go,' Ellie said to Jean without hesitation, and she ran out with the woman and found an elderly Labrador lying in the back of a car, shaking and whimpering, one leg bent at an ominous angle.

'I was bringing her to Hugo to put to sleep because of her cancer, but she slipped off the ramp getting into the car and...'

She broke off, sobbing, and Ellie gave her a quick hug. 'I'll go and get the drugs and find Hugo. Don't worry, I'll be really quick. You stay with her.'

She ran back in and found Hugo on his way out to them.

'What's up with Nell?' he asked.

'Fractured femur. She slipped getting in the car.'

He swore. 'I'll get the stuff. Can you help, please?'

It wasn't really a question that needed answering. They went out together, and found Nell's owner sitting under the tailgate by her head, stroking her side, her face grief-stricken, and she looked up at Hugo through eyes filled with tears.

'Hugo, this is all my fault, please don't let her hurt any more,' she said, and he hugged her briefly.

'Don't worry, Jenny, it'll be quick and I'll be very gentle.'

She moved out of the way, and he leant into the car.

'Hello, sweetheart,' he murmured tenderly, stroking Nell's head, and the dog looked up at him with pleading eyes. 'It's OK, Nell, it's all going to be OK, good girl,' he said, his voice low and soothing, and as soon as Ellie had clipped the little area of hair on her front leg and pressed her thumb on the vein to raise it, he took the syringe and slid in the needle, and as Ellie stepped out of the way, Nell's head sank down and she gave a quiet sigh.

'There we go, Nell,' he crooned softly, stroking her head with gentle fingers. 'It's all over now.' He put the stethoscope on her chest to listen to her heart, then turned to Jenny. 'She's gone now,' he said quietly, and stroked the old dog's head again tenderly as he straightened up.

'It's my fault,' she said, sobbing and cradling Nell's lolling head against her. 'I should have listened to you before...'

'You weren't to know she'd slip like that,' Hugo said, his voice gentle, one hand rubbing her shoulder to comfort her. 'Will you be OK to drive home?'

She nodded. 'I will be now. Thank you so much.' She sniffed and straightened up, visibly pulling herself together. 'Um—I need to pay you.'

'Don't worry about that now. Do you still want her cremated?'

'Please. That would be so kind, Hugo. We've buried the others but since I lost George...'

He squeezed her shoulder. 'It's no problem. You take care. I'll be in touch.'

Hugo lifted Nell out of the car as gently as he would an

injured child, her owner kissed her goodbye and he carried her into the back of the practice while Ellie held Jenny as she sobbed, her own eyes filling with tears.

She felt Jenny drag in a huge breath and straighten up, swiping at her eyes and fumbling for a tissue.

'Are you going to be OK?' Ellie asked her.

Her smile was sad, but her face was calmer. 'I will be. It's just the shock. She was our fifth dog, and I don't know why we kept doing it, setting ourselves up for heartache. I don't know why anyone does it.'

'Because we love them, and they bring us so much joy in their short lives. Just try and remember the good times.'

'I will, but I'll never forgive myself. Since George died she's always been by my side, and the guilt will live with me for ever. She was my best friend in my darkest hours, and I let her down...'

'No, you didn't, it was an accident. You loved her till the end, and she knew that. Don't worry, we'll take good care of her and Hugo will give you a call about her ashes.'

'Thank you,' she said, and as she drove away Ellie watched her go, tears blurring her view.

She turned and went back inside, and walked straight into Hugo's arms. They wrapped around her like a protective cocoon, and she rested her head against his shoulder for a moment, soaking up his warmth and strength. She could have stayed there for ever, breathing in the scent of his body, listening to the steady, reassuring thud of his heart beneath her ear.

'You OK?' he murmured softly, and she nodded and straightened up, and he gave her shoulders a quick squeeze before letting her go.

She followed him into the prep room where Nell was lying on the table, and she walked over to her and stroked her head tenderly. 'Poor Nell. Such a sad end. You know I hate it, we were talking about it last night, but when it's like that…'

He nodded. 'I know. I'm just sorry Jenny didn't let me do it the last time she was here and then this wouldn't have happened.'

'She told me Nell was her best friend and she let her down. She said she'll never forgive herself.'

'It's always easy to be wise after the event. They've listened to advice in the past, but maybe Nell was the last link to George. I wonder if she'll get another.'

Ellie looked down at Nell and stroked her again. 'I expect she will, the house will seem awfully empty without a dog. She said they've had five.'

'They have. I've known them all.'

She studied his face, searching his eyes as he held her gaze. There was something in his eyes, something dark and—angry? No, not angry. More…

'There's something else.'

He gave a soft laugh that wasn't a laugh at all, and looked away. 'You don't miss much, do you?' he murmured, then went on, 'My mother had a pathological fracture of her femur—she stumbled in the garden and it went. Luckily I was there with her. They took her to hospital and pinned it, then she moved to a hospice and never went home again. That was when I came to live with Peter and Sally. So—yeah, pathological fractures are a bit of a sore point.'

She could see why. How traumatic for a fourteen-year-old to witness that. 'You hid it well from Jenny.'

He shrugged. 'That's what we do. We keep our own feelings under wraps, and manage theirs. And sometimes it's harder than others. Nell was a lovely dog. I was very fond of her, and so was Jenny, but I understand how hard it is to say goodbye. It's a difficult decision. Grief is always difficult, but this just made it a whole lot harder for them both. And yet we do it to ourselves over and over again,' he added quietly, looking down at Rufus who was leaning devotedly against his leg as if he knew he needed comfort.

He reached down and Rufus licked his hand, and she smiled round the lump in her throat.

He straightened up, his eyes glittering a little before he turned away. 'I need to take Nell to the cremation guy, and I've got a couple of others to drop off as well. If you're not busy you could come with me?'

She stared at his back, trying to work out if he wanted her there or not. Should she go?

Probably, but Lola had had a boring day in her kennel, and Rufus had been in the office all day. 'Is it far?'

'About twenty minutes away.'

She hesitated again. 'Wouldn't it be better if I stayed with the dogs? And I need to go and buy some food.'

'Do that tomorrow. I've got stuff in my fridge that needs eating—I could knock us up something when I get back?'

She was so tempted, partly because of Nell and how it had affected him, but—another meal eaten with him? That would make it the fifth night on the trot. Every night, in fact, since she'd arrived at the practice with Lola trying to bleed to death. And he hadn't turned *her* away, either. No wonder he looked exhausted. The man didn't know how to say no.

'It's not that hard to decide, is it?' he asked, a smile tugging at his lips, and she gave a little laugh.

'No, it's not that hard, but I'll cook. It's definitely my turn.'

'Well, use the food in my fridge or it'll turn up its toes. I shouldn't be more than an hour. I'll take Rufus, he likes a run in the car.'

* * *

While he loaded the car and set off, she removed Lola's cone and took her out into the garden briefly, and then fed her and sat beside her on the floor in the office, Lola's head on her lap and her good leg raised for a tummy rub.

The wound on her other one was healing nicely, thanks to Hugo. She chewed her lip and wondered how much her bill was going to be. She owed him so much for last Friday night, not to mention the inpatient fees, and every time she raised the subject Hugo brushed it aside.

She'd have to pin him down—or ask Jean. She'd do that tomorrow.

Lola rolled her head round and stared up at her. 'Yes, I will,' she said to her. 'I'll ask Jean tomorrow, but right now, sweetie, you need to go back in your kennel and I need to go and see what Hugo's got in his fridge.'

Lots, was the answer. Some chicken thighs with a short date, lots of fresh green veg, a small pot of crème fraiche, again with a short date, the remains of the parmesan he'd used on Friday night, and there was even a pot of basil growing on the windowsill.

She found dried herbs, stock cubes and olive oil in a cupboard near the hob and another rummage in the fridge came up with garlic and a small jar of sundried tomatoes.

She smiled. Excellent. She had everything she needed.

She'd just finished cooking when she heard his car pull up, and by the time she'd put the veg in the pan ready to steam and a pouch of rice in the microwave, she heard the door at the bottom of the stairs open.

Rufus arrived first, of course, rushing in to greet her and

sniff around for anything she might have dropped, followed by Hugo, also sniffing.

'Wow, what are you cooking? It smells amazing.'

'It is amazing, and it's also super easy and you just happened to have all the ingredients. I hope you weren't saving any of them for anything special?'

'No, nothing. So what is it?'

She felt him close, his breath teasing her cheek as he peered over her shoulder into the pan.

'It's vaguely Italian. For some ludicrous reason it's called Marry Me Chicken,' she said, turning her head as his eyes widened, and she gave a stifled laugh and turned away again, wishing she hadn't told him. 'Don't panic, that's not significant, it's just one of the few things I can cook.'

She heard a low chuckle. 'Well, if it tastes as good as it smells I can imagine why it got the name. How long will it be?'

'Three minutes? I just need to steam the veg.'

'I'll go and change. Dish up when it's ready, I won't be long.'

He walked into his bedroom, closed the door and leant on it, letting out a long, slow breath.

Yes, it smelt amazing, but so did she, and standing that close, the combination of the rich sauce and the drift of something tantalising from her hair had sent a shiver of something powerful and potent streaking through his body.

Three minutes? He'd need three hours in a cold shower to unravel that. But then again, Marry Me Chicken? Really?

In another world, at another time—but not here, not now. Not ever. Not since—

He felt his chest tighten and slammed the door on that

thought, peeled off his clothes, dragged on a pair of jeans and a long-sleeved T and went back out to find she'd laid the table under the window and was about to dish up.

Good. He wouldn't need to make small talk.

'Thanks for your help with Nell,' he said, propping himself up against the worktop and folding his arms.

She looked slightly surprised at that. 'You don't need to thank me. And for what it's worth, if I was ever in any doubt about you genuinely needing another vet, it's gone. Today was crazy.'

'It was, and I was very grateful for your help. My job offer still stands, just so you know. Oh, and I have a message for you from Mrs Grey, she wanted me to thank you. She said you were very kind to her and really great with Chester. She was impressed. And he's doing fine so far. I rang and checked on the way back and his blood glucose level's picked up and he's stable now.'

'Good. We weren't sure how much he'd had, really, but I didn't want to take any chances.'

'No, very wise. Right, let's eat this, I'm starving,' he said, and he sat down with his plate and took a mouthful.

Wow. His taste buds all but cried with joy, and he gave up any attempt at small talk and scraped the plate clean. If he'd been on his own, he might even have licked it. Instead he swallowed and met her eyes.

'That is *the best* chicken dish I've ever tasted. I don't care what it's called, I want the recipe.'

She gave a tiny laugh and looked away, and he wasn't sure if her cheeks were turning a soft shade of pink or if it was just the heat from cooking. Whatever, he had to fight the urge to kiss her—

'Sure. I'll zap the link to your phone. There's enough left for you tomorrow.'

He swallowed. 'Excellent. And thank you.'

'You're welcome—and thank *you*. It was your food.'

His laugh sounded a little hollow. 'If you can do that with my ingredients, you can cook for me any time you want.'

This time her laugh was real. 'Don't push your luck. It's about the only thing I can cook apart from pasta and jacket potatoes. Right, I'll clear this lot up, and then I'd better get Lola settled for the night.'

'And I'd better take Rufus for a walk, and then I really need to do some admin. See you tomorrow?'

'Sure, since you clearly need me.'

Something flickered in his eyes for a second, and then he bent down and ruffled Rufus's ears again, her words hanging in the air between them.

'Yes, we need you,' he said, his voice oddly gruff. He pushed back his chair and headed for the door without meeting her eyes. 'Thanks again, Ellie. I'll see you in the morning. Rufus, come.'

Ellie stared after him, trying to work out what if anything had just happened there.

No. She was imagining it, trying to make something out of nothing. He was simply grateful for another pair of hands, and it was nothing more than that, however much she might want it to be.

And anyway, now wasn't the time. She had a new life to build, to find her place in the world now it had been turned upside down.

He'd be such a wonderful father...

And where had that thought come from? She'd barely met him and she was dreaming about his babies!

She felt a curious stab of longing, and stifled it. Getting tangled up with Hugo would be silly right now.

However much she wanted it...

How could it *be* so difficult?

She wasn't interested in him—or at least not in the job. She'd made that clear enough—and yet there was something that drew him relentlessly to her.

Why? She was a vet, and he needed a vet more than he needed anything else in the world right now, or his health would start to suffer and his practice would collapse. And that wouldn't help anyone. And even if he *was* interested in her, there was no way, not with the little he had to offer. Apart from the fact that his dedication to his job screwed up every relationship before it really got off the ground, like it had with Emma, he couldn't offer her anything like the relationship she deserved.

She needed someone kind, someone who was able to love her whole-heartedly. Someone who'd give her the family life she'd never had. And that wasn't him. Didn't stop him wanting her...

He swallowed hard. Time to start advertising again. Maybe if he chucked in the flat he might get a couple of decent candidates. With rents sky-rocketing and an uncertain housing market, free accommodation could be a winner. If he could get anyone else competent enough to do the job.

Someone as competent and capable and caring as Ellie... *Never going to happen.*

'Come on, Rufus,' he said with a sigh, and he put the little dog on a lead and headed out of the door. A good brisk walk along the sea front would clear his head and sort it out.

Except he'd only got halfway to the gates when he realised there was a cardboard box outside them. Rufus tugged him towards it, and as he unlocked the gate and bent to open it he heard a distressed miaow coming from inside the box.

His heart sinking, he picked up the box carefully, went back inside, shut the confused Rufus in the office and went into a consulting room, closing the door behind him before he opened the lid in case the cat escaped.

There was no way the tiny little cat was going anywhere. She stared up at him, hugely pregnant, utterly exhausted and clearly in need of help. He lifted her out carefully and examined her, and as her abdomen went rigid with a contraction, he noticed a tiny paw protruding.

The kitten was still alive, the paw flexing slightly when he touched it, but it was clearly obstructed. And he didn't have much time. Damn.

He called Ellie and she picked up on the second ring.

'I've got a very pregnant cat in obstructed labour. Fancy some overtime?'

'Give me ten seconds to change and I'll come down.'

He hung up and carried the poor little cat through to the prep room, laid her down, shaved her leg in readiness then put her back in the box and quickly got out all the things they'd need for a C section, then stripped and pulled on some scrubs. By the time he'd done that Ellie was there. She'd had the sense to put scrubs on, too, and they anaesthetised the little cat and opened her up and carefully eased out the kittens. Six were alive, and the seventh, the one that had been stuck and that he finally managed to free by easing it back, was borderline.

He took the borderline one and worked on it while Ellie rubbed the live ones and got them mewling and tucked them under a heat lamp, and then she took the limp, barely alive kitten from him and breathed into its mouth while he closed up the mother.

'How is he?' he asked.

'I think he's trying to breathe—yes, he's breathing!'

'Wow. I thought he wouldn't make it. I reckon he'd been stuck for ages, but I think we deserved some luck after Nell. But there you go, you win some, you lose some. Right, can you monitor mum while I finish closing, please? And then we need to get these babies snuggled up to her.'

She put the little kitten down with the others under the heat lamp, and turned back to the mother with a quiet groan.

'Problem?' he asked, and she shook her head.

'No, she seems OK at the moment, but it's going to be a long night and my bed's calling me already,' she said, and he gave a short laugh. Her bed was calling him, too, but hey...

'Tell me about it,' he said, his voice irritatingly gruff. 'We'll finish off and then you can go up to bed. I'll sit up with them and feed them.'

She cocked her head on one side. 'Does this happen often?'

That dragged a laugh out of him. 'Things rocking up at the door when we're shut? All the time—like you with Lola. If I had more cover, I'd still be running a night service, but I just haven't been able to recruit enough staff and when I do they leave because their partners have moved away with jobs or they're off on mat leave or they want a senior vet job—it just got relentless. So if this happens, it's all down to me to sort out.'

'Does everyone know you don't turn anything away?'

He grunted. 'Probably. I've no idea where she's come

from, she was in a box by the gate. I expect someone got her on a whim and didn't follow through with a spay, and then didn't know what to do.'

'Is she microchipped?'

He shrugged wearily. 'I don't know. I haven't had time to check her yet. I'll do it when I've finished this, but I doubt I'll find anything. Let's get this done and get her settled and we can worry about it then.'

The little cat survived her ordeal, and so did all the kittens, but after a night spent taking it in turns to feed them, Ellie was drained.

So, by the look of him when he came down just before seven, was Hugo.

'You look about as good as I feel,' she said, and he gave a grunt of laughter.

'Don't. Coffee?'

'Please. Lots. And toast.'

'You do it, I'll check on the kitties and scan her for a microchip. And then I really need to take Rufus out for a run before we start.'

She looked at him a bit more closely and realised he was dressed in running gear. 'Really a run?'

'Really a run. We do it every day.'

'Wow. Where do you get your energy?'

His hollow laugh echoed in the empty air behind him as he went through to check on their little patients, and she went into the kitchen and realised she was smiling.

He was really getting under her skin…

The little cat had been microchipped, to his surprise, and she'd been reported as lost by her owners three months previously on the day they'd moved from Yoxburgh to Norfolk. Hugo rang them and they were delighted to hear she was OK, and came later that day. They left smiling with their little cat and her family, armed with cat food, kitten milk to supplement if necessary, and an advice leaflet.

'Nice to have a happy ending,' Hugo said to Jean after he'd waved them off.

'Nice to have your bill paid, even if it was heavily discounted,' she pointed out, and he laughed.

'Yeah, well, it wasn't their fault and I had to do it. Oh, and Ellie needs some overtime pay for that, too.'

'Overtime pay for what?' Ellie asked, walking into the office at the critical moment, and he left Jean to explain that to her. She'd only argue with him.

'What overtime pay?'

'For the cat. Her owners just came and collected them all. Didn't Hugo tell you?'

'No, I haven't seen him all day. So, what overtime pay?'

'Last night.'

'I don't need overtime pay for last night. And he needs to bill me for Lola.'

'Take it up with Hugo. I'm just doing as I'm told,' Jean said, and Ellie gave a little huff of irritation and went to find him.

'Why overtime?'

'Because you worked all night.'

'So did you. We did it for the kittens.'

'The owners came and got her and they paid the bill. It's covered.'

She tilted her head on one side and studied him. 'What, all of it, the whole, proper, everything-accounted-for bill?

Or a figure you pulled out of the air because you felt sorry for them and the cat?'

'I'm not that magnanimous, but there may have been an element of that,' he admitted, but then trashed it by adding, 'and regardless of that, you still need paying for the overtime. And incidentally, while we're on the subject of magnanimous, you won't let me pay you locum rates, so you actually don't have a leg to stand on.'

'Fair cop,' she said with a chuckle, and walked away, but she hadn't forgotten that she owed him for Lola's treatment. She'd sort it out with Jean in a quiet moment, if there ever was such a thing...

CHAPTER FIVE

MERCIFULLY THE REST of the week was quieter—not that it was quiet, exactly, but certainly more manageable with the other two vets there on alternate days, and then it was Friday night.

To her relief she wasn't scheduled to work on Saturday morning, and she'd have time to spend with Lola at last.

She was still on cage rest, but she was well enough to move now. And Ellie really, really wanted to go to her house, even if it was only for the weekend. It would get them out of Hugo's hair and give her something else to think about apart from him.

She found him in the office at the computer, and she perched on the edge of the desk and waited for him to pause.

'Give me two seconds,' he said, and then pressed save and looked up with a smile. 'Sorry. You OK?'

'Yes, I'm fine. I'm going to my house tonight with Lola.'

He blinked. 'Really? I thought you were staying until she was off cage rest?'

'I know, but I'd like to be there, at least for the weekend, to give Lola a change of scenery if nothing else, and I need to get on with tackling it properly, as well. She can lie and watch me while I do stuff.'

'I'll give you a hand,' he said, without asking her if she needed help. Typical Hugo, and actually it was the last thing she needed when she was trying to get some distance between her and the man who was occupying all too much of her head space.

She shook her head. 'Don't worry, I can manage, but could I borrow your big crate for a while? Just until her stitches are out?'

'Sure, if you really feel you need to go, but you're welcome to stay here, you know that. The flat's just sitting there.'

'Yes, I know, but—'

'You want your own home,' he said softly, because of course, being Hugo, he understood.

She smiled. 'That sounds ungrateful, and I'm not, not after all you've done for me and Lola in the last week, but I thought if I spend the weekend there, I won't have to worry about her, I can get on with sorting my stuff out, and we can see how it goes. I'm assuming you won't mind if I bring Lola to work every day if I decide to stay there?'

'Of course I won't. She can lie in here in the day. She'll have plenty of company.'

'She will, and she was fine doing that at the other practice. If you don't mind, that would be brilliant.'

'Of course I don't mind. The crate probably won't fit in your car, but I can drop it over later, after I've taken Rufus out. Then I'll give you a hand, if you like?'

Did she like? She was torn, for all sorts of reasons. He'd done so much for her, and being independent was hard-wired into her DNA, but nevertheless it seemed churlish to refuse his help, like throwing his kindness back in his face.

'That's very kind of you, Hugo, but I can probably manage if you could drop the crate off,' she said, and hoped she could and it wasn't just a big fat optimistic lie…

* * *

Ellie pulled up on the drive with a feeling of déjà vu.

Was it really only a week since she'd arrived here so full of optimism and then everything had fallen apart? Just seven days, and without Hugo she had no idea what she would have done. Would Lola even have survived?

She felt her eyes prickling, and pulled herself together. No time for sentiment, she had things to do. She opened the front door and carried Lola in from the car and put her down, then looked around. She'd forgotten how tired it all was, how much in need of some love. She really needed to phone the agent and have a serious conversation.

She opened the back door and led her reluctant dog out into the garden. It was the first time Lola had been here since her accident, and she was a bit wary of it, but after a few moments of hesitation she was persuaded to step onto the grass—only for long enough to bop down and do a wee, and then she was back on the patio and staring pleadingly up at Ellie.

She clearly hadn't forgotten that the garden was full of terrors. Maybe tomorrow in full daylight would be better— under strict supervision, because even though Hugo had been meticulous, there might still be something lurking there and she'd never forgive herself if Lola was hurt again.

They went back inside, and Ellie took Lola's cone off. She wasn't allowed to jump up or go on the stairs until her sutures were out, so Ellie dug a throw out of the pile of bags still decorating the living room, spread it out in front of the sofa and sat down, patting the space beside her. Lola looked at the sofa, then at her, and lay down beside her with a sigh, head on Ellie's lap, and she fondled her ears.

'You're such a good girl,' she murmured, and Lola

thumped her tail and sighed again. She could understand that. She'd be sighing all the time if she didn't stop herself.

'What am I going to do, Lola?' she asked, her voice weary. 'I wish I knew, but there's no hurry now, thanks to Hugo. Shall we see how it goes?' she asked the dog, and got another little tail thump in reply.

Not much of an answer, but heart-warming. Maybe it *could* be a home. And maybe Hugo really was as decent as he seemed. Should she take the job he'd offered?

Her chest tightened a little at the thought, and she shook her head. Too soon. There was no hurry, and besides, he still had to find a replacement, so she'd be locuming anyway for a while. She'd do as she'd promised and stick it out until then...

A car pulled up outside, and she heard the dull thunk of a door closing, then footsteps. She glanced out and saw him walking up her path, as if she'd conjured him up out of her imagination, and her heart gave a little skip. He was carrying a bag, and she opened the door as he rang the bell.

'Hi.'

'Hi.' He held the bag out to her, his mouth tipped in a crooked smile. 'I brought you something to eat. I wasn't sure if you'd had time to do a shop, so I dived into the supermarket.'

'Oh, Hugo, you didn't have to—thank you! That's so kind of you—or are you still trying to buy me?' she added, only half joking, and he gave a soft huff of laughter.

'You don't take anything at face value, do you?' he said, giving Lola a little tickle, and turned away and went back to his car.

Now she'd offended him—except he opened the boot, pulled out the crate, then leant in again and emerged carrying a plant in a pot. An orchid, the beautiful white flowers almost luminous in the dusk.

'What's that for?' she asked, expecting him to say yet another thank you for bailing him out, but he didn't.

His mouth tipped into another of those crooked smiles. 'Housewarming present. A little something to cheer the place up a bit—oh, and I've brought a body sleeve for Lola,' he said, and for a second she had the ridiculous urge to cry.

'Thank you, Hugo,' she murmured, absurdly moved by his simple but thoughtful gestures. She took the plant and beckoned him in.

'Sorry, it's still a mess. I haven't done a thing since I got here except sit down with Lola. Come on through.'

He followed her and Lola into the kitchen and put the shopping bag on the worktop. 'Does the microwave work?'

'I think so. I've cleaned it so I hope so.'

She put the orchid on the kitchen windowsill while he emptied the bag. Milk, eggs, bread, butter, tea, coffee, Greek yogurt, some fruit—and two ready meals.

'They're not exactly the healthiest, but I didn't think you'd want to start cooking on top of everything else. And I bought two, in case you fancied company?'

She searched his eyes, and all she found was that bone-deep kindness and consideration that seemed to be his trademark, and possibly her undoing.

'I don't have to stay,' he added, when she said nothing, and she swallowed another urge to cry—where was that coming from?—and found a smile from somewhere.

'Sorry. Yes, of course stay. What do I owe you for the shopping?'

'You don't give up, do you?' he said mildly.

'Not often.'

His lips twitched, and he pulled the receipt out of his pocket and glanced at it. 'Twelve pounds and seventy-four pence.'

She didn't believe him for an instant, but the receipt was back in his pocket and she tipped out her purse and found something close to it while he pricked the top of the ready meals and stuck them in the microwave.

While they heated she put the body sleeve on Lola and he erected the crate. He'd even brought a new sheet of thick vet fleece cut to fit it, something she hadn't even got round to thinking about.

She found a couple of plates that weren't too chipped, and they took their food into the sitting room and settled down on the sofa, Lola on the floor between them looking hopeful.

'Where's Rufus?' she asked, to break the yawning silence.

'In his bed. He's fine, he's had a busy day keeping an eye on things and he's had a bit of a run around in the garden, so I'll take him out later.'

The silence descended again, and she finished her meal—surprisingly delicious and very welcome—and then picked up their plates and took them back to the kitchen. He followed her and propped himself up against the worktop as she dumped them in the sink.

'Anything I can do? Carry stuff upstairs, shift furniture, help you make the bed?'

No way was he going anywhere near her bed, but the carrying…

'That would be great. I'll stick Lola in her crate while we do that, or she'll try and come up.'

'I'd put the cone back on, she'll need that unless she's under supervision,' Hugo said.

Lola wasn't impressed, but she went into the crate reluctantly and lay down with a great sigh, the plastic cone framing her mournful face.

'She does that martyr thing for England,' Ellie said with a chuckle, and led him back to the sitting room. 'Well, this is it. Grab a bag or two and follow me.'

She took the garment bag on top, followed by a couple of carrier bags, and went up into her bedroom—*her bedroom? How odd*—and turned to find him right behind her with three bags in each hand.

'Where do you want them?'

'On the bed. That way I'll have to deal with them before I can go to sleep. Otherwise I won't get round to it.'

And it avoided the issue of him helping her to make it.

Except, of course, he had a better idea.

'Why don't we make it first, then dump the stuff on it? That way when you've finished emptying them you can fall straight into it.'

It made sense. Of course it did, so she searched the bags, found the bedding and quickly whipped out the mattress protector, the sheet and the pillow cases and dropped them on the mattress.

By the time she'd wrestled the duvet out of its bag he'd nearly done the sheet. In seconds the bed was made, and if it hadn't been for common sense she would have been tempted to fall straight into it there and then.

With him?

As they straightened up their eyes met, and she looked quickly away before he could see what she was thinking.

Madness. Tempted or not, there was no way she was going there. Not with Hugo, or any vet who was a prospective employer. Not after Craig, who'd made it impossible for her to stay in the job she'd only stayed in out of loyalty to Jim.

And Hugo was a charmer. Her father had been a charmer, according to her mother, and she was never going to let herself fall for that.

But he was hoisting the bags back onto the bed, and she forced herself to meet his eyes again over the top of the heap.

'Coffee?' she asked lightly.

'Sure, if you've got time?'

'Of course I've got time.' And as he'd brought the coffee, it would have been churlish to kick him out without offering.

They ended up on the floor in the living room, Lola lying between them making the most of stereo cuddles, her head draped over Hugo's lap this time. The body sleeve had hind legs to cover the stitches, and she was groaning softly as he scratched her neck where the cone had been, and tugged her ears gently.

The movement of his hands was mesmerising, and Ellie looked away. She had to work with him, at least for the next few weeks or maybe months, and letting herself fantasise about his gentle, knowing hands on her body wasn't the way to do it. Especially with that freshly made bed right overhead...

Get a grip!

'So, what's your plan?' he asked, and she blinked at him.

'Plan?'

'For the house.'

She looked fleetingly relieved, for some reason, and he wondered if she'd thought he meant about the job. He already knew the answer to that, and it wasn't even as positive as a maybe.

'I don't really have one yet. Obviously it needs decorating

from top to bottom, so I'll presumably start there, a room at a time, and then it'll need new carpets and furniture, really.'

'Especially if you're going to live in it for any length of time.'

She shot him a sideways glance and gave a wry smile. 'Nice thought, but I can't afford to replace anything yet.' She sighed. 'I need to phone the agent tomorrow morning. It's time I told him what it was like. And I still need to wipe down all the woodwork.'

'I can give you a hand tomorrow after we close if you like?' he offered without engaging his brain, and she glanced at him with that wry smile and looked away again.

'Hugo, I'm fine. I just need to put on my big-girl pants and get on with it.'

Why did she have to say that? He really, really didn't need to think about her pants...

'Well, the offer's there if you want to take me up on it,' he said, and looked down at Lola. 'Sorry, sweetie, you need to let me get up, I have to go home and get on.'

'Admin again?'

He laughed, and it sounded hollow even to his ears. 'Always admin. Well, admin and Rufus. He needs a walk, or at the very least I need to play with him in the garden for a while. And I need to get that advert out there.'

He waited a heartbeat in case she picked it up, but she didn't, so he lifted Lola's head gently and slid out from underneath it.

'I'll see you out,' Ellie said, but he shook his head.

'You stay there with Lola. She looks comfortable. I'll let myself out. See you tomorrow?'

She tilted her head and smiled up at him, and he felt a

jolt of something warm surge through him and settle in the region of his heart.

'You really don't need to help me. You've done enough already—more than enough. I can cope.'

'Big-girl pants,' he murmured, trying not to think about her bed right over their heads, and she smiled.

'Absolutely—and, Hugo?'

She reached up and caught his hand as he passed her, and the warmth turned to fire and burned through his body.

'Thank you. I don't know what I would have done without you this last week. You've been a lifesaver. Literally, for Lola.'

He gave a little huff of laughter, and his smile felt crooked. 'I only did what you would have done, and as for Lola, that's what we do, isn't it? That's why we're here.'

He squeezed her hand, then disentangled his fingers and made his escape before he did something really, really foolish that would only hurt them both.

The front door closed with a firm click, and she rested her head back against the arm of the sofa and listened to the sound of his car driving away.

She could still feel the warmth of his hand in hers, still feel the unexpected quiver that had travelled through her like lightning, leaving longing in its wake.

No! No, no, no! She wasn't going to go there. Not that he'd suggested anything in any way, but...

'You're an idiot. He's just being nice.'

Lola lifted her head and stared at her, and she stroked her gently. 'Come on, baby, let's take you out in that beastly garden again and then put you to bed, hmm?'

She put their mugs in the dishwasher, then took Lola out,

put the cone back on her and settled her in her crate before heading up to bed.

A strange bed, in a strange room, with all her worldly goods piled on top of it, but she was too tired now to deal with that, so she dumped the bags on the floor, found her wash things and cleaned her teeth, then lay down on the unfamiliar mattress, staring at the ceiling.

Her own bedroom, in her own home.

It should have felt wonderful, but it didn't, it felt oddly wrong, temporary, uncertain. There was still so much that was undecided, so many ways to go, different paths to travel.

Should she take the job? Or just locum for now and take the time to do up the house a bit and then re-let it and move on? But where to? She'd have to find accommodation that would take Lola, and that was tricky. And she couldn't take her with her into practices if she was locuming, it wouldn't be fair on any of them.

Only one thing was certain. If she stayed here, she'd definitely need a better bed…

She spent Saturday morning washing the woodwork downstairs with Lola, but she needed to pull out the washing machine and dishwasher so she could clean under them.

Except that meant asking Hugo for *another* favour.

'Oh, Lola, what am I thinking? I need to leave him alone! He's got a life, and he doesn't need us clogging it up.'

Lola lifted her head and thumped her tail gently on the floor. Thank goodness she'd got her. She'd go mad otherwise.

And she'd still be in her old practice working with the odious Craig.

'It's a lovely day, let's go and have a look in the garden, shall we?'

She managed to drag and lift the crate out onto the patio, and Lola went hastily into it the moment she opened the door. She left it open, so Lola could come out if she wanted to, and then spent an hour or more peering down into the grass to see if she could find anything else that might present a hazard.

Not easy, as it needed another cut already and of course the lawnmower in the little shed was useless, the cable sliced through as if it had been mown by accident.

By the time she was satisfied that it was safe, Lola had come out of her crate and was lying on the patio in the sun watching her, so she sat down beside her, a hand on her side, and stared blankly at the garden.

If you could even call it that. Another thing on her endless to-do list.

She took Lola inside, hauled the crate back in—harder than bringing it out, of course—and put her back into it, then went into town. First stop the rental agent, only the office was closed, so she found a supermarket, bought a few food essentials, a pot of violas in full bloom to cheer up the garden, a packet of drawer liners and some dishwasher and washing machine cleaner, then headed back.

The first thing she did was run the empty dishwasher and the washing machine on a hot wash with the cleaner, then spent an hour adding to her to-do list and emailing the letting agent, then went for a short stroll while Lola was napping, trying to find some nice walks for her once she was able to start controlled exercise again.

She did the same thing the next day, heading towards the sea this time, and of course she bumped into Hugo and Rufus out on a run.

He slowed to a halt and stopped in front of her, his chest heaving, sweat dribbling down his neck and into the running vest that clung to his lean, toned frame, and her heart lurched in her chest.

How is it that, even hot and sweaty, he's so darned sexy?

'Hi,' he said, his eyes crinkling into a smile, and she smiled back and bent to say hello to Rufus. Not that Rufus really cared, but it was a good excuse and got her eyes off his body.

Except his legs were now right in front of her, and they were every bit as distracting as the rest.

'You look hot,' she said, and then could have kicked herself, but he just laughed.

'I am hot. I'm steaming. We've just done ten K, ready for the race next weekend.'

'Race?'

'Yes, there's one every year in aid of the local children's hospice. I've been tapping the clients for sponsorship.' His grin was cheeky and made her heart hiccup, and she had to look away again. 'So how's it going?'

'Oh, OK. I'm just taking a little stroll to keep my muscles working and to get to know the area ready for taking Lola out,' she told him, distracting her brain from the subject of his hot sweatiness and his support for charity, both of which made him even more attractive than he had been.

Why does he have to be so nice?

'How's she doing?'

'OK, but she's bored to death. I reckon in another week her leg should be healed enough so she can come out of prison. She'll love that.'

'She will. It's nine days now.'

'Yes, I suppose it is.' Ten since her world had been turned upside down, and nine since she'd met him—

He shifted from foot to foot. 'I'd better go or I'll stiffen up, I need a shower and some stretches, but what are you doing later?'

How to find an excuse to avoid him? 'Trying to tame the house?' she said truthfully, and then without permission her mouth tacked on, 'Why?'

He shrugged. 'I thought, as the weather seems so much warmer today, I could crack out the barbecue? Then Rufus and Lola can spend a bit of time together and it'll give her a change of scenery. She must have serious cabin fever.'

She wasn't alone, just the thought of tackling the house made Ellie want to run away, and the offer was so tempting. Still, she really shouldn't...

'That sounds lovely. Anything I can bring?' her mouth asked, and she contemplated sewing it shut.

'No, nothing. I've got some stuff in the freezer and I'm going shopping after I've showered. Two-thirty?'

She nodded, cross with herself for being weak and yet looking forward to it because she felt oddly lonely here. Lovely though everyone here was, she missed her friends in the old practice, and her house with all that needed doing was overwhelming. And a barbecue with Hugo...

'Two-thirty's fine. Are you sure I can't bring anything?'

'Just yourselves,' he said, and she told herself that the invitation was as much about Lola as it was about her. If not more so.

'OK. I'll see you then.'

He threw her a smile and set off again, Rufus running beside him, and she watched him go, those long, strong legs eating up the pavement, and kicked herself for being so weak-willed.

Maybe she should start applying for other jobs.

And leave him in the lurch, after all his kindness?

No. She couldn't. And she knew in her heart of hearts that

she ought to put him out of his misery and take the job, but she was scared of doing it, scared of making another mistake, another wrong decision, another error of judgement—

'He's nothing like Craig,' she told herself crossly as she walked back into the house, and Lola looked up at her and whined. She opened the crate and stroked her head.

'I'm sorry, sweetie, you have to stay in there. You need a rest before this afternoon, and I need to get *something* done on the house. Maybe it's time to fire up the washing machine. What do you think?'

It didn't really matter what Lola thought about that as an idea, because the washing machine needed another hot cleaner wash before she'd want to use it, and anyway, she didn't have time to dry the clothes before tomorrow. She phoned Hugo.

'Can I ask a favour? Can I use the practice washing machine? I'm running out of clothes.'

'Of course you can. Bring everything over when you come. In fact why don't you just come back today instead of tomorrow? It would save moving Lola backwards and forwards and you won't have to rush in the morning.'

She hesitated, torn between her need for distance from him and the lure of the blissfully comfortable bed in the flat.

The flat won hands down, and she didn't really want the distance, anyway, if she was honest. 'Thanks, you're a star. I'll do that.'

She hung up, had a shower, threw all her washing into a bag and then rummaged through her clothes.

'It's not a date!' she told herself crossly, and threw on a pair of jeans and a top, then changed the top for a nicer one, grabbed a jumper just in case it got chilly later, and then loaded Lola and the laundry into the car and headed back to the practice.

He'd opened the gate for her, and she shut it behind herself and parked in her usual place, then picked Lola up and carried her round to the staff entrance. She could see Hugo in the office, and she put Lola gently on the floor and took her in there so she could say hello.

'Are we interrupting?'

He gave a wry, tired laugh and reached out to give Lola a little love. 'Not really. I'm posting an ad for the vet job. I thought I'd throw in the flat, see if it tempts a few applicants.' He tilted his head to one side. 'Since I clearly can't tempt you?'

Oh, she was so tempted, but there was no way he was knowing that...

'What?' he asked, his brows crunching together, his eyes searching. 'Are you having second thoughts?'

She looked away. 'I'm not sure. Right now I'm not sure about anything.'

He gave a grunt of laughter. 'Well, if it helps give you a little certainty, how about I take you on as maternity cover for Lucy, then that gives you time to decide and me time to find a permanent replacement if you really don't want to stay?'

'When's she due back?'

'Six months, give or take.'

Six months...

She held his eyes for a moment, then looked away again. 'Can I think about it?'

'Sure. Of course you can. And I'll hold fire on the advert for now.' He pressed save, closed his laptop and got to his feet. 'Let's go and cook. I'm starving.'

'Can I put my washing on first?'

'Help yourself. I'll get started, come on out when you're done. I'll take Lola with me, I can tie her to the bench and she can lie in the sun and hang out with Rufus.'

CHAPTER SIX

BY THE TIME she'd put the first load into the washing machine there was a delicious waft of barbecue in the air.

She went out into the garden and found Hugo, armed with tongs, standing by the barbecue with the contented look of a man making fire, Rufus and Lola gazing up at him hopefully.

'It really smells of summer out here,' she said, and he turned his head and grinned.

'About time. It's been cold too long. I've got a very attentive audience.'

'Yes, I can see that,' she said with a smile. 'Lola's leg certainly hasn't affected her appetite.'

'Have you had a look at it today?'

'Yes. It's healing beautifully, thanks to you.' She peered at the laden griddle. 'That looks delicious. Anything I can do?'

'Yes, you can relax.'

Relax? It was so long since she'd truly relaxed she wasn't sure how to do it, but she parked herself on a sun lounger, lay back and closed her eyes and let the sounds of the garden wash over her.

She could hear the hiss and spit of the barbecue, the scrape of the tongs as he turned things on the griddle. A bird was singing somewhere in the garden, and she could hear another answering it. Blackbirds? Maybe.

The sun was warm on her skin, not the fierce heat of summer, but the gentle warmth of spring that relaxed her muscles, emptied her mind of her worries and lured her into sleep…

It was ready. Hugo turned the barbecue down, piled all the food on the warming rack and closed the lid.

He turned, his mouth open to speak, and then stopped.

'Ellie?' His voice was low, no more than a murmur, but she didn't respond, and his mouth softened into a rueful smile. He didn't have the heart to wake her.

Her chest was rising and falling slowly, her limbs relaxed, and he made himself look away. He really didn't need to know what she looked like when she was asleep, her face unguarded, her body motionless apart from the gentle lift of her breasts towards the sun with every slow breath…

God, he wanted her. He wanted her so much it hurt, but she deserved so much more than he could offer.

He closed his eyes, but he could still see her, see the soft curves, the peep of cleavage in the vee of her top—

Should he wake her? She clearly needed to sleep.

He opened his eyes and saw a wasp on her cheek. Her eyelids flickered as her hand came up to swat it away.

'Don't move, it's a wasp,' he said quietly. 'Just keep still and it'll go.'

It flew off, and she sat up and turned towards him, looking a little confused, her eyes blinking against the sun.

'Sorry, I must have dropped off. How long have I been asleep?'

He shrugged. 'I don't know, I've been busy. Five minutes, max? I was about to wake you when the wasp landed. The food's ready when you are. I'll bring out the salads.'

* * *

Had he been watching her sleep?

Idiot, of course he hadn't. She was reading far too much into it. Why would he want to watch her anyway?

He came back out with a tray and set it down on the table, and her smile felt awkward. 'I'm sorry, I didn't mean to drop off like that, but it was just so relaxing in the sun.'

'You obviously needed it.'

She nodded. 'Yes, I guess I did. I didn't sleep well last night.' Or the night before...

He paused in mid-unwrapping of the salads and turned to look at her searchingly. 'Why?'

She shrugged. 'I don't know. Maybe the bed? It's not because I'm not tired, but—I don't really know. I just feel so unsettled.' Partly because of him, but there was no way she was telling him that—

'I'm sure you do. There's been a lot of sudden change in your life and it must have been pretty overwhelming. I know how that feels, but you've got a job here for as long as you want it, and a very decent reference if you want to move on, so you don't need to worry about that.'

Except she did, because somehow it all seemed too cosy. And it wasn't that she couldn't trust Hugo professionally, that was a given, but she felt this weird pull towards him, an almost visceral yearning, and it was herself she didn't trust. She was in danger of falling in love with him, and that wasn't in any way a good idea. Not personally, not professionally, and certainly not now.

'I know,' she said, breaking away from that searching gaze, 'and I am very grateful for all of that, but it's everything else as well,' she said, making excuses now. 'There's so much to do on the house, and I don't know where or how to begin. I need to speak to the letting agent, really. I've emailed him asking for a meeting. I might need to take some time off for that, if it's OK?'

'Sure.'

'Not that it'll make any difference. He'll probably just say it was "wear and tear", knowing my luck.'

Hugo grunted and picked up the tongs. 'Very likely. Right, we're good to go. Grab a plate and come and load it up.'

They ate in silence, the dogs lined up watching every mouthful while he watched Ellie.

She looked troubled, and after what she'd said, he wasn't surprised. He could offer to help with the decorating, but he really didn't have time while they were so short-staffed. And if he offered to pay a decorator, she'd only say no.

'Do you want this last sausage?'

She shook her head, so he put the leftover salads in the fridge for lunch tomorrow and shared the sausage between Rufus and Lola.

It was starting to cool down now, the sun dropping lower in the sky, and despite her thin jumper he saw her shiver.

'Coffee?' he suggested, and she gave a tiny shrug.

'I feel so guilty. I really ought to be at home getting on with something,' she said. 'My to-do list is ridiculous.'

And she didn't sound as if she wanted to do any of it.

'It'll keep. Come on, let's go and get a coffee. It'll be warmer inside and we can talk through what needs doing before you speak to the agent.'

She hesitated, a host of emotions flickering in her eyes, and then she nodded. 'That sounds good. You're right, the house can wait.'

She had a message from the agent just before eight the next morning, suggesting he meet her at the house. Now.

She stared at her phone, sighed and went to find Hugo.

He was in the office with Kerry, running over the list of consults and electives while Jean answered the phone and slotted in another client.

'Hugo, I'm so sorry to do this, but is there any way I can meet the agent at my house now? He's just messaged me.'

He hesitated for a second, holding her eyes, then shrugged. 'Sure. We can cope.'

'Thanks. I've fed Lola and she's been out, so she should be fine. I'll be as quick as I can,' she promised, and headed off armed with a list of issues and very few expectations. It was going to be a difficult meeting and it needed to be done, but she was so not looking forward to it…

While Jean went out to Reception, he and Kerry rejigged the first couple of appointments. Difficult, as he didn't know how long she'd be. Would she get any joy from the agent? He doubted it, and he certainly wasn't holding his breath—

'Hugo? Hello?'

He shook his head to break his train of thought, and looked back at Kerry. 'Yeah. Sorry. What?'

'Is Ellie OK?'

'Yes, she's fine, she's just got issues with her house. The tenants pretty much trashed it.'

'Mmm, she said that the other day. It sounds a nightmare.'

'It is a nightmare, and it all needs decorating, which is difficult when she's living in it.'

Kerry pounced on that immediately.

'Let her stay on in the flat as long as she's here. You aren't going to find a new vet that quickly, not anyone worth having, anyway. They'll have to give notice. And it's just sitting there doing nothing. It's the obvious solution.'

It was, and he'd already thought about it.

'It would give you a chance to get to know her better, too,' Kerry went on, and he searched her eyes and turned away, letting out a frustrated huff of laughter.

'Don't start that. I don't need you matchmaking.'

'But she's lovely, Hugo, and you're lonely—'

'I'm not lonely, I don't have time to be lonely, and I'm hardly a monk.'

'I'm not talking about your sex life, Hugo, I'm talking about a meaningful relationship. You've been on hold for ten years—'

His heart crashed against his ribs. 'You don't have to tell me that, I'm well aware,' he said shortly.

'Don't you think it's time—'

He glared at her. 'Don't go there, Kerry. I'm warning you...'

'She'd be so perfect for you.'

She would be. She was. She wasn't the problem, he was. Not that he was telling Kerry that. 'Just because you're all loved-up—'

'That doesn't mean you can't be. James and I don't have the monopoly. You deserve to be happy.'

He shoved a hand through his hair. 'Dammit, do I have to fire you to get you to shut up?' he growled, his pent-up frustration threatening to boil over, but she'd known him a long time and she just smiled gently and shook her head.

'Have it your way, Hugo, but you know I'm right. I just want you to be happy,' she added over her shoulder as a parting shot, and he waited till she'd gone and punched the wall.

Hard.

He rubbed his knuckles, the pain bringing him to his senses. Kerry was right. Ellie was perfect for him, in every way. But he was very far from being perfect for her, and the past kept coming back to haunt him.

He clenched his fist again, but it was already sore enough so he left the wall alone before he broke a metacarpal and went and called in his first client.

The flat idea was still kicking around in his brain, though. He'd initially offered it to Ellie as the obvious solution while Lola was on cage rest, but she was almost better now, and Ellie still hadn't committed to cover Lucy's mat leave.

Even though he knew letting her stay on in the flat for longer was the ideal solution for her, it would put them in very close proximity for however long it took to fix her house, which would do nothing to help keep any distance between them.

Except she needed to get the house sorted, and that would give her a chance. And then there was his other idea that would help her even more—although it would throw them together for even longer, so that was still kicking around in the back of his mind.

He was such a sucker for punishment…

Ellie headed back to the practice, still not quite believing how the meeting had turned out, and Kerry grabbed her on the way in.

'How did you get on with the agent?'

'He's agreed to refund his commission, which means I can afford to get it decorated. I can't believe it.'

Kerry blinked. 'Wow. That's a result.'

'Isn't it?' She just hoped Hugo wouldn't mind her staying on in the flat a bit longer, but then Kerry pre-empted that.

'You won't be able to live in it while that's happening, of

course,' she said, ever practical, 'but Hugo won't mind if you stay on in the flat. It's sitting there doing nothing.'

'At the moment, but he's going to offer it to a new vet so he won't want me there for long.'

'You're covering Lucy's mat leave, aren't you?'

'Well—only for now. I haven't agreed to stay—'

'Well, that's fine, he can still advertise the job with the flat. The decorating won't take long, will it?'

It wouldn't, once she'd found someone to do it, but…

Then Kerry moved on. 'Anyway, enough of that, I've been meaning to ask you if you'd like to come to my wedding in three weeks? The day's for family, but the evening's a party and I'd love you to be there. Everyone here's coming, and you're one of us now.'

Was she? Was she really 'one of them'?

She waited for that familiar feeling of the net tightening, like it had in her last practice whenever Craig had organised social events for them and she'd felt obliged to go, but it didn't happen, because this wasn't Craig, it was Hugo. His practice, his head nurse. All she felt was the steady, gentle warmth of welcome, and she felt her eyes fill with unexpected tears.

'Oh, Kerry, that's so sweet of you. I'd love—'

Kerry beamed. 'Great. I'll add you to the list. You can be Hugo's plus one.'

She stared at Kerry. 'Hugo's…? But surely he's got someone to bring? A girlfriend?' she added, now blatantly fishing, but Kerry just shook her head.

'Hugo? No, or certainly not one he'd bring to the wedding. He doesn't have time.'

Didn't he? Or was he just lonely, and filling time with busy work? What a waste of his life—and actually, none of her business.

* * *

'Kerry's invited me to her wedding,' she told him later between consults, and he gave a wry smile.

'I didn't think it would take her long.'

Really?

'So how did you get on with the letting agent?' he asked, changing the subject swiftly.

Ellie shook her head slowly and laughed. 'Weird. He was a bit defensive, but then acutely embarrassed when he looked through my photos, said he'd sent a new member of the team out to deal with it and should have done it himself. And, amazingly, he's refunding me all the commission from the last six months, which means I can afford to get it decorated.'

She let it hang, wondering how to bring up the flat, not wanting to put him in a difficult situation because knowing Hugo he'd just say yes regardless of his own feelings.

'That's great news. Look, I don't have time to talk now, I've got a Lab with an obstruction, but let's get this morning out of the way, and we can talk over lunch. I've got an idea I want to put to you.'

'Is this the mat leave thing?'

'No. Later.'

Except that lunch didn't happen for either of them, not surprisingly, and it was after six before her last client left. She walked out of Reception and bumped into him in the corridor.

'Sorry about lunch,' he said, 'the Lab took longer than I thought.'

'What was it?'

He rolled his eyes. 'Foam balls from the park. He'd eaten at least two, judging by the colours, and his gut was choked with bits, some of them huge. I don't know why people give them to dogs. They get chopped up when they mow the grass and some dogs just can't resist. Have you got time now to talk?'

'Sure, I'm not busy. I just need to eat pretty soon, so as long as it doesn't take more than a few minutes I'm fine, otherwise we can do it after I've eaten. And I need to spend time with Lola.'

He laughed. 'It'll take seconds. Let's do it now, and then I'll cook us something while we talk about it.'

'It's not your turn,' she pointed out, but he just laughed and headed upstairs anyway.

She left Lola in the kennel and followed him up, curious. His door was open, so she walked in and propped herself against the worktop in his kitchen while he pulled stuff out of the fridge.

'What have you done to your hand?' she asked, eyeing a nasty bruise on his knuckles.

'Oh, nothing, I misjudged a doorway,' he said, sounding a bit short, and carried on sorting through the fridge.

'So what did you want to talk about?' she asked as he straightened up.

'The flat.' He had his back to her as he chopped veg, so she couldn't read his expression, but his shoulders seemed a bit tense. 'I know what it's like trying to work on a property and live in it, and it's not easy, but if you're going to get a decorator, it'd be much easier for you and for him if you'd moved out, and the flat's the obvious answer.'

'Kerry said I should ask you about doing that, but I thought you might not want me in it for that long,' she said carefully.

He glanced at her then looked away again, turning his attention back to the onion he was dicing into a million pieces. 'Why wouldn't I want you in it?'

Why wouldn't he look at her?

'I don't know. Because you want it for the permanent vet, when you get one? Because I'll be in your way?' she tacked on, wondering if that was it, but he shook his head.

'You won't be in my way.'

'But it's not necessary. I don't have to move out, Hugo, I can just stay there and they can work round me.'

'You don't need to do that, not when the flat's just sitting here, and anyway, I'd already assumed you'd be here. That's not really what I wanted to talk to you about,' he said, scraping the onion into the pan before turning to face her and coming up with something that took her completely by surprise.

'I've been thinking. If you cover the rest of Lucy's mat leave, which is six months, that takes us to mid-October. If you move into the flat and stay here all summer, rent free, which is the vet's deal, then you could get the house done up a bit and rent it as a holiday let. They're in very short supply at the moment, and Yoxburgh's really popular in the summer.'

She stared at him, vaguely stunned because it had never occurred to her, and it was a genius idea. Except…

'I know. We used to holiday here when I was a kid, and I loved it, which is why I bought the house, but that isn't the point. What if you find a really good vet who's available sooner and they need accommodation? I'd have nowhere to go.'

He shrugged. 'Then let your house as a late last-minute deal. If you want to, of course. I just thought it might help pay the mortgage.'

She stared at him, stunned.

It would. It absolutely would, and the money would be really useful, because having lost nearly three months' rent due to the tenant, she didn't have much of a buffer, even with the commission being refunded. But…

'Can I think about it?'

'Sure. I'm doing Thai paneer curry. Red or green?'

She stared at him blankly for a second, then gave a soft laugh. 'Green would be lovely. Thank you. Let me go and feed Lola and take her out for a minute, and I'll be with you.'

By the time she'd done that he was dishing up, to her relief, and they sat at the table and ate without speaking until their plates were cleared.

Then he pushed his plate away and looked up, his head cocked on one side as he met her eyes. 'So, has the agent suggested a decorator?'

Ellie swallowed the last delicious mouthful and shook her head. 'No, and I wouldn't know where to start looking.'

'I spoke to Ryan, the guy I use, while you were downstairs with Lola. He's got a gap next week if you're interested. I said I'd call him back if you were.'

Another thing to be beholden to him for? He'd picked up their plates and headed over to the dishwasher with them. Was it her, or was he really avoiding her eyes?

'Is he expensive?'

'Yes and no, because he's quick, so he doesn't waste time and he's very, very good, and he clears up after himself. He used to do work for Peter, and he's done quite a bit for me. Or you can find someone else? Up to you.'

'How is he available, if he's any good?' she asked sceptically.

He shrugged. 'People pull out for all sorts of reasons. Financial pressure, mostly.'

She stared at his back, knowing that it made sense, debating the 'beholden' thing again, since they were talking about financial pressure. But if he was a known quantity…

She gave up. 'OK. If you give me his number I'll call him.'

'I'll do it, I said I'd come back to him.'

Which probably meant he'd offered him some financial incentive, she thought, knowing Hugo, but he handed her his phone after a few brief words, and two minutes later she had a decorator lined up, an appointment to meet him at the house tomorrow evening at six thirty, and a promise that he could start on Monday.

She gave Hugo his phone back and chewed the inside of her cheek.

'What?' he asked, studying her with those eyes that saw altogether too much and right now gave away too little.

'Nothing. It just seems too easy—'

'That again? Life doesn't have to be difficult, Ellie, and you can trust Ryan. Yogurt and berries?'

'On one condition. I'm cooking tomorrow, as soon as I get back from the house.'

He held her eyes, and one corner of his mouth twitched. 'You're on. Do you want some colour charts to look at? I've got some somewhere.'

The decorator was bang on time, and she was back in the practice by seven. Hugo, predictably, was in the office, Lola and Rufus at his feet, and he turned to her as she went in, his eyes searching her face.

'How did you get on?'

'Quite well, I think,' she said, giving Lola a love. 'He said he could get it all done next week. He's sending me a quote this evening. It'll probably be hideous.'

'Great. I've done my run, so are you cooking, or am I ordering a takeaway?'

'I'm cooking. Give me ten minutes.'

The quote pinged into her phone while she was cooking. It made her wince a little, but the house would be transformed in a few days and she could move on with her life. If nothing else, she'd have options, and Hugo's suggestion of letting it over the summer was growing more tempting by the minute.

She showed the email to Hugo when he appeared. 'What do you think? Is that fair?'

He nodded thoughtfully and handed her phone back. 'I would say so. It's about what I expected, maybe a bit less. I'd bite his hand off. What colour are you going for on the walls?'

'White everywhere except the front door, because it's cheaper and easy to touch up. I'm just worried it'll look too clinical.'

'No. It'll look clean and fresh, especially if you're going to let it?'

She searched his eyes. 'Are you really OK with that? Because it seems a brilliant idea—short term, only, obviously, and no longer than Lucy's mat leave, but it would give me a buffer.'

'Of course I'm OK with it. I wouldn't have suggested it if I wasn't.' He leant over and peered into the pan she was stirring. 'That smells good. I'm starving. Anything I can do?'

She emailed Ryan and accepted his quote, and then the next two days were so busy she didn't have time to worry about her house. Hugo's charity ten K was coming up on Sunday and he went running every evening after work, sometimes for half an hour, sometimes for longer, and she took the time to take Lola out into the garden and let her wander around for a good while before going inside to cook for both of them.

He argued, of course, but she pointed out she owed him, and if nothing else it was good for her pride.

'Chosen a colour for the front door yet?' he asked on Thursday while she was cooking, and she shook her head.

'I have no idea.'

So after they'd eaten they went down to his flat and he dug out the colour charts and they sat together on his sofa poring over the coloured squares and drinking coffee.

'That's nice,' he said, pointing to a very dark blue. 'Sort of charcoal navy. It could look very smart.'

She peered at the colour he'd picked out, leaning closer and catching a delicious whiff of shampoo and warm skin. She straightened up, her own skin warming, her heart rate kicking up a notch.

Why? Really, why? I need to get out of here...

She shifted away. 'Yes, I think that one could look great. Can I hang on to the chart and show it to Ryan?'

'Of course. Or drop him a text. He'll pick it up then before he starts. More coffee?'

'Uh, no, thanks, I've got stuff to do, and I want to take Lola out for a little stroll. I think she's healed enough now and she must be so bored.'

'I'm sure she is. That's fine. I'll see you in the morning.'

He listened to the door close, and dropped his head back and blew his breath out slowly. Why on earth had he suggested she should do this? It was bad enough bumping into her during the day, but the evenings, eating together, sitting together over coffee, chatting about this and that, it was all too cosy, too—dammit, too tempting.

That worried him. There was no way this was going anywhere, however tempted he was. He wasn't in the market for anything other than a decent vet to cover Lucy's mat leave. Nothing more, and certainly nothing like what his body was screaming at him to do. He saved that for women who didn't expect anything from him but a good time. And now he and Ellie would be living cheek by jowl for months.

This was all Kerry's fault.

No, it isn't. You brought it on yourself.

He flexed his fist, but it was still sore, so he left the wall alone...

Ellie ran upstairs, closed the door of her flat and leant back against it. Why was she reacting like this to him? She'd known him two weeks now—two weeks tomorrow. She worked with him, ate with him, and mostly it was fine, but then every now and again he'd be that little bit closer, close enough to smell the scent of his skin, feel the warmth radiating from his body, and her heart would somersault in her chest and she'd feel breathless until he moved away.

It was ridiculous. And if she was going to be living here over the summer, letting her house, she was going to have to get a grip. And maybe a bit more space. Fewer cosy evenings...

That was fine. She could do that. Lola was almost better now, so every evening she could take her for a walk, a nice slow stroll onto the clifftop to look at the sea, then a stroll back via the other road. Starting now.

She put on her trainers, ran back downstairs and let Lola out of her kennel. 'Come on, sweetie, I've got a lovely treat for you. We're going for walkies.'

Lola's ears pricked, and she seemed more than ready to go

out. They wouldn't be long, Ellie wouldn't do that to her on her first proper outing, but she needed to build her strength and have a change of scenery, and so did Ellie.

Especially scenery that didn't have Hugo in it...

The sun was setting as they reached the clifftop, and she watched the light on the water, the slow, lazy swell of the waves washing away the stress. The tide had reached its height, she guessed, and she sat on the grass, Lola lying down by her side, and they watched the sky turn a glorious orange streaked with purple while all the tension faded away.

Lola nudged her with her nose, and she gave her a hug and got to her feet. 'Come on, little lady, let's take you home.'

And hopefully Hugo wouldn't be in the office...

Sunday dawned cool and sunny, with a light breeze, to Hugo's relief.

The run kicked off at ten, and he was mercilessly collecting last-minute sponsorship from anyone he could.

He'd already tapped the practice team, and Ellie had chipped in with twenty pounds that he knew she couldn't afford until she was on a better footing, but he'd taken it anyway.

He couldn't see her here today. Maybe she was at the house getting it ready for Ryan to start tomorrow, or maybe she just didn't want to come, but as he scanned the crowd he saw Peter and Sally waving as they made their way towards him.

Bless them, they never failed to support this event, and he knew they'd sponsor him generously. They always did.

'Hugo,' Peter said, wrapping him in a hug and slapping his back fondly. 'How are you? Ready for this?'

'I reckon. I've been putting in some pretty good times.'

'I'm sure you have,' Sally said, kissing his cheek and hugging him. 'Where's your form?'

He handed it to her, and over her shoulder he caught sight of Ellie. He beckoned her over. 'Ellie, I'd like you to meet Peter and Sally. Ellie's the vet covering Lucy's maternity leave.'

'Good to meet you, Ellie, I've heard great things about you,' Peter said, shaking her hand warmly.

'Good to meet you, too, and I've heard wonderful things about you both. It's nice to put faces to the names.' Her smile seemed warm and genuine to Hugo's eyes as she shook their hands, but he noticed she didn't really look at him. Well, not in the eye, at least—

No! He didn't need to think about her now, he needed to focus on the run and remember why he was doing it. Not that he could ever forget… 'Right, guys, I'm going to shoot off and warm up. I'll see you when it's over.'

'We'll be here,' Sally told him, and handed back the form.

He glanced at it. 'That's ridiculously generous.'

'It's not for you,' she pointed out, and he hugged her hard and headed for the group gathered behind the start line, his heart pumping.

As he jogged away, leaving Rufus with Peter, Ellie's shoulders dropped a notch, as did her heart rate, and yet again she wondered what on earth she'd committed herself to by agreeing to locum until October—never mind living in the flat!

Sally smiled at her, but her eyes were assessing and Ellie wondered what his godmother was thinking. Peter, thankfully, had better things to do making friends with Lola.

'This must be the invalid we heard about,' he said, rubbing her tummy and studying the faint line of the scar on the inside of her thigh.

'Yes—well, she was. She's not now, she's pretty much healed, but Hugo was—amazing. Not that I gave him much choice, I pretty much bullied him into treating her, but without him I don't know what would have happened to either of us.'

Peter gave Lola a last pat and straightened up. 'No, he told us a little about it and I don't think you had to bully him. He's a good lad. Always has been. Priorities in the right place, but he—he's had a lot to deal with.'

She met his eyes and read a warning there, a gentle reminder that Hugo, too, had been damaged and needed care.

'I know, he told me. He also told me how wonderful you both are, and how much love and support you've given him. And judging by you being here today, I guess you still do.'

'We do. Right, I think we need to head over there, Sally. We can catch up later, Ellie. I think we're all going to the pub.'

He and Rufus walked away, heading after Hugo, but Sally hung back.

'Peter's right, we do try to support him however we can, but there are some things we can't fix,' she said, her eyes following Peter as he walked towards Hugo at the race start point then looking back at her as she added softly, a gentle warning in her eyes, 'Please don't hurt him.'

Ellie shook her head. 'I—I'm just working there. We're not...'

'He said you've become a friend.'

'Did he?' That warmed her in a way she hadn't expected. 'Yes—yes, I suppose I have, in a way, but—that's all it is. We're not...'

'That's a shame,' Sally said softly under her breath, and followed Peter to the start line, leaving Ellie staring after her, not knowing what to make of that.

'Hey, Ellie, come on, we have to watch them set off,' Kerry said, linking her arm through Ellie's and towing her and Lola towards the start.

She went, a little reluctantly, Sally's words echoing in her head. 'Please don't hurt him.'

And what about me?

CHAPTER SEVEN

THEY WATCHED THEM set off, Hugo at the front of the pack, and as the runners streamed past them, Kerry turned to her.

'Right, let's go and find a coffee and a doughnut and have a look round the stalls. There are all sorts of things—puzzles, books, clothing, local produce, tombola, splat the rat, a bouncy castle for the kids, and it's all in aid of the hospice so I hope you've brought lots of money?'

'I brought some,' she said, wishing now that she'd brought more cash because she'd had no idea there'd be so many stalls. 'How long have we got?'

'Before the front runners get back? About forty-five minutes.'

'And Hugo?' she asked, wondering if that sounded too needy, but Kerry just chuckled.

'Hugo won it the year before last, but last year someone pipped him, so he'll be right up there trying to get that title back.'

'Is that why he's been training so hard?'

'Oh, no, he always pushes himself. He's a bit driven, really, but it's not surprising. He's had so much to deal with.'

'Yes, he told me. It was awful.'

'He told you?' Kerry glanced at her, her face surprised.

'Yes. We had a long heart-to-heart,' Ellie said softly, remembering their conversations about his parents, and his mother dying in a hospice would explain his support for this one.

Kerry sighed. 'I'm so glad he felt he could open up about it. They took such wonderful care of them all for the short time he was in there.'

He? Ellie stopped in her tracks. 'He?'

She stared at Kerry blankly, and Kerry stared just as blankly back, then let out a long groan.

'He didn't tell you, did he? Oh, no…'

'Tell me what?'

Kerry closed her eyes and bit her lips. 'Oh, Ellie. I should have realised he wouldn't have told you. He never talks about it.'

'About *what,* Kerry? What does he never talk about? I know he lost both his parents. I thought you must mean his mother dying in a hospice?'

Kerry shook her head, and Ellie could see she was fighting back tears. She felt a cold chill spread through her.

'Who is "he", Kerry?' she asked, dreading the answer.

She hesitated, then said softly, 'His baby.'

His baby? His…son?

'No…'

'Don't say anything to him, please? I shouldn't have told you, and it'll only upset him.'

She shook her head. 'No, no, of course I won't. I…'

'Come on, let's go and get a coffee and sit down for a bit,' Kerry said, and steered her towards a picnic bench by a refreshments stand.

'So—what happened? Where is he now?' she asked, half of her not wanting to hear the answer, but Kerry's face was enough. 'He died. Didn't he?'

Kerry nodded wordlessly, and Ellie felt the air sucked

out of her lungs. Her eyes filled with tears and she blinked them away, but they slid down her cheeks and she swiped them away. 'I had no idea,' she said, heartbroken for him. 'How—that's…'

'Sorry. Look, I'll get us a coffee. Stay here.'

Stay? She couldn't have moved if she'd tried. She sat down on the bench as if her strings were cut, staring numbly across the field while Lola sat pressed against her leg. To comfort her?

She could see runners in the distance through a gap in the hedge, streaming past. Was Hugo at the front, driven by the need to support the place that must mean so much to him? Or just running away from it, trying to forget…

No. He'd never forget. You couldn't. But how could he live with that? Live with such a horrendous, soul-destroying loss? It must have torn his heart out…

She closed her eyes, the tears leaking through her lids and streaming down her face, and she felt something pushed into her hand. A paper napkin, offered to her by Kerry who was sitting beside her with a coffee in her hand and a bag of doughnuts on her lap.

She scrubbed her face, blew her nose and sniffed hard. 'Sorry. It just—'

'I know. And I'm the one who's sorry, I didn't mean to dump that on you. I shouldn't have—'

'When?' she asked, her voice sounding weird and some-how remote. 'When did he die?'

'Nearly ten years ago? I'd just started there. It was before Peter retired, and Hugo dropped off the face of the earth for a lot of the time in those few months. How he would have coped without Peter and Sally I don't know, and of course it was the nearest they'd get to a grandchild, so they felt the loss almost as deeply. And he hasn't had a meaningful relationship since. It broke him, and I think he's scared of the what-ifs.'

'What what-ifs?'

'In case it happens again—maybe. I don't know. He just shuts down if you raise the subject. He'll talk about anything else, but not that.'

That made sense. 'He told me about himself, about his parents dying—and actually, when he was telling me that, I was sure there was something else. There was just some undercurrent, and he suddenly changed the subject and asked me about myself. It was right back at the beginning—I hardly knew him at all, and we told each other all sorts of stuff, but not that. Never, ever that—'

She pressed a hand to her mouth to hold in a sob, and Kerry put an arm round her shoulders and hugged her.

'I should have realised he wouldn't. I don't think anyone else at the practice knows apart from Jean who's been there for ever, and she never gossips. Here, have a doughnut. They're still warm, and you probably need that sugar hit.'

She took one, the sugary crunch followed by soft, sweet dough and the comforting squelch of jam. She took another bite, and another and another, almost absently, then handed the last bit to Lola, dusting off her fingers and dredging up a smile.

'Thanks. You were right, I needed that.'

'You're welcome. Come on, let's drink our coffee and have a wander round before we go back and wait for them. We've got twenty minutes or so.'

They stood at the finish with Peter and Sally and other members of the team. While she was still trying to make sense of what she'd been told, they were yelling and cheering as he ran through the timer beam, then slowed and ducked under the tape to join them. He bent over, hands on his knees, chest heaving, his body driven to the limit, slowly getting his breath back.

Then he straightened up and checked with the stewards, and came back to them with a broad smile.

'Ten seconds off my PB,' he said, but the smile didn't quite reach his eyes—not now she knew what to look for.

'Congratulations,' she said, and then turned and slipped quietly away, the tears threatening again as she left him, surrounded by the nearest thing he had to family.

Ten years of sorrow, ten years of loss, ten years of denying himself a family, the children he'd be such a good, kind, loving father to.

Don't hurt him.

We're just friends.

That's a shame.

She walked quickly away, taking a reluctant Lola with her, and a moment later she felt a firm, warm hand on her shoulder.

'Hey, where are you going? I thought we were all going to the pub?'

She couldn't look at him, not now, with those tears still threatening, not knowing what she knew.

'Sorry, I need to get on with the house. Ryan's coming in the morning and I need to get it ready. But well done. I'm really pleased for you.'

She glanced up fleetingly then and caught the flicker of a frown on his face as she forced a smile. 'I'll see you tomorrow.'

'OK,' he said, the words coming after the briefest hesitation. 'Shout if I can help.'

'I'll be fine,' she told him, her voice much firmer now, but her smile was probably no more convincing, so she turned and walked away, taking a still reluctant Lola with her.

Hugo watched her go, torn between the people behind him and the woman in front.

Something was wrong, he had no idea what, but she didn't want to talk to him. Sure, there must be things she had to do at the house, but he didn't think sorting the house was enough to make her cry. And she'd been crying, without a shadow of a doubt. Why?

He turned and walked slowly back to the others, endured a stream of hugs and back-slapping and handshakes as the results revealed that he'd won, and then he caught Kerry looking at him with an odd expression on her face.

He moved to her side. 'What's up with Ellie? Why's she crying?'

She shook her head slowly, biting her lip. 'We need to talk.'

'Well, go on, then, spit it out.'

She closed her eyes and shook her head again. 'It's my fault, Hugo, I'm so sorry. She was asking why winning was so important to you, and I said you always push yourself hard. I said you were a bit driven, you'd had a lot to deal with, and she said she knew, you'd told her, and I just assumed...'

'You told her.' He crushed it down, the rush of emotion he thought he'd outrun, but he hadn't. He never could.

'Not in so many words, but you seem to be so close—'

'Not that close.'

Never that close, not to anyone, never again...

'I just said the hospice had been very supportive while he was in there, and she just stared at me. She thought I was talking about your mum, and after that I had to tell her—had to explain. I'm so sorry, Hugo, you know I would never have told her if I hadn't thought she knew.'

Her eyes were welling up, and he sighed and gave her a quick hug. 'It's OK, it doesn't matter, it's done now. I'll talk to her later. Right now I need a shower, and then we're going to the pub to celebrate.'

'Really?'

'Yes, really. We don't have a choice. Chin up, Kerry, what's done is done and it's not the end of the world.'

She heard a knock at the door in mid-afternoon, and she froze.

Hugo? Who else? Anyone else, hopefully, because if it was Hugo she wouldn't know how to look him in the eye.

She peered out of the window, but there was no car outside. Not that that meant anything, he was quite likely to have walked. Or it could be one of the neighbours come for a nose round. Please God…

Except Lola was whining and scratching at the door. The knock came again, and she braced herself and opened it.

He was standing there with Rufus, hands rammed in his jeans pockets, unsmiling, and she could see the pulse beating at the base of his throat.

'Hugo, I said I didn't need your help.'

'I know.'

She closed her eyes, not sure what to say, not sure what to do, but he took the decision out of her hands.

'Can we go for a walk?'

She looked at him again, her heart pounding, but his eyes were blank, giving nothing away. Not so the tension in his body. Had Kerry told him?

'Yes, of course. I'll put Lola in her crate.'

They walked side by side in an awkward silence, Rufus sniffing along the way, and when they reached the cliff top they made their way down the steps and along the concrete walkway, the sea stretching away to their right, the water glinting in the sunlight.

She didn't say anything, she had no idea what to say or where to start, so she left it up to him. A couple passed them, going the other way, and still she waited. And then finally they reached a point where the concrete ran out and the rocky sea defences took over, and at last he stopped walking.

'I spoke to Kerry.'

What was she supposed to say to that? She had no idea, so she said nothing, and he carried on.

'I asked what was wrong with you. She said—' He sucked in a breath, then let it out in a shaky rush. 'She said she'd told you about Samuel. Thought you knew.'

Samuel. She hadn't known his name, and somehow knowing it made her hurt for him even more.

She closed her eyes, and the tears slid silently down her cheeks. She felt him brush them away with a gentle hand.

'Hey, come on. Let's sit down.'

They sat side by side on the shingle, shoulders not quite touching, Rufus wedged between them.

He laid a hand on the dog's head, stroking it gently, and then he started to speak, his voice low, sombre.

'We weren't married—we'd been on and off for a bit and we weren't together any more, and it was a while before Emma realised she was pregnant. She had a scan at twenty weeks which showed that the baby had all sorts of issues and he might not even survive the pregnancy. She contacted me then to tell me about it, so even though we weren't together,

I was there for her. I had to be. He was my child as much as hers, and I blamed myself for her getting pregnant. She didn't want a termination, she wanted to let nature take its course, and he was born at thirty-seven weeks.

'His DNA had three copies of chromosome eighteen in each cell, instead of the usual two. It's called Edwards' syndrome, or trisomy 18, and the fault could have come from either of us. They said it wasn't a heritable defect, just one of those things, a failure in the cell division of the ovum or sperm, but in his case it was incompatible with life.

'His head was small, and he had cysts in his brain, which meant sometimes he stopped breathing, and he had difficulty swallowing so he had to be tube-fed. His heart wasn't plumbed right so his circulation was impaired, so he was on oxygen, but he wasn't in pain and he wasn't in imminent danger of dying and he didn't need to be in the noisy hospital, so we got him moved to the hospice so we could be with him in a quieter, more normal environment for as long as he had.

'And they were wonderful in there. He needed round the clock care, so with their support we took it in shifts, and then when he was eight weeks old he got a chest infection, and he died in my arms—'

His voice cracked, and she rested her head against his shoulder, her hand on his arm.

'I'm so sorry, Hugo.'

His hand covered hers. 'Don't be. He couldn't have lived, his body was too compromised, but that time we had with him was so precious. It'll be with me for ever, but I couldn't go through all that again.'

'What about Emma? She must have been devastated.'

'Oh, she was, of course, but she's moved on. She's married now, she's had three children. I don't know how she could do that. It would seem all wrong to me, somehow, to have another child, as if I'd airbrushed him away because he didn't matter. But he did—'

His voice cracked again, and he stopped talking, the tension vibrating through him, and a single tear leaked out of the corner of his eye.

Oh, Hugo...

She closed her eyes, and he put an arm around her and leant his head against hers as they sat in silence, listening to the sound of the sea lapping on the shingle, each lost in their thoughts.

And then he straightened up, sucked in a breath and gave her a crooked little smile. 'We need to go and get your house sorted out.'

He stood up, held out his hand and pulled her to her feet, then wrapped his arms around her, folding her against his body as if to comfort her, and as he spoke she could feel the low rumble of his voice.

'Don't be sad for me, Ellie. I'm OK.'

Was he? Was he really? She didn't think so, not for a second.

She kissed his cheek, and he turned his head and his mouth brushed hers and lingered for a moment, then he lifted his head, leaving her lips bereft and her body aching to comfort his.

She laid her head against his chest, felt the slow, heavy thud of his heart against her ear, and after the longest moment she straightened up and moved out of his arms, but he didn't let her go, just slid his hand down her arm and took hold of her hand and held it all the way back to her house while she thought of his baby and tried not to cry.

She unlocked the door and went in, and he followed her

and the silence closed around them, still unbroken, the tension now replaced by sorrow.

'I don't have any dust sheets,' she said inconsequentially, dragging them both back into the here and now, and his mouth twitched into a smile that didn't quite reach his eyes.

'Ryan has hundreds of dust sheets. Let's get your stuff out, give him a clear field.'

An hour later her possessions were stacked in her bedroom at the practice.

All except the beautiful orchid he'd given her, and she'd put that on the worktop in the kitchen so she could see it every day.

'Have you eaten?' he asked, and she shook her head.

'You have, though, haven't you? You went to the pub.'

His smile was a little twisted. 'I didn't eat a lot. How about we try again, just the two of us and the dogs?'

So he took her to the Harbour Inn, and they had fish and chips and shared some with the dogs, and gradually she began to relax again.

He drove them home—funny how the practice and not her house seemed like home—they went upstairs together and he kissed her, another gentle touch of his lips on hers that left her heart and her body aching.

'Goodnight, Ellie,' he said after a breath-stealing pause, and turned away.

She nearly called him back, but that would have been foolish, and anyway she needed some time alone to think. She heard the door on the landing click shut, and she closed her eyes.

'Goodnight, my love,' she whispered, and closed the door, walked into her bedroom, lay down on the bed and cried for him.

* * *

Within days the house was transformed.

So was her relationship with Hugo.

She felt she had a much greater understanding of him, and she could absolutely understand Sally's 'don't hurt him'. Her 'that's a shame' was echoed in her heart, but there was no way he was going to take their relationship any further, so they focussed on the friendship that they'd formed.

With the run over for another year, their evenings were spent walking the dogs, often strolling along the beach or beside the river. Sometimes they'd eat out, sometimes she'd cook for them, sometimes he would.

And as soon as Ryan was finished, she got her house ready for holiday letting, found a site where she could advertise it and within moments she had her first tenants lined up.

'Wow, that was quick,' he said when she told him.

'It was. I'm stunned. I just hope they don't trash it. And of course it's taken my eye off the ball for this wedding and I don't even know if I've got anything to wear. What's the dress code? And do you have any idea what I could buy for them?'

'Black tie, and no. She's got a gift list on a website, I believe. Ask her.'

'I will. And I might have to go dress shopping. I've only got three days and I've got to get the house ready, they come on Sunday.'

'That's fine, you can do that whenever. There are some good shops in Yoxburgh, nice little independents and they aren't outrageous.'

They didn't need to be outrageous, because she didn't have money to fling around after the expense of the house.

She asked some of the others what they were wearing, and they were all going in long. And she didn't have a long dress.

Unless she wore the wrap dress she'd got for Jim's retirement party...

It was hanging in her bedroom in the flat, and at lunchtime she ran up and pulled it out. Would it do? She'd felt good in it, she'd only worn it once, it had been expensive, and it was long.

Well, it was at the back, but not at the front where it wrapped across. That was mid-calf.

Long enough? Probably. And it was a beautiful dress.

She stripped off her scrubs, put it on, tied the waist and looked in the mirror, but it wasn't a full-length mirror so it was hard to judge. A bit too much cleavage? And if it was windy...

But she owned it, it suited her, and it picked up the colour of her eyes.

'It'll be fine,' she told herself, and hung it back up.

Job done. Now she just had to buy a present.

Hugo gave his bow tie a last little tug to straighten it, looked at himself in the mirror and closed his eyes.

He really, really needed to find a smile or he'd upset everyone, but he wasn't looking forward to the wedding.

It would have been easier without Ellie being his 'plus one' as Kerry, so blatantly matchmaking, had described it. They'd grown closer since the race, and he was finding it difficult enough to keep his distance as it was, especially since he'd kissed her. OK, it had been pretty platonic, but that had only been because he'd firmly kept it that way.

If she'd been anyone else, they would have ended up in bed weeks ago, but she wasn't a woman he could sleep with and kiss goodbye, and that was as much of a commitment he'd been prepared to make for years. And he cared about her far too much to want to treat her like that.

But with all the romantic wedding vibes, the alcohol, the dancing—hell, especially the dancing.

His heart sank. He'd be expected to dance with Ellie. They'd all be watching and waiting for it, and he'd bet his life that as soon as they were up on the dance floor Kerry would get the DJ to play some slow numbers, and she'd end up in his arms.

No alcohol, then. The only thing left for him to influence. Unless she hated dancing. He could only hope—

There was a quiet tap on the door, and he opened it to find Ellie there, looking drop-dead gorgeous in a beautiful dress that did absolutely nothing for his increasingly fragile self-control. It was bad enough when she was wearing scrubs—

'Will I be all right in this?' she asked doubtfully.

If it was any more all right he'd die of a heart attack, but that was his business, not hers. He dragged his eyes off the soft swell of her breasts so perfectly framed by the vee.

'Yes, it's fine,' he said, his voice gruffer that usual because that dress had totally emptied his brain. 'It's lovely. Are you ready?'

'Yes, I'm good to go.'

She needn't have worried about her dress. It was just right for the tone of the occasion, and she felt good in it.

They'd left the dogs together in his flat and walked to the venue, arriving bang on time, and after she'd changed into heels and left her wrap and flats in the cloakroom, they'd gone in and found some of the others from the practice there clustered around the bar talking to Kerry and her new husband James.

'Oh, she looks gorgeous,' Ellie said softly, 'and so happy, both of them.'

'They are, and she deserves it. I'm really happy for her.'

Kerry turned then and spotted them, and after all the kisses and hugs and handshakes were done and they moved on, Hugo turned to her.

'What would you like to drink?' he asked her, and she hesitated, then threw caution to the winds.

'White wine? Just a small one, not massive, I'm a bit of a lightweight and I haven't eaten yet.'

'No, nor have I. We'll have to raid the buffet later.'

He ordered drinks for all the practice members there, got himself an alcohol-free beer, handed her the wine and they mingled with the others.

'Hello, you,' a voice said behind them, and Hugo turned and gave the woman a warm hug.

'Lucy! Great to see you, I'm so glad you're here. Lucy, this is Ellie, she's covering your mat leave.'

Ellie met her eyes—curious, assessing—and smiled at her. 'Hi.'

'Hi. I've heard a lot about you from everyone. I hope Hugo's not working you too hard.'

She laughed, wondering what she'd heard, hoping none of it was idle speculation. 'Not as hard as he works himself, that's for sure. And everyone's been lovely.'

'They are lovely. I miss them.'

'I hope that means you're coming back,' Hugo said, and Lucy laughed.

'Never say never,' she said, 'although I might pop in soon.'

'Do. You're always welcome. So, how's it going?'

'Great. I love being a mum. Sleep would be nice, but—
yeah, it's all good. Anyway, I need to mingle, we're not
here for long and I've got loads of catching up to do. See
you soon?'

'Sure.'

Lucy turned away and went back to the others, and Ellie
met Hugo's eyes and smiled. 'She's nice.'

'She is. Right, somewhere there's a buffet table, and I need
to eat. I had half a sandwich for lunch.'

They grazed on the buffet, mingled a bit more, and then
it was time for the first dance.

They all clustered round to watch, phones clicking as photos were taken, videos filmed, and then everyone clapped
and cheered and headed onto the dance floor.

Hugo looked down at her with a smile she couldn't quite
read. 'Shall we?' he said, and held out his hand.

She put hers in it, and a shiver of something strange ran
up her arm and settled in her chest, robbing her of breath.
She should have had a bigger glass of wine, she thought, and
let him lead her onto the dance floor.

The music was typical wedding dance stuff, and despite
his apparent reluctance, he was a natural. It didn't surprise
her, because he always moved fluidly, but it was years since
she'd danced with anyone who didn't have two left feet, and
it was a joy to dance with someone who loved it as much
as she did.

And then the music slowed, and he held out his arms and
she moved into them. Not too close, but close enough that
she could smell the subtle fragrance of his cologne, feel the
light touch of his hand on her back, the occasional nudge of
his legs against hers, and her body caught fire.

She glanced at his face and met his eyes, and with a quiet

sigh he eased her closer; she rested her head on his shoulder, his cheek against hers, his body close now, his legs brushing hers as they swayed together to the music. She felt his lips graze her cheek, and she turned her head a fraction and his mouth met hers, a light, fleeting kiss that seared all the way down through her body, leaving her feeling more alive than she had for years.

He swore softly, then turned his head a fraction, his mouth by her ear, his voice a low murmur.

'We need to get out of here.'

They did, but she had no idea where it would lead, and she had no more idea where she wanted it to lead, either.

She just knew that for now, she wanted Hugo, and he wanted her, as simple and as complicated as that.

Except there was nothing simple about leaving, because Kerry caught them on the way out and gave them both a knowing look.

'Damn,' he said after they'd made the feeble excuse of needing to get back to the dogs and headed for the foyer.

'Don't worry, she's had way too much to drink, she probably won't even remember,' Ellie said, hoping it was true.

She retrieved her ballet flats, slung her wrap around her shoulders and they walked back to the practice, not quite touching, not quite apart.

So what now?

What was he doing? What was he *thinking* about?

He had no idea, he just knew that the only sure way to find out where this was going was to go with it, and go with it they would, he knew that much.

Either that or he'd die wondering what it would be like to—

He put his key in the lock, let them in and led her up to his flat.

The dogs gave them a rapturous welcome, and he took them out into the garden for a moment and came back up, wondering if she'd still be there or if she would have come to her senses and gone up to her flat.

No such luck.

'Stay and have a drink?' he suggested, leaving her a way out, just in case, hoping to God she didn't—

'Sure.'

She didn't look sure, and he wasn't, either, but it made no difference. He headed to the kitchen. 'Coffee or wine? I have both.'

'What are you having?'

Second thoughts, but he didn't say that, because she turned and he caught a flash of leg where the two sides of the dress met, and his brain left the building.

He swallowed. 'I don't really want a drink,' he said, and held her eyes.

Then what...?

'Nor do I.'

He held out his hand, and she let him draw her into his arms.

'I want you.' His voice was gruff, and she could feel the tension vibrating through his body. It matched the tension in her own, and she lifted her head and met his eyes.

'I want you, too,' she whispered, and he closed his eyes.

His mouth found hers, tentatively at first, then bolder, his teeth nipping lightly at her lips, his tongue teasing, coaxing, and then hot, so hot as she opened her mouth to him.

He rocked against her, his erection hard against her abdomen, one leg nudging between hers as he lifted her against him, his mouth doing incredible things to hers.

And then he broke away and let her go.

'I think we need to take this somewhere—'

'Horizontal?' she offered, and he gave a strangled laugh.

'I was going to say without the dogs, but yeah, that too.'

He shut the dogs in the sitting room, then caught her hand in his and led her into his bedroom and closed the door.

'So, where were we?'

'Not horizontal yet,' she said with a shaky smile, and tugged at his bow tie. 'Oh. It's real.'

'Of course it's real.' He slid it out from under the collar and laid it on his chair, shrugged off his jacket, heeled off his shoes and turned back to her. Then he stopped, took her by the hands and stared down into her eyes.

'This isn't going anywhere, you know that, don't you?'

She nodded, not at all sure if that was how she felt but willing to go along with it. So long as he was...

'If you don't want this, I can go,' she said, but he shook his head and his mouth tilted into a wry smile.

'Oh, I want. Believe me, I want.'

He cupped her face in his hands and kissed her again, slowly and thoroughly, then let her go and took a step back. 'We have way too much on,' he said, his voice hoarse, gravelly with need, his eyes so dark they looked almost black.

He turned off the top light, put on a bedside light and stripped off his shirt—or tried to. 'Stupid cufflinks,' he muttered, and she took his hands and slipped the cufflinks out one by one, dropping them on his bedside table.

When she turned back his shirt was gone, and his hand was on his belt buckle. She stopped him, removed his hands, undid the buckle, slipped the leather free, then reached for the waistband. Two clips. Why so many?

And then his zip was sliding down, and she let go and his trousers slid down his legs and puddled round his ankles.

She closed her eyes then, unable to look at him without touching. She heard the soft rustle of fabric, a muted clunk as the belt buckle hit the floor again, then his hands were on her waist.

'How does this undo?'

She reached for the bow and he caught her hands and eased them aside, then she felt the waist fall away, the cool air of his bedroom brushing her skin as he opened the front of the dress.

She heard the sharp hiss of indrawn breath, felt the touch of his hands on her shoulders brushing the dress aside so it slid to the floor, then his hands reached around her and un-clipped her bra and freed her aching breasts.

She opened her eyes and they locked with his as he reached for her and drew her into his arms, his chest heaving as if he'd been running, the soft hairs chafing lightly at her nipples with every breath.

His kiss was long and slow, one leg nudging between hers, the thin layers of fabric between them annoying now.

'Hugo, please,' she said, her voice cracking, and he tugged back the covers, stripped off his shorts and then slowly, inch by inch, he drew that last tiny scrap of lace away, his mouth following it.

She sucked in her breath, and he straightened up, lifted her and laid her on the bed, following her down and strad-dling her. Then he reached into the bedside table and pulled out a small foil packet, tore it open and took out a condom.

'I'm on the pill,' she told him, but he just shook his head.

'I still want this.'

'Let me,' she said, and, in the gentle light that gilded his body, she saw the muscles in his abdomen clench as she touched him, carrying out the intimate task with deliberate and meticulous care. He tipped his head back and swore softly as she trailed her trembling fingers slowly back up.

He took her hand away. 'Are you done torturing me?' he said, his voice uneven, his breathing ragged.

She couldn't stop the smile. 'I think so. For now.'

He stared down at her, his mouth tipping into an answering smile, and then the smile faded as his hands reached down and cupped her breasts, taking his sweet time as he rolled her nipples gently between thumb and forefinger, then shifted down her body, bending his head to draw her nipples one at a time into his hot, hungry mouth.

His tongue toyed with them, his teeth nipping gently, his lips closing over them as he suckled. She bucked and writhed under him, and finally, when she thought she was going to cry with frustration, he nudged her legs apart and slid slowly, deeply inside her.

A long, shuddering groan echoed through his body and into hers, then his mouth found hers in a kiss that nearly sent her over the brink as he began to move. His hands were everywhere, nothing off limits, and so were hers. She loved the feel of his body, the taut muscles of his shoulders, the feel of his hair sifting through her fingers, the slight roughness of his beard against her cheek as his tongue flicked against the pulse in her neck. The tension she could feel building in him…

She was close, so close, and then he shifted again, his clever, knowing fingers touching her, coaxing her, taking

her over the edge and then following her with a guttural cry
as his body stiffened against hers.

He lowered his head and rested it against hers, and she
could feel his breath hot against her shoulder.

And then, as the echoes faded and their breathing slowed,
he rolled away from her, got up and went into his bathroom,
closing the door behind him with a soft but definite click.

CHAPTER EIGHT

HUGO DEALT WITH the condom, then propped his hands on the washbasin and stared at himself in the mirror, shaken to the core.

What the hell just happened?

Apart from the fact that he'd just had the most profound sex of his life. He closed his eyes and groaned.

Why? Why the hell did you do that?

No idea. No idea at all, except it had seemed like a good idea at the time, get rid of the urge, take the edge off it. But it hadn't, had it? No. It was worse than ever, because now he *knew.* He knew just how good it was with her, and it scared him, because sure, the sex had been good, but it had been more than that.

Far more.

He felt like he'd given her his soul, and taken hers. So now what did he do with it? Hand it back? Tell her it was all a stupid, rash mistake and they should never have done it?

He had no idea. He just knew he wanted her like he'd never wanted anyone ever before and, whatever happened, it was going to hurt them both.

She tugged the covers over herself and lay there motionless, staring at his bathroom door, her body still thrumming with the last echoes of her climax.

So what happens now? Is that it? Is he done with me now?

No idea. Should she get up and leave before he told her to go? Get up and put her dress back on and go and sit with the dogs? She could hear them whining in the other room, wondering what was going on.

They weren't alone.

The bathroom door opened and he walked out, gloriously, beautifully naked, and she wanted to touch him, to hold him, to make love with him again. But she didn't have the right to do that, because it would make it more than just a one-off drunken quickie.

Not that it had felt like that, at least for her. Quick, yes, but something much more powerful, more meaningful than she'd expected. And neither of them were drunk, or at least not on alcohol, so that meant—what, exactly?

'The dogs are whining, and I'm still hungry. Fancy a snack and a cup of tea?'

He turned away before she could read his eyes, and she stared at his back. He was lifting a bathrobe off the back of the door, shrugging into it, covering that glorious, wonderful body that had just taken her to places she'd never been before and stolen her heart along the way.

'Sure,' she said, although she wasn't sure of anything right then. 'I'll run upstairs and put something on.' Something sensible that didn't give out such blatant signals...

'I'll be in the kitchen.'

He left the room, and she scrambled out of bed, flung her dress back on, scooped up her underwear and shoes and ran up to her flat, closing the door behind her and leaning back on it with a shaky sigh.

She had no idea what was going on in his head, and his

eyes had been unreadable. Mostly because he'd had his back to her for nearly all of that very brief conversation…

She hung up her dress, pulled on fresh underwear and her jersey PJs, and then after a glance in the mirror she took off her makeup and went back down to his flat, her heart beating a tattoo behind her ribs.

He'd pulled on sweat pants and a hoodie, and he was busy in the kitchen, the dogs at his feet looking hopeful.

'That smells good,' she offered, trying to sound normal.

'I made cheese on toast,' he said over his shoulder. 'Hope that's OK.'

And he turned then and smiled at her, and she still couldn't read his face, but at least he wasn't frowning. He picked up the laden plate.

'Here, you take the tea and I'll bring this. I don't want Rufus to steal it, he loves cheese.'

'He'd have to fight Lola for it,' she said drily, and smiled back, not sure if it would look like a smile or some kind of weird rictus, but it was the best she could do. She picked up the mugs and followed him.

Rufus and Lola, as predicted, were all about the cheese, dancing around under Hugo's feet, their eyes fixed on the plate.

'No. Lie down.'

They lay, obeying him but eyeing the plate longingly as Hugo sat down beside her with it on his lap.

'Here, let's eat it quick while it's still hot and before they drool everywhere.'

She took a slice, the melted cheese running off the edges of the toast, stretching into strings as she lifted it. She scooped it up, wiped it off on the crust and sucked the tip of her finger, then glanced at Hugo.

He was watching her, transfixed, and she could read his face easily now. Want, need, the white heat of that visceral urge that had brought them together just a short while ago.

'Did you have to do that?' he said, his smile wry, his voice not quite managing to be casual.

'I'm sorry—'

'Don't apologise,' he told her, and leant over and kissed her. Just a touch, a light brush of his mouth on hers, the flick of his tongue to catch the taste of that melted cheese.

Then he leant back, his shoulder against hers, and picked up a slice, biting into it with a groan that dragged her mind straight back to his bed. 'Oh, that's *so-o-o* good! I'm starving.'

She couldn't watch him. Too tempting, too—just too *Hugo*...

His arm settled round her shoulders, pulling her in against his side as he rested his head against hers.

'Are we OK, Ellie?'

His voice was low, a little gruff, and she turned her head a fraction so she could see him, the food forgotten.

'I don't know,' she told him frankly. 'Are we?'

His mouth twisted a little. 'I hope so. But I think we need to talk.'

She looked down at her cheese, cooling now, congealing on the toast as it cooled. 'Can we eat and talk at the same time?'

She felt as much as heard his chuckle.

'Yes, we can eat and talk.'

But he didn't talk, so she prompted him.

'So what did you want to say?'

He'd just taken another bite, so he shook his head and chewed and swallowed, a smile playing on his lips. She was happy to see the smile, because she had no idea what was coming and until he got on with whatever it was he wanted to say—

'Sorry. OK. Firstly, I have absolutely no regrets about what happened. But if we're going to do it again, we need some ground rules first,' he added, his smile fading.

Ground rules? 'OK,' she said slowly. 'Such as?'

He hesitated, his smile well and truly gone, his face serious now. 'I don't do permanent. I don't do long-term, I don't make promises I can't keep—and I don't want anyone else here knowing. And there's no way you're getting pregnant if I have anything to do with it.'

The last one was clearly a veiled reference to Samuel, and maybe all the rest of his rules, too. She chewed and swallowed, taking her time while she tried to work out exactly what he was saying. 'So, is that it?'

He turned his head and studied her face for a moment. 'I think so, for now. Your turn,' he added, but she shook her head.

'I haven't—I didn't ask for permanent, I didn't ask for long-term—'

'You didn't ask me to leave the wedding with you so abruptly and come back here and—'

He broke off, and she wondered, for a moment, what he'd been going to say.

'Make love to me?' she suggested, her words hanging in the silence, and he met her eyes again, his utterly unreadable this time.

'I don't do love,' he said.

Because love hurt, she realised, and he'd already lost too much. Oh, Hugo…

She felt something in her chest squeeze a little tighter. 'OK, so what do you do?' she asked, and then added bluntly, 'Apart from having mind-blowing, earth-shaking no-strings sex?'

She'd felt it, too?

The blown mind, the shaken earth.

The soul-sharing? She hadn't mentioned that. Maybe she hadn't felt it the way he had.

'That's pretty much it,' he said, his voice a little terse because he wanted to deny it and couldn't. He wasn't going to talk about the soul-sharing, not now, not ever. He had nothing to offer her. Nothing that would expose him to any more losses in his life. His heart was like a hollow shell already. Letting himself fall for her would just tear out the little that was left of it when she went. Which she would, in the end. And she deserved better than the little he had to offer.

'OK.'

He stared at her, his mind distracted. 'OK?'

'Yes. OK. Your terms.'

He pulled himself together. 'And what are yours?'

Something raw and hurt flickered in her eyes and was gone before he was sure.

'I don't do Ts & Cs, Hugo, and I'm on the pill and you're using condoms, so that takes care of that one. All I'd ask is that you don't slag me off to all the practice staff when you decide you're done with me.'

He swore, dumped the plate and turned her face towards him, appalled. 'I would never do that to you. *Ever.* And the last thing I want to do is hurt you.'

He leant in and kissed her, just a fleeting, gentle touch, an apology for sounding like a—

'No!'

He swore again, snatched up the empty plate and glared at the dogs. They were gulping down the last few pieces, and they didn't even have the grace to look guilty...

'Come back to bed,' he said, and then added, as a belated afterthought, 'Please?'

She couldn't have said no to him if her life had depended on it.

They took it slower this time, savouring every touch, every tremor, every kiss, and when it was over he kissed her gently, rolled away and went into the bathroom.

She watched him go, wondering what would happen now, what his protocol was for this kind of event. Would he expect her to go up to her room for the rest of the night? Stay here with him? And what about the dogs? Lola was used to being upstairs with her now. Where would *she* sleep?

Maybe she should just be proactive and get up—

The bathroom light clicked off, and he walked back to the bed, turning off the bedside light as he got back under the covers. 'Come here,' he said softly.

He rolled towards her, drawing her into his arms again, and his kiss was tender. 'You OK?'

'Mm-hm. You?'

'I'm very OK.'

He kissed her again, then rolled onto his back, leaving his arm around her, and she lay with her arm draped over his chest and her head on his shoulder, listening to the beat of his heart and the slow rhythm of his breathing.

I don't do love.

Maybe not, but he did mind-blowing, earth-shaking no-strings sex with bells on. Maybe she should have said heart stealing, too. Because that was what it was. She felt as if he'd reached inside her chest and cradled her heart in his hands, and nothing would ever feel the same again, and she wanted to cry...

He woke in the night to raging thirst and a dead arm.

She was fast asleep, her body lax, her breathing slow and regular. He eased his arm out from under her, tucking the pillow in its place, and went quietly out of the room, snagging his robe off the back of the door and wincing as the blood flowed through his arm again.

The dogs were silent, so he left them alone and went into the kitchen, downed a glass of water and then made a cup of tea and sat and drank it, his mind lost in thought.

Was she really OK? Would they be able to do this? He didn't know, and the very last thing he wanted to do was hurt her, hurt anyone, but she was young, only early thirties, and she had so much life to live, so much love to give.

It would be so easy to let himself love her, but she deserved a family, not a no-strings contract, and that was all he could offer her. All he *dared* to offer her. And it wasn't enough.

Idiot. You shouldn't have touched her.

He swore softly under his breath, and stared blankly out of the window. The sky was still dark, not even the slightest touch of pale along the horizon, but he was too wired to sleep. He scrolled through the photos he'd taken last night, Kerry dancing with James, a group one of the practice members, and then one of Ellie laughing at him that got him right in the solar plexus.

And then just because why not torture himself, he scrolled back through the photos, right back to ten years ago and his photos of Samuel.

There was one of him lying in Emma's arms, another in his own, one of his little finger in Samuel's tiny fist, another with Peter and Sally.

Four broken hearts, four lives plunged into grief and despair. A salutary reminder of why it could never happen again…

He switched off his phone, put it on charge and went quietly back into the bedroom. She was motionless, silent, and he let his robe drop to the floor and lay down, easing the duvet over himself.

'Are you OK?'

Her voice was soft, concerned, her hand finding his shoulder in the darkness, and he shifted to face her. 'I'm fine,' he lied. 'I was just thirsty.'

'You've been ages.'

'I made tea. We didn't drink the last one.'

'I know. I'm thirsty, too. What's the time?'

'Three twenty-eight the last time I looked. Want me to get you tea?'

'Tea would be lovely. Thank you.'

He made them both one, and took them back to the bedroom. She'd turned on the bedside light and she was in the bathroom, and she came out naked and beautiful and he wanted her all over again.

Yet again, the tea went ignored.

The dogs woke them at eight, and she ran up to her flat and showered and dressed while Hugo let the dogs out.

He was in the shower when she came down, so she made coffee and put some toast in, then sat on the sofa, Lola's head on her lap and Rufus curled up under her arm, wondering what would happen next.

He hadn't outlined the rules beyond the 'don't do long-term' etc., but was she expected to move in with him? Sleep in her own bed unless and until either of them wanted to be together? 'The Rules', as she was starting to think of them, needed a little clarification. And maybe some of her own.

He appeared a few moments later, while her list was still a work in progress.

'Well, you all look comfy,' he said, and perched on the arm of the sofa, the only place left for him. 'I can smell coffee.'

'You can. And toast. It's only just done. Come on, dogs, shift, it's time for breakfast.'

The dogs leapt off the sofa, and Hugo stood and pulled her up into his arms. His hug was brief, and then he let her go and led the way into the kitchen, the dogs trotting at his heels.

After breakfast they walked the dogs along the beach, and as they headed back she broke the comfortable silence.

'What are your plans for the rest of the day?' she asked him, because it was that or wait for him to tell her.

'I don't really have any. I mean, there's always admin to do.'

'Well, while you're doing that, you can do a bill for Lola's treatment,' she told him, and raised an eyebrow when he opened his mouth.

He ignored the gesture. 'Don't you think we're rather past that?'

'Or I can do it myself.'

'So what are your plans?'

'First I need to go over to my house to make sure it's ready for my first booking. They're coming this afternoon.'

'Can I come?'

'Sure. You can give me your first impression of it.'

They let the dogs in, rubbed them down with towels to get the sand off their feet, and then headed over to her house on foot.

'It looks really good,' he told her as they walked round, and she smiled in relief.

'I did my best. I just hope they don't trash it.'

'Who is it, do you know?'

'A couple with a baby, and their parents, his or hers, I don't know.'

He chuckled. 'They don't sound like they'll trash it.'

'No, they don't. It was a good idea of yours.'

So long as nothing happened between them to upset the status quo. Not that she was entirely sure yet quite what that was...

They went back to the practice, and while Hugo busied himself in the office, she went food shopping.

She had to drop a welcome pack in for her tenants, so she picked up those things and some stuff for the barbecue. His idea, and of course because it was a glorious early May day, everyone else had the same idea and the shelves were a bit depleted.

She threw a selection of things into the basket, then detoured up the last aisle and dropped a packet of condoms in on the rest. Just in case...

By the time she'd been to the house and got back it was getting hotter, and she carried the food upstairs and then hesitated. His fridge or hers? Or both?

They definitely needed to lay down more rules...

Hugo heard her come in, and followed her upstairs.

'What did you get?'

'All sorts of stuff. I just don't know where to put it,' she told him, turning to meet his eyes. 'Are we living together? Cooking together? Sleeping together? Or living independently and meeting up for sex when the mood takes us? Are we lovers? Friends with benefits? What the hell are we, Hugo?'

He blinked at that. 'Wow. Um—are you OK, Ellie? Because that sounds…'

'Confused? Uncertain? I mean, you have all these *rules*, but they're so vague—'

'OK, so we have sex on Sunday evening, Tuesday lunchtime, Wednesday morning—oh, and we might cram a quickie in between consults—'

'Don't be sarcastic.'

He scrubbed a hand through his hair and sighed. 'I'm not being sarcastic, Ellie, and frankly, I don't know the answers either.' His voice gentled. 'And I don't know what we call this. I hate friends with benefits, it's—it's not what it is. It feels—I don't know, more than that. And I certainly don't want to call all the shots, that's not what this is about. Maybe we just need to be honest with each other, like say, *I want to spend the night alone*, or *Let's eat in mine tonight*, or…' he shrugged '…*I want you now.*'

She stared at him, her eyes searching. 'Do you?'

He felt his body react instantly, and he couldn't stop the little huff of laughter. He closed his eyes briefly. 'Of course I do. I always have done. Right from day one. But only if you do.'

She was still staring at him, something primal stirring in her eyes. Her lips parted, then shut, pursing a little. He could almost hear her mind work.

'Um—maybe we should put the food away first?' she suggested after a sizzling pause, and he laughed and pulled her into his arms, folding her against his chest in a gentle hug.

'We probably should.'

Over the next few days, things sorted themselves out, because it turned out neither of them wanted to sleep alone, and it was easier with the dogs if they were in his flat rather than up the extra flight to hers.

And because they were there all the time, they cooked and ate in his kitchen, and hung out in his sitting room playing backgammon or watching TV or just talking about this and that.

Work was busier than usual, because people were going on holiday and so there were the usual panicked vaccinations that had been overlooked or forms to fill in for going abroad, and of course Kerry and James were on their honeymoon so they were a nurse down for that first week.

Then Kerry sent a group message, full of her honeymoon photos, both of them looking blissfully happy with life. And Ellie felt a pang of sadness that this wasn't ever going to be the case with her and Hugo.

Not in his rules. And yes, she understood where he was coming from, and in a way she was glad she knew where she stood with him, but underneath it all was an aching sadness that it couldn't be more, because she loved him.

She'd loved him since the day she'd met him, the day he saved Lola's life, and with every day she loved him more.

And he didn't do love.

So she kept smiling, got on with her work, and then on Thursday, just as she was about to take her lunch break, a client she'd seen before came in on the verge of tears. Ellie was in Reception at the time, and she ushered her into a consult room and closed the door.

'What's wrong?' she asked gently, because the dog looked absolutely fine, and her owner shook her head.

'My husband's—we've split up, and he doesn't want Bailey and I work full-time and I don't know where I'm going to live because I can't find a place I can afford where they allow dogs, and I can't leave him alone all day, and I can't work from home—'

'Do you want us to find a new home for him? Is that it?'

She nodded, fumbling in her pockets, and Ellie handed her a tissue. 'Thanks.'

She blew her nose and blinked away tears and met Ellie's eyes. 'It's just—he's such a lovely, gentle, kind dog, and I can't bear to think of him going to someone awful who doesn't understand dogs...'

'Let me talk to Hugo—in fact, hang on, if you can, and I'll see if he's free now?'

She went out the back into the corridor and heard his voice. He was in the office talking to Jean, and he looked up at her and broke off.

'Hi, what's up?'

'Client wants—no, she *needs* to rehome a dog. He's a Golden Retriever, three years old, absolutely lovely dog, they've split up and she can't find accommodation that'll allow her to keep him, she works full-time. I was thinking, Jenny?'

Jenny, who'd lost Nell in Ellie's first week, and was alone now.

'Who is he?'

'Mrs Williams' Bailey.'

'*Bailey?* I know Bailey, he'd be perfect for Jenny. Oh, she must be heartbroken. Is she still here with him?'

'Yes, she's in the consult room.'

'Jean, I'll be back. Ellie, let's go and talk to her.'

Bailey recognised him instantly and greeted him, tail wagging, smiling in the way that only a Golden Retriever could smile. He crouched down and gave him a fuss, then straightened up.

'I'm so sorry to hear about your circumstances, Mrs Williams. Are you OK to keep him a day or so while we make some enquiries? We have someone in mind, a lady who lost her dog recently who could be just right for him. She has grandchildren, and they visit her often and are used to dogs. They've had five over the years and she certainly knows what she's doing with them. I could call her? Would you mind?'

'Oh, could you? He loves children. I've got a baby nephew and he adores him, he's so gentle, and we thought…'

The tears started again, and it wasn't hard to work out why. A family dog, for a family that was never going to happen.

'I tell you what, why don't you stay here for a minute and let me go and make a call. OK?'

She nodded, and they left her there and went back to the office. Jean, reading his mind as ever, thrust a piece of paper at him.

'Jenny's number.'

'Thanks.' She picked up almost immediately, and after asking how she was, he said carefully, 'Look, I know it's still early days, but have you given any thought to getting another dog?'

'Oh, Hugo—I don't know. The house just feels so *wrong*

without a dog, but I can't cope with a puppy right now, and an older rescue dog might come with all sorts of issues.'

'How about a three-year-old Golden Retriever? Lovely boy, sweet, friendly, gentle dog, loves everybody, good with children, fit and healthy, and needs a new home through no fault of his own. Change of personal circumstances, but he's very much loved.'

'Oh, poor boy, he sounds… Oh, Hugo, I don't know. Is he with you?'

'He is at the moment.'

There was a long pause, then she said, 'Can I come now?'

'Sure. Come to the back door, you can meet him in the office.'

They sent Mrs Williams back to the waiting room and took Bailey through to the office, put Lola and Rufus in the kennels out of the way, and after a very few minutes Jenny arrived.

Hugo met her at the back door and ushered her in, and she took one look at Bailey and fell in love.

'Oh, the dear, dear boy…'

'Here, have a seat.' He turned a chair round and she sat on it and held out a hand, and the dog came over and licked it and sat beside her and leant against her leg, his head tilted up, staring at her as if she was his best friend.

'Oh, he's such a sweetheart… He reminds me of Rupert.'

'I'm sure he can be naughty.'

Jenny laughed and looked up at him, smiling the first real smile he'd seen on her in months. 'Hugo, all dogs can be naughty. It's part of their charm. Nell was still naughty. Oh, the poor, sweet boy. Can I ask why?'

'Divorce, and she works full-time.'

'Oh, no, that wouldn't work, Goldens need all the love all the time. Oh, Bailey. Are you a good boy? Are you?'

Bailey wagged his tail, tongue lolling, a silly smile on his face, and that was it. 'I'll take him.'

'Are you sure? You don't have to make a decision now. Do you want to think about it?'

She looked up and met his eyes. 'Hugo, I've thought about nothing else since Nell, and she would have loved him. I don't need to think any more. I want to take him home as soon as I can.'

'Let me fetch his owner. I'm sure she'd love to meet you.'

Half an hour later a tearful Mrs Williams said goodbye to Bailey and left him with his new owner. He whined for a moment, but a bit of a cuddle and a gravy bone treat brought him back to Jenny.

'She's left a bag of his toys and blankets in Reception, and also his bed, so you can take them home with you. I'll give you a hand out to the car.'

He saw her off, then went back inside and found Ellie up to her eyes with consults, and he took some of them off her.

Jo, their Thursday vet, was busy doing the first of two dentals, and Ellie was in dire need of a break. So was he, but hey, he was the boss.

'Are you sure you've got time? I thought you were busy with Jenny.'

'No, she's gone home with Bailey. Go and eat something, and after we've finished tonight we'll take the dogs for a walk by the river and go to the pub.'

It was a lovely walk, the dogs enjoying the change of scenery as much as she was, and she breathed in deeply and sighed.

'There's something so evocative about the smell of river mud at low tide,' she murmured, and Hugo chuckled.

'Only when it's in the river. When it's on the dogs it's less great.'

She laughed, picturing the two of them if they'd been off the lead. They couldn't be, of course, because of the ground-nesting wetland birds, but they were still having fun.

'So how did it go with Jenny?'

'Oh, she's in love. I think they'll be fine. She knows what she's doing.'

Ellie didn't reply. She was busy thinking about the comparison between them, Jenny in love with Bailey, who wouldn't have any rules or restrictions on the breadth and depth of her love for him, and her, falling deeper and deeper in love with an enigmatic loner with a broken heart and a rule book that lay between them like a minefield.

What on earth was she doing with him? Unlike Jenny with Bailey, she didn't have a clue. She just knew it was bound to end in tears...

CHAPTER NINE

FRIDAY WAS AS hectic as ever, and as soon as all her consults were done, she headed over to her house.

Her tenants had left this morning, and a new family were coming in tomorrow. She opened the front door with a feeling of trepidation, but the house was immaculate, and there was a note on the worktop thanking her for a lovely break and saying they'd like to book again later in the summer.

They'd be more than welcome. The bathroom and kitchen had both been cleaned, the beds stripped and the carpeted floors vacuumed, so there wasn't much for her to do. She put on the fresh bedding, ran a duster round the house, emptied the dishwasher and then headed back to Hugo.

She found him in his kitchen, busy stirring something on the hob, and she wrapped her arms round him and peered down into the pan. Chilli? 'That smells delicious.'

'Hopefully. So how was the house?'

'Brilliant. I couldn't believe it. They'd cleaned everything.'

'Wow. That's good. So when do your next tenants come?'

'Tomorrow afternoon, and they're here till Wednesday. I'll need to pop over first thing tomorrow with a welcome pack before we start. Then I've got another family from next Saturday for two weeks. Have the dogs been out?'

'Yes. Not far, but they've been out in the garden quite a bit today. They get on really well. Oh, and I heard from Jenny.

Bailey cried a bit in the night, but then he settled and she's really happy. She brought us some chocolates as a thank you.'

She rolled her eyes. 'More chocolates? We'll all be obese and diabetic.'

He threw her a wry grin. 'Don't worry about that, some days it's all that keeps us going. I have to say I'm glad Kerry's back on Monday, we've been picking up all sorts of things she usually does, so we might get time to eat actual food.'

It was a vain hope.

They were every bit as busy, and the week flew by. She went over late on Wednesday to get her house ready for the new people coming on Saturday, and then on Friday afternoon, as it was all winding down at the end of the day, Lucy walked in via the back door with her baby in her arms, and everyone who could downed tools and congregated in the office for a look at the new arrival.

Ellie was still busy while they were all cooing over baby Freya, but when she emerged after her last consult ended, she went in there for a peek.

'Oh, she's gorgeous,' she said softly, just as Hugo walked in, and Lucy laughed.

'She'd be more gorgeous if she slept through the night. Hey, Hugo, do me a favour and hold her while I nip to the loo?'

And without waiting for an answer, she dumped Freya into his arms.

For a fleeting second he looked paralysed, then Freya cried and instinct kicked in and he shifted her gently into a better position, smiling at her and murmuring reassuring nothings to soothe her, and Ellie stared at him, gazing down at Freya with such tenderness that she wanted to cry.

And then he looked up and met her eyes.

For a moment he froze, his face filled with longing, a deep yearning he'd never let her see before, and then his eyes went blank as the shutters came down. He turned away and walked out, still talking to Freya, but away from Ellie, away from the others.

Lucy appeared, and he handed Freya back instantly.

'Has she been OK?'

'Fine. Sorry, got to go. Congratulations, she's beautiful.'

He dropped a kiss on her cheek and walked away, heading for the door to his flat with Rufus at his heels, leaving Ellie standing there staring at the space where he'd been. She'd thought he was OK until he'd looked up, and then she'd seen the longing in his eyes—for Samuel, or for a child he'd never let himself have?

Oh, Hugo. Had that shown in her own eyes? The ache in her heart for him, and for a child of his that she'd never be able to hold?

Or the ache in his own heart, reflected back at him...

She needed to go to him.

He turned the latch on his door, went upstairs and locked the door to the back stairs, then walked into the sitting room and dropped onto the sofa.

He could still smell the baby—that evocative, unforgettable mixture of milk and nappy cream.

How? How can I remember that?

How could he forget?

He closed his eyes to shut out the images, but it didn't work. Of course it didn't work.

And nor did this thing he had going with Ellie. He'd been OK until she'd rocked up in his life and invaded the safe little cocoon he'd built around himself. He'd let her in because he couldn't help himself, but he couldn't do it any more, couldn't let her stay there, knocking down the protective walls around his heart brick by brick with every kiss, every touch, because he knew what would come next.

He'd seen the need in her eyes, the longing he could never dare to fulfil. It was a longing that was all too familiar to him, but Samuel was gone and he'd never get him back—

He heard her on the back stairs, the rattle of the door handle, the knock.

'Hugo? Hugo, let me in.'

Rufus ran to the door and scratched at it, whining, and he closed his eyes.

'Hugo, please, don't do this. We need to talk.'

She was right, they did.

And he knew exactly what he had to say...

Ellie rested her head against the door, her heart pounding, dread running through her veins.

Why wouldn't he talk to her? Why—

She heard the key turn, and the door opened.

Oh, Hugo...

He looked awful, jaw clenched, eyes blank and yet not. He turned away and she followed him into the sitting room. He walked straight past the sofa where they sat each night, over to the window, staring through it as if he was looking for something.

Words?

'Hugo, please talk to me.'

He turned, hands still rammed in his pockets, his back to the light, and she sat down on the arm of the sofa as if her strings were cut.

He was going to end it. She couldn't read the expression on his face but she didn't need to, she could see it in every defensive line of his body.

'We can't do this any more. You're getting in too deep, and I can't let you do that. I don't want it, and if you had any sense, nor would you. You deserve better. You deserve someone who can give you what you need, give you a family, a stable home life, the love you deserve, and that's never going to be me.'

No...

'Why don't you let me be the judge of what I need?'

'Because your judgement's clouded. Yes, the sex is great, but that's all it is, all it could ever be.'

'You're wrong, Hugo. I don't care about the sex, it's neither here nor there. It's way more than that—'

'Only for you. And I don't want it any more.' He closed his eyes and she saw him swallow. 'I can't love you, Ellie. And you need a man who will. A man who *can*.'

She stood up, legs shaking like jelly, and took a step towards him, but he held up his hand to ward her off.

'Don't—'

Don't what? Don't go and put your arms around him and tell him you love him? Don't tell him he's all you'll ever need, that you don't care about having a family, so long as you have him?

His face blurred, but for a few more seconds she stood her ground, and then she sucked in a breath and drew herself up. She wasn't going to grovel.

'Goodbye, Hugo,' she said softly.

And then she turned and walked out of his flat, her heart in shreds. Lola was torn between the two of them, and she called her, closing the door behind them and heading up the stairs on trembling legs.

Seven weeks. Seven weeks today since she'd hit the road and driven here, into his life. How was it only that?

She reached her flat and closed the door, somehow holding it together, her heart numb. She knew it wouldn't stay that way, but for now, she had to escape from here and get as far away from him as she could before the tears came.

She packed her things—not all of them, she didn't have enough bags or enough energy. Just the things she and Lola would need.

She carried it all downstairs, put it into her car, came back for Lola's bed, her food, her toys, and then put Lola in the car and drove away.

Hugo stood at the window and watched her go, his eyes dry, his heart thudding against his ribcage.

He'd done the right thing, for her, for him.

The only thing.

He just hadn't expected it to hurt quite so much.

His chest heaved and he fought down the sob, but it tore its way out of his chest anyway. He walked into his bedroom and lay on the bed, but it smelt of her, the lingering trace of her scent wrapping around him, engulfing him in pain.

Rufus whined and licked his face, and he realised tears were leaking out of the corners of his eyes and dribbling down onto the pillow. He let them fall. He owed her that, at least...

She didn't know where to go.

Her house? Too close, and anyway she had holidaymakers arriving tomorrow.

Oh, no. Welcome pack.

She pulled over into the forecourt of a mini-supermarket, left Lola in the car and grabbed a few things—milk, tea-bags, bread, butter, eggs, cheese, biscuits, jam—just something to tide them over after a journey—and dropped them off at the house.

Seven weeks ago today, almost to the hour, she'd let Lola out into the garden and she'd been injured. Seven short weeks that had been the best and worst weeks of her life.

And now here she was again, back to square one, only now with an intact dog and a broken heart.

Where could she go?

Nowhere, at this time of night, but she couldn't stay here in Yoxburgh. Too close, too many memories of Hugo.

So she locked the house, left the key in the key safe she'd had installed and drove away.

Instinct and adrenaline got her down the A12 and round the M25, and then a near-miss as she went up the slip road and onto the M40 brought her to her senses. She drove to the motel she'd stayed at before, checked into a dog-friendly room and fed Lola, then lay on the bed, dry-eyed, cast adrift once more on the sea of life without a rudder or a compass to guide her, the future a yawning void...

Where could she go? What should she do?

Somehow she slept, Lola on the bed beside her, and when she woke it was just gone five. Too early for breakfast, not that she was hungry, but she fed Lola, picked up her bag, clipped her on her lead and left the room, dropping her key in the slot on her way out.

She drove on autopilot, and shortly after six she turned onto Jim's drive and cut the engine. The light was on in his kitchen. Of course it was, because her old boss and mentor had always been an early riser and the kettle would be on. His face appeared in the window, then the front door opened and he stood there, a familiar silhouette in a world that seemed suddenly alien.

She got out of the car and walked towards him, and he took one look at her and held out his arms. She fell into them, felt the warmth and strength of them close around her, holding her safe, and felt herself starting to fall apart.

'Oh, dear, dear girl. Come inside and have a cup of tea.'

'Lola,' she said, and he let the dog out of the car and brought her inside, ushering Ellie into the kitchen.

'This one looks as if she could do with a run in the garden, and you look as if you could do with a nice cup of tea,' he said, and while he opened the back door and took Lola outside, she sat down at his kitchen table where she'd sat so many times before, and finally, finally, the tears fell.

He didn't say a word when he came back in with Lola, just put a mug down on the table in front of her and handed her a wad of tissues.

'I'm sorry,' she managed, sniffing and scrubbing at her eyes, but he squeezed her hand briefly.

'No need to apologise. You're safe here, and you don't have to tell me anything.'

Just as well, because right then she was beyond making any sense. She cradled the mug, warming her ice-cold hands on it, but she didn't drink.

'I should have rung—'

'Nonsense. My door's always open to you, Ellie. You know that. I wish you'd come to me before.'

So did she, now, looking back, but then she'd never have met Hugo, never known just how beautiful love could be.

Or how painful.

The tears welled again, and she swiped at them, her hands shaking.

'When did you last eat anything?'

She stared blankly at him. 'Eat...? I—I don't remember, Jim. Maybe lunch yesterday? I'm not sure, maybe a chocolate? I had a biscuit in the motel last night, but—no, not really.'

She wasn't even making sense, but Jim just tutted softly and got up and put some bread in the toaster, took eggs out of a bowl and a pan from the rack and cracked the eggs into it, added milk, a knob of butter, a twist of salt and pepper, beat them together and set them on the hob while he buttered the toast.

Moments later he put their two plates down on the table and sat down.

'Come on, eat up,' he told her, pushing the plate of scrambled eggs towards her, and she suddenly realised how hungry she was.

She ate, and then when she'd finished every last morsel, Jim cleared the plates away, sat down again and met her eyes.

'Is this about Hugo?'

The kindness and sympathy in his eyes were too much for her, so she looked down at her hands, finding a crumb on the table and pushing it around with her fingertip until she couldn't see it any longer.

'I should have known better,' she said unevenly. 'God knows he warned me, Jim. He told me it wasn't going anywhere, and he gave me a whole list of rules, things he didn't do, like permanent or long-term or love, said he didn't make promises he couldn't keep—and I somehow managed to forget all about that and fall in love with him anyway—'

Jim's firm, kindly hand closed over hers and gave it a gentle squeeze.

'I'm so sorry. I thought you'd be all right with Hugo, I thought he'd take care of you.'

'Oh, he did. He was so kind, so decent, so—and he still is, Jim. That's the awful thing. It's not about us, it's about—'

She sucked in a shaky breath. 'He had a baby. Ten years ago, and he was born with a chromosomal disorder that was incompatible with life, and he died when he was eight weeks old. And it broke him, Jim. It broke him more than I'd realised. I suppose I thought at first I could stick to his stupid rules, but then I couldn't, I went and fell in love with him, and still I thought we'd be OK, and then… I'm—no, I *was* covering someone's maternity leave, and she brought her baby in, and she's about the same age as his baby was, I guess, and she gave her to him to hold, and the way he looked at her, the tenderness, the longing—I just wanted to cry for him, and then he saw my face, and…'

'And?'

'I went after him, asked him to talk to me, and he told me it was over, he didn't love me, he told me I needed to go and find a nice man and have babies with him, but I don't want to have babies with a nice man, I want to have babies with Hugo, and if I can't have babies, well, tough, but I want him, I love him, and he won't even give us a chance—'

The tears erupted again, and she felt Jim's hand on her shoulder giving it a gentle squeeze.

'Oh, dear, oh, dear. I'm so sorry, Ellie. Love can be a hard thing to bear at times.'

And then she felt a wave of guilt because Marion, his wife

of more than forty years, was in a care home and didn't know who he was any more.

She scrubbed away the tears and looked at him. 'How's Marion?'

'Oh, you know. Some days are better than others. But it is what it is, and we put one foot in front of the other and keep on going. That's what it's all about, isn't it?'

Was that what Hugo had been doing for the last ten years, putting one foot in front of the other? And then she'd come along and upset the fragile equilibrium of his life, and it had all come tumbling down on top of them.

'I'm so sorry. I shouldn't be here, you've got enough to deal with.'

He laid a hand on Lola's head, and Ellie realised she'd left her side and was leaning against his leg as if to comfort him. She looked around, puzzled, but there was no sign...

'Jim, where's Milo?' she asked softly, knowing the answer but not ready to believe it.

'He died—a month ago. His heart. I found him in the morning, curled up in his bed asleep. And the house doesn't feel the same without him or Marion.'

Like Jenny, when she'd lost her beloved Nell so soon after George. And now there was Bailey...

'Do you think you'll get another dog?'

He gave a soft, humourless little laugh. 'I'm not sure I've got the stamina for it, or the time. I spend most days with Marion—not that she realises, half the time. But I do, and I'm there because she's still my wife and I still love her.'

Of course he did—and she still loved Hugo. The difference was Hugo knew exactly who she was and he didn't want her there, didn't want her love...

'He may come round, you know.'

She could have laughed at that. 'Hugo? No. He's too—oh, gosh. Principled? Decent? He really seems to believe that being a mother is what I'm on the earth for, and it's not, or not the only thing. I'm thirty-two, Jim, and this is the first time I've ever met anyone I loved enough to even consider having a child with. And now it's not even for me, it's for Hugo.'

'Having another baby won't bring his dead baby back, Ellie. Was it planned, do you know?'

She shook her head. 'No. They were off and on, as he put it, and it was just a tragic accident. And it's broken him, Jim. He said he'll never have another child, and he'd be such a good father.'

'Maybe he doesn't want to be? Not everyone's cut out for it.'

'You've got four and I don't remember you complaining,' she reminded him, and he gave a rueful chuckle.

'No, and we've three grandchildren, now, and I wouldn't change it for the world, but if it hadn't happened for us, we would still have been happy together.'

'Maybe I should give you his number so you can tell him that.'

'It's not me that has to tell him that, Ellie. It's you. But not yet. Let the dust settle. Stay here, you and Lola, for as long as you need, and then when you're ready, go and talk to him.'

'He won't talk. He's got a stubborn streak a mile wide.'

'He's not alone in that. Don't give up on him yet, Ellie. Give him time. He'll be missing you, too.'

How could he miss her so much?

He hadn't slept all night—changing the sheets had got rid of her scent, but it didn't do anything for the memories of her lying there with him. So he'd got up and gone down to the office and changed the rota, emailed Jo and asked her to do Saturday morning, juggled things around later in the week so he or Jo were picking up the times Ellie would have been in surgery, then he took Rufus out for a run at stupid o'clock, ran for an hour and came back and showered, sent Jo a text to be sure she'd got his message, and then went downstairs to get on with the day.

Thank goodness it was only Saturday and he didn't have a full day of electives to fit in, but that didn't really help his mood. He was terse with everyone, and Kerry took him on one side after a short while and told him to get a grip or they'd all be leaving.

'It's not their fault you and Ellie have had a row—'

'We haven't had a row. She had to go away.'

'Had to? Is that why you're like a bear with a sore head? I wasn't born yesterday. You've obviously split up—'

'We weren't together—'

'Oh, come on, Hugo, tell it to the fairies! It's been blindingly obvious since the wedding. Everybody knows.'

'Nothing happened at the wedding.'

'Oh, don't give me that. The way you two were dancing? There was only one place you were going when you left—and don't bother to deny it. So why's she gone? What did you say to her?'

'It's none of your business, Kerry.'

'It's my business when you upset my nurses.'

He scraped a hand through his hair and gave a sharp sigh. 'I told her to go. She's left.'

'*Left?* You mean she's not coming back?'

'No. She's not coming back.'

Kerry stared at him for an age, then light dawned in her

eyes and her voice softened. 'Oh, Hugo… This is because of Lucy's baby, isn't it?'

He swallowed hard. 'Don't go there, Kerry, please.'

'Oh, Hugo…'

She hugged him hard, then told him to go. 'You don't need to be here. We can manage, Jo's in, she can do the consults. I'll shut up shop. Go and see Peter and Sally. Talk to them.'

'I can't just leave you all—'

'You can. Seriously, we can cope and you're no use to us anyway like this. Go.'

So he went, taking Rufus with him and leaving the practice in Kerry's very capable hands. Not that he had the slightest clue what to say to his godparents when he turned up on the doorstep at ten on a Saturday morning, but it turned out he didn't have to.

'Come in, Hugo,' Peter said, and he walked in and found Sally in the kitchen.

'Oh, you're here, darling. Sit down, coffee'll be ready in a minute. Would you like something to eat?'

'No, I'm—I'm fine.'

'Are you? Because you don't look it.' She pointed to a chair. 'Sit down, you're cluttering the place up. I'll make some toast.'

The light dawned. 'Kerry rang you, didn't she?'

'She might have done.'

'Interfering—'

'She's got your best interests at heart, Hugo,' Peter said quietly. 'We all have. And we're here if you need to talk.'

'I don't want to talk,' he said tightly. 'There's nothing to say. She's gone. End of.'

'Because of the baby?' Sally, this time, not knowing when to leave well alone. What was it with the women in his life?

'You, too? It's nothing to do with Lucy's baby—'

'I wasn't talking about Lucy's baby, Hugo,' she said softly. 'I was talking about Samuel.'

He felt himself flinch and looked away.

'So what happened with Ellie?'

She wasn't going to give up, but then nor was he.

She plonked a plate of hot buttered toast in the middle of the table, poured the coffee and sat down, waiting.

He picked up a slice of toast and bit into it, but he could hardly swallow past the tightness of his throat. He gave up and put it down again.

'Lucy came in with Freya, and I thought I ought to show my face, and she just handed her to me and went to the loo. And then Freya cried, and I—just knew what to do. It all came back, and the smell—it was so familiar, so—'

'So what happened then?'

'Ellie was looking at me, and her face—' He broke off and looked down, poking at the slice of toast for something to do, crumbling it into little bits between his fingers. 'She doesn't need me. She needs someone to give her children. She'd be a brilliant mother. She *needs* to be a mother.'

'And you need to be a father.'

'No. I've *been* a father. I *am* a father. Never again.'

'Why? Why, when you were so good with Samuel?'

'*Because* of him. I don't want—don't want to overlay my memories. I don't want to forget—'

His voice cracked, and he felt Sally's hand on his shoulder.

'You'll never forget him,' she said gently. 'He'll live in you for ever, Hugo. That's what happens, but it doesn't mean you can't try again—and even if you don't, even if you never have children, you'd have each other.'

She took Peter's hand and squeezed it, and he covered her hand with his.

'We were never blessed with children,' he said quietly, 'it just never happened for us, but there's no way we'd rather not have been together. We've had a wonderful life, we've been together for forty-five years, and we're still in love. And if we'd known at the start that one of us couldn't have a child, there's no way it would have made the slightest difference to how much we love each other and want to be together.'

'You weren't really childless, though, were you? You were lumbered with me—'

'We were never *lumbered* with you,' Sally said firmly. 'We were more than happy to have you, and you've brought so much richness into our lives, but even without you, we would still have felt the same. It isn't children that make a marriage, Hugo, it's love, first and foremost.'

'But—what if she really wanted a baby? What if she got pregnant? I can't—I'm not brave enough.'

'They said it was a one-off,' Peter reminded him.

'But it could be something else next time. I can't lose anyone else—'

'You've lost Ellie. Doesn't that matter?'

He sucked in a breath. 'Of course it matters! But a child— it would just open the wound...'

'Which will never heal unless you let it, Hugo,' Sally said softly, taking his hands in hers. 'You need to let yourself grieve.'

He snatched his hands back.

'Don't tell me about grief, Sally. I know enough about grief. I could write a book about it.'

'You've never grieved for Samuel. You just threw yourself back into work and carried on, business as usual—except it wasn't, was it? That's why you've worked so hard, spent all your time keeping busy, and you've never really let yourself love anyone since your parents died.'

'That's not true, I love you.'

'You already loved us, just as we loved you.'

They had. 'I was horrible to you.'

'You'd just lost your parents! That's huge. And we understood, of course we did, but you've never had a serious relationship, and ever since Samuel you've sabotaged anything that might lead to love. And now it's even worse, because you've found someone to love and you've sent her away. You're just hiding from your grief, Hugo, and you've been doing it ever since he died.'

Had he?

He pushed back his chair. 'I don't need to listen to this—'

'Maybe not, but maybe it's time to listen to your heart.'

CHAPTER TEN

HE DROVE AWAY, no fixed idea of where he was going, just anywhere away from the people who loved him and thought it was their business to sort him out.

If only it were that easy.

He couldn't go back to the practice while they were all there, so he drove down to the harbour, parked the car and took Rufus for a walk. Not that he needed one, not after their run that he'd thought was a good idea well before dawn. He had no idea what time he'd left or how long they'd run for, but he'd been back at five thirty and he'd felt wiped.

Still did, but he couldn't rest, couldn't settle to anything, so he walked, until Rufus finally sat down and refused to move. He sat beside him on the edge of the path, legs resting on the bank down to the river, the smell of the estuary reminding him of Ellie.

He'd walked here with her and Lola, the day Jenny had taken Bailey home because she missed Nell and she missed George.

He sighed, and laid a hand on Rufus.

'I miss her, Rufe,' he said softly. 'I had to let her go, but I miss her.' Just another ache, another loss to carry with him.

He blinked to clear his vision and got to his feet, picking up the exhausted Rufus and carrying him back to the car.

Listen to your heart.

That was what Sally had said to him, but he had no idea what it was trying to say. All he could hear was all the reasons why he'd done the right thing letting her go.

Had he?

Although actually he hadn't *let* her go, he'd sent her away. And he'd lied to her, but he'd do it again if she came back.

He'd have to, for her sake, because she wanted something he could never give her.

He drove away from the harbour on autopilot, turned off and found himself somewhere he hadn't been for ten years, his heart apparently leading him where he needed to go. He drove slowly into the almost empty car park and stopped the engine.

'Come on, Rufus, let's go for a little walk. It's not far.'

He clipped his lead on, and they left the car park and wandered along the pretty, tree-lined path. It led between gravestones, some ancient, others newer, and then it came to another area, set aside from the rest, with tiny headstones set among the bobbing heads of wildflowers coming into bloom.

His feet led him in the right direction, and he knelt down in front of the simple headstone and laid his hand gently on the grass.

Maybe it's time to listen to your heart.

He didn't have a choice. It was beating so hard it was deafening, but it brought him no answers.

Why?

But nothing answered his silent scream. Rufus leant against him, and he sat down cross-legged and pulled him onto his lap and held him against his flailing heart while he let the memories flood in.

Samuel, his poor body compromised, his brave little heart doing its best against impossible odds, but his eyes would look up as clear as day, follow you, watch you. He'd recognised people, would turn towards the voices of the people he knew, kick his legs in delight, and sometimes he'd reward them with a smile. He loved to be sung to, would listen intently to voices, react to their tone.

He remembered singing to him, an old-fashioned lullaby his mother had sung him as a child. He used to sing it to him every night, and Samuel had loved it. He'd sung it to him softly as he lay dying in his arms...

He hummed it now, rocking gently, his hand still lying on the grass, and as he sang his heart slowed and steadied. Yes, it still ached, and it always would, but coming here, singing that tender lullaby, had reminded him of the good things that he'd forgotten.

He stayed there an age, lost in his memories, until Rufus started to fidget. He had no idea how long he'd been there, but Rufus was telling him it was time to go, and he unfolded his legs and got stiffly to his knees, kissing his fingers and pressing them to the grass where his baby lay, surrounded by all the other little ones who'd gone too young.

'I'm sorry I've been such a rubbish father. I should have come before, but I'll come again soon, I promise. I love you.'

He slept that night, then spent the next day going through his photos, printing some out and framing them. He propped them on the bookcase in his study with the one of himself with his parents, and put one, his favourite, on his bedside table.

The memories still tore him apart, but in a good way, now, and he realised just how much of himself he'd shut away for the last ten years since Samuel died.

And on Monday morning, he apologised to all the staff.

'I've not been in a good place—that's nothing new, I've not been in a good place for a long time, but Saturday was— well, anyway, I'm sorry. Sorry I took it out on you when it was nothing to do with any of you, but it won't happen again.'

There were a few murmurs, and then one of the junior nurses said cautiously, 'Is Ellie coming back?'

He swallowed hard. 'I don't know. Probably not. But I'm going to start advertising in earnest for a new vet, and I'm going to try and get a locum in the meantime, and until then I guess we all need to work a bit harder, but I'll do my best to sort it.'

More murmuring, and then, realising he'd finished, they went back to their tasks.

'Well done.' Kerry patted his shoulder on the way past, and Jean met his eyes.

'Are you really all right?'

He smiled. 'As all right as I can be.'

'Peter rang. He said he could come and help out if we need him.'

Hugo swallowed hard. 'I think we'll be OK, Jean. I'll give him a call.'

He sent him a quick message, and then there in his messaging app was Ellie's photo. He was so tempted to message her, but he needed to get his head straight before he could do that.

She couldn't ignore it any longer.

She'd been with Jim for two weeks, and there'd been nothing from Hugo. Not that she'd expected to hear from him, but she'd hoped…

Would he talk to her now? Hear what she had to say? Because if these weeks away from him had proved one thing, it was that she couldn't live without him. And if that meant they never had a family, well, so be it. Lots of people were in that situation, some because it had never happened for them, others by choice.

And it could be their choice.

Jim was with Marion, so she wasn't able to talk to him, but she wrote him a note thanking him for all his kindness and understanding and promising to be in touch, and then she stripped her bed, packed up all their things and loaded them and Lola into the car.

Her tenants would have left this morning and she'd kept the next two weeks clear, so if all else failed she could live at her house while she worked out what to do with her life, but for now, at least, she wasn't giving up on Hugo.

He needed her every bit as much as she needed him, and she knew—she just *knew*—that he loved her. He'd lied to protect her, and for that she loved him even more, but she had to convince him that it wasn't necessary. She didn't need protecting, she needed him. Nothing else.

She was on the M25 when her phone tinged, but it was probably nothing, so she ignored it until she got to the South Mimms service area at the A1 junction. She found a space, dug her phone out of her bag and glanced at it.

Hugo?

She tapped to open it, her heart pounding.

Where are you?

She stared at it, the text blurring, her heart trying to escape from her chest. Why did he want to know?

She struggled to get her shaking fingers to work.

On M25. Why?

His reply was instant.

Need to talk to you.

To say what? She had no idea. She hesitated, then:

I'm on my way back.

Come on, Hugo...

Drive carefully. Call me when you get here.

She got Lola out of the car, her legs shaking, her whole body trembling, and led her to a patch of grass at the edge of the car park.

He wants to talk...

Her heart was pounding so hard she could hardly think, and she couldn't drive like this. She needed a drink and something to eat, so she put Lola back in the car, ran into the services, bought a bottle of water and a sandwich and ran back out. She shared the water with Lola, and sat in the car and took a bite of the sandwich and made herself swallow it, and the next one, and the next, until her heart had slowed a little.

Then she screwed the lid back on the water, put her seat belt on and headed back onto the M25.

Hugo sat on the sofa, staring at his phone.

She's coming back. Why?

Tenant change-over day, he realised. Of course.

His heart sank. For a moment there he'd thought…

No. He'd told her he didn't want her, didn't love her. Who in their right mind would want to talk to him again?

But maybe…

He went shopping. Just in case. He knew exactly what he was going to buy, and he had the recipe on his phone to remind him.

He found everything he needed, went home, did all the necessary prep and followed the recipe meticulously. And then, when it was done, he turned the heat off under the casserole dish, closed the kitchen door and went into the study, stood at the window and waited for her car to appear.

She turned into the practice, parked the car and sat there, her heart in her mouth.

Lola was standing up, tail thrashing, and she got out of the car and unclipped her harness. She shot out of the car, lead trailing, and ran straight up to Rufus, who was wagging furiously in delight.

And then she looked past them, and there was Hugo.

He looked drawn, thinner, his mouth unsmiling, and she walked towards him, her legs like jelly.

'You made good time,' he said.

It was the last thing she'd expected him to say, and her heart sank. Until she saw the muscle clenching in his jaw, and realised his heart was beating so hard she could see the pulse at his throat.

She walked up to him and then stopped, not knowing how to greet him or what to say. He saved her the trouble.

'Let's go up to my flat. I've cooked for us,' he said, and led the way.

She followed him, all her carefully rehearsed speeches forgotten. This was Hugo's gig, she'd let him do the talking.

For now.

He didn't know what to say, where to start. Except...

'I'm sorry.'

They were on the sofa in his sitting room, the room where two weeks ago he'd told her to leave. Told her he didn't love her. Told her to go and find a nice man and make babies with him.

Her eyes were fixed on his, searching.

'What for?'

'Lying to you. I said I didn't want you in my life any more, but it was a lie. I told myself I was trying to protect you, but I wasn't, I was trying to protect myself, and I wasn't ready to acknowledge the truth.'

'And now?'

'And now, I am. I've spent the last two weeks sorting my head out, dealing with a lot of stuff I should have dealt with years ago.' He took a breath. 'Losing Samuel was brutal. It broke my heart, and so I shut down and I didn't let myself feel any more. I didn't want to feel, didn't want to love. I just wanted to carry on being numb, because it was safe.

'What happened after the wedding really shouldn't have happened. I wasn't ready for what it made me feel, and I couldn't handle it. I hadn't dealt with Samuel's death—hell, I probably hadn't dealt with my parents' deaths, and I've never let myself love anyone. I've avoided it like the plague because I couldn't bear to expose myself to losing anyone else. And then you came along and blew all that out the water, and it scared the hell out of me.

'You'd broken through my defences, and you made me

want more in my life than I could bear, more than was safe. And so I lashed out, because I was afraid of unleashing all the feelings I'd denied for the last ten years.

'I didn't mean to love you, but I did, and I hadn't even realised. It hit me like a train, and I was scared. I was so scared. And I'm so sorry I hurt you.'

'So what now?' she asked, her face guarded, but she wasn't giving anything away and he had no idea where she was in her head. He could only hope.

'That's all down to you,' he said, and waited.

And then finally, she spoke.

'I thought I could cope with us being friends,' she said quietly, 'but I wanted more. I'd never found anyone I could trust with my heart, and then I met you, and you were so kind, so caring, so generous, and I thought I might be safe with you, that you wouldn't leave me like my father left my mother…' Her voice cracked and she swallowed, then went on, 'I thought you were different. And then you sent me away.'

His face creased with pain. 'Oh, Ellie… I only did it for you. I was too scared of the future, too scared we might lose a child, and I knew you wanted children. The way you looked at me when I was holding Freya—the longing. And I felt it, too, and I just couldn't deal with it.'

'So what's different now?' she asked, her heart pounding as she waited for his answer. She could see the sincerity in his eyes, but could she trust it?

'I am. I told Sally and Peter I was afraid of losing anyone else, and Sally pointed out I'd lost you anyway. And she was right. I had, and it left this yawning void…'

'So—what now, Hugo?'

'I want you back.'

'Really?' she asked, pushing him for the truth. 'For ever, or just for this week? Because right now you're sounding a lot like my father apparently did and I'm not sure I can dare to believe anything you tell me.'

His eyes prickled and he turned away. 'I guess I deserve that.'

'So why do you really need me back? Because you need a locum?'

He stared at her, shocked that she could even think that, but then what had he ever done that might make her think differently?

'Absolutely not. I have a locum. What I don't have is you, Ellie, and I love you, and I'm lost without you.'

His voice cracked, and she stared at him, searching his eyes, so readable now, if she only dared to trust what they were telling her.

'You really want me back?'

'Yes.'

'What, just to take up where we left off?'

'No—well, yes, but—no.'

'Hugo, you're not making any sense. Do you want me back, or do you not want me back?'

'Yes, I do want you back. Of course I want you back!'

'OK. And what about your rules?'

He looked puzzled. 'My rules?'

'"I don't do long term, I don't do—"'

He held up his hand. 'No rules—well, that's not quite true. There is one. We tell the truth. Always. And the truth is, I love you, and I want to be with you.'

Could it really be so easy?

No. It never was, and they'd only had nine weeks to get to this point, and they'd been apart for two of them.

'You honestly love me?'

'Yes, Ellie. I honestly love you. Honestly and truly and with all my heart, tattered though it is. And no, I'm not perfect, I know that, but I promise I'll do my best not to hurt you ever again.'

Her eyes were welling up, but she blinked hard and pulled herself together.

'And no rules? Because I don't want to get in any deeper and have you change your mind because you realise that actually you *don't* do long term after all.'

He smiled, a rueful flicker of his lips, a softening of his eyes. 'No rules. Only the truth.'

She swallowed, looked away, looked back at him.

'And this stuff you had to deal with…?'

His smile faded. 'Ah. When I went to see Peter and Sally, Sally pointed out I'd never let myself grieve for Samuel, never let myself move on. I'd cut myself off from any joy, any love—until I met you. And then I still wouldn't let it in. And then I lost you and everything seemed pointless— my work, my life—all of it. I went to Samuel's grave, and I talked to him, and then I came home and I cried. I'd never cried for him—'

'Oh, Hugo…'

She reached out to him, and then she was in his arms, and he was holding her close, his lips pressed against her cheek, and she tilted her head back and met his eyes. 'Are you OK now?' she asked, cradling his jaw in her hand, and he smiled.

It was a bit crooked, but it was there. 'I think so. It's still a work in progress, but I'm getting there.' He turned his head and kissed her hand, then stood up. 'I need to go and finish off in the kitchen.'

'Want any help?'

'No, you stay here and talk to the dogs. I won't be long.'

He warmed the food up, stirring it gently on the hob, blanched the green beans, drained the baby new potatoes and laid the table.

Nothing fancy, no candles, since it was four in the afternoon and candles might look a bit ridiculous. And he checked his back pocket, just in case.

Lord, he was nervous. What if—

'Are you sure I can't help?'

He turned and smiled, or tried to, but it was probably a pretty poor effort. 'No, you're fine, I'm done. Come and sit down.'

She sat, watching him curiously. 'Smells good,' she said, and he put the dishes down on the table and took the lid off the casserole dish.

She looked at it, then up at him, her heart starting to race.

'Is that…what I think it is?'

She saw his throat work as he swallowed. 'Yes, it is.'

He'd cooked her Marry Me Chicken?

She looked away, wondering if…then looked back up at him. Was she imagining it, or did he look nervous? She'd *never* seen Hugo look nervous. And now he was fumbling in his back pocket, pulling something out.

A—ring?

He knelt down beside her and met her eyes, and she bit her lips and tried not to cry.

'I love you, Eleanor Radcliffe,' he said, his voice low, soft and a little shaky. 'I know I'm a basket case, but I'm working on it, and I promise you that whatever happens, whatever goes wrong, whatever life throws at us, I will *always* love you. Will you marry me?'

'What about children?' she asked, not because she wanted them, but because she needed to hear his answer, whatever it was, before she gave him hers.

'What about them? If you want my children, then if it happens, I'm fine with it. More than fine. Yes, it might hurt, but it would also heal, and I'd love us to be a family. But there's no hurry, and I don't mind either way, so long as I've got you. But the thought of you with another man...' He hauled in a breath. 'I wouldn't try to stop you if it was what you wanted, but it would break my heart if I knew I'd driven you into someone else's arms.'

She cradled his cheek in her hand. 'I can't give you Samuel back, you do know that, don't you?' she said gently, unable even to imagine the depth of his pain, but he just smiled a sad little smile.

'Of course I do, and I wouldn't want that. He was incredibly special to me, but we always knew we would lose him. What I didn't know was how much it was possible to love someone so small, and how much it would hurt to lose them.'

'Oh, Hugo...'

'Don't be sad for me. I'm OK. And if you want to have a family, we can do that, but I don't want to put any pressure on you one way or the other. I just need to be with you. That's all I ask. Anything else would be a bonus.'

She leant in and kissed him, just a gentle touch, then sat back.

'I was coming back to tell you that I don't need to have a baby to make me happy. Yes, I'd always hoped that one day I'd meet a man, the sort of man who wouldn't leave me like my father left my mother, and that we'd get married and have a family, but nobody's ever made me feel even remotely like this before. I fell in love with you weeks ago, and then I found out you'd lost a baby, and my heart just broke for you.'

'Oh, Ellie…'

'I can't replace him for you, I know that, and I know you'll always feel a tinge of sadness around babies, but, children or no children, I want to be with you. I love you, Hugo. I know it's ridiculously quick, but I think I've loved you since you saved Lola's life and we sat and had that long talk and I realised what a truly decent and wonderful human being you are.'

He gave a choked laugh. 'Don't go too mad, I'm very far from perfect.'

She smiled at him, the love of her life. 'Aren't we all? I still love you. And yes, I'll marry you, of course I will. I'd be honoured.'

'I thought you'd never get round to saying that,' he said, and he started to laugh, then his eyes softened and he took her hand.

'I don't know if this will fit you. It—' He broke off and swallowed hard. 'It was my mother's engagement ring, and I know she'd be so happy for you to wear it. She would have loved you very much, and so would my father.'

'Even though I'm a vet?'

He smiled. 'Even though you're a vet.'

He slid the ring onto her finger, and it fitted as if it had been made for her. She looked down at it, a row of five simple but beautifully cut graduated diamonds, sparkling in the light. She touched it with shaking fingers, and bit her lip to try and stop the tears.

'It's beautiful,' she said. 'Thank you.'

He stood up and pulled her to her feet, and he wrapped her in his arms and held her as if he'd never let her go.

'Make love to me, Hugo,' she said, and the meaning wasn't lost on him.

'Nothing would make me happier.'

He put the lid back on the casserole dish with a smile. There'd be time to eat it later, but right now they had better things to do, and its job was done…

EPILOGUE

ANOTHER SCORCHING EARLY September day, just like it had been this time last year for their wedding day.

Hugo locked the gates and the front door, ran upstairs and showered, pulled on shorts and a T-shirt and went out into the garden.

A year ago, there'd been a marquee on the lawn for their wedding reception. They'd closed the practice at lunchtime on that Friday so all the staff could join them, and he and Ellie had had a quiet wedding with all the people that mattered to them.

Peter and Sally, of course, and Ellie's mother and her partner from Spain; Jim Harkness, all the practice staff, old friends—nobody had been left out. Ellie wore his mother's ring, he his father's dress watch, and in his breast pocket against his heart he had a picture of Samuel—they'd all been there in their thoughts and in their hearts.

And since then, there'd been a new arrival.

He could see them in the shade under the copper beech. Ellie had spread a rug on the grass, and they were all lying on it, Ellie on her side, head propped up on one hand, watching Lola and Rufus, who were, in turn, lying with their heads on their front paws and watching the newest member of the family.

She'd been born so fast he'd delivered her himself on the

bathroom floor, bright red and screaming with rage and utterly beautiful. It was a moment he'd been dreading, but it had been the best and most wonderful moment of his life.

The dogs lifted their heads and wagged their tails as he walked barefoot across the grass towards them, and he stopped and looked down at them all with a wry smile, his heart filled with love.

'You all look very relaxed,' he said, and knelt down beside Ellie and gave her a kiss. 'Everything OK?'

'Very OK, thank you. It's blissful.'

'How long's she been asleep?'

'I'm not sure. I fed her a little while ago but I'm sure she wouldn't say no to a cuddle.'

He smiled. 'I can't wake her, she needs her sleep and so do I. She was up most of the night.'

'Tell me about it.' She shuffled across and made room for him, and he lay down between them and drew her into his arms and kissed her.

'I love you, Mrs Alexander.'

'I love you, too. I'm glad it's the weekend, we've missed you.'

'I was never far away.' He kissed her again, his body stirring, but he ignored it. It wasn't the only thing stirring, and he snagged another kiss and propped himself up so he could look down at their baby. Charlotte, after his mother, but Lottie to them.

'Hello, my gorgeous girl,' he crooned softly, and she kicked her legs and smiled at him, just the way Samuel used to.

He swallowed the lump in his throat, scooped her up and cradled her in the crook of his arm. She was so precious, so easy to love, but it hadn't been easy. The first few weeks of the pregnancy he'd lived on a knife-edge, and only after the first scan had he dared to believe in her. And here she was, perfect in every way, three months old and the image of her mother, and he loved her more than he would ever have believed possible.

'Now, little Lottie, listen to your daddy,' he murmured, still smiling. 'You need to be a good girl tonight and sleep, because it's our wedding anniversary and we would like to celebrate it by sleeping all night...'

'*All* night?'

He dragged his eyes off the baby and looked at Ellie—his wife, his soulmate, his saviour. And he smiled.

'Well, maybe not *all* night...'

* * * * *

Flirting With The Florida Heart Doctor

Janice Lynn

MILLS & BOON

Also by Janice Lynn

The Single Mum He Can't Resist
Heart Doctor's Summer Reunion
Breaking the Nurse's No-Dating Rule
Risking It All with the Paramedic

Discover more at
millsandboon.com.au.

USA TODAY and *Wall Street Journal* bestselling author **Janice Lynn** has a Master's in nursing from Vanderbilt University and works as a nurse practitioner in a family practice. She lives in the southern United States with her Prince Charming, their children, their Maltese named Halo and a lot of unnamed dust bunnies that have moved in after she started her writing career. Readers can visit Janice via her website at: www.janicelynn.com.

To Kimberly Bradford Scott.

You're amazing.

CHAPTER ONE

DR. HAILEY EASTON didn't like the cold. Tired of northern Ohio winters, her past life, and the toxic relationship she'd left behind, she welcomed Venice, Florida's sunshine. However, when she'd moved south, she'd been thinking of warm weather and new beginnings, not her heated reaction to Dr. Cayden Wilton.

Having never experienced such awareness, Hailey's instant attraction to the cardiologist coming down the hallway wasn't something she could have foreseen, especially not after the drawn-out ten-year destruction of her belief in the opposite sex. Sometimes life threw in surprises. Her surprises had rarely been good ones, but things were going to be different in Florida.

Things were already different.

With a complete head-to-toe makeover, *she* was different. It was more than just her outer appearance that had changed. She was lighter, freer, and determined to shake her past. In her new sunshine-filled life she planned to erase the wasted years of John demolishing her already miniscule self-confidence and making her believe she hadn't deserved anything better than what little he'd given. Since she'd stayed for so long in the relationship, hoping he'd change, maybe she hadn't. Either way, with finishing medical school and acknowledging that it was now or never, she'd said goodbye to her old self, Ohio, John, and to silly dreams. Hello, Florida and the improved Hailey.

"I see who you're looking at and you're wasting your time." Her coworker Renee confirmed what Hailey had known. Dr. Wilton was way out of her league.

No, stop that, she scolded herself.

She wouldn't let John's voice reign any longer.

Being realistic wasn't being negative, though. Hailey was no beauty queen, but she had a good heart, loved people, and as far as looks, well, she had nice teeth and had always liked her eyes. They were her best feature, in her opinion, which was fitting as one's eyes were the window to one's soul. Thanks to the corrective eye surgery she'd gifted herself as a finishing-residency present, her thick glasses no longer obscured that window. Even with her radical revamping, she was more along the lines of an average, slightly overweight person, and not someone who turned heads. Cayden Wilton must be a leading cause of whiplash. The man was gorgeous.

"He's taken," Renee continued, glancing from the cardiologist to Hailey.

Just as well; she'd made her move to work on herself, to find her inner happiness, not to jump into another relationship. When she was ready to date again, it would be light, fun, about her, and she could play in any league that valued the things that mattered most.

"Taken?" Asking was way outside the old Hailey's comfort zone, but she couldn't hold back her curiosity, so maybe all those self-help books she'd been devouring were working. Dr. Wilton hadn't been wearing a wedding ring, but that didn't mean he was single. Of course, he wasn't. Like John, Dr. Wilton was one of the beautiful people of the world—everyone flocked to them with no effort on their part.

"Claimed would be a more accurate description," the charge nurse clarified from where she sat next to Hailey in the small open office cubby behind the nurses' station. The hospital walls were a light gray and were offset with stark white ceilings and trim. White tiled floors added to the calming, clean feel. The unit boasted a fresh clean linen scent that was a positive testament to housekeeping. "When he is ready to settle down, everyone expects him to marry Leanna Moore, especially Leanna. They're the hospital's very own 'celebrity' couple. We refer to them as Caydna."

Caydna? Venice General Hospital's drama was on a whole new level. She couldn't recall any couple name combos at her Ohio hospital other than someone occasionally referring to "Bennifer," "Brangelina," or "Tayvis" celebrity couples.

Hailey had seen Dr. Wilton three times. Once from across the hospital cafeteria during her orientation, yesterday during her first shift as Venice General's newest inpatient physician, and right now. Each time, she'd wondered if she was hitting menopause prior to her thirtieth birthday as she instantly flushed hot.

Dragging her gaze from the scrub-wearing cardiologist walking down the med-surg unit's hallway was impossible. Tall, athletically built, gorgeous hazel eyes, and brown, slightly wavy hair, he commandeered her attention and refused to let go.

As Cayden passed, Sharla Little rushed from her

husband's room, calling out to him. Melvin Little had required an emergency appendectomy for a ruptured appendix the previous night. After Hailey rounded on him at his transfer to the medical/surgical floor that morning, she had entered the cardiac consult to keep close tabs on his significant history of congestive heart failure. Now, fatigue and worry etched upon her face, Mrs. Little swiped at the tears that had started. Whatever she said had Cayden placing his arm around her shoulder and giving a hug. His unabashed show of compassion surprised Hailey. Good-looking, smart, and kind.

"Leanna Moore?" Why had Hailey spoken on his personal life? She did not want to get caught up in hospital gossip. As she said the name out loud an image of a pretty blonde on a billboard popped into her mind. "The radio personality?"

"The one and only."

Embarrassed she'd voiced an interest, Hailey forced her gaze to the computer screen where she should be addressing messages—she had a ton of new employee ones filling her inbox.

"It doesn't surprise me that you know who Leanna is despite having just moved to the area a few weeks ago. Born and raised here, she's Venice's darling. She wants Dr. Wilton and doesn't care who knows it. After they met at a charity event, she convinced him to do a weekly heart health segment during her morning show. He doesn't go out with any woman more than a few times, but Leanna lasted several months and they've kept in touch since, which makes her different from all the rest. Of course, their continued relationship may just be that he's a softie for raising money for the needy or promoting a good cause. I think he sits on every volunteer committee the hospital has."

"That's admirable."

Watching where Dr. Wilton still spoke with Mrs. Little, Renee nodded. "He's admirable. In lots of ways that go beyond that fabulous smile of his. Despite his playboy reputation, we all adore him and most of us have crushed on him."

Hailey arched a brow at the nurse who'd claimed to be happily married when they'd been chitchatting the previous day. "Even you?"

"Touché." Renee leaned back in her chair and grinned. "Not crush, per se, but my eyes can see. Mmm-hmm. He is fine."

Hailey smiled as the fifty-something woman fanned her face.

"So, what you're saying is that for a fun, no-strings-attached evening I should invite him to check out that tiki bar in Manasota that you were telling me about?" She had no intentions of doing so, had never asked out a man, but teasing Renee was fun. Even thinking that someday she might be so bold was mind-boggling. She'd always been demure, letting John dictate their relationship, and doing her best to keep the peace. That hadn't worked out well.

Renee's eyes widened as did her smile. "I tell you what, new girl, you forget everything I said and you have your fun. Just keep your heart in check so it doesn't get broken."

Her heart had already been broken. Just once, because she'd only had one romantic relationship. It had been a long and painful breaking, piece by shattered piece.

Taking a deep breath and forcing a smile, Hailey shook

her head. "I was joking, but like you, my eyes appreciate beauty. Dr. Wilton looks as if he belongs on a television medical drama rather than in a real hospital. He'd be an instant heartthrob." Ha ha. Look at her making a pun with his being a cardiologist. As far as her own heart, when and if she dated again, she'd keep it locked up tighter than Fort Knox. "Now, tell me about these volunteer committees and charities. I want to get involved in my new hometown."

She wanted to do more, to give back more, to focus on things beyond just remaking herself, but to also contribute to making the world a better place. In Ohio, John hadn't wanted her to have a life outside of residency and their relationship. Looking back, she was ashamed of how she'd let him rob her of so much joy. She had gifts to give and wanted to do just that. That volunteering was a great way to meet people and make friends was an added bonus.

Eyes twinkling, Renee turned toward where Cayden was stepping behind the nurses' station counter. "Good morning, Doctor Wilton. Saw you talking with Mrs. Little. Do I need to enter new orders?" She jerked her thumb toward Hailey. "Also, Dr. Easton wants to volunteer with Venice Has Heart. Can you help her?"

Hailey's jaw dropped. *That* was not what she'd meant when she'd asked about the charities. She never should have teased Renee.

Cayden's gaze shifted toward them, going first to Renee, then settling on Hailey. An amused light shone in his gorgeous eyes. His lips curved, digging dimples into his cheeks that matched the one on his chin. The man had a strong, yet friendly facial structure. From what

Hailey could tell, he had great everything, but she'd been wrong before.

"You want to volunteer for Venice Has Heart?" he asked.

She didn't even know what Venice Has Heart was, but that didn't stop her from saying, "Renee thinks I should and suggested I talk to you about doing so." Hailey glanced toward the charge nurse who looked all innocent although she was far from it, then returned her attention to him. "Where do I find out more?"

"That's great. We're always looking for more volunteers." His phone dinged and he glanced down at the message that appeared on his watch face. "Sorry, one sec." Brows veeing, he typed out a quick response, then smiled at Hailey, causing a major rhythm hiccup. "As far as where to find out more, I'd love to tell you about Venice Has Heart. I've got to round on a few patients, then get back to the clinic, but maybe we can meet this evening, I can give you the lowdown then."

Hailey's face heated. Meet that evening? How long was giving her the "lowdown" going to take? Unless he was using her volunteering as an excuse to make plans with her and if so, how did she feel about that? She'd just moved to Florida a few weeks before. She'd intended to focus on building a life, not a romantic relationship.

Drastic makeover or not, she knew Cayden was just being kind as he had been with Sharla Little. She shouldn't read anything into his invitation other than at face value he wanted to tell a new colleague about a beloved charity.

Beside her, Renee elbowed her arm. "Hailey was just saying she wanted to try out that fabulous tiki bar in

Manasota and check out some of our Florida nightlife."
Her coworker smiled big at Dr. Wilton. "Maybe you could
have dinner, listen to the band, watch the sunset, tell her
about Venice Has Heart, and all the reasons why moving
to our little sunny part of the world was a great decision."

The hospital floor could just open and swallow Hailey,
chair and all. The sooner, the better. But Cayden didn't
seem to mind. If anything, he seemed intrigued by Renee's comment.

"That sounds like a great idea." He looked directly
at Hailey, making her forget to breathe as she stared
into eyes that were a deep green with golden flecks and
rimmed with an intense blue. "Shall I pick you up at six?"

Feeling panicky, she reminded herself that it was just
an innocent meeting between colleagues to discuss a volunteer opportunity and shook her head. "My shift ends at
six, Dr. Wilton, but I'll meet you there at seven." Look at
her taking charge with the time suggestion. Such a small
thing, but after years of following John's dictates, pride
filled her that she hadn't just said yes.

"It's Cayden. Thought I mentioned that yesterday," he
said, his smile revving up her heart rate even more. His
phone dinged a second time, and, glancing down at his
watch to view the message, he sighed. "Sorry. Duty calls.
I'm going to see Mr. Little and the other cardiac consult."
He shot one last smile toward her. "Looking forward to
seeing you at seven, *Hailey.*"

"Okay." She didn't say *Cayden* back, couldn't even
wrap her brain around doing so, which was silly. She'd
been on a first-name basis with coworkers in the past. But
saying Cayden's name out loud felt as if it would be more

than something casual and not something she should do in front of Renee.

What is wrong with me?

He moved to leave the nurses' station area to head down the hospital hallway. Renee grabbed her arm, giving an excited squeeze, and mouthed, "Girl!" However, the nurse rapidly straightened when Cayden turned back toward them, standing just to the other side of the counter separating the nurses' area from the hallway but still in close proximity of the office cubby along the back wall. A fresh heatwave infused Hailey's face because no way had he missed Renee's theatrical shimmy.

His gaze dropped to where Renee's fingers wrapped around her arm, then lifted to Hailey. A twinkly light shone there, making the golden flecks glisten. "We should exchange numbers in case something comes up and one of us is running late."

"Or if one of us needs to cancel."

His brow lifted. "Changing your mind already?"

"I meant in case you were too busy to meet and just wanted to call."

"Why would I do that?" He made it sound as if the idea was preposterous.

Taking a deep breath, she cleared her throat. "You're a cardiologist. I can think of a few scenarios that could prevent you from meeting me."

"A few," he agreed, grinning as he handed her his phone to punch in her number. "But I'm not on call tonight, so we should be good. I was more concerned that you might get hung up here at shift change." A realistic possibility, she thought as she typed in her number with shaky fingers. He took the phone, glanced down at what she'd input, then hit Dial, causing her phone to vibrate in her scrub pocket. "Now you have my number, too. I'm looking forward to a relaxing evening of a good food, music, sunset, and great company. See you at seven."

This time when he turned to leave, it was a stunned, wobbly-legged Hailey grabbing Renee's arm.

"I thought you weren't on call tonight," Hailey reminded Cayden from where she sat catty-corner from him at an outdoor table at The Manasota Mango. After he'd pulled out her chair and waited for her to sit, she'd thought he'd move across from her. Instead, he'd chosen the closer seat to where they could both easily see the band on the far end of the outdoor patio. When the hostess had seated them, he'd requested to be in easy line of vision, but not so close that the music would be too loud for them to hear each other when talking. The young lady had chosen the perfect spot.

"I'm not." Cayden slid the phone back into his pocket. "But, as you could tell, that was the hospital. You know how it is. In our profession, you're always working on some level. I like to keep up-to-date on any changes in my hospitalized patients."

Taking a sip of the fruity nonalcoholic drink she'd ordered, Hailey nodded. She did know how it was for many in her profession. With solely overseeing inpatient care as a hospitalist, she didn't get a ton of after-hour calls. At least, she hadn't in Ohio as a resident and wasn't expecting to in Florida.

Although she'd been nervous when she'd first arrived at the restaurant, she'd mostly relaxed as they'd eaten their meal and chatted, assuring herself that Cayden's invitation had been nothing more than a casual one of convenience for telling her about Venice Has Heart. His easy laughs, frequent compliments, and seeming fascination with whatever she said was enough to make a woman's head spin, though.

"That was Dr. Bentley who came on at the end of your shift," he continued. "Melvin Little has increased shortness of breath. Dr. Bentley ordered a chest X-ray and additional labs. He questioned if there were any other tests that I'd like done prior to my rechecking Melvin in the morning."

"Sorry to hear that his breathing has worsened." Neither Melvin nor his wife had mentioned anything when she'd rounded prior to the end of her shift. "I'll be there in the morning."

"Ah, so if you completely avoid me, I'll know I failed miserably tonight." His eyes twinkled.

She made a noise that was a somewhat embarrassing cross between a snort and laugh. "You already know you're a success. Your passion for educating our community on heart health through a fun event completely wowed me. All you're missing is my name signed on the dotted line to have me locked in for a full day of providing medical consults with anyone who has an abnormal screen."

"I'll bring the ironclad contract in the morning," he teased. "My grandfather died of a heart attack when I was young. I've often wondered how different things would have been if he'd just known how to take care of himself, things like a proper diet and lifestyle habits." His expression had gone momentarily serious, then he smiled. "But you're right. Tonight is a success because I got to spend time getting to know you."

Remember what Renee said. Have fun, but don't take him too seriously.

"Yes, since we'll be seeing each other with the Venice Has Heart event." Cheeks burning, she took another sip of her pineapple and coconut drink, thinking maybe she should have gone for the real deal for liquid courage. She'd not wanted to dull her senses while talking to him in hopes that she would be less likely to say or do silly things. But, being with him, knowing people were looking their way and likely wondering why he was with her, twisted her stomach into knots.

Quit, she reminded herself. *Quit. Quit. Quit. Cayden asked you here, is smiling at you, and seems to be enjoying himself. Being with him was great practice for if you ever do risk dating again.*

Just like her "as friends" Saturday night plans with a neighbor was great practice. She'd bumped into Ryan several times at neighborhood events and the gym. His offer to introduce her to his friend group had been kind and she looked forward to the cookout. When ready, she'd need all the help she could get she'd not been on a first date in ten years. Although she and John had officially called their relationship quits with Hailey moving into their guest bedroom three months prior to leaving Ohio, she'd not dated. Having done so in Ohio would have antagonized an already bad situation. Not to mention that she'd had zero interest. Apparently, the Florida sunshine was thawing something inside her, though, because her body was logging all kinds of interest where Cayden was concerned.

"You'll definitely be seeing me with Venice Has Heart." His smile deepened his dimples.

"Um, yeah." Hailey gulped. She was a novice when it came to men, but good grief, what she saw in his eyes. His gaze burned so hot it was a wonder she didn't spontaneously combust. "I look forward to volunteering. I love that you have the local nursing programs involved to take blood pressures and random blood sugar readings."

Could she sound any cornier? She wasn't used to having dinner with gorgeous single, flirty men. The emotions hitting her and having to deal with them weren't things she could learn about from her self-help books, that was for sure.

"It's a great experience for them on a lot of different levels as they get real-world experience. Their instructors always provide positive feedback that the students have shared."

"Anytime one can get hands-on experience is a good thing. The band is good."

His brow arched. "Do you like classic rock?"

Although somewhat familiar with it, she didn't even know the name of the song that was currently being sung. "I like most music," she answered honestly. "But even if not my favorite genre, I appreciate the band's musical skills. They're talented, don't you think?" She smiled. Wasn't that what her books said to do and to do frequently? Smile because a smile went a long way to making most situations better.

"They are." Something in the way that he said it made her wonder if he had paid any more attention to what song was playing than she had. "What's your favorite genre?"

For years Hailey had listened to rap because that had

been John's favorite. Her favorite hadn't been something she'd thought much about, maybe ever. For far too long she hadn't thought about what her favorite anything was. No more. In her new life, she was finding herself, her likes, and her dislikes. She'd never be purposefully oppositional, but she wasn't going to be a doormat ever again. She considered what she'd listened to while she'd been unpacking her few belongings into the house she'd bought not too far from where they currently were. "I listen to a variety of music, but when alone, I tend to listen to pop. I'm going with that as my favorite."

"When you're not concerned about whether or not someone else is enjoying what is playing, you listen to pop." His observation was so on the money that she blushed. He took a drink from his bottle, then placed it back on the table. "Who is your favorite artist?"

"Elvis," she said without hesitation, smiling as memories assailed her of listening to the Memphis crooner with the couple who'd rescued her from bouncing from one foster family to another. He'd been her adopted parents' favorite and she'd grown up listening to him and other iconic performers from the sixties and seventies. She'd been eleven when she'd been adopted by the older couple who'd never had children of their own. Hailey equated the singer with having a home and a family because she never had prior to being introduced to his silky voice.

Cayden chuckled. "Not what I was expecting you to say. As the known King of Rock 'n' Roll and not a pop artist, I have to ask, why Elvis?"

"Why not Elvis? After all, like you said, he is the 'King of Rock 'n' Roll.' But if you meant a more modern artist or band, I'll go with Ed Sheeran."

"Nice. I saw him in concert back during my early college days," he surprised her by saying, although she wasn't sure why she was surprised. No doubt Cayden had an active social life that had included numerous concerts over the years. "He is a super-talented musician. My friends and I had a great time."

"He did a show in Columbus at the beginning of my freshman year. A group of classmates sold a kidney or two to come up with enough money to go see him and invited me to tag along." She smiled at the memory, trying not to question herself too much on why she'd let John systematically cut her off from everyone in her life. With moving from one foster home to another and her adopted parents opting to homeschool her, she'd never had any close friendships. She had been thrilled when her classmates had asked her to go with them to the concert. She'd thought she was on top of the world—making friends and having a boyfriend for the first time ever. The concert had been one of her few friend outings. John had thrown a fit. He'd thrown a fit for her breaking things off and moving to Florida, too, telling her she'd regret leaving and come running home, lonely and begging for his forgiveness for her "stupidity." There was no level of loneliness that would send her back to him. Being with John the past ten years had been some of her loneliest and with her childhood, that was saying something. Thank God she'd had her lifelong dream of being a doctor to focus on and keep her from sinking into despair.

"Willing to sacrifice body parts for great music—making a note of it," Cayden teased, taking a sip of his drink and pulling her back to the present. A present where she had achieved her greatest goal and now planned to heal the holes in who she was, to get to know that person, and learn to love herself completely and know that she was enough and didn't need anyone else in her life. "You went to school in Columbus?"

"I had a scholarship to Ohio State for my undergraduate studies. Staying for medical school made sense." John had been there. After her parents died, without him she would have been completely alone in the world, as he'd pointed out on a regular basis. Looking back, she wondered what her life would have been like if she'd left Ohio. Better in many ways, but she had learned powerful lessons. She hadn't been a fast learner, but she had eventually caught on. She'd never wear that in-a-serious-relationship cage again. "What about you? Are you originally from Florida?"

Cayden took another drink from his bottle. "I grew up around Gainesville, did residency in Kentucky and a fellowship in Kansas. I missed the ocean enough to know I didn't want to live anywhere that didn't offer a sunset over the water."

Having already fallen in love with being near the sea, Hailey understood. She ran her finger over condensation forming on her glass. The moisture was cool beneath her fingertips and as welcome as the breeze cutting the evening's heat. "Because sunsets are what you like best about being near the ocean?"

"More that I wanted to remind you that Renee mentioned our watching the sunset." He grinned in a way that had Hailey gulping. His smile was lethal. Maybe he couldn't help himself and just naturally flirted with every woman. Not that she'd seen him do so with anyone else, not even the hostess who'd definitely given him the eye. "I'm fine with staying here, listening to the band," he continued. "Or we could walk across the street and watch the sunset from the beach. There are just enough clouds in the sky that the colors should be spectacular."

A spectacular sunset over the water with a gorgeous man sounded surreal. Scary, too. But Hailey had moved to Florida to be different, to step outside her comfort zone, and to create the life she wanted. That life should include spectacular sunsets.

"Watching the sun set while sitting on the beach would be great and something I've not done since moving here."

He feigned horror. "What? How is that even possible? That should have been one of the first things anyone who moves here does."

"It's not that I haven't wanted to." She glanced toward the band who'd started singing a Lynyrd Skynyrd classic. "But I wasn't sure how safe it would be for me to be on the beach and walk back to my car by myself after dark. I've not heard of any safety issues, but I'm new to the area and trying to make good choices, not put myself in compromising situations."

Unlike the past. She'd made a terrible choice with John and compromised for almost a decade. Had she stayed so long because she'd been grieving her parents, in school, then in residency, and she just hadn't had the energy to break free? Was that why she'd turned a blind eye and forgiven so many things? Or had the fear of being alone kept her there?

"I doubt you'd have any problems, but it's always best to be safe." Cayden finished his drink, placed the bottle on the table, then motioned for their waitress to bring their check. Hailey reached for her purse, pulled out her wallet, but Cayden shook his head. "Tonight is my treat."

Clutching her wallet, she met his gaze and hoped her face wasn't as rosy as it felt. "I don't expect you to pay for my meal."

His brows scrunched together. "When a man invites you to dinner, you should expect him to pay. My advice is that if he expects you to pay, next time, tell him to hit the road."

"Duly noted." She was so used to paying for everything with John that she'd just automatically planned to do the same. John's thoughts had been that she should just be grateful for the opportunity to support him. If she'd let him, he would have broken her financially the way he had her heart. Fortunately, most of her parents' estate had been tied up until a few months back. Acid burned her throat, and she took another sip of the virgin drink, letting the cold liquid glide down her throat to ease the heat. The fruity sweetness did little to dissolve her bitterness at her own foolishness that she'd once again let John into her head. Maybe it was natural for him to pop into her mind since tonight was the first time she'd ever had dinner with a man who wasn't John.

"To be fair, though, Renee instigated our dinner tonight."

Cayden shook his head. "Renee might have made the initial suggestion, but I asked. Dinner is my treat."

"In that case, thank you." She slipped her slim wallet back into her cross-body and assured herself that it was okay that she was letting him pay even though doing so felt awkward. The new her did not pay when she met a man for dinner. Okay, got it. "For the record, what about if I ask someone to dinner? Who should I expect to pay then?"

Not that she'd probably ever be so bold, but this new Florida Hailey was a work in progress. She refused to be boring, walked-all-over Ohio Hailey ever again. Talking with Cayden was insightful and wonderful and reinforced that she'd been right to start fresh in a place of her choosing. The hospitalist position in Venice had been a godsend.

Cayden shrugged. "That one is okay either way. If he insists, its fine for you to let him pay. But he doesn't lose points if he lets you since you asked." He paused, then added, "Not the first time. If there's a second, call me old-fashioned, but he needs to man up."

It was difficult to think of the charming man sitting across from her as old-fashioned, but there was something about him that made her think he had an old soul. She liked whatever that something was.

"Tonight is enlightening." And an unexpected bonus to her new Florida life. "You're easy to talk to and seem quite the expert. Being new to the area, I should come to you for all my dating advice."

Hilarious. Unless one counted tonight, which she didn't since it wasn't one, she hadn't been on a first date in years. With the way John had shredded her heart, she might never risk letting someone in to mess with the woman she was working to become.

Certainly, she'd fight to protect the new her and would

steer clear of anyone who threatened her hard-won peace. There were worse things than being alone.

She didn't need Cayden's, or anyone's, advice to know that.

Life had taught her that painful lesson well.

CHAPTER TWO

CAYDEN AND HAILEY crossed the street, paused at his SUV long enough to grab a blanket, then headed to the beach. When they reached the sand, he took off his shoes and Hailey did the same. Hot pink covered her toenails and her big toes each had a palm tree emblem in the middle of the polish. Liking the glimpse at her whimsy, Cayden grinned.

The Gulf's breeze whipped at her long blond hair, dancing the strands about her lovely face. She'd had her hair pulled back at the hospital. He loved that she'd loosened it for their dinner. She'd also changed and wore white capris, a bright blue top, and plain white canvas shoes.

Her heavily lashed eyes were cloudy with uncertainty, as if she was trying to decide if he'd really been eyeing her toenails. That he understood. He wasn't a feet guy, or at least, he never had been. But those brightly painted toenails were downright sexy. Of course, looking at her curvy figure, he couldn't name one part of Hailey that he didn't find attractive. She fascinated him, which explained why he was on the beach with a coworker. He liked women and wasn't shy about it, but he didn't spend personal time with women he worked with. Doing that was much too complicated when it didn't work out and it never worked out. He no longer wanted it to. He'd been cured of that ailment. He had a great life, was never lonely when he wanted company, and was completely happy with lifelong bachelorhood. He only spent time with women with an exit plan already in place, and never coworkers. Apparently, Hailey was the exception to that rule because none of that had kept him from asking her to dinner to discuss her volunteering with Venice Has Heart when he could have just sent her to their website.

"I'd thought it would be more crowded," Hailey mused as, their shoes dangling from their fingers and the blanket folded over his arm, they made their way across the warm sand.

"It's later in the day on a weeknight so not too busy, but it can get crowded at times." When they were about halfway to the water, he stopped. "This okay?"

She nodded, watching as he spread the blanket, then sat to face where the sun was making its descent toward the horizon. A seagull squawked in the distance and a couple of sandpipers darted to and fro at the edge of the surf. The golden light reflected off the water, casting a picturesque view for what was in many ways the most interesting evening he'd had in a long time. So long, in fact, that he couldn't recall having felt the excitement that buzzed through him when he looked at the woman next to him. He'd felt the buzz the first time he'd seen her and each time since. While grabbing something to eat with a colleague, he'd noticed the smiling blonde chatting with the hospital administrator. Yesterday, he'd practically tripped over introducing himself to her.

Hailey stared out at where small waves were racing

ashore. She hugged her knees and appeared to relax to the calming sea sounds. He'd always found peace in being near the water and was pleased she seemed to do the same.

Hailey twisted toward him. The sun's setting rays cast a hue to her face, making the blue of her eyes seem almost electric. "Are you always this nice?"

"Nope." Take this moment for example. He felt more naughty than nice. "Why did the phrase, 'Nice guys finish last,' pop into my head?"

As he'd hoped, she smiled. "I can't imagine that you ever finish last."

"There have been times I've finished last." But not because he hadn't given his best effort.

"Look at you. You're a successful cardiologist and gor—" She paused. Her cheeks glowed brighter than the setting sun.

Suspecting what she was going to say and pleased that she thought so, he grinned. "Go on, Hailey. Finish what you were about to say."

Odd, as he wasn't one to fish for compliments, but he craved hers.

Her lips twitched. "I was going to say that you're easy on the eyes, but I stopped because I didn't want to give you a big head."

Her compliment did funny things to his chest, like make his heart jerk. What was it about her that made him feel as if he'd morphed back to high school days?

"You think I'm easy on the eyes?" he teased, but deep down, he admitted that he was encouraging her to elaborate because he still wanted to hear more.

"Don't pretend you're not aware. You've looked in a mirror. You know how blessed you are."

Interesting that her tone almost held accusation.

"I could say the same in regard to you," he said. She was a beautiful woman who took great care with her appearance, although he suspected that beneath the makeup she was just as stunning. Beneath the powder and paint, she had a natural beauty that shined through.

She rolled her eyes in a way that made him wonder if, when looking in her mirror, she saw the same person he did. He didn't think so. Which might explain why her cheeks turned such a rosy shade each time he complimented her, and she seemed so unaccustomed to the praise. Could she really not know how beautiful she was?

"Looks fade, Hailey. Mine, yours, everyone's. It's what's on the inside that matters."

"I agree with you, of course. But, in the real world, most people never look to see what's on the inside unless it's nicely packaged on the outside." Her words held too much hurt for them to be a casual observation point. Who had punched the holes in her? And why did the urge to patch those holes hit so hard? Not just repair the broken pieces, but to kintsugi them with the finest gold so that the new was better than the former version? They'd just met and he was not a white knight and didn't want to be.

"I'm not most people, Hailey." When her face remained serious, he added, "Just ask my mother and she'll gladly tell you all my finer points."

Her expression lightening, Hailey snorted. "Hmm, not sure I trust your mother to give an unbiased opinion. But I don't need to ask her because, surprisingly, I believe you."

"Thank you, I think." He chuckled, wondering if his

own cheeks now matched the streaked sky. "I'm torn on whether that was a compliment or a backhanded insult."

"Compliment." She smiled a big, real smile that stole his breath, then turned to look at the water. The fading sunlight highlighted her features, showcasing her beauty that far outshone their surroundings.

"Then thank you," he told her.

She stared at where the sun was inching beneath the horizon's edge. Cayden couldn't drag his gaze from her. The breeze coming in off the Gulf ruffled her hair, and the sun's glow cast her in a golden hue that gave her an ethereal appearance, as if she couldn't possibly be real. Maybe she wasn't because she sure triggered other-worldly reactions.

"I can't believe I've not been coming out here in the evening when I'm so close. This is so peaceful, and feels safe." Cayden wouldn't call sitting next to her watching the sun go down "safe." *Dangerous* was the description that came to mind.

"You've ruined me," she continued. "I'm going to want to come back again and again."

"We can anytime you want. Being near the water is my thing and I don't mind company." At least, he didn't tonight. Usually, he preferred being at the beach alone.

"Ha, after so many years of being landlocked, I may want to be out here day and night, but I promise I wasn't implying that we come together." She laughed. "There's something mesmerizing about the sound of the water, isn't there?"

There was something mesmerizing about the sound of her laughter, something that should have him leery of further developing a friendship with her. "Just let me know whenever you want company for a beach sunset or walk," he offered anyway. "Or we can go to Caspersen Beach to look for shark teeth. It's just down the coast and something a lot of folks around here enjoy."

Her eyes widened. "Look for shark teeth?"

He chuckled at her expression. "Did you not realize you moved to the shark tooth capital of the world?"

"The hospital forgot to list that in their job description. Does that mean there's more sharks here than anywhere else?" Her face squished. "For the record, that would not be a selling point for me. Although, I guess it's too late now since I'm here."

"Not sure about the number of sharks compared to other places, but the number of shark teeth has to do with the area having favorable conditions to fossilize the teeth. If you've never been shark tooth hunting, you're in for a treat."

"Ohio girl. I've never found a shark tooth, much less been shark tooth hunting. I didn't even know that was a thing or that there was a shark tooth capital of the world."

He tsked. "You can't live here and not ever go shark tooth hunting."

She eyed him. "You say that as if you're confident I'd find a shark tooth."

"I am."

Her expression grew suspicious. "Am I missing something? Are they just lying around on the sand or something?"

He laughed. "Sometimes you can find them lying on the beach. Here, too, for that matter, especially after a storm. But the best ones are in the water at Caspersen, even the occasional megalodon tooth can be found."

"You want me to hunt shark teeth *in the water* after you just told me the beach is the shark tooth capital of the world and that there are sharks?" She gave him an I-don't-think-so look. "No, thank you."

He couldn't resist teasing. "You'll be fine so long as you stay away from the teeth still attached to the shark."

She snorted and made a funny face that had him liking her more and more. "No worries there. I'm not knowingly going anywhere near a shark."

"Lucky for you then that the teeth we would be hunting aren't attached." He chuckled, thinking the lightness in her tone was more beautiful than any sunset he'd even seen.

"But they once were, so maybe shark tooth hunting isn't my thing. Although, I'll admit you have me intrigued that you're so confident I'd find one. I've never been that lucky on those types of things. I've never even found a four-leaf clover my whole life."

"Then your luck is about to change."

Her smile was slow, innocently seductive, as she said, "I'm tempted to say yes simply from curiosity, but then I recall what they say about curiosity and the cat."

"Fortunately, you're not a cat."

"Ha! When it comes to sharks, I admit to being a big scaredy-cat. I mean, I know they are just animals doing what nature intended, but nature also dictates my survival instinct to stay away."

"I promise to protect you."

Her humor faded, as did his, and his assurance felt like more than just part of their fun banter.

"I can protect myself." Her chin tilt dared him to say otherwise even as he recognized the forced gusto in her eyes. Wondering what, or who, had made her so prickly, Cayden longed for the return of lightness.

"Even from sharks?"

Taking a deep breath, she swallowed and relaxed a little. "I'll defer dealing with sharks to you."

"Good idea. You're acing this listening to advice thing." Too bad he wasn't listening to the warning bells going off in his own head about what he was doing with her, a coworker, watching the sunset on a beach, and flirting with her despite all the reasons he shouldn't.

"Being a good student was never a problem. It's the rest of life that I've struggled with." She sighed, then with a soft smile back on her face she rested her chin atop her knees and stared at the sunset with deep appreciation. "This is so much better than when I watched while sitting in my car."

Cayden wanted to know more, to know what struggles she'd faced, but sensed she wouldn't tell him, so kept his questions to himself. The thought of her sitting in her car, watching the sunset by herself, tugged at his insides.

Her gaze cut to him and after a moment, she smiled. "I...thank you, Cayden. For dinner, the expert dating advice—" her smile widened when she said that one "—for the sunset, for asking me to go shark tooth hunting, for making me feel happy, for, just, well, for an enjoyable evening with someone who I feel is a new friend. It's been really nice."

"Seriously, anytime you want to watch the sunset from the beach, just call. I'll meet you so you don't have to worry about being alone." For safety reasons. That was why he kept offering. To keep her safe.

Who was going to keep him safe from his growing attraction to her was another matter completely.

"Are you going to tell me about last night?"

Even prior to arriving at the hospital, Hailey had known Renee would ask about her evening with Cayden. What she hadn't known was what she wanted to share. How could she explain what she didn't understand. Despite his "playboy reputation," Cayden had been a perfect gentleman. She'd had a great time, even agreeing to go shark tooth hunting with him, because why not? The new her was supposed to be adventurous and open to new experiences. Shark tooth hunting, from the beach as she wouldn't be going in the water, would certainly be that. She wanted to make friends, to have a social life, and be involved with her community. Going with Cayden just made sense, right? So, why did butterflies dance her in her belly at the thought that she'd be spending more time with him?

Knowing she couldn't ignore Renee, she smiled. "We ate dinner, listened to the band, and discussed Venice Has Heart. Thank you for suggesting that. Venice Has Heart sounds like an amazing community outreach program."

"It is." Renee literally rubbed her hands together. "Now, tell me more. Being happily married as I am, I have to live vicariously through you when it comes to Cayden."

Attempting to look casual, Hailey shrugged. "There's nothing more to tell."

Renee jerked her head back in disbelief. "Oh, come on. You were with the hospital's most notorious bachelor and I saw how he looked at you yesterday like he wanted to devour you in one bite. There has to be something more to tell."

Hailey fought gulping at Renee's assessment. Cayden hadn't looked at her that way. Sure, there had been moments the night before when she'd swear his flirting went beyond friendliness and making a new coworker feel welcomed. But she couldn't convince herself that her makeover was so good that Cayden would be interested in her, and yet…no, his offer to meet her for future sunsets and to take her shark tooth hunting weren't date offers. As surprising as it was, Cayden had been easy to talk to, had made her smile, and was hopefully destined to be a friend. That he was the sexiest man she'd ever met had no bearing on how much she'd liked him other than to make her uncomfortably aware of her body's reaction to his hotness.

"I see you stalling. Tell me." Renee wasn't going to let up. Hailey's silent mulling had made it seem as if more had happened than what had, so she glanced up from where she'd been charting a note on the patient she'd seen first thing that morning.

Looking her coworker directly in the eyes, she smiled as big as her plumped-up lips would allow. "As you know, we met at the bar you recommended. The food and music were wonderful. He told me about Venice Has Heart. I'm volunteering for the event."

Renee frowned. "What about drinks and a sunset with our favorite cardiologist? Please tell me you didn't waste that fabulous opportunity by just talking shop all evening."

"You are who told me that he's already claimed for whenever he tires of being a bachelor." Did he have an emotional involvement with the radio deejay beyond friendship? Hailey hadn't gotten that impression. What she had gotten was the impression that he liked the shiny new her. Absently, she reached up to touch where she had her hair extensions pulled back. He'd sounded so sincere in his claim of outer beauty fading that she wondered what he'd think if he knew just how much she'd done to enhance her appearance. Would he have noticed Ohio Hailey? What was she thinking? She didn't want him to notice Florida Hailey. She wasn't in the market for a relationship. She wasn't ready for one. Only, she couldn't deny that his flirting had made her feel…good.

Renee's brows scrunched. "Yes, but Cayden is way in the future. No reason you can't have fun in the here and now."

"He seems like a great guy to be so involved with the event. I enjoyed dinner and talking with him, but I'm just coming out of a long and unhealthy relationship. I'm really not interested in anything more than friendship with any man." There. Maybe that truth would appease Renee because Hailey did like her and hoped their working relationship would develop into friendship. To say anything further was setting herself up for gossip. "I need to check on Melvin Little. Is Sharla with him this morning?"

Frustrated that Hailey wasn't telling her more, Renee sighed. "She barely leaves his side. She tells me they've been together for over fifty years."

"He's fortunate to have her." What would it be like to have someone who cared that much about you for that long? Sharla adored her husband and the sentiment seemed to be mutual. In many ways they reminded her of her adoptive parents. The Eastons had loved each other and given Hailey the only real affection she'd ever known. Prior to them, she'd been bounced from place to place from the point her birth mother had died from an overdose and if her birth mother had known who Hailey's father was, she'd not listed it on her birth certificate. When her adoptive mother had died from breast cancer, her father hadn't lived a year before succumbing to a heart attack. All the old feelings of being alone in the world had hit and she'd clung to John no matter what he did. As unhealthy as it had been, his was the longest relationship of her life. Maybe she could forgive herself a little for trying so hard to make things work.

"I was told that Dr. Wilton would be by this morning to check on him and the sick sinus syndrome patient in Room 204." Renee looked at Hailey as if she expected some type of reaction. If she got one, it would be over Hailey falling down memory lane, which felt more like nightmare street.

Meeting Renee's gaze was her only reaction to her coworker's comment.

"Great. With Mr. Little's ruptured appendix then surgery putting a toll on his body, his heart needs to be watched closely." She didn't mention that she already knew Cayden would be by. "Are you going with me to see him, then?"

"Do you need me to?" Renee crossed her arms, pouting a little that Hailey wasn't revealing what she wanted to hear and that, perhaps, Hailey truly had "wasted" the opportunity. What had Renee expected her to do? Make out with Cayden under the stars?

Knowing her color was rising and her coworker was sure to notice, Hailey shook her head. "No, I was just checking."

Yikes. Her voice had broken a little.

"Then I'm going to stay here to do paperwork, maybe scribble notes on how you should have taken advantage of who you were with last night. Just because I told you to guard your heart didn't mean you couldn't have fun. Life is short. Sometimes you have to live a little." Renee waggled her brows. "Or a lot, if you get my drift."

Face aflame, Hailey grimaced. Yeah, that had never been that much fun for her. Maybe because it had always been about her trying to please John, doing whatever he wanted to try to make him so happy that he wouldn't want anyone else. Her best efforts hadn't worked, so maybe neither of them had been having much fun.

Knowing she had to get away from Renee's watchful eyes, Hailey headed to check on Melvin. Some of the medical floor rooms were doubles and some were private. Whether by luck or design, he was in a private room. Hailey knocked on the open door before stepping into the pale gray room with its white tiles. Although he was still on a liquid-only diet, the room smelled of oranges and Hailey noted peels on the wheeled bed tray that was pulled closer to Sharla than her husband. As long as his exam was okay, she planned to start him on bland soft foods that morning and would have Dietary bring breakfast.

"Good morning," she greeted as she took in the pale man lying in the hospital bed. He had the head of the bed raised and a couple of pillows stuffed behind him, propping himself up farther. He was in his midseventies, had thick white hair, and was too thin. All except his feet and ankles, which were swollen. They weren't weeping through the compression hose that she'd put on him the previous day, though. He hadn't been thrilled but hadn't had the energy to refuse. "How are you feeling today?"

"Like I'm starving and want to go home." He coughed. The cough had been wet, as if he'd needed to clear phlegm from his throat and struggled to do so.

"I'm hoping to do something about the starving part," she assured him, smiling. "As far as the going home, the charge nurse informed me that you had chest flutters last night and the night staff consulted with your cardiologist." Recalling where Cayden had been, who he'd been with during that consultation, Hailey's heart fluttered, too. "No symptoms since last night?"

Grunting as he cautiously scooted up farther on his hospital bed, Melvin shook his head. "I think it was just indigestion but after what happened with my stomach, I wasn't keeping quiet."

"Understood." His ruptured appendix had required his lower abdomen to be surgically opened and "cleaned" because he'd ignored his pain. Sepsis had quickly set in, increasing the criticalness of his situation. "How's your surgical site?"

He adjusted the white cotton hospital blanket covering him. "Okay, I guess. Just aggravating I had to have my appendix taken out. I thought that was something that happened to kids, not grown men."

She shrugged. "A bad appendix can happen at any age."

"Apparently," he muttered. "Too bad I didn't realize

that was what was causing my pain. I thought I was trying to pass another kidney stone."

"Since both are painful, I understand how you could make that assumption. Besides my planning to let you eat, I've got more good news this morning. Your white blood cell count is trending downward so going home is getting closer."

Although he looked relieved, he grumbled, "No wonder with as much medication as you people have pumped into me."

"All those medications seem to be working." Hailey shifted her gaze to the tired-appearing woman sitting in the chair beside her husband's hospital bed. Had she eaten anything other than the orange? Hailey made a note to request Dietary bring an extra breakfast tray, if available. When Hailey had entered the room, Sharla's fingers had paused in the crocheting she was doing on making an afghan. The colors reminded Hailey of the previous night's sunset with its mix of warm red, orange, and golds. Her fingers itched to reach out to see if the yarn was as soft as it appeared. "That's beautiful."

Brightening at the compliment, Sharla held up the piece for Hailey to better see what she had done. "It's all my favorite colors. Working with my hands helps me not be so nervous at being here." Arranging the piece back into her lap, she chuckled. "I found that crocheting was good therapy years ago when we lived up north. I usually make several a year."

With med school, then residency, Hailey hadn't had time for hobbies since high school other than occasionally losing herself in a book. She hoped to find a few interests that would fill her with passion. Her adoptive mother had painted, and Hailey had dabbled with that on occasion during her teens. Wanting to please her talented mother who'd hoped Hailey would possess artistic ability, she'd never been able to relax enough to truly enjoy what she was doing, though. Hailey's talent had been reading, studying, and making excellent grades. She'd been great at doing those, but not so much on anything creative that she'd tried thus far in life. Maybe she'd try her hand at some new creative ventures, but for now, she was excited to learn more about her new hometown, to meet people, volunteer, and get involved in the community.

She wanted to have a life, because she'd not had one since…since before her parents died, since before John, and residency. Only during those few years after the Eastons adopted her up until they'd passed had she belonged anywhere and had a life.

With her move to Florida, she was changing that.

She examined Melvin, taking care with his surgical site as she checked the incision, and was glad that he continued to progress. "Let's see how you do with soft food, then we'll advance your diet as tolerated. If you don't have any reoccurrence of chest symptoms and your labs continue to improve when I review them in the morning, we will discuss a discharge plan."

Hailey made notes in his electronic record, putting in for the dietary order changes and the tray for Sharla. She also ordered labs to be drawn the following morning. She spoke with the couple a few more minutes, making sure to address questions, then went to check on another patient. Hopefully, Larry Davis would be able to be discharged that day or the following morning.

After disinfecting her hands with the wall sanitizer

pump just outside his doorway, Hailey entered the gentleman's room, expecting to see him watching old Westerns as he'd been doing the previous two mornings. Instead, he appeared to be sleeping.

"Good morning, Mr. Davis," she greeted, not wanting to startle him as she approached his bed. His chest was rising and falling, but when he hadn't roused when she reached his bedside, nervousness set in. "Mr. Davis? I'm going to touch your arm."

She placed her hands on his arm and gave a gentle shake. He didn't react to the stimulation. She did a quick pulse check. There, but thready.

"Mr. Davis, this is Dr. Easton. I'm going to listen to your chest," she told him in hope that he was aware of her presence. She placed the diaphragm of her stethoscope on his chest. Grimacing at what she heard, she pulled out her phone to call for assistance.

CHAPTER THREE

"CODE BLUE. CODE BLUE," the announcer blared over Venice General Hospital's PA system then proceeded to give the location of the emergency, citing the medical floor and patient room number. Cayden recognized the number as the one he'd been headed to. Larry Davis had been admitted with sick sinus syndrome earlier in the week and had been improving. He'd been transferred out of the at-full-capacity cardiac care unit to the medical floor two days prior. He'd been somewhat better the previous day and Cayden had planned to recommend he be sent home that day or the next. What had changed?

The man's vital signs, apparently.

Having been in the medical floor hallway, Cayden rushed to Mr. Davis's room, not surprised to see part of the code team in action. That Hailey led the code had his stomach buzzing with excitement the same as it did each time that he saw her. He'd enjoyed their evening together and was looking forward to introducing her to shark tooth hunting. As a friend, he assured himself, despite his attraction to her. Friendship worked with their being co-workers. Being lovers did not. He needed to remember that. You'd think with the beating Cynthia had given his heart he wouldn't need to remind himself. Then again, she hadn't been the first to trample on his affections. Fortunately, she was the last and would remain so as he'd permanently taken his heart off the market.

"Dr. Wilton," Renee said, noticing he had entered the room. While Hailey did chest compressions, the charge nurse delivered oxygen via a bag valve mask.

At his name, Hailey's blue gaze lifted from where she'd been observing Larry, met Cayden's for a millisecond, then returned to her patient, all without her palms pausing from where she rhythmically compressed the man's chest. That brief meeting of their gazes had Cayden sucking in a deep breath before he hit the ground from lack of oxygen himself.

"You want me to take over compressions?" He moved beside her, knowing the lifesaving actions quickly wore out one's arms. Depending upon how long she'd been doing the hundred-plus compressions per minute routine her arms might already be trembling. They'd just called the code, so probably not long, but he wanted to help.

"Either that or you can lead the code until the compression nurse arrives to take this over."

Cayden had been so close he wasn't surprised he'd beat the rest of the code team to the room. His gut instinct told him to let Hailey run the code. Today was her third day on the floor. He'd assist and jump in where needed. He leaned in next to her, clasped his hands, and held them just above Larry's chest. "On the count of three, I'll take over compressions. One. Two. Three." His hands replaced hers in pushing in Larry's chest just over two inches with each downward push. "Fill me in on what happened."

"I came to check him. He looked to be asleep and wouldn't rouse," Hailey told him. "He was breathing, just, but pulse was thready. Systolic blood pressure was in the low sixties. Oxygen saturation was upper seventies then and now."

A nurse rushed in with the crash cart and, while Cayden continued to compress Larry's chest, Renee continued to deliver oxygen via the bag valve mask ventilator. Hailey and the nurse who'd arrived with the supplies dug into the cart, one going for medication while the other opened the defibrillator.

A documenter, security guard, and a respiratory therapist rushed into the room, along with another nurse. The respiratory therapist took over the bag valve mask delivering air. Renee shifted to the crash cart, taking over opening the defibrillator leads and freeing Hailey to assess the situation and direct the code.

A nurse cut Larry's gown out of the way, and Renee pressed the defibrillator leads to the man's chest. Glancing toward the display, Hailey waited the few seconds while the machine assessed Larry's heart's electrical activity.

The defibrillator didn't recommend a shock and Hailey advised, "Keep doing CPR."

"Trade on compressions." The code team's compression nurse leaned in to take over Cayden's role. On the count of three, Cayden shifted back as the nurse immediately started pressing the man's chest.

Stretching out his arms, he stepped back, then moved beside Hailey to assess the situation, his gaze going from the telemetry to the defibrillator's display. The machine screen changed, flashing its new recommendation. She was on top of it, immediately reacting.

"Prepare to deliver shock," Hailey said, then warned, "All clear."

Everyone who'd been administering care stepped back, making sure they weren't touching the patient. First glancing to check that everyone truly appeared all clear, Hailey pushed the button that administered the electrical pulse that would hopefully jolt the patient's heart back into rhythm.

Immediately, Cayden and the others were poised, ready for whatever was needed, all the while holding their breath as they waited for the machine's analysis of Larry's heart rhythm. He was in ventricular tachycardia where his heart was essentially quivering without pumping sufficient blood to supply his body with oxygen.

"Give epinephrine," Hailey ordered, not glancing up as an anesthesiologist entered the room. Good. If the patient warranted intubation, the specialist would be the one to do so. Efficiency of time was of the essence since compression would have to be stopped for tube placement. Cayden could do it, as no doubt could Hailey, but neither of them had the experience the specialist did.

Everyone performing their roles, they continued giving lifesaving measures. As soon as the defibrillator monitor advised to do so, Hailey ordered everyone to step back so she could administer another electrical shock.

"All clear," she said, then pushed the machine's button for a second shock in continued hope of restoring a normal rhythm.

Holding his breath, Cayden watched the screen. There. A normal beat, then another. Another. And another. *Yes.*

"Equipment is showing a normal sinus rhythm," Hailey informed them, her voice calm, but relieved.

A collective sigh went up around the hospital room. Not that Larry was out of the woods, but he was alive, and his heart was currently pumping oxygen out to his body. How long that lasted was another matter. His heart could stay in rhythm or jump right back out. Or worse. His heart could completely stop beating.

"Let's get him ready to transfer to the Cardiac Care Unit," Hailey ordered.

Within minutes, Larry was being transferred to the CCU and would soon thereafter be in the cardiac lab for testing to find out what had triggered his dangerous arrhythmia. Cayden and Hailey traveled down the hallway with the team as they rolled the patient's bed and equipment. Once their patient had been handed off to the CCU, Hailey took a deep breath.

"What a morning, huh?" Cayden asked from where he stood beside her, watching as the CCU team took over Larry's care. "Not even working on the floor a week and you've already saved a man's life. Congratulations."

Hailey gave him a *Yeah, right* look. "Some third day on the job. Not counting orientation, of course." Her gaze going back to their patient, she let out a long sigh.

His heart went out to her. Having a patient to code was never easy. To have one happen so quickly into starting a new job was diving in headfirst. "You did good."

Looking surprised at his compliment, she smiled, but it was a weak one. "Thank you. I'm just glad he didn't die. For so many reasons, that would have been terrible."

"You saved him."

She didn't look convinced, instead shaking her head. "The team saved him."

"The team under your lead," he reminded her, surprised at just how rattled she appeared. Thinking back, he'd probably been rattled on his first few codes, as well.

"Honestly, I was hoping to send him home. I'd thought possibly today." She eyed where the CCU team was setting up Larry's equipment in his new high-intensity care room that was really more of a three-sided area open to the hallway with a large sliding glass door that could be pulled closed for privacy. "Thank goodness I hadn't."

"I'd planned to recommend he go home today, too. The reality is that one's health can change in a heartbeat." He nudged her arm. "Some things can be predicted. Some can't." She knew that but with her so fresh out of residency, he understood why she was being critical of herself. As far as things that could and couldn't be predicted, take his reaction to her, for instance. Because his simple nudge had him intensely aware that he'd touched her. Given where they were, what they'd just experienced, he wouldn't have predicted the zings shooting through him. Yet, there they went. *Zing. Zing. Zing.* He swallowed, then added, "Pun intended, and you have to smile that the heart specialist has jokes."

"Thanks." She smiled and it was a little more real. "The whole team showed up quickly and worked well together. Plus, we had you there. Not every code is lucky enough to have a cardiologist to give a hand." She cut her gaze toward him and surprised him with a nudge of her own, eliciting another flare of zings. "I appreciated you being there, Cayden. To have you and Renee in the room definitely made me feel better just because you were familiar and friendly faces."

Her admission had his stomach flopping. Familiar and friendly. That's what they were destined to be. Not that those zings felt familiar or friendly, but more of an attack on logic and good intentions. "Then I'm glad I arrived when I did. But I have no doubt that you would have been just fine. You ran the code exactly the way I would have done."

Giving an appreciative smile, she stood a little taller and nodded. "You're right. I worked plenty of codes during residency. However, this is my first one while not a resident, the first one at a new hospital, the first one during my first week on the job, and that made it feel different," she admitted, brushing a strayed-from-her-ponytail lock of hair back behind her ear and meeting his gaze. "I'm not sure if that makes sense, but like I said, it was nice knowing I had you there. Is the med-surg floor always this exciting?"

He was glad she'd had him there, too. Not because she'd needed him, but because she'd said his presence had comforted her. He liked that she felt that way, that she'd viewed his presence as a plus. What he wasn't sure of was how much he liked those things or how much he liked the way she was looking at him with more than a little awe mingled in with appreciation.

"Med-surg has it's days, but most are relatively calm compared to the other hospital units." He grinned. "Apparently, despite having never found a four-leaf clover, you're just lucky that way."

She snorted. "The cardiologist really does have jokes. However, that we got him back into rhythm makes me feel lucky." She glanced around the busy CCU room where Larry was being attended to by the nurses, respiratory therapist, and anesthesiologist. "No one wants to lose a patient, but especially not during your first week on a new job." Hesitating a moment, she stared directly into Cayden's eyes, making him feel as if he needed to loosen his collar and his scrub top didn't have one. "I'm no longer needed here and should head back to the medical floor. I've got a few more patients to see for my morning rounds."

She turned to go and had taken a few steps before Cayden caught up to walk beside her. "Me, too. That's why I was so close when the code was called."

She continued toward the elevator bank. "You being so close is something else that makes me feel lucky. Maybe four-leaf clovers are overrated."

"Maybe." He was glad she seemed to have gotten her composure back and was making jokes. "We should celebrate."

Now where had that come from? They didn't need to celebrate her doing her job. Yet he wanted to take her out to do just that. To celebrate her because his gut instinct said Hailey wasn't used to being celebrated. He probably wasn't the guy who should be doing so, since he was deeply attracted to her physically and they were coworkers. That wasn't a good combination. Just look at the messy situation he'd been in when Cynthia had cheated on him. He'd been ready to promise his future to her and she'd not been faithfully committed to him in the present. Which shouldn't have surprised him. His own parents hadn't been faithful to each other.

Hailey looked at him with confusion. "Celebrate?"

"Life should be celebrated." None of his meanderings of the past made that any less true. "And especially when it's the result of a successful code during one's first work week."

"Ah, I see." Her lips twitched. "In that case, what did you have in mind, Dr. Wilton?"

"Dinner and a toast to the unnecessity of four-leaf clovers for good fortune?"

She hesitated, waiting until they'd reached the elevator bank and she'd pressed the up arrow prior to turning toward him. The elevator door opened. No one was in the car and they stepped inside.

"Dinner two nights in a row?" Her eyes flickered with uncertainty as they met his. "I'm not sure that's a good idea."

Cayden couldn't argue. Somehow, though, he suspected her reasons ran deeper than them working together. "I asked so I'm paying. A free dinner could be called good luck, too."

Her lips twitched, hinting that she was fighting a smile. Good. He wanted to make her smile. "Hasn't anyone ever told you that there's no such thing as a free dinner?"

She was probably right. There was always a price to be paid, but that didn't keep his insides from lighting up like the Fourth of July when she agreed.

Incoming waves lapped at Hailey's feet as she walked along the shore. She and Cayden had eaten dinner on the same blanket he'd had from the previous night. When they'd finished, she'd said she'd like to walk, and he'd immediately stood. Spending time with a man who didn't purposely do the opposite of whatever she suggested was such an oddity that she'd caught herself staring at him for much longer than she should have. He hadn't seemed to mind, just smiled at her as if it was the most normal thing in the world. The light breeze coming off the water and the temperature felt perfect after a long day spent inside the hospital. The company was perfect, too. Too perfect.

"Tell me about Leanna Moore." What was she doing? Trying to prove to herself that he wasn't perfect? She knew he wasn't. No one was, including and especially her. Or maybe she was trying to sabotage the sense of contentment that being with him filled her with. Contentment? That wasn't the most accurate way to describe how she responded to him. Besides, there was no reason for Cayden to tell her anything about the woman he'd once dated. He and Hailey were just friends…right?

But Cayden didn't seem upset by her inappropriate and out-of-the-blue request. "She and I hit it off for a while. We worked when neither of us was interested in anything long-term. She started wanting something more." He squinted at how the evening sun hit his face. "She's a great person. I was upfront with her that I wouldn't ever want more and we ended the physical side of our friendship before things got too messy for us to remain friends."

Hailey walked closest to the water, and a fresh wave lapped at her feet.

"It's good you remained friends." She and John sure weren't. The unfriendly sentiment was mutual except when he was trying to convince her to return to Ohio. He'd called the night before, but not wanting her enjoyable evening with Cayden spoiled, she'd let the call go to voicemail. "Renee mentioned that you do a weekly segment during her morning radio show."

"I'm flattered that you were talking about me with Renee and curious as to why she would mention Leanna. Not that I go around broadcasting my personal life, but it's no secret that I've been involved with women."

Involved. Hailey mentally gulped at what he likely meant by that. "Renee must have gotten the wrong impression that you were more serious."

"That we've remained close friends may confuse some." He shrugged. "But, to be fair, at one time Leanna had hoped for a proposal, but that was never going to happen. Not from me. I've no desire to ever get married."

The water pulled back toward the sea, causing the sand to shift beneath Hailey's feet and she fought to keep from stumbling.

"Me, either." Heat infused her cheeks the moment the claim left her lips and she felt compelled to rush on. "Marriage is overrated." Not that she knew firsthand, but by some standards she'd been John's common-law wife due to how long they lived together. Ten wasted years. She wouldn't be risking that again. Relationships never lasted in her life, anyway.

Just as another wave rushed around them, this one climbing midway up Hailey's calf, Cayden stopped walking. "You continue to surprise me, Hailey. Why is it that you agree with my sentiments on marriage?"

"I was in my last relationship for almost a decade." Her *only* relationship. "Between that, school, and residency, I've missed out on a lot in life, you know?" Which was true and easier to admit than going into the details of just how hollow that relationship had been. "I want to do things with friends, the things most people did during their teens and university days, but I didn't. I was too busy making sure I made good grades and working." Next to her, he was quiet, and she wondered if she'd admitted too much. "I'm not sure if that makes sense, but it's where I'm at in my life journey and for the first time in a long time, I feel at peace."

As she said the words, she acknowledged their validity. Not that she'd achieved all or even most of her self-improvement goals, but because she'd taken control of her life and was making steps in the right direction. That she was telling him those things was further validation of how far she'd come. How could he make her so jittery inside and yet be so easy to talk to that she told him things that were so personal? Things that she was just realizing as she was saying them?

"As I said, you surprise me." He met her gaze and she fought to keep from looking away. "Being near the water gives me that sense of peace. I run here most mornings because my day goes better when I've spent time near the water."

Staring into his eyes, she wondered if diving in would bring further peace or throw her into complete turmoil. "If being near the water is what brings peace, then I should have moved long ago."

Concern shone on his face. "I take it your life in Ohio wasn't that great?"

"It led me to here so I'm not going to complain." Because, right here, next to this delicious and kind man who she was pouring her most inner thoughts out to felt like a marvelous place to be. She could tell that he wanted to ask more, but he just nodded. Maybe that was part of why he was so easy to talk to. He seemed to instinctively recognize her comfort zone and didn't push beyond it.

"I'm glad you're here, Hailey." It was probably just how the sun shone, how it hit his gorgeous hazel eyes, how the soft waves lapped at her feet that had her feeling more in sync than she'd ever felt with another person. What was it about him?

"Why?" She couldn't believe she'd asked. Even after all the time they'd lived together, having such an open, honest conversation with John would have been difficult. Impossible even. He hadn't been one for deep conversations. Or conversations at all unless the topic was something that interested him.

"Why not?" Cayden gave a sheepish grin and reached for her hand, entwining his fingers with hers. They were warm, strong, firm, full of electricity that zapped from him to her. Hailey was completely stunned.

Why is he holding my hand?

Heart pounding, she gulped. Taking a deep breath, she reminded herself that she was the new Hailey. The new Hailey could hold a gorgeous man's hand if she wanted to. It didn't mean anything. Maybe this was what friends did. Or maybe he wanted to be more than friends. What was it Renee had said about guarding her heart but still having fun? Being with Cayden was fun. How long had it been since she'd been more than an inconvenience and wallet? Since she'd felt attractive? Wanted? Feminine in all the best ways? Had she ever? When Cayden looked at her, she felt those things. Those scary, wonderful, addictive things.

Why not?

Yeah, she could think of a million reasons, but none of them had her pulling her hand from where it was clasped with his.

Later, orange and red hues painted the sky. Hailey sat on the blanket they had left spread during their walk and Cayden had gone to his car.

"Dessert and our toast to good luck," he proclaimed when he returned, holding up a small bag cooler and wine holder.

She eyed them with mixed feelings. "If I keep hanging out with you, I'm going to gain back the progress I've made in losing weight and will never reach my goal."

His forehead wrinkled. "You're dieting?"

"For my whole life it seems." Mainly, she'd just gotten a bit down after her parents died and the resulting extra pounds had added up over time. Food comforted her, making her feel better in the moment. She didn't like the trait but recognized it as her reality. It was a wonder she hadn't gained a lot more than she had over the last ten years.

Cayden ran his gaze over her, which should have made her want to suck everything in as tightly as she could, but she sat still under his scrutiny.

"The only diet you need is one where you eat healthy."

She snorted. "Says the man who brought appetizers and dessert in addition to the side salad, asparagus, and salmon I ordered for dinner."

"I didn't know I was sabotaging something that was important to you. Fortunately, you're perfect as you are. Besides, I chose fresh strawberries. They're a great source of vitamin C and good for you." He handed her the plastic champagne glasses, then removed the bottle's foil cover.

"No cork?" she asked, having imagined that he'd pop the top. Or was that just something that happened in movies?

"No cork." He grinned mischievously. "You may fault me for a technicality."

Wondering what he meant, she arched a brow. "Uh-oh. What have you done?"

He turned the bottle so that she could read the label.

"Sparkling apple cider?" She tsked as he poured bubbly liquid into one glass and then the other. Why did her insides feel just as bubbly? "You're right. I may deduct points from your celebration skills." Although, not really. She was blown away that he'd brought the bottle.

"I should get an A for effort since I noticed you didn't drink anything alcoholic last night and so I opted for an alternative, just in case." He twisted the top onto the bottle, then slid it back into the cooler bag. She held out one of the plastic glasses. Grinning, he took it, then clinked it to hers. "Here's to your first code's success."

He'd noticed that and adjusted what he'd bought to accommodate what he'd thought she'd want? Gulping back the emotions hitting her, Hailey raised her glass, touching it to his.

"And to points not deducted."

CHAPTER FOUR

ALTHOUGH THEY TEXTED, Hailey didn't see Cayden again until Sunday morning for their planned shark tooth hunt. At least, not outside of her mind, she hadn't. How could she think so much of someone she'd just met? How could she miss him? She'd been off from the hospital on Thursday. It was her designated self-care day. She exercised, got a massage, had her lashes, hair, and nails done on rotation in Sarasota, had her weekly online mental health therapy session, and furniture shopped. She'd not had a lot of things to move as most of her parents' things had been auctioned off after they'd passed. She'd been eighteen and had agreed with what the estate trustee recommended.

With the exception of a few mementoes and a painting of her mother's that John had never liked and insisted stay in the closet, she'd left most things at the apartment she'd shared with him, including the majority of her clothes. She'd wanted very little from her former life, just a few books and things from school, and had taken off from Ohio with what fit into her car. Upon arrival, she'd unpacked at the house she'd bought with only having seen it online, but knowing it was the right one. Next, she'd traded her boring sedan for the shiny blue convertible that had caught her eye when she'd driven by the lot in Sarasota. Her new life would be filled with things she'd picked, things she liked, starting with a bright, airy home, lots of whites and turquoise colors making up the sea theme she'd chosen. With initially focusing on her physical appearance and mindset, her new job, and attending neighborhood events, she'd not had much time for home decor shopping. When she had gone, she'd been picky so the process was slow. The week she'd arrived, she'd bought a bed, chest of drawers, nightstand, and an oversized amazing reading chair. She'd made a department store run for bedding, bath linens, and odd and ends. The following week, she'd found a four-person dining room table and chairs to put in the window nook off her kitchen. For a sofa, she'd been willing to wait until she found just the right one. Happily, she'd found the one today, along with a comfy chair, and bleached wooden coffee and end tables. She made arrangements for the items to be delivered the following evening, so, despite how she couldn't stop thinking of Cayden, she'd declined his phoned invitation to listen to a band playing at a nearby community village shopping area.

On Saturday, she went to the cookout with Ryan. He'd been fun, a gentleman, opening the car door and introducing her to his friends. Even though the evening was "just as friends," his attention had made her feel good, but in such a different way from how she felt with Cayden that she'd not been able to prevent comparing the outing with when she was with him. Unfortunately, she'd also not been able to stop wondering what Cayden was doing. Had he gone to listen to music the night before, only with someone as a date rather than friend? Perhaps with Leanna Moore. The green in Hailey's veins didn't bode well for someone who wasn't ready to date and, although innocent and arranged prior to meeting Cayden, was with another man.

Cayden muddied the waters of her somewhat clear vision for her future. She was more attracted to him than she'd known possible. After the horror of her relationship with John, the last thing she should be thinking about was a man. But Cayden was never far from her mind. Had she truly only known him a week?

Was that the real reason she'd not gone with him Friday evening? Fear of how he'd already gotten beneath her skin? After all, she could have invited him to wait with her on her furniture delivery and they could have gone to listen to the music afterward. Was she scared of how he made her feel? And if so, wasn't being afraid letting John still wield control over her life?

On Sunday morning, a beach-adventure-ready Hailey watched for Cayden's arrival and rushed to meet him before he'd much more than gotten out of his car. Her home was still too bare for her to let him in, which didn't make a lot of sense since she'd gotten the new pieces Friday and she'd let Ryan come in when he'd retrieved her for the cookout. It hadn't seemed to matter so much what *he* thought of her bare walls. It shouldn't matter what Cayden thought of her home. It was hers and as long as she loved it, that was what mattered. She didn't have to please anyone else.

"You're very quiet." Cayden glanced her way from the driver's seat of his SUV. As Ryan had, he'd opened the passenger door for her, something John never did. Of course, they'd been very young when they'd first gotten together and that probably made a difference. Maybe. Either way, she'd felt giddy inside like a silly schoolgirl at the gesture. How low were her standards if it took so little to impress her?

Something else to work on—have higher expectations from everyone she let into her life.

"I was thinking about needing to shop for my apartment." The truth, just that she'd had several other thoughts, too. "I've been to several places, but not found what I'm looking for. My walls are very blah." Other than in her bedroom where she had her mother's painting that she cherished. She'd have hung it in her apartment with John if she hadn't feared that he might do something to it if she'd left it in plain sight. "Not that I want clutter, but I hope to find a few special pieces to give the place a splash of me."

"A splash of you?" Cayden chuckled, glancing her way briefly as he maneuvered his vehicle through the light traffic. "That sounds intriguing and possibly painful."

"Ha. Ha. You knew what I meant." She'd wondered how things would be between them with her saying no to going with him Friday. She'd explained about the furniture, but she half expected him to be upset that she'd not done as he wished. His smile and nature were so relaxed that any uncertainty over saying no had quickly dissolved.

As silly as it was since she was similarly dressed, he'd caught her completely off guard with his bare legs as she'd only seen him with scrubs or rolled-up casual slacks. For their shark tooth hunting adventure, he wore a Venice Has Heart T-shirt complete with various local sponsors listed on the back and a pair of yellow with little pink flamingos swim trunks that came to just above his knees. He'd opted for leather sandals. Casual Cayden was just as hot as Dr. Cayden. Maybe more so as he seemed more approachable in his "play" clothes.

More approachable? Ha! If he'd been any more approachable she'd have been pushing him back on the sand after their "celebration" toast and strawberries. That he had a playboy reputation and hadn't made any moves on her should clue her in that, despite his occasional flirty comment and the spark she saw in his eyes that she'd swear was desire, ultimately, he wasn't interested in anything more than friendship.

"What are you needing? Maybe I can help," he offered, fortunately oblivious to her mental ramblings.

"You have spare lamps, pictures, and such lying around to give my house personality?" She didn't know exactly what she wanted, just knew she'd recognize the right additions when she came across them.

"You wouldn't want what's in my house." He tapped his thumbs against the steering wheel. "My condo is the ultimate bachelor pad, right down to the bicycle and surfboard in my living room. But I'm game to changing our plans to going shopping instead of to Caspersen."

Fighting a smile, she eyed him with suspicion. "Afraid you won't be able to live up to your promise of helping me find a shark tooth?"

"I keep my promises." His gaze cut to hers, emphasizing his point with its intensity and having her swallow. "We've plenty of time for finding shark teeth. Just say the word and we'll save that for another time and go shopping today."

That Cayden was willing to change their plans so readily, that he was willing to go shopping with her, had her eyeing him with renewed awe. John would have complained and only have agreed if she'd begged and they'd been shopping for him. He'd do all kinds of things when there was something in it for him.

"I'm not going to be contacted by a home makeover show anytime soon," his grin widened, "but I have decent taste. Plus, having two spare arms to carry things would be helpful."

"Or I could just use a shopping cart," she teased trying not to let her gaze go to where his arms were on display. He looked as if he could carry a lot of things. He wasn't bulky muscled, just really fit, as if he took his role as a cardiologist and promoting good heart health seriously. Hailey swallowed. Yeah, he looked like the poster child—man—for good heart health. Or maybe a poster for a heartthrob, because he was certainly that, too. Take her heart for instance. It was throbbing so hard that she was surprised it didn't drown out the music he had playing.

He chuckled. "You could, but where's the fun in that?"

"We're not dressed for shopping." She had on her bathing suit beneath her loose shorts and baggy T-shirt. They definitely had a we're-heading-to-the-beach vibe.

"You're in Florida. Beach attire works for most occasions."

She twisted in the passenger seat to more fully look at him. "You would skip going to the beach to go shopping with me?"

He nodded.

"Okay, you may regret this, because I'm going to take you up on your offer." Not that she didn't want to go to the beach with him, but she would like to find a few things for her house and she was curious about shopping with Cayden.

"Just point me in the direction you want to go and that's where I'll drive." He didn't seem the slightest fazed by their change of plans.

"Yeah, that's not a good idea. I'm still learning where things are so you may have to help. Plus, I've searched around here and haven't found what I want. I'm looking for lamps, pictures for my walls, a few cool knickknacks, that kind of thing. As cliché as it may seem, my home theme is the water."

"I'm impressed you have a home theme."

"Other than 'bachelor pad'?" Had she really just batted her lashes when his gaze was on the road, anyway?

"Yeah, I don't see that one working for you." He grinned, then glanced her way. "If you don't mind the drive, there's a place just outside Sarasota that might have what you're looking for."

"I'm good with Sarasota. It's less than an hour and where I purchased my living room furniture." She made the drive every Thursday for her big makeover maintenance.

"To Sarasota it is, then."

Cayden drove her to a large warehouse-type store that offered a variety of new and locally made items. Shopping with him was an adventure. He was funny, made hilarious suggestions, and yet, fairly quickly homed in on her taste preferences. When he pointed out two lamps that had been made by a local artisan, excitement hit.

"Those are amazing." She ran her fingertip over the intricate piece of smooth bleached driftwood that made up the base and neck of one of the lamps. The artist had covered the lower portion of the base with seashells. "Do you think I'm going overboard with my beach theme?"

"You do recall that you didn't let me see your house so I've no basis to answer with any accuracy?"

She gave a sheepish smile. "Sorry."

"But, for whatever its worth, my thought is that if you like the lamps, and you obviously do, buy them." He shrugged. "If, down the road, you decide that you want to change them out, you can. You're not stuck with today's decision forever."

He made a good point and she suspected that she'd regret it if she didn't buy one. She could even envision the piece in her living room next to her new sofa.

"Which do you like best?" She knew which she preferred but was curious if he agreed. Part of her hoped he didn't as he seemed much too in sync with her thoughts.

He ran his gaze over each lamp, then pointed to the one that had originally drawn her attention. "That one. Both pieces are great, but I like how the artist seeped the turquoise into the variances in the wood. It's subtle enough that you barely see it initially, but is a testament to its connection to the sea."

"Sold." Because, seriously, how could she not choose that one since he'd picked the lamp she'd liked best? Or ever get rid of the piece when he'd described the design exactly how she'd seen it? The subtle hint of color inflected into the wood added just the right pizzazz. She suspected she'd never look at it without being reminded of him, which gave her a moment's pause. She didn't want her home to remind her of him or anyone. It was supposed to be about her, her safe place and haven from the world. Still, she had chosen prior to his description and truly, the lamp was perfect. "Let's put those 'spare arms' to use."

Grinning, he picked up the lamp. "While you finish looking, I'll take this to the cashier for them to hold until we're ready to check out."

Hailey didn't find anything else that jumped out at the shop, but she loved the lamp and paid for it. Cayden loaded the artsy light onto the back floorboard of his SUV. He placed the shade on the seat, then used the towels he'd brought for their beach excursion to protectively place around the lamp.

"I could sit back there and make sure it doesn't get banged around," she offered. Truth was, she was impressed by his thoughtfulness in how he arranged the lamp.

"And have me looking like I'm driving Miss Hailey?" He wrinkled his nose. After one last check to make sure the lamp was secure, he got into the driver's seat. "I prefer to have you up here next to me." He buckled his safety belt, then started the car. "Are you in a hurry?"

"Not necessarily. What do you have in mind?"

"The bigger farmers markets are on Saturday but there are some that carry over onto Sundays. They usually have a variety of vendors ranging from food to artisans. There's one not too far from here," he told her. "We could grab lunch, walk around to see if we can find any other treasures for your home."

Her home. Not her apartment, but her home. Because that was what she was making in Florida. A home for herself.

A home and a new life that she liked more and more.

* * *

A couple of hours later, Cayden watched as Hailey surveyed the ice cream selection with eyes as big as any child's. Rather than order, she turned to him and shook her head.

"I'm going to pass. Thanks, though."

"It's organic and made with all-natural ingredients," he said. They'd eaten a healthy lunch and he'd been the one to suggest ice cream. Ice cream was his weakness. Not that he did, but he could eat it every single day and not get tired of the cold dessert. He wasn't even picky on what flavor. He liked them all. Some better than others. In his book, there were no bad ice cream flavors.

"That's not it. You go ahead."

Then he remembered she'd mentioned dieting. How did he convince her that her curves were perfect without making her self-conscious or have her to think he was being a jerk? Because he really liked the ease in which they'd enjoyed their day and didn't want to do anything that jeopardized that comradery. It had been a good day. A great day. Surely, she must think so, too.

Sure, he'd been a bit prickly Friday evening when they'd been on the phone and she'd said she had to wait on her furniture. Her reason had felt as flat as if she'd said she had to wash her hair. That he'd been disappointed had bothered him. He had no right to be bothered that she'd said no, but he'd spent most of his on call day mulling over just how much it had.

He didn't want more than friendship with her, and yet…he did. Hailey was refreshing, with an air of innocence mingled with an irresistible feminine allure that sucked him right in.

"I'm not eating ice cream if you're not, Hailey." He would be a jerk if he did that when he knew she wanted ice cream, too. But he didn't want her to feel he was sabotaging her if he pushed. He wanted her happy with herself. If she could see herself as he saw her, she would be. He'd hoped that with their plans being to go to the beach that she'd have foregone the makeup, because he longed to see her without it, but she'd been fully made up. He knew she was just as stunning barefaced as she was with all the latest beauty aids. How much he longed to see what she didn't readily reveal to the world should have Cynthia's name flashing through his mind like a warning beacon, but instead was muffled by how protective he felt at Hailey's vulnerability. He suspected someone had done a real number on her body image and although it wasn't Cayden's place to clear her vision to her true beauty, he wanted to do just that. Seeing how she still longingly stared at the display, he suggested, "How about if I order a small bowl and share a few bites?"

"I—" She glanced toward him, a slow smile spreading across her lovely mouth. "Okay, but just a few bites."

That a girl. "Which flavor do you want?"

She pointed to his favorite and he grinned. Incredible how in tune they were. "Great choice."

He ordered two scoops in a small bowl, then paid the cashier while another employee prepared their order. He slid his money clip into his pocket and took the ice cream bowl. Hailey had walked over to where a wide ledge served as a bar top–style table at the base of the storefront window. She sat on a stool and stared out at the boardwalk. Yeah, she should see what he saw. She was so beautiful she stole his breath and yet, it was the pureness in her eyes, in how she looked through the glass with appreciation of everything she was seeing, in how she smiled when she glanced up and saw him. That sweet, genuinely-happy-he'd-bought-ice-cream smile got him right in the feels.

"Remember, this is guilt-free ice cream." He pulled one of the spoons from the ice cream and handed it to her. "Enjoy."

"I didn't see 'guilt-free' written anywhere in the description."

"It should have been. For real, this place is known for using all-natural ingredients, nothing GMO or processed." He pulled the other spoon from the ice cream, a large glob sticking to the utensil. He stuck the cold confection in his mouth and savored the fruity flavor. "Mmm. Good and good for you."

"Next thing, you'll be trying to sell me oceanfront property in Arizona." Watching him, Hailey toyed with her spoon. "It's not fair that men can eat whatever they want and still look like you."

He scooped a second bite. "That's not an accurate statement."

"Do you eat whatever you want?" she challenged, still not using her spoon for anything other than to point it toward him.

Fortunately, other than his ice cream addiction, he ate a healthy Mediterranean diet and was lucky that he preferred eating clean. Ice cream was his guilty pleasure, and even then, he sought ones made with natural ingredients.

"I exercise regularly," he defended.

"No doubt."

Her tone made him smile and he flexed a little. "You like these?"

Snorting, she rolled her eyes with great exaggeration. "It's mostly your modesty that impresses me."

"I get that a lot." Laughing, he gestured to the bowl. "Eat up before it melts and you have a strawberry milk-shake instead of ice cream."

Hailey ate one bite to his every three, and her bites were tiny in comparison to his, but at least she did eat some of the dessert and seemed to savor each bite. He refrained from saying anything more for fear she'd stop eating altogether. He didn't want to be a stumbling block, but whoever had made her think she needed to diet de-served a hardy talking to.

When they'd finished their dessert, they headed back out onto the blocked-off street where numerous vendors were selling their wares. The smell of roasted cinnamon pecans and almonds from a nearby booth filled the air and lured several passersby.

"Admit it," he said, glancing toward where she was taking in the busy booths and their various goods. "The ice cream was worth it."

"Sure, it was." Amused sarcasm laced her words. "At the moment," she added. "However, if you ask me when I'm in the gym huffing and puffing and it takes me more than an hour to burn off what I just ate..." She let her voice trail off, then clicked her tongue. "I really shouldn't have."

"You know you look fabulous, right?"

Her cheeks went bright pink. "Thank you for saying so, but I'm well aware that I've always been a little pudgy. I gained extra weight on top of that during med school.

I want to get it back off. I've lost some since completing residency and I plan to keep working on the rest. I don't fool myself that I'll ever be thin, but I'd like to be healthy, you know?"

He ran his gaze over her and shook his head. "What you call pudgy, I call sexy."

"And my ex called fat." Her color heightened after her words slipped out, letting him know she hadn't meant to say them.

Right in the middle of the busy-with-pedestrians street, he stopped walking to look directly at her, letting the crowd weave around them. "For the record, your ex was an idiot."

Looking stunned, Hailey's blue eyes lifted to his, then her mouth slowly curved upward. "You're right. He was."

That smile... She obviously had no clue how seductive her mouth was, how the curve of her neck should be listed as lethal to a man's peace of mind because he was so wanted to nuzzle her there. How—*get yourself together*, he ordered. Where were they...oh, yeah.

"Good, we're in agreement. Don't let his lack of good sense influence how you see yourself. You're beautiful. Inside and out. Now, let's go check out those paintings at that booth just up ahead." With that, he grabbed her hand, lacing his fingers with hers, and took off walking as if it weren't a big deal that he was holding her hand.

But, just as when they'd been walking on the beach, Hailey's soft hand clasped within his felt as if touching her was a very big deal. Even more so than during their sunset stroll. Which meant he probably shouldn't be holding her hand. But he wasn't letting go.

Not when Hailey held on to his hand as if he'd offered

her a lifeline to lift her from some terrible place she'd
been stuck for much too long.

"I love it!" Hailey exclaimed of the artwork Cayden had
just hung on her living room wall. She'd been anxious
about letting him inside her house, wondering what he'd
think of what she'd done thus far. As he'd been helping her carry her purchases inside, she'd not had much
choice short of turning him away at the door. The truth
was, she'd enjoyed their day, enjoyed being with him.
And, as nervous as she'd thought she'd be at his seeing
her incompletely put together house, when he'd walked
in, he'd glanced around and that he'd liked what he'd
seen was obvious.

His approval shouldn't matter. She'd lived on edge trying to get John's approval. She sure didn't want to be in
a relationship where that misery became part of her day-
to-day existence again. A big difference, she reminded
herself, was that no matter what she did, John never really gave his approval regarding anything that wasn't to
his benefit. Cayden seemed to selflessly give his time
and again. That made her smile big. How wonderful to be
with someone who made you feel better about yourself?

With his hands resting on his hips, he stared at her
new picture. "She's growing on me."

"Ha! Don't give me that. You were the one to point her
out to me." Pulling her gaze from him, Hailey admired
the mermaid with her soulful eyes, turquoise tendrils and
tail, and the chaotic sea. Wild waves crashed about the
mermaid, but she appeared at ease, her expression one of
being at peace with the world. The artist had used broken
shells to create the mixed media rock emerging from the

sea that the mermaid perched upon and nacre to make a pearly bikini top. Hailey had immediately fallen in love with the piece and how well it would look with her living room decor. She'd been right.

"You thought that meant I liked her?" He clicked his tongue. "I was joking when I said you should buy her."

Unfazed by his ragging, she shook her head. "No, you weren't. You like her as much as I do." His poor attempt to look innocent of her accusation failed miserably. "That's why you insisted upon buying her as a housewarming gift," she reminded him, still stunned by his generosity after a lifetime of only gifts from her parents. John had come through with holiday gifts, but they'd always been generic types of things. Supermarket flowers on her birthday. A small box of chocolates on Valentine's. New department store gloves and scarf set at Christmas year after year. Thank God she had no need of his gloves and scarfs in Florida. She'd left them all. Not that there would have been anything wrong with his gifts if they'd come with feeling rather than an obligatory holiday appeasement and expectation that she'd have done something extravagant for him. Besides, how many gloves and scarf sets had she needed? None now, because she had finally stepped into the sunshine. She met his gaze and hoped he could see how much she appreciated him. "Thank you, again, Cayden."

His brow lifted, but after a moment in which he looked torn on what he might say, he returned his attention to the artwork. "There is something about her that latches on to you and won't let go, isn't there? And you're welcome. I'm glad you gave in to my gifting her to you."

She hadn't wanted to, but he'd insisted that he'd spotted the artwork first and called dibs, saying that it was the perfect housewarming gift for a friend who'd just moved to town. He was smooth with the lines. Yet she didn't doubt his sincerity or that she would always treasure the piece. "Even the colors are perfect. As if she was meant to come home with me."

He gestured to where she'd put her new lamp. "That looks great, like it was made for this room, too. Great find."

"You're an expert at this shopping thing, too." He really was, and she'd had tons of fun in the process. "Maybe instead of shark tooth hunting, we can look for big shells. I'd like to have one to put on the table there."

He looked at her in question. "A conch shell?"

She nodded. "I think that's what they're called."

"You don't need to buy one. We can find good shells around here, but if we don't find what you're looking for, then we can go to Sanibel Island."

Sanibel Island. She'd heard of it at some point but couldn't place where it was in her mind. "How far away is that?"

He shrugged. "Just a couple of hours drive."

She gave a horrified look. "A couple of hours is too far to drive to find a seashell."

He laughed. "Where's your adventurous spirit?"

"Hidden beneath my practicality that says driving a couple of hours to find a seashell doesn't make good common sense. Especially when there are dozens of tourist shops around here that sell shells."

"We could say that we're going to Sanibel Island for sightseeing, rather than for shell hunting. Or maybe we will find one when we go shark tooth hunting. The catch to finding great ones really is to either go early or to dive to find them, though."

She adjusted where the lamp sat on the end table. Happiness bubbled inside. The lamp and the painting truly were the perfect finds and she'd had the most perfect day. "Dive?"

"Snorkeling," he clarified. "Although, we could scuba, too. Truthfully, if you were game to learn, that would be the best way to find what you want."

She shook her head. She could wait on finding a shell. There was no rush. "Ohio girl, remember? I'm not used to the ocean. I'd never been prior to moving here and the idea of snorkeling or diving makes me feel claustrophobic."

He looked taken aback. "You moved here without ever having visited? Where was your practicality when you made that decision?" His teasing tone filtered out any real judgment in his question.

"It seemed like a good idea at the time." Glancing around her bright, airy house, which made her feel free and light by just being in it, then at him, she lowered her lashes and smiled. "It's early yet, but so far, I'd say moving here was a great idea."

His eyes crinkled with his return smile. "You're liking our subtropical climate and good-natured natives, eh?"

"Absolutely." Everyone she'd met had been kind, especially him. That he was also the hottest man she'd ever met…she fought fanning her face. "The sunsets are beautiful, too."

"Some say they're spectacular."

Had he just stepped closer? Oh, heaven above, she really was about to fan her face.

"Speaking of sunsets, last night's was amazing. Did you see it?" he asked.

"Not really," she admitted. "I was at a cookout with a friend, and after eating, we were playing games in a small fenced-in backyard where the view wasn't that great so I didn't pay much attention."

An odd look settled onto his face as his gaze met hers. "A male friend?"

"Yes. A neighbor offered to introduce me to his friend group. They were a fun bunch. You'd like them."

The cookout, meeting Ryan's friends, playing cornhole, terrible as she'd been, had been fun. She'd been a little giddy that she was checking another box of having her new life.

"Are you going to see this neighbor again?" Cayden's eyes darkened and even though the evening had been innocent, she had trouble holding his gaze. She took a step back.

"I'm sure I will." She'd bumped into Ryan each time she'd gone to the community room events and he was frequently in the workout room while she was there for her early morning torture sessions. He'd been sweet and she'd enjoyed meeting his friends. They hadn't made any specific plans, but he'd asked if it was okay to call, and she'd said it was. Making friends was a priority and Ryan was one of the first she'd met.

"Oh." Cayden's face blanched of color, then red splotched his cheeks.

His "oh" held so much disappointment and negativity that she couldn't let it pass. She'd dealt with both much too often. Fingers curling into her palms, she said, "Go on."

"What do you want me to say, Hailey? That I'm glad that you went out with this guy last night and that you're planning to see him again?" He harrumphed. "I can't do that."

"Ryan," she supplied prior to thinking better of it.

"That's his name?" Cayden asked. She nodded, and he continued, "Okay, you told me to go on, so I will." He flexed his jaw. "I'd rather you not go out with Ryan again."

She fought flinching. John telling her what she could and couldn't do echoed through her mind. He wouldn't have said "rather you not" but would have just told her that she wasn't going to. That didn't seem to matter though as she lifted her chin.

"The cookout was just as friends, but for the record, you don't get a say in whether or not I go on a date with someone." Even as she said it, she questioned the validity of her bravado. Disappointing Cayden bothered her. She didn't want to disappoint him and that irked. She'd spent ten years trying not to disappoint John. Ten years that she'd never get back. She needed to focus on not disappointing herself and not another man.

"It's just—" Cayden stopped, raked his fingers through his hair, and closed his eyes as if he was at a loss for words.

"Just what?" Barely able to breathe, she crossed her arms and stared at him.

"The truth is that I'm jealous you were with another man last night, Hailey." He appeared as shocked as she was by his confession. Shocked, and perhaps a bit self-disgusted. "How's that for a truthful admission?"

Hailey's knees threatened to give way. "Why would you be jealous?"

"I like you." He didn't sound thrilled by his admission, but he'd said the words without hesitation.

Her heart pounded. She was standing in her living room, staring at the most gorgeous man she'd ever known, and he'd just said he liked her. Was this what it felt like to have the most popular guy in school notice you when you were of the wallflower variety?

"I like you, too."

Cayden's gaze didn't waver from hers. "Yet you were with another man last night? Why would you do that?"

She hadn't done anything wrong. His questions made her feel like bringing up all kinds of protective walls. Her evening had just been "as friends," but if it had been a date, she was well within her rights to have gone. She was not wrong to want to experience life.

"I just met you this past week," she reminded him, trying to choose her words wisely because she didn't want to argue with Cayden. How surreal was it that she felt as if she'd known him much longer? In reality, she'd been to the beach with him twice, seen him at work, and spent today with him. They were strangers. And yet, they weren't. She felt as if she knew him better than the man she'd lived with for almost ten years. "I can't even believe we're having this conversation."

"You're right." Frowning, he worked his jaw from one side then to the other. "Does *Ryan* know about me?"

Stunned, Hailey stared at him. "Why would I have told Ryan about you? A week ago today, he invited me to the cookout so I could get to know people because I'm new in town. You and I are coworkers." She put her fisted hands on her hips. "Please explain why Ryan would need to know anything about you?"

Cayden stared at the woman glaring at him and thought her well within her right to do so. Everything she said was true. What was wrong with him? He was acting like a jealous boyfriend.

He didn't do boyfriend. Hadn't in years. Sure, he'd gone out, but he'd only been involved with women who knew the score and didn't have false expectations. He'd let his romantic involvement with Leanna go on too long as she'd started wanting more and losing their friendship would have been a shame. Cynthia had been his last real girlfriend where his heart had been involved and, after that had ended as disastrously as his previous attempts at being in a supposedly committed relationship, he'd given up on happy-ever-after and was quite content with his happy-right-now status. Why he'd ever thought such a mythical thing existed was beyond him. It sure hadn't been the example his parents had set. Great as they were individually, together they'd been malignant. As far as jealous? Yeah, he didn't do that, either. Why had he told Hailey he was jealous?

Because it was true. Right or wrong, for the first time in forever the thought of a woman being with anyone other than him had him seeing green.

"You're right." Because what else could he say?

Her jaw dropped. "I am? I mean, of course, I am. I'm just surprised that you're admitting it. That's a new one for me."

"I've said it before, but your ex was an idiot." He paced across the room, staring at her mixed-media mermaid and battling emotions that felt as tumultuous as the artwork's churning sea. "That you were out with another man last night caught me off guard, Hailey. That's all."

He couldn't call it cheating because that implied something existed between him and Hailey that didn't. But he couldn't squelch his dislike of the idea of her with another man, even if only as friends. Years had passed since the last time he'd cared about what a woman did with her time away from him. He wasn't the jealous type. Yet he wanted to beat his chest and warn this Ryan guy to stay away.

What's wrong with me?

"Am I missing something, Cayden?" Hailey pushed.

He turned back, taking in the stubborn tilt to her chin, the just as determined glint in her eyes. How was he supposed to explain that he didn't want a relationship, but he didn't want her out with other men? He couldn't tell her that. She'd laugh in his face or tell him to get out or both. Rightly so.

"Cayden?" She came to stand a foot in front of him when he remained silent. "We had such a great day. I don't want to argue with you. I don't understand what's happening."

What was happening was that his gaze had dropped to her mouth, watching as her lips formed each word, and now, all he could think, feel, was how much he wanted to kiss her. Out of desire, but also, as a way of staking his claim.

Frustrated with himself, he shook his head. "Nothing. I just—it's time I go."

Because as easy as it would be to give in to what he wanted to do, to kiss her, how strongly that he didn't want anyone else doing the same, made his head spin. He did not want to stake a claim. He didn't care what women did when they weren't with him. He hadn't since he'd found out Cynthia had been screwing around with another man. Beyond that, hadn't he decided that he and Hailey were coworkers, and anything more than friendship would be complicated?

Friendship with Hailey was already complicated.

Even so, unable to resist, he leaned in, and kissed her forehead. "Good night, Hailey."

With that, he hightailed it out of her house. Denying just how much Hailey got under his skin had become impossible. That quick peck to her forehead had done little to appease the culminating burn within him.

Since she claimed to not want marriage any more than he did, and he saw how she looked at him, sometimes so innocently that he wasn't even sure if she was aware how hot desire burned in her eyes, maybe he shouldn't deny either of them.

But if they became lovers, could they remain friends after the fires died down?

He liked Hailey more than as just the woman he wanted to devour from head to toe. They may have only known each other for a week as she'd so sassily pointed out, but he was positive he'd miss her if he lost her friendship.

CHAPTER FIVE

"GOOD MORNING," a tired Hailey greeted Melvin Little and his wife the following morning. Mondays had always been just another day as during residency she was just as likely to work on weekends as weekdays. More so, usually. With her new Monday through Wednesday work schedule, she rotated out with other physicians and would cover one weekend a month. Had she not tossed and turned all night with thoughts of Cayden, of trying to figure out what that little kiss had meant and why he'd left, then she might feel rested. Instead, she'd used drops to try to clear her red eyes and applied extra powder to hide her dark circles. Maybe no one would notice. She smiled a little brighter at her patient. "I hoped you'd be recovered enough that you'd have been dismissed prior to my returning to work this morning."

The bushy white-haired man scooted up in his hospital bed, grimacing a little as he did so, but moving easier than he had the last time she'd examined him. "Hoping to not have to see me again, Doc?"

She shook her head. "Just wishing you well." She glanced at the blanket in Sharla's lap. "Wow. You've gotten a lot of your afghan completed. That's wonderful."

"Thank you." Keeping a tight hold on her needle and

yarn, Sharla proudly held up the sunset-colored piece. "I'll probably have it finished within the next couple of days if he doesn't go home."

"Is that a request to keep him here until you've finished?" Hailey teased, running her hand beneath a hand sanitizer dispenser, then moving beside where Melvin lay. He still appeared pale, but his color was better.

"Could you?" Laughing, Sharla shot her husband a loving look. "When I get him home, he's going to be his usual cantankerous self and thinking I'm supposed to wait on him hand and foot. Having him here is like a vacation for me."

Melvin grunted at his wife's poking. "Don't let her fool you. She lives to dote on me. She did the same with the kids and now the grandkids. They came by yesterday. The whole lot of them. This room was a madhouse for an hour or so. Be glad you missed the chaos."

Hailey couldn't imagine having a big family and what it must feel like to have them be there for you. Those too-short years she'd had with the Eastons had just given her a taste of family life and then it had been ripped away.

She cleared her throat and her thoughts. "That's good you got to see them, but I hope you didn't overdo it."

He shrugged. "Hard to overdo anything when I'm just lying in a hospital bed and waiting on this old body to heal."

"There are different ways to overdo it." After first gloving up, Hailey listened to his heart, his lungs, then checked his abdomen. Everything sounded, looked, and felt as it should other than his chronic heart issues. He seemed to be improving from his surgical emergency and was slowly getting his strength back. "I think I have bad news for you,

Sharla. His white blood cell count was completely normal this morning. His surgical site is healing with no redness, drainage, or other sign of infection from his ruptured appendix. His BNP, that stands for brain natriuretic peptide, is still elevated, but not so elevated that home management of his heart failure shouldn't be sufficient. His numbers may have come down enough to be at his baseline, even. But either way, the levels are safe to further address in an outpatient setting. Dr. Wilton—" her heart squeezed as she said his name out loud "—will be by this morning and will be able to give you more information regarding your outpatient heart failure follow-up. As long as he's in agreement, then you'll be discharged later today."

"That's wonderful." Sharla smiled at her husband.

"Doc, that's the best news I've heard since I showed up at this place," Melvin said, coughing as he did so.

Hailey hadn't heard any rattles in his chest, nor had his chest X-ray picked up on any fluid buildup in his lungs. His cough and continued elevated BNP concerned her, but when everything was overall so improved, those weren't sufficient reasons to maintain acute inpatient care.

She talked with the couple a few more minutes, then left his room to round on the remainder of her patients. The unit was full, but no one had anything too exciting going on. When Hailey returned to the office cubicle behind the nurses' station to make further chart notations, Renee glanced up from where she worked and grinned big.

"You just missed Dr. Wilton." The nurse manager eyed Hailey curiously as if she was expecting a reaction. Hailey did her best not to give one as Renee continued, "I think he was going to Room 211." Renee waggled her drawn-on brows. "If you hurry, you can catch him."

Catch Cayden. Hailey's heart sped up. She hadn't been able to quit thinking of him the night before. Mostly, she marveled that he liked her enough that he was upset that she had gone to the cookout with Ryan and had admitted that he was jealous. Even with the hair color, extensions, weight loss, and the rest of her big makeover, how was that even possible?

Struggling to hide how knowing he was near affected her, Hailey adjusted her stethoscope from where the tubing poked up from her scrub top's pocket. "Did he need to consult with me on a patient?"

Hopefully oblivious to the thundering in Hailey's chest, Renee shook her head. "Not that I'm aware of. I was just letting you know that he came by so that, you know, you could find a reason to bump into him, talk to him, maybe mention sharing dinner and another romantic sunset with him. That kind of thing."

"Not once have I said I shared a romantic sunset with Dr. Wilton." Not out loud, but they had been romantic. *Spectacular.* "Nor is there a reason for me to purposely bump into him, Renee." No reason other than she yearned to see him, to know if he was upset with her, to know if frustration would still shine in his gorgeous eyes when he looked at her. Maybe she didn't want to see him, because if he gave her a cold shoulder, how was she going to hide her disappointment? Why would he give her a cold shoulder when he'd kissed her good-night? A peck, but it had been a kiss. Plus, he'd said he was jealous. That had to mean something.

What do I want it to mean?

"Did he make any notes on Mr. Little? I'm planning to discharge him today unless Dr. Wilton prefers he be kept one more night for further observation."

"He hasn't yet." Renee gave a sly grin that hinted she wasn't buying Hailey's lack of forthcoming details. Her coworker would have a field day if she knew Hailey had seen him outside of work two additional times since their Manasota sunset and that Cayden's lips had touched her the night before. Her forehead. But they had touched her. Perhaps her coworker could see the scorch marks, because she was fairly positive her skin was branded from the simple caress. "He's in with Mr. Little now."

Hailey's belly churned. How would Cayden act around her? Would he be friendly or standoffish? If the latter, would it be from being professional or as a carryover from his displeasure at her having gone to the cookout with Ryan? Whatever Cayden's reaction, he'd be professional. He wouldn't cause a scene or purposely trigger hospital gossip.

"Oh, goody. You don't have to not purposely bump into him, because there he is now." Renee gestured to behind where Hailey stood. "Hello, Dr. Wilton. Your timing is perfect. Look who is back at the nurses' station."

Yeah, Cayden was professional and wouldn't cause hospital gossip. Renee, on the other hand, had no issue with saying whatever popped into her mind. Despite her warnings to guard her heart, her coworker had completely gotten on board with the idea of Cayden and Hailey. Maybe because she considered herself the cupid who had shot the arrow and felt invested in their relationship. Either way, Hailey believed Renee's intentions weren't malicious, but, oh, how she wished she wouldn't be so obvious.

Taking a quick breath, Hailey turned, met Cayden's gaze and attempted to read his mood. Instantly, she realized that he was doing the same. Had he been concerned that she'd be upset with him? In the entirety of their relationship, John had never cared if he'd upset her. If he had, she'd been expected to get over it and to not do whatever had caused him to upset her again. Even with his cheating, he'd blamed her, citing that she had been too distracted with medical school and residency to meet his needs.

Why did I forgive him time and again?

Swallowing at her own past follies, she smiled at Cayden and after only a moment's hesitation, his lips curved upward, too. Hailey's entire body lightened as her muscles released from the tension that had bound them.

No matter what happened, she wanted to end up as friends with Cayden. Maybe that's all they should be to preserve that future friendship and their working relationship. But how could she insist upon something that she wasn't sure she could do? Because the bubbles of giddiness filling her at his smile weren't bubbles of just wanting to be his friend.

"Good morning, Dr. Wilton." She kept it more formal for Renee's benefit, but knew he'd know why she had. He wore his standard hospital navy scrubs that pulled out the golden flecks in his hazel eyes and she had to fight the strong urge to hug him because he'd so readily smiled back. He didn't seem to play the games she'd come to expect.

Do not put him on a pedestal. You've only known him a week, she reminded herself.

Why did it feel as if she'd known him on some level her entire existence? Thinking she'd lost her mind, she cleared her throat. "What are your thoughts on Mr. Little?"

"He has high hopes of going home today." Cayden grasped the tip of the stethoscope he had draped around his neck, the muscles in his arms flexing as he did so and drawing Hailey's gaze. His teasing flashed through her mind and her belly clenched at the memory. It was too late to think of Cayden as just a friend. Maybe at some point in the future she'd be able to, but the man tangled up her nerve endings into a hormonal mess she hadn't known she was capable of being.

The real question was what was she going to do about how he affected her? He didn't want anything serious. She didn't want anything serious. Why couldn't they just have fun together? Why couldn't he truly impart some of his expert advice to guide her through her initial "dating" debut? She wanted to explore the joy he triggered within her, to flirt and revel in his attention for however long it lasted. As long as she kept her heart safely tucked away, what would be wrong with soaking up the deliciousness of time spent with him?

Biting into her lower lip, Hailey forced her gaze back to his face, realized Cayden knew exactly what she'd looked at, thought, and she gulped. "Are you on board with his being discharged today?"

Okay, so her voice might have been a slightly higher pitch than normal, but for the most part she'd managed to sound professional.

"His heart failure is chronic, stable overall, and had nothing to do with his initial admission. His surgical complications from his ruptured appendix are resolving." Cayden's gaze stayed connected to hers to the point where Hailey felt the conversation was something personal rather than purely professional, that there were two conversations occurring. One with words and another with their eyes. "From an acute cardiac standpoint, Melvin is safe to go home and will definitely be more comfortable there while he recuperates. His wife will keep close tabs and will get him back here if anything changes."

"Absolutely," she agreed, grateful his assessment had been the same as hers and even more grateful that he seemed as relieved that everything was okay between them as she was. They'd talk soon, away from the hospital. She'd figure out how to say she wanted to spend time with him, to date him, even. But that she would date other men, too, if the opportunity and desire to presented itself. The new Hailey wouldn't be bound by an exclusive relationship that could a man power to dictate her life the way John had. She wouldn't risk getting too close to Cayden and falling into old habits. Seeing other men would be a constant reminder not to get too attached because she and Cayden were casual. "I'll write up discharge orders and have a hospital follow-up appointment scheduled with his primary care provider. Do you want to see him in your office in a few days, as well? Or to just have him follow up with you at his regularly scheduled cardiac checkup?"

"Within the next two weeks would be best."

I'm sorry about last night. That's what his eyes were saying, what her heart was hearing.

"Have my office get him worked in on my schedule."
Me, too, she told him back.

At least she hoped her eyes were broadcasting as clearly as his were. Were hers also transmitting the hesitation she saw in his? He wasn't his usual, teasing self, making reading him difficult and she was far from an expert at her best moments.

"I'll get it noted." Listen to them sounding all business. Standing there, staring at each other, Renee watching them with a Cheshire cat grin, Hailey felt self-conscious because she wasn't sure what to say or do with their audience. She looked at the charge nurse. "What?"

"Nothing." But Renee was smiling when she turned back to her computer screen. When the charge nurse started humming, Hailey shook her head and gave Cayden a *Sorry...* look.

"Don't forget that this Thursday evening is a meeting regarding the Venice Has Heart event," Cayden continued. "It's at six in the Main Street Community Room. I hope you're planning to be there."

"Of course." Avoiding looking directly toward Renee in case her coworker glanced up, Hailey nodded. No way would she be able to hide her thoughts if she met Renee's gaze. "Thursday works perfectly as I'm off from the hospital. I truly do want to get involved in community events and to be helpful wherever I can. I planned to volunteer with some charities even before I moved to Florida. I feel lucky to have done so this quickly thanks to Renee."

"That's great. We appreciate everyone who volunteers." Yeah, she doubted their conversation was fooling Renee.

"I'm looking forward to meeting the other volunteers."

She was. Making friends was high on her priority list for her big move to Florida. She'd been so isolated for so long. She was getting to know some of her neighbors via their HOA neighborhood activities and community gym, and she'd met Ryan's group at the cookout. Slowly, but surely, she'd make friends.

"We have the best volunteers at Venice Has Heart. I..." He hesitated then seemed to change his mind about whatever he'd considered saying. She assumed that Renee being able and eager to hear their discussion limited what he was saying as it did for Hailey.

There was a quiet pause where they just looked at each other, then Hailey gave a nervous laugh. "I should get Mr. Little's discharge started. He'll be excited that you're in agreement for him to go home. Sharla is going to have her hands full."

She'd hoped he'd say something more, but after a moment of obvious debating with himself that had Renee looking back and forth between them, he just nodded. "Sounds good, Hailey. Thanks for taking care of that."

She didn't see him again that day and considered texting him, but decided she shouldn't. No matter how many self-confidence podcasts she listened to while doing household chores and therapy sessions she attended, she wasn't sure she'd ever get over her insecurities. What if Cayden had realized he wasn't interested in anything more than friendship and being her coworker? Either way, she'd be fine, she assured herself. She did not need him or any man for affirmation of her value. She was enough. Just ask her therapist.

After work, Hailey stopped by a home goods store and purchased an outdoor patio set that included a propane-fueled fire pit and arranged to have it delivered early Thursday as she didn't have any self-care appointments until later in the day. She found an outdoor rug that matched and managed to finagle it into her new car by lowering the convertible top and buckling it into the passenger seat. If she envisioned having friends to come over to visit, socializing with them while sitting on her patio, it would happen, right?

The following two days, one of Cayden's partners was on call for the cardiology rounds. In his late forties, Dr. Brothers was polite, to the point, and there and gone in under fifteen minutes each morning. Having known the posted call schedule didn't keep Hailey from feeling disappointed as each day passed without her seeing or hearing from Cayden. On Wednesday evening, she started a yoga class and ended up with a coffee date for the following morning with another newcomer who worked as a nurse at an extended living facility.

After an hour at her community gym and her patio furniture delivery, she met Jamie, and had a low-carb protein smoothie that tasted pretty good. They ended up walking around the man-made lake near the shopping center, chatting away as they continued to get to know each other. Jamie had recently moved to the area and was as eager to make friends as Hailey. They promised to make their Thursday mornings a new tradition. Hailey would have to adjust the timing on her Sarasota beauty session trips, but that should be easy enough by planning ahead.

That evening, Hailey debated on what one would wear to a Venice Has Heart volunteer meeting. She ended up settling on a casual power-red skirt, white eyelet top, and comfy sandals from her new wardrobe. Not too casual and not too dressy.

When she arrived at the community center, she wasn't sure where to go, but met up with a very tan and fit late sixties couple. They claimed to be longtime volunteers and advised her to follow them. They were dressed casually in shorts, T-shirts, and sandals so she was glad she'd not chosen anything dressier. When they entered the room, there were already around thirty volunteers present, including Cayden and Leanna Moore. Most everyone was somewhere between the Krandalls' level of casual and Hailey's, but not Leanna. She stunned in white capris pants and a turquoise top that matched her eyes, chunky jewelry, and not a hair out of place. As beautiful as the radio personality had appeared on the billboards, the signs didn't do her justice. No wonder Renee had said they all believed Cayden and the woman would eventually end up together. They were absolutely fantastic standing next to each other, as if they'd both won the best of the best in the gene pool. Seriously, had she come there tonight hoping to invite him to spend time together? Why would he want to when he had someone as dynamic as the radio deejay vying for his attention. The woman looked at Cayden with pure adoration.

Perhaps sensing that Hailey had arrived and was staring at him, Cayden spotted her and smiled. The curving of his lips instantly sent her pulse upward. Seeing him, Leanna glanced toward Hailey. She smiled, too, but it wasn't nearly as bright as Cayden's had been. As if to stake her claim, Leanna placed her hand on his arm, saying something to recover his attention.

"Come sit with us," the Krandalls offered, oblivious

to Hailey having been put in her place by Leanna that had just occurred. "Just know that our plan in keeping you close is to have you signed up to help with the half marathon."

"I think I'm already signed up to help elsewhere. Although, to be honest, I really don't know specific details other than the event is in a couple of months." Confused, she smiled at the couple. "Venice Has Heart is a race?"

Mr. Krandall chuckled. "Venice Has Heart is much more than a race and will be here before we know it. The day starts out with the half marathon that Saturday morning," he said as they made their way toward a group in the corner. "Afterward, there are different booths, all geared to make people more heart healthy. There will be blood pressure checks, educational bits, relay races and bouncy houses for the kids, that kind of thing."

"There's a vegan cook-off competition. Some of the vendors will be selling veggie burgers and other vegan food options to broaden dietary palates and introduce things folks may not have ever tried so they can know how tasty healthy eating can actually be," Mrs. Krandall added, waving to someone as they passed a table. "There will be relay races for the kids, face painting, that kind of thing, too. It's just a great day all the way around with something for everyone. It's one of our favorite days of the entire year and takes about a year's worth of planning."

"It sounds wonderful." She smiled at the woman. "If you're signing me up to help with the race, I assume you're in charge of it?"

"This is the third year of the Venice Has Heart event," Mrs. Krandall explained. "Bobby and I have put together the half marathon portion each year. Usually, we get to meetings early, but we picked our grandson up from band practice and ran him home this evening. He's involved in so much that his mom and dad can't always get him to and fro. We're glad to come to the rescue."

Her husband chuckled. "Listen at her acting as if we're late when we still arrived on time despite picking our Robert up from middle school."

Hailey smiled as the couple bantered back and forth all the while introducing her to the other race volunteers. Their energy was impressive, as was how welcoming they were. This, she thought. This was exactly the sort of thing she'd been hoping to become a part of. She liked these people already and they strove to do good in the world.

"Linda, you aren't trying to steal away one of my medical volunteers, are you?" Cayden hugged the woman, then shook Mr. Krandall's hand. "Hello, Bob."

The older couple beamed at him with obvious affection.

"Hailey didn't tell me that she was one of your volunteers or I *might* have left her alone." Mrs. Krandall laughed. "Probably not, but maybe."

"No?" Cayden tsked his tongue. "Sorry, Linda, but I have other plans for Dr. Easton during Venice Has Heart."

"Doctor? Good for you." Linda glanced toward Hailey, admiration on her face. "You should have told me that there was little chance he'd let me have you."

"Sorry," she apologized at the woman's playful scolding. "I honestly didn't know what all Cayden had in line for me."

"He'll have you doing more than refilling water bottles and cheering on our runners," Linda chuckled. "But he could stick you in the medical tent that morning in case any of our runners have issues. We'd love to have you with us."

"For the record, I was going to let Hailey choose what time frame she wants to volunteer, but if she wants to come early for the half marathon, that works for me."

"I'd love to," Hailey assured them, earning smiles from the couple.

They chatted a few minutes. Then Cayden placed his hand on Hailey's back and steered her away from the others. "You came." Had he thought she wouldn't show? "I didn't know if you would change your mind or have other plans."

Had that been a dig at her possibly having gone out with Ryan or someone else? She straightened her spine to stand tall.

"We haven't known each other long." Yes, she was purposely pointing that out yet again. "But I do my best to follow through on things I say I will do. If I'm physically able to do something I've said I would do, then that's what I will be doing."

"Noted and good to know." His lips twitched, letting her know that her response had amused him. Perhaps because her hands had gone to her hips which she hadn't realized until that moment.

She ordered her tense muscles to relax. "You're in charge of the medical volunteers?"

"Darling, Cayden is in charge of the whole production. Venice Has Heart is his baby." In a waft of something that smelled absolutely fabulous, Leanna stuck out her hand. "Hi, I'm Leanna Moore."

Not surprised that the woman had soon followed Cayden, Hailey shook her hand. "I know who you are. I've seen your billboards, but they fail to do you justice." The woman beamed. "I'm Hailey Easton," she continued. "I work with Cayden at the hospital and offered to volunteer."

The woman glanced back and forth between them. "You're a nurse?"

Hailey greatly admired nurses, but that Leanna immediately assumed that must be her role irked.

"Hailey is a hospitalist at Venice General. The hospital was lucky enough to have her start a few weeks ago," Cayden supplied, then returned his gaze to Hailey. "And, really, although Leanna says I'm in charge, it's the people like her, Linda, and Bob, and so many others who put the individual pieces together who make the event such a success."

"He's much too modest." With a plump-lipped smile and her eyes conveying so much more than mere admiration, Leanna patted Cayden's cheek with familiarity. Her beautifully manicured hand lingered on the last pat prior to slowly gliding down his chin.

Was this what he'd felt when he'd said he was jealous that she'd gone to the cookout with Ryan? Hailey didn't want to feel jealousy. She'd known Cayden less than two weeks so how could such intense green be filling her veins? She was getting too caught up in Cayden. Especially with how much she'd missed him that week. How could she miss someone she'd only known existed for such a short time? Especially when he had never been hers to begin with?

"Dr. Wilton's modesty was one of the first things I noticed about him." Hailey hadn't been sure if he'd catch her reference to the teasing comment she'd previously made to him, but his grin said he knew exactly what she'd meant. He didn't call her out on addressing him so formally and Hailey wasn't quite sure how she felt about that. Despite what he'd said, was he glad she'd kept it formal when Leanna was around to witness their conversation? Enough dwelling on Cayden's relationship with the radio beauty. It wasn't any of Hailey's business and she needed to remember that. "Nice to meet you, Leanna," she automatically told the woman from a lifetime of good manners. Then she looked at Cayden, meeting his gaze. "Point me in the direction where I can be useful or at least learn what I need to know. I want to help."

Cayden introduced her to Benny Lewis, a gem of a woman who was a retired nurse and who headed up the event's medical volunteers. Hailey got the impression that Cayden might have stuck around, but Leanna called him to where she was now with another group, saying she needed his input.

"How long are you willing to volunteer, and do you have any special interests in the day's events?" Benny asked. "Knowing that will help me know best where to place you. We want to keep our volunteers happy, so they'll be back year after year."

"This is all new to me, so no special interests other than wanting to be useful. As far as how long—" she shrugged "—how long do you need me?"

Benny chuckled. "Honey, I'll use you all day if you're willing."

Hailey glanced toward Cayden. The group he was with spoke animatedly about whatever it was they were discussing, smiling and laughing as they did so. Leanna's hand rested on his upper arm, and she leaned in to tell him something, making him laugh. Hailey's heart hiccupped.

"If it's helpful, I can be there all day." Perhaps seeing him with the radio personality would be helpful to Hailey, ingraining just how out of her league he really was despite his attention the previous week. She did want to spend time with him, but it was just as well that she didn't want a happy-ever-after as she'd only get her heart broken again. "Linda and Bob mentioned helping with the race. If there's something I can do to be useful, I'd love to assist with that."

"You want to help from start to finish? That would be amazing." Benny hugged her. "It'll be a long day. But there are several of us who do just that and think it's one of the best days of each year. I'll start you in the medical tent for the half marathon, then transition you to volunteering in the blood pressure reading area. We have nursing student volunteers taking the pressures, checking blood glucose readings, that kind of thing. Any people with abnormal results are offered a brief consult with one of the provider volunteers on what they need to do to decrease their heart disease risk."

"What a wonderful event for the community," Hailey said and meant. Education was everything in living a healthier life. She knew that firsthand. Her adoptive parents had been wonderful people, but sedentary and she'd followed in their footsteps until recently.

"It is. By the end of the day, you'll be mutually exhilarated and exhausted." Benny motioned to a table where several other volunteers were gathered. "Come on. Let me introduce you to the rest of the medical crew. At least the ones who are here tonight. We have a few who couldn't attend. And, of course, you already know Dr. Wilton. He's there from start to finish. The man is tireless when it comes to getting the word out about having a healthy heart and living your best life."

Hailey had been living her best life since meeting him. Not that he was why, she assured herself, but because she was living the life she had envisioned and was creating for herself. Cayden was just one small part of her "best life."

After the introductions, Benny ran through items she had listed out on a clipboard, making sure their team would have all the necessary equipment for the day. Apparently, they'd be set up inside a large tent. A church was supplying tables and chairs and more volunteers. Another was supplying water and heart-healthy snacks. Home health, hospice, private ambulance services, and several other health agencies would have booths and activities for attendees. During the afternoon there would be a live band and a charity auction. According to Benny they'd start closing things down around six and hopefully be done between seven and eight. As she'd asked for the half marathon medical volunteers to arrive at around six that morning, Hailey agreed that it was going to be a long day. Most of the other medical volunteers were working in half-day or shorter shifts, but Hailey looked forward to being there all day. She really did want to be involved and give back to her new community and what a great way to do so. She'd even mentioned the meeting to Jamie that morning and her new nurse friend might volunteer, as well. How cool to have a friend who wanted to spend time with her?

The meeting lasted about an hour, then ended. Hailey enjoyed getting to know the medical team and said goodbye to them. Cayden made it over to them once but had quickly been summoned back to where Leanna had wanted his opinion yet again. Apparently, the woman still needed his attention as they were deep in conversation. Hailey had caught him looking her way a few times, but he'd not made it back to speak directly to her since right after she'd arrived. Not a big deal, she assured herself. The event was what was the big deal and why she was there, why they were both there. He was busy with making sure all the last-minute details were in place.

Hailey considered going to tell him bye, but decided it would feel awkward with the others around to witness her doing so. She said a few words to Benny, then to Linda and Bob, letting them know that she had volunteered for the medical tent, and would see them early on the Saturday morning of the Venice Has Heart event which was a month away.

Glad she'd gone, excited about volunteering, and conflicted about Cayden, Hailey had made it to her car when she heard him calling to her from where he'd apparently followed her out of the building.

"Hailey, wait up."

Fingers on her door handle, she turned and saw him jogging toward her. Her heart raced as if she was the one jogging. He'd come after her. That had to mean something beyond his being grateful she was volunteering, right? "Practicing for the race?"

Catching up to where she stood next to her car, he grinned. "Something like that. Are you in a rush to go?"

Her breath caught. "Not necessarily. Why?"

"I've not eaten. Do you want to grab something with me?"

She considered saying yes. She wanted to say yes. However, she forced herself to admit the truth. "I actually ate before coming to the meeting. Sorry."

He regarded her a moment. "Can I tempt you with a drink and a sunset, then? That seems to be our thing."

She was tempted. Oh, how she was tempted. But she shook her head because as much as she wanted to go, to talk with him, her emotions were running rampant after seeing him with Leanna and just how jealous that had made her. "Not tonight, Cayden, but thanks for asking."

He nodded as if he understood, but he failed miserably if he was trying to hide his disappointment and that boosted Hailey's courage.

She opened her car door, then paused. "If you're willing, I would take you up on the offer to go shark tooth hunting, still, though. If you aren't busy, maybe we could go this weekend?"

He regarded her a few moments, then arched his brow. "You don't have other plans?"

She knew what he was asking. She'd declined Ryan's offer to go to a concert in Tampa with others she'd met at the cookout. It had sounded like a fun outing, and yet, she'd made an excuse rather than say yes.

"I don't have plans on Saturday or Sunday morning and truly would like to go to the beach." Not that she had to have him with her to do so, but going with him would be nice and she didn't see herself shark tooth hunting without him. "Maybe I'll get lucky and find the perfect big shell for my table."

"We'd have better odds of that in Sanibel," he reminded her.

"It's okay if I don't find just what I'm looking for as I'm not in a rush. If I do find a great shell, well, that's just an added bonus to spending time with you." Heat flushed her cheeks. There. She'd been obvious in that she liked him. She might as well confess, at least to herself, that she'd turned Ryan's invitation down and purposely left her weekend open in hopes of spending time with Cayden. Which was okay, just so long as she didn't get too caught up in thinking time with Cayden was something more than just fun.

"I… Sure. I'd love to take you on your first shark tooth hunt. Does Saturday morning work? Around seven?" His eyes sparkled with the glittery gold flecks that fascinated her. Ha! Everything about Cayden fascinated her. He was a fascinating man. A fascinating man who was smiling at her in a way that had her cheeks flushing further because he made her feel pretty fascinating, too. How did he do that? When he was so fabulously gorgeous, how did he make her feel as if she were the one who was worthy of adoration? Would he have looked at her the same way if he'd met her pre-makeover? If he'd seen her prior to the hair and lash extensions, prior to the dull brown to blond, prior to the weight loss? Did it matter? She didn't even like that person she'd been. Not so much because of her outer appearance, but because of how timid she'd been on the inside, allowing John to take such advantage of her heart.

"Seven works great for me." She was used to getting

up early to exercise prior to having to be at the hospital. She tended to wake early even on her off days. She smiled up at him, thinking he truly was the most handsome man she'd ever met. "I look forward to finally finding a shark tooth, and maybe getting lucky and finding a shell."

"Then I'll see you Saturday morning. Don't forget to bring your water shoes and sense of adventure."

Before she chickened out, Hailey stood on her tiptoes and kissed his cheek. "Good night, Cayden. Sweet dreams."

CHAPTER SIX

"So, I take this sifter thing and I wade out into the water and just scoop up a bunch of sand and shells and whatever it picks up and I'm to hope I get a shark tooth?" Hailey eyed Cayden as if he'd lost his mind. Toes digging into the sand, her big straw hat with its tied strap beneath her chin, her baggy T-shirt and loose shorts over her bathing suit, she clutched the screened scoop. "As in, go in the water where the sharks who lost these teeth are?"

"The sharks who lost these teeth are long past," Cayden reminded her, wondering what it was about her that had him so tied up in knots, that had him thinking about her more often than not. She was beautiful, but he'd dated beautiful women in the past. It was something much more potent than physical beauty that had him so hooked. And that good-night kiss…yeah, his dreams had been sweet, all right. He'd barely thought of anything else day or night. With his work schedule not having him in the hospital Tuesday and Wednesday, and her being off Thursday and Friday, he'd missed her and considered texting her a hundred times. He should have. His reasons for not doing so had been petty. Even after her tentative smile on Monday morning, he'd let his jealousy over her going to the cookout with another man dictate that he put some distance between him and Hailey. The moment he'd spotted her with Mrs. Krandall he'd admitted to himself that he was behaving like a Neanderthal and was only depriving himself of the most fascinating woman he'd ever met. No more. "Besides," he continued. "You don't have to go out into the water that far. Just follow me, do what I do, and you'll be fine."

She eyed him skeptically, not budging from where she stood next to where he'd placed their things on the sand. He'd not unpacked their bag but would later if they decided they wanted to relax and watch the waves. He'd packed a blanket, sunscreen, the small medical kit that was always in his beach backpack, and even a small cooler with drinks and snacks in hope of extending their time together. Maybe she'd agree to lunch at one of the restaurants they'd drive past on their way back to her place.

A strong breeze whipped at them and she grasped hold of the brim of her hat, the other clasping the sifter. "What if I don't want to do what you do? What if I prefer to watch?"

"You want to just watch?" He arched a brow. "Do I need to remind you that you're the one who suggested we do this today? That you are here to find your first shark tooth? No sitting on the sidelines allowed."

She wrinkled her nose. "A woman has a right to change her mind."

He laughed at her dubious expression. "Come on, Hailey. You're going to have fun. I promise."

That's when he noticed the gleam in her eyes. "You big faker. You're already having fun."

Her lips twitched and her eyes danced with mischief. "Who says I'm having fun?"

If ever he'd heard a challenge, she'd just issued one with her flirty tone and lowered lashes.

"Me." Catching her off guard, he grabbed her at the waist, hoisted her over his shoulder, and headed toward the water.

"Cayden! Stop! What are you doing?" she demanded, laughing. "Oh, no, you're not," she warned as he waded into the water, his feet sluicing through the incoming wave. "Cayden, put me down. Seriously, you're going to hurt yourself. Put. Me. Down."

Enjoying having her in his grasp, Cayden walked farther into the water. "Don't worry. I plan to."

"Put me down on my feet while I'm not in the water," she clarified, squirming in his grasp. Her body was warm against his and she smelled good, like citrus blossoms. Probably an aftereffect of her sunscreen, but he wanted to breathe in and let her permeate every part of him.

"Why would I want to do that when the view is so great from where I'm at?" he teased.

"I wouldn't know. All I can see is your backside!"

He laughed. "Poor you."

"It's not that bad, but—"

"You trying to sweet-talk me by saying you like my bum?" He definitely liked the sweet curve of hers in his periphery as he had her draped over his shoulder, the feel of her in his grasp.

"No, I'm not saying I like your bum." She wiggled as he continued farther out. "I'm saying you're going to drop me. Seriously, Cayden, put me down before you do."

Cayden took another step, using caution to make sure

he had solid footing as another wave came in, hitting him just above knee level. He was far enough out now that the water would be midthigh if a bigger wave came in.

"Cayden, the water is going to knock you down."

"Then you should be still so I can keep my balance," he warned jokingly. Surprising him, she instantly quit wiggling. "That was quick."

"I don't want to end up in the water." She was still stiff in his hold.

"Now, where's the fun in going to the beach and not getting wet?" A wave came in and water splashed onto his shorts hem.

"That's what you're supposed to be showing me, how fun looking for shark teeth is, right?" Her voice held an edge and he tried to decide if she was playing him again. "Getting tossed into the water was not part of the plan."

He gave an exaggerated sigh. "I guess you're right." He slowly slid her down his body, keeping a tight hold until her feet were firmly planted on the sand with the water rushing around their legs. To keep her hat out of the way of his chest, she had to look up and she remained doing so when she was set upright on her own two feet. Whether from the coolness of the water or how she pressed against him, goose bumps prickled her skin. His, too, but he knew exactly what had elicited his reaction. It wasn't the water. As her body had lowered, she'd wrapped her arms around his neck and if he held her this way much longer, he'd have to dunk himself prior to heading back to shore to keep from embarrassing himself. He cleared his throat. "I must be getting soft in my old age because in my younger years you'd be swimming back to shore about now."

"You're wrong." Her arms clinging tightly around his neck, almost as if she were afraid to let go, she shook her head. "I wouldn't."

"No?" Something about her tone, the way she clung to him, had him looking at her closer. The teasing light in her eyes was gone and he knew the apprehension that shone there had nothing to do with their flush bodies. His stomach knotted. "Can you swim, Hailey?"

She shivered against him. "No."

He tightened his hold at her waist. "Why didn't you say so earlier?"

Pink tinged her cheeks. "It's a bit embarrassing to not be able to swim at my age."

"Nothing to be embarrassed about, but something we should rectify." As much as he was enjoying having her pressed to him, knowing she couldn't swim, he wanted her out of the water. He scooped her back up and began carrying her back to shore. Only this time, he didn't toss her over his shoulder, but rather, held her against him where he could see her face.

"We don't need to rectify anything, and I can walk, you know," she protested, but she wasn't trying to get down and almost seemed relieved that he held her. Although, probably it was more a relief that she would soon be back on the beach. Rather than immediately put her down when they reached the shoreline, he brought her beyond where the waves stretched to powdery dry sand, then he lowered her.

"I know and it's a lovely walk you have, too." He hoped to ease the twists in his gut. Whether the idea that he could have tossed her into the water without knowing she couldn't swim or from how her warm body had been pressed to his had caused the kinks, he wasn't sure. Probably a combination of both. "If you're going to live in Florida, you need to know how to swim."

Not that he had any say in the matter, but he wouldn't let her not learn how.

From beneath her oversized hat, she stared at him. "Is it a prerequisite or something? No one gave me that memo when I bought my house."

"No, but it should be." He appreciated her attempt at humor now that she was safely on ground, but he saw the vulnerability in her gaze, the self-disgust that she couldn't do something she thought she should. Heart squeezing at her vulnerability, he brushed his fingertip over her chin. "How is it that you never learned to swim, Hailey?"

Swallowing, she shrugged and stepped back from him. "My parents were older and weren't interested in water activities. As I reached an age where I could have learned on my own, I was busy with studying and school stuff. Learning just never came up."

"Until you decided to move to a state that is surrounded by water on three of its four sides," he pointed out, missing the warmth of her body against his. To distract himself, he bent to pull the blanket from his backpack and spread it upon the sand and tossed his sandals onto opposite corners to keep the wind from lifting them. He'd changed into his water shoes earlier but didn't want to wear them now as he didn't like the feel of wet sand in his shoes. He'd switch to his sandals prior to their leaving. He put his backpack down on the other end to hold the blanket in place.

"My moving to Florida shouldn't be a problem since I plan to stay out of the water. I can enjoy living in Florida without getting more than my feet wet. Well, except for perhaps when you're around." Her color had returned now that she was safely on the beach, but her teasing smile wasn't enough to dissuade him.

"You need to know how to swim, Hailey." He wasn't sure why her knowing seemed imperative to him. But it did. What if he'd tossed her into the waves? What if she went to the beach with someone else and didn't reveal her inability to them and they tossed her? What if something happened to her? His rib cage caved in around his chest, squeezing so tightly he couldn't breathe. Yeah, she needed to know how to swim.

"You want me to enroll in a class?" She furrowed her brows. "I'd be in there with all the little kids. No thanks. This has caused me enough humiliation for one lifetime."

Which sounded as if there was a lot more to the story.

"No need for classes with kids. I can teach you," he offered. He wanted to teach her. For lots of different reasons.

"You?" She eyed him through narrowed eyes.

"Don't sound so incredulous. I know what I'm doing. I worked as a lifeguard during high school. We offered swimming courses that I assisted in teaching."

She snorted. "Of course, you did."

"What's that supposed to mean?"

She shook her head. "Nothing."

He lifted her chin. "Tell me."

"It's just not surprising that you're an expert at swimming."

"I'm not sure I'd say I'm an expert, but I am qualified to teach you and you need to learn. The good news is that with me teaching you, you'll have private one-on-one instructions."

From where she stood on the other side of the blanket, she eyed him. The rise and fall of her chest was a little too rapid for her to be as indifferent as she pretended. "Just as you're teaching me to find shark teeth? Because so far, we're batting zero."

"The day has barely begun."

Her chin lifted, pulling free from where he touched her, but a smile played about her lips. "True, but all I'm saying is that I haven't found any teeth yet and you did promise that I'd find one."

How she went from vulnerable to using those big blue eyes to turn him inside out in a completely different way was testament to just how under her spell he was. That had nagged at him all week, but at the moment, basking in her smile, all that mattered was Hailey.

"You will, Hailey. Just as you will learn to swim."

Hailey did find a shark tooth. She found around twenty fossilized shark teeth of various sizes and breeds. Not that they'd looked them up yet, but Cayden had identified several of the teeth as makos and one as a sand tiger tooth. She'd sifted out several fossilized stingray bones and a horse tooth, too. Not that she'd have known what they were had Cayden not told her.

She'd not gone out beyond midcalf into the water. When she did so, she was fully aware that Cayden's return trips into the sea to dip out more sand and shells coincided with hers and that he always put himself out farther in what was a protective move in case she lost her footing. His automatic chivalry was sweet and something she wasn't accustomed to. John had teased her mercilessly about her inability to do something so "childish" as knowing how to swim. As she was making herself into the woman she wanted to be, she really should learn to swim.

Now they sat back on the familiar blanket that she'd become quite fond of, eating apples he'd stored in a small cooler. The cold juicy fruit was delicious.

"Thank you for bringing snacks. I wasn't expecting to be so hungry."

"Being in and around the water always works up my appetite." He gestured to the apple. "These are always a good option for a quick pick-me-up."

She nodded. "How long have you been coming out here?"

He shrugged. "All my life that I can recall. When I was a child, prior to their divorce, and separately after, my parents often rented a vacation house in Venice. It was always my favorite beach to visit."

"Because of the shark teeth?"

He grinned. "Probably. That was something different from the other places where we vacationed, and I was all boy."

He was still all boy. Well, man. In the water, his body pressed against hers had been all solid, strong man. She'd never been picked up and thrown over someone's shoulder. Cayden hadn't hesitated when doing so, making lifting her seem effortless. As apprehensive as she'd been of being in the water, deep down she'd known he wouldn't let anything happen to her and she'd been stunned at someone lifting her that way, that someone *could* lift her that way. He made her feel...dainty and feminine.

"Were you serious about teaching me to swim?"

His gaze cut to hers. "Absolutely. I want to teach you. I don't like the thought of you not knowing how to safely get yourself out of the water."

Her as in her specifically or just that he didn't like anyone not knowing how?

"Why?"

His grin was lethal as he said, "Because you never know when some man is going to toss you over his shoulder and throw you into the sea."

"You didn't throw me into the sea," she reminded him, swallowing back how being with him made her feel, with how just sitting on a blanket and eating fruit felt surreal and special.

"No, but I could have since I didn't know. Good beach advice would be to make whomever you're with aware that you don't swim."

"Now you're my beach expert, too?" At his look, she relented. "Fine. I should have told you. Like I mentioned, my parents were older and there were a lot of things I didn't do during my childhood that many would consider as standards, like learning to swim." Ecstatic to be out of the foster system, she'd been content to be in her room with a good book and her parents had never discouraged her from doing just that since they'd also been lifelong readers. She'd loved the peace, the stability they'd brought into her chaotic life, but maybe she should have stepped outside of the comfort zone they'd created for her. "In the future, I promise to make anyone I go to the beach with aware of my inability to swim."

He crunched into the last bite of his apple, put the core into a bag in his backpack, then wiped juice from his fingers. "In the future you won't need to since you're going to learn."

He sounded so confident that Hailey had no choice but to believe him. Why not? Thus far he had proved brilliant at all he did. Why should teaching her to swim be any different?

"Just when and where are these lessons going to take place?"

"My condo complex has a pool. I can teach you there or we can go—"

A scream sounded from down the beach, preventing Cayden from finishing his answer. Immediately to his feet, he took off down the beach in the direction the distressed cry had come from. Grabbing up his backpack where she'd noticed a first aid kit earlier, Hailey quickly followed.

Please don't be a shark attack, she prayed, hating that her brain immediately had gone there. *Please don't be a shark attack.*

Seeming paralyzed in the waist-deep water, a teenaged girl flailed her arms. Hailey didn't see any red discoloration the way it seemed to instantly appear in the movies when a shark attacked so maybe it was something else. But all she could think was that they were at the shark tooth capital of the world and there had to be a reason that it was the perfect environment for creating fossils like Cayden had told her.

Regardless of what it was, the other teens who'd been in the water with her seemed frozen, too, staring at their friend rather than going to where she was until finally one young man snapped out of whatever had taken over him and he began cutting through the ten or so feet that separated him from where the girl screamed in panicked agony. That Cayden reached her at about the same time the teen did said something about how fast he'd gotten there. Perhaps because of his lifeguard training, or maybe just because of his natural athleticism, the man could move. Again, there didn't seem to be much he couldn't do and do well.

"What happened?" he called as he closed in on where the girl was still thrashing her hands as if trying to shoo something away.

Scared to go into the water and knowing she shouldn't as she might create another emergency, Hailey hesitated at the shoreline, a cold wave lapping at her ankles and sending shivers over her body. What if Cayden needed the first aid kit?

What if whatever had hurt the girl hurt him?

"Something bit me. On my leg," the girl cried between sobs. "It burns bad."

Burns. That wouldn't be a shark bite, would it?

"Careful in case whatever got her is still around," he warned the teen boy who seemed as unsure of what to do as Hailey felt from where she stood. "Sounds as if it may have been a jellyfish. Let's get her out of the water so we can figure out what's going on."

A jellyfish. That was way better than a shark in Hailey's eyes, although with the way the girl was crying, perhaps she didn't think so.

Cayden was still talking, but the waves drowned out whatever he was saying. Feeling helpless as she waited, Hailey reminded herself that for her to go into the water would be more of a hindrance than a benefit. For her to go out as far as the girl was when she couldn't swim could possibly create a second crisis, so logic said to stay put and to just be ready to help once they got the girl to shore.

Logic also said to call for emergency help. Pulling her phone from where they'd put it into his bag earlier in the day, Hailey dialed the three-digit emergency number, all the while keeping her gaze on the trio in the water. Please, please, please be okay. The girl and Cayden.

"This is Dr. Hailey Easton. I'm at Caspersen Beach. A teenaged girl is injured and is currently being assisted out of the water. Not certain as to the cause or extent of her injuries at this point."

Cayden and the young man guided the sobbing girl to the beach. Once beyond the water break, they lowered her onto the sand.

"Good. You called for help and grabbed my bag," Cayden praised, noting what Hailey held and that she was on the phone with emergency services.

Hailey had zero experience in acute emergency care of aquatic animal attack injuries. Not that she was sure that it was a jelly that had injured the woman. Her knowledge of jellyfish was limited to books and movies. Beyond her inability to swim, she felt ill prepared to deal with the current situation and she didn't like it. She'd always aimed high, to be the best she could be, not incompetent. At the moment, she felt at a huge disadvantage.

"Definitely a jellyfish injury," Hailey informed the dispatcher as she grimaced at the girl's left leg where a clearish purple tentacle wrapped around her thigh and ran down her leg. The skin beneath the detached tentacle welted a deep red as did an area on the girl's right palm, probably caused from when she'd reacted to the jelly's tentacle at her leg and tried to remove it. Wanting to help medically if needed, she handed the phone to the teen boy who'd aided Cayden getting the victim out of the water. "Here, talk to the dispatcher and keep her informed of whatever we say."

The boy looked unsure, but took the phone while Hailey knelt next to where they'd laid the girl on the sand.

Rather than immediately check her, Cayden glanced around them on the sand. Quickly spotting a shell, he got it. "This isn't going to be pleasant for you," he told the teen, "but I need to get the tentacle off you immediately. Hold still."

Hailey's Ohio hospital and emergency room rotations hadn't prepared her for jellyfish sting injury. Inadequacy hit. She wasn't working in the emergency room and by the time an admitted patient made their way to her, any acute reaction would have been handled in the emergency department. But she needed to know basics of emergency care when living near the ocean. The girl was hysterical and going into shock, possibly even beginning an allergic reaction to the venom, and that, Hailey could assist with. So, while Cayden used the shell to scrap where the tentacle clung to the girl's skin, taking care to press with enough force to remove all bits of the tentacle to stop the release of more venom into her system, Hailey placed her hand on her inner wrist for the dual purpose of checking her pulse and in hopes of distracting the teen from what Cayden was doing. They needed to calm her down as her hysteria would only exacerbate her reaction to the jellyfish's venom.

"What's your name?" she asked, making mental note of the girl's tachycardic heart rate.

"Sasha," the teen boy answered when the girl continued to sob rather than answer Hailey. Her hysterics made getting a respiration count a bit trickier, but Hailey paid close attention to her breathing pattern.

"Hi, Sasha. I'm Dr. Easton and that's Dr. Wilton. We work at Venice General," she told the girl, keeping her voice calm and hoping to reassure both her, the boy, their other friends and the small crowd that were gathering around them.

The girl's panicked gaze cut to Hailey and her cries eased enough for her to ask, "Am I going to die?"

"No, you're not going to die," Hailey answered, even though it was possible if the girl had an intense enough reaction to the venom. Sasha was crying so profusely that it was difficult to tell if her runny nose and breathiness were from her sobs or if she was having a more intense than normal reaction to the sting. Hailey winced as blotchy red whelps that seemed to be multiplying while Hailey watched began covering Sasha's arms and legs.

"We're going to take good care of you and more help is on the way." She took the girl's uninjured hand into hers and gave it a gentle squeeze. She didn't want to alarm Sasha further but if Cayden had an antihistamine they could give her, then the sooner the better. "Cayden, Sasha has a rash. Do you have anything in your medical kit that I can give her for that?"

Apparently, he'd satisfied himself with the removal of the tentacle from her skin or decided that treating the rash took precedence. "Hand me my bag. I should have something to help."

She did so, and he pulled out the first aid kit, along with a water bottle. He handed the water bottle to a bystander.

"Pour out the water in this and fill it with sea water," he instructed as he unzipped the medical kit. "Sasha, have you ever had an allergic reaction to anything?"

"She's allergic to peanuts," the teen on the phone with the emergency dispatcher replied, answering for the girl again.

"Anything else?" Cayden asked, his gaze on the girl.

Tears streaming from her puffy eyes and down her face, Sasha shook her head, then swiped at her runny nose. She coughed and it had a wheezy sound.

"Sasha, I want you to open your mouth for me," Cayden instructed. "I need to look at your throat."

The girl did so. Cayden didn't say anything as he looked, but his gaze flicked to Hailey's for a millisecond and she knew what he'd seen, what she'd already suspected was happening.

Sasha's throat was swelling.

Why didn't it surprise her when Cayden dug into his medical kit and pulled out an epinephrine auto-injector? Was the man ever not prepared?

"You're not allergic to a medication called epinephrine?" he asked yet again, wanting to be sure the girl didn't have an allergy to the adrenaline.

"Not," the girl said, coughing again. "Just peanuts."

"She used a pen like that when she reacted to peanuts on a school trip once," the young man supplied.

"Sasha, most people don't react to jellyfish stings so intensely, but unfortunately, you are," Cayden told the girl whose brows lifted above her puffy eyes. "I'm going to give you the injection into your leg to slow, and hopefully stop, the reaction you're having to the jellyfish venom."

He didn't give the girl time to protest, just popped the

injector against her injured leg in the thigh, delivering the possibly lifesaving medication in the process. When done, he tossed the device by the backpack, then took the water bottle from the bystander who'd done as he'd instructed. Cayden poured the seawater over the area the jelly fish had stung, then gently patted the area dry with a towel from his bag. Digging through his medical kit, he pulled out a tube of steroid cream and squeezed some onto the girl's leg, gently spreading a thin layer over where she'd been stung.

Hailey noticed the red line across Cayden's hand and winced. "You're stung, too."

"Got that when we were still in the water." He didn't look up from where he worked on Sasha's leg. When satisfied that the sting on her leg and hand were coated, he squirted a bit of the cream on his own hand.

In the distance, sirens blared and Hailey sighed in relief that the girl would soon be on her way to the hospital. She'd be treated in the emergency department, and the determination would be made of whether or not she needed to be admitted for overnight observation based upon how she responded to the epinephrine, any additional medications the paramedics administered, and how she did after a few hours of being watched.

Within minutes, the girl was loaded into the back of the ambulance and on her way to the hospital.

"Thank you," the teen boy told them, taking off so he could follow the ambulance to the hospital with his friend.

Clapping erupted around them. Hailey joined in, clapping for Cayden and what he'd done for the girl. His cheeks turned pink, and he tried dismissing what he'd done. "Just doing what anyone else would have done."

Hailey's heart squeezed at his humility. She didn't want to keep comparing the two men, but she couldn't help herself. John would have been calling every media outlet in the area, expecting to be heralded a hero on the nightly news. Cayden on the other hand, got a phone number from one of the teens who'd been with the girl so he could call and check on her progress.

As the bystanders dissipated, Hailey gathered his things, putting them into the backpack and waited for him to finish talking with the girl's friends. When he had, they headed back to where they'd left their things farther down the beach.

"What just happened made me realize I need a living-near-the-sea emergency medicine crash course," she admitted as they made their way over the sandy beach.

"You'd have been fine if I hadn't been here."

She shook her head. "I wouldn't have. Beyond the fact that I couldn't have gotten her out of the water, not once have I ever treated a jellyfish sting. I mean, what other living on the Gulf of Mexico things do I need to know?"

"Other than how to swim?"

"After what just happened you may never get me to agree to go in the water again." But even as she said it, she acknowledged that she did want to learn. She'd hated knowing that if Cayden had needed her that she'd have had to stand ashore and helplessly watch, that if he hadn't been there, she wouldn't have been able to help Sasha to shore.

"What happened with Sasha is a rarity when you consider how many people get into the water. Beyond that, most who encounter jellyfish and do have the misfortune to be stung, don't have anaphylactic reactions." He held up his hand. "Like me for instance."

"True, but I don't think I'm going back in beyond where I can walk and see all around me." She winced at the red mark on his hand. "I'm sorry you got hurt. Is there anything I can do?"

"Kiss it and make it better?"

Hailey's breath caught. "If you think that would help."

He held out his hand. "Only one way to know for sure."

Swallowing, Hailey touched her lips to his hand, taking care to avoid the steroid cream by kissing just to the side of his injury.

"Better already," he assured her, smiling at her in a way that could almost convince her that her kiss truly had made him feel better. "For the record, I plan to teach you to swim in a pool, Hailey. Not in the open sea."

"I… I do want to learn." Because she didn't want to limit herself. Not ever again. "However, learning to swim isn't likely to change how I feel about getting into the ocean. But we'll see."

Because if she truly didn't want to limit herself then she had to be open to the possibility that she might change her mind.

"We'll start with learning to swim. If, after you've mastered swimming, you want to venture outside the pool, then we will. No pressure."

She didn't comment on his "we will." Who knew what the future held? For now, she was just going to appreciate that she got to spend the day with an amazing man who was kind and patient and had acted heroically with his only motivation being to help the teenager. Plus, he acted as if own injury was no big deal rather than milking it for all it was worth. Since she'd asked if there was anything she could do, she didn't count his request for her to kiss his hand and make it better. She'd been so fearful for him and the girl when they'd been in the water, she wanted to wrap her arms around his neck and kiss him for real in gratitude that he was okay, that he'd saved Sasha, both in the water and on land.

"I'm quite impressed that you had an epinephrine pen in your medical kit. I wasn't expecting that level of preparedness."

"No?" The corners of his eyes crinkled with his smile. "My sister is allergic to bees. I always keep a pen handy, just in case."

"You have a sister?" Did she sound as envious as she felt? How often had she wished for siblings?

He nodded. "Casey is older than me by a couple of years. She and her husband live in Atlanta, where my mother now lives, too, so she can be close to the grands. Dad lives in Tampa, so not too far away. During a visit a few years ago, Casey forgot her emergency medication injector and had to go to the emergency room to get treated. Since then, I keep one on hand."

"Amongst the many things I'm grateful for, I'm glad you had one today."

"Me, too." As they reached the blanket they'd abandoned in a rush, he asked, "You want to sit here a while, walk, or look for more shark teeth?"

"Ha, that's a trick question, right? We have already established that I'm not going back into the water."

"I'd be willing to scoop for you if you want to search for more shark teeth. Maybe you'll find a megalodon."

He would do that. But the truth was, she didn't want

him back in the water, either. She was being a total wimp, but she preferred all of his body parts being where she could see them.

"As cool as finding a fossilized prehistoric shark tooth would be, I think I've had enough beach time for the day." Sasha's jellyfish encounter had been a great reminder of all the reasons she needed to be cautious with water activities beyond her inability to swim. "If you're not in a hurry, we could grab something to eat. My treat. Something took off with the rest of my apple. When Sasha screamed, I'd tossed it onto the blanket, and now it's gone."

He chuckled. "Some seagull or crab thought it was its lucky day."

Being with Cayden had Hailey thinking it really was *her* lucky day.

CHAPTER SEVEN

CAYDEN GRINNED AT how excited Hailey looked when she glanced up from where she was reviewing a patient's chart on the small office alcove behind the medical floor's nurses' station and saw him. She'd gone from calm professional to sparkling. Spotting him had given her joy and he liked the thought of his being able to make her happy. Over the past month, she'd certainly made him happy.

"Hello, Dr. Wilton," she greeted, sounding all businesslike as she glanced around to see if any of their co-workers were close by. There weren't. Keeping her voice to barely above a whisper, she asked, "Would you be interested in going on a double date with my friend Jamie and her boyfriend? She's my nurse friend from my yoga class. Remember that I mentioned she plans to volunteer at the Venice Has Heart event, too?"

"Hello, Dr. Easton." The bluest sea had nothing on Hailey's eyes. He wanted to dive in and lose himself. "Are you asking me on a date?"

Glancing around again, letting him know that despite their having seen each other numerous times outside of work, she preferred to keep their personal relationship just between them. Since neither of them wanted anything serious, it was honestly for the best that she preferred their coworkers not in on the time they were spending together outside the hospital. He doubted they were fooling many, though, especially Renee.

"Before you say yes," she warned, brushing a hair back behind her ear, "it's a working double date."

Intrigued, he leaned against her desk. "A working double date? You'll have to explain that one to me as I have no idea what you're talking about."

She laughed. "Probably not, but no worries. It's not anything too strenuous. I'm not putting you to doing landscaping or some other type of tough manual labor."

"I wouldn't be opposed to helping you with your landscaping or any other manual labor that you need to have done." He enjoyed the time they spent together.

"Good to know and something I'll keep in mind. But this is much better than that. It's a restaurant that my friend wants to try." She sounded so excited that he couldn't help but smile. He did that a lot around her. "You pay to learn how to cook a particular meal and do so with a chef guiding you through each step. Afterward, everyone sits down to eat the meal together. Someone Jamie works with mentioned to her how much fun they'd had when they went, and we agreed it sounded like something interesting to try." The term puppy dog eyes came to mind with how she looked at him. "Say you'll go with me."

"You know I'm not going to tell you no, right?"

Hailey grinned. "I'm hoping you're not because she's already made reservations for this Saturday night. We were afraid to wait because the only reason we got an opening on such short notice is that we were the first to reach out after they'd had a last-minute cancellation."

Saturday night. Cayden's excitement tanked. "I'm the cardiologist on call for the hospital this weekend."

Her excitement visibly fizzled.

"Sometimes I only get a few calls. Sometimes I'm there the whole weekend." He'd never really minded too much, but the disappointment on Hailey's face had him wishing he could assure her he would be able to be there the entire time for their double date. "But I usually don't make any big plans because my time isn't my own and I should be prepared for whatever the shift throws at me."

"I forgot about you being on call," she admitted, her disheartenment palpable. "I definitely understand that you have to work. Actually, that will be me having to be at the hospital next weekend for my turn on the weekend work rotation."

Which meant his seeing her would be limited to whether or not she wanted to go out after her shift ended rather than spending an entire day with her as they'd done the past two weekends.

"Just because I usually keep my schedule clear doesn't mean I can't go with you, Hailey. I just can't guarantee that I won't have to bail last minute if I get called in to the hospital." He looked directly into her big eyes, wanting to see the sparkle back in them. "I'm willing to chance it if you are."

Because he didn't want her to ask someone else to go on the double date. She hadn't mentioned the Ryan guy and Cayden hadn't asked. What had been the point when he and Hailey had been together more often than not? Either of them were free to see someone else if they chose. Neither wanted forever and eventually, they would go to just being friends.

"I'm not sure how much fun it would be to take a couples cooking class by myself if you got called away, but..." She seemed to be considering and for a moment he thought she was going to say she'd just ask someone else, and despite his previous thoughts, his breath caught as he waited for her to continue. "Let's try," she suggested, "and I'll keep my fingers crossed that you don't get called in."

Yeah, he would keep his crossed, too. She'd understand work-related things came up. The past two weeks had been fun.

"Perfect. It's a date." As he said the words, he realized what he'd said. A date. He didn't date.

"A double date," she corrected, then smiled at him so brilliantly that his heart did a funny flip-flop. Did she have any idea how much she dazzled him? He really didn't think so as most of the time she seemed to question herself. She was such a sweet contradiction, one moment exuding bold confidence and another completely blind to how great she was.

"It's been a long time since I've been on a double date," he mused from where he still leaned against the desk. Not since Cynthia. Double dating felt more serious than just going out as a couple having fun. He wouldn't back out on Hailey. He didn't really want to. But perhaps it wouldn't be a bad thing if he got called in to the hospital.

"I've got you beat." She made a soft snort sound. "For me, it's been a lifetime."

"Meaning you have never been on a double date?" That surprised him. She'd been in a long-term relationship prior to moving to Florida. Then again, he'd already deduced that her ex was a loser who was responsible for a lot of her insecurities. Cayden would have a hard time not punching the guy if he ever had the displeasure of running into the jerk.

"That's correct." She averted her gaze, looking embarrassed and as if she regretted her admission. The vulnerability on her face had Cayden retracting his thoughts on getting called in to the hospital. Hailey deserved double dates and whatever else she wanted.

"Then I'll have to make sure this first one is a good one." Which he wouldn't be able to do if he was at the hospital. She was an amazing woman and Cayden did not want to let her down the way her ex had.

"I...uh... I'm sure it will be." Her cheeks still a little pink, she lifted her gaze to his and changed the subject. "Have you been in to see Room 208 yet? The patient was admitted for a bacterial urinary tract infection that was resistant to oral antibiotic options. He's here so he can receive intravenous medication that his culture and sensitivity test showed should resolve his infection. He doesn't have a cardiac disease history other than controlled hypertension, however, when I listened to him this morning, he threw several partial beats. The EKG I ordered only showed numerous pre-ventricular contractions so that's likely what I heard. But my gut instinct was that I should have you take a look at him so I entered the consult."

"Maybe you just wanted me to have an excuse to stop by so you could ask me out," he teased, pushing himself up from where he'd been half sitting on the edge of her desk.

Her eyes widened. "No. I didn't enter the consult for personal reasons. I wouldn't do that."

She looked so horrified that he relented rather than tease her further.

"I'm joking, Hailey. I know you wouldn't. Just as I didn't stop by here just to see you, but I admit that getting to see you is an added bonus to making my rounds these days."

She regarded him a moment, then keeping her gaze locked with his, bestowed him with the sweetest smile. "Thank you. Seeing you is an added bonus, too."

Cayden's heart threw a few wild beats, thudding against his ribcage. Reminding himself that they were at work, that someone could return to the nurses' area any moment so he shouldn't pull her to him so he could kiss her plump lips, he cleared his throat. "You want to go with me to examine 208?"

She clicked a button to close the electronic medical record program, then stood. "I'd love to, Dr. Wilton."

Later that day at Cayden's office, Dr. Pennington knocked on Cayden's office door while he was at his desk, dictating his last patient's consult note. He motioned for his coworker to come in while he finished the section he'd been working on, then paused the dictation program on his phone.

"I know it's last minute," his colleague began from where he'd sat down across from Cayden's desk, "but would you swap call weekends with me? I'm on for next weekend and Layla's parents have decided to come visit."

"You want to swap call for you to take this weekend and me to cover next weekend?" Him be off during the double date and be on call next weekend when Hailey would be working—could he be that lucky that his partner was asking to do that?

"I completely understand if you can't," the cardiologist continued. "I started not to ask because of how last-minute it was, but thought I would at least check on the off chance that you didn't have anything going on. I'd asked Rob and he already had plans so he couldn't."

Excited, Cayden leaned back in his chair. "Swapping works great for me as it's this weekend that I have something going on that I was concerned I'd get called away from."

"Seriously?" Dr. Pennington looked relieved. "That's fantastic. I owe you big, pal."

"Ditto." Cayden liked it when life worked for the better for all concerned. It seemed it rarely did, but this time he'd certainly lucked out.

That evening, he and Hailey tried a restaurant in Punta Gorda and she agreed to go to dinner with him the next evening after her shift as well, but they stayed close, choosing a seafood place that had open seating next to the water. She ordered a salmon appetizer that she insisted was some of the best fish she'd ever eaten and insisted he try. She was right.

He'd have spent every evening with her, but the following evening she had her yoga class and on Thursday evening she'd said she had other plans and hadn't elaborated. He'd offered to come by on Saturday so they could do her first swim lesson, but just as she'd done each time he'd mentioned doing so over the past few weeks, she'd put him off yet again.

He wasn't used to women putting him off when he wanted to see them. He wasn't used to caring. With Hailey, he craved every moment with her. He wasn't thrilled by that truth and assumed the excitement of being with her would soon wear off. Only, he'd never experienced the excitement he felt with being with Hailey. She made everything feel new.

On Friday evening when he arrived at her house to pick her up for their cooking date, the scent of sunshine and the sea met him. Whatever air freshener she used, he liked the clean, nonperfume fragrance. It fit the crispness of her white walls and furniture with their turquoise and sea-themed accents, including the pieces they'd picked up in Sarasota that first weekend together. The place felt homey, relaxing, and an extension of her, especially the mermaid mixed-media painting he'd gifted her. He looked at the piece and saw Hailey. It's what he'd seen from the beginning, calm amidst chaos. She did calm him. She also made his world a bit chaotic.

She confused him, had him behaving in ways he didn't understand and that were completely out of his norm. For instance, why hadn't he seduced her? He wasn't blind. She wanted him. But there was something so innocent about her sexuality that, despite knowing she'd lived with a man, he'd held himself back from taking what he wanted. Maybe he even worried that sex would change things between them in ways that would be the end.

He wasn't ready for the end. Not yet.

"These are for you." He handed her the brightly colored bouquet of assorted flowers that he'd swung into the hospital gift shop to buy when they'd caught his eye on his way out of the hospital. He'd liked the yellows and bright pinks mixed in with the daisies and other flowers. The colorful bouquet had made him think of her.

"Aw, thank you. They're beautiful." She went to the kitchen and pulled out a shell-encrusted vase they'd picked up the previous weekend at a shop they'd stopped at on their drive back from Sanibel Island. She placed the flower vase on the end table beside her driftwood lamp and the shell she'd selected from the bounty they'd found. "When I bought this and said it would be perfect for flowers, I wasn't hinting for you to buy me some."

"I didn't think you were," he assured her. "I'm glad you like them."

"I do. Tonight is going to be fun," she promised, walking to the back patio door to check to make sure she'd locked it. He imagined the enclosed area's outer door stayed locked, but he was glad she took the extra precautions even with living inside a gated community. The thought had him pausing. Had he ever considered whether or not a woman in his life locked her doors?

"If I have to cook my own meal, at least I get to do it with you." Not that he minded cooking his own meal. He'd been doing so pretty much from the time his parents divorced. Casey had helped, but Cayden had definitely surpassed his sister's cooking skills.

"You say that, but you've never cooked with me to know whether I'm more of a hindrance than a help." She grabbed her purse from the kitchen bar and turned to him, smiling big as she did so. His chest did funny things when Hailey smiled at him. Things like make up beats of its own rather than follow the usual *lub-dub* normal sinus rhythm. Her face powder didn't hide the pink tinge to her nose and cheeks.

"You got too much sun today." Which surprised him as she'd diligently protected her skin during their outings.

"Yeah, it's not too bad, fortunately, but I should have reapplied my sunscreen sooner." Moving toward her front door, she smiled at whatever ran through her mind. "I was sweating it off faster than I could have reapplied, anyway."

He'd not noticed anything different outdoors, but he'd not really been paying attention, either and she might really have worked on her landscaping. "What were you doing? Lawn work? I was serious in that I'd help you."

Not that it was any of his business, but everything about her fascinated him and he wanted to do things to make her life easier.

She'd been heading toward her front door but turned to look at him and grin. "Would you believe that I was playing pickleball?"

She sounded so proud that he did believe that's what she'd been doing.

"I didn't know you played."

"A more accurate statement would have been if I'd said that I was learning to play pickleball." She gave a self-deprecating laugh. "Unfortunately, I have the athleticism of a slug so it's slow going, but I'm enjoying learning and am already better than when I started."

She moved with such grace that he couldn't imagine her not being able to do anything she wanted, but he wasn't going to argue. What he would do is take advantage of something else they had in common. He'd been playing for years as it was something he and his buddies had enjoyed since college days.

"What you're saying is that if we play, I currently have a decent chance of winning?"

She snorted. "Oh, you're pretty much guaranteed to

win. I've never been good at sports, but I'm determined to up my game since it's a popular activity at our community center. Barry says I keep getting better each time we play."

Barry. Cayden's insides withered into green mush. How could she be so nonchalant about seeing another man? He bit back an expletive.

"Barry is a neighbor, by the way. He's married and I'd guess to be in his seventies."

Had she sensed his reaction? Or maybe he'd just thought he'd held back his frustrated curse. He and Hailey were just casually dating, not moving toward anything serious, so he shouldn't care who Barry was and he sure shouldn't feel such relief that the man was nothing more than a friendly neighbor.

That he did was concerning, but not something he wanted to delve into too closely.

To do that might be having to admit things he didn't want to admit and tonight was about making Hailey's first double date dream worthy.

Later that evening at the Be the Chef cooking venue, Hailey tossed a piece of rice at Cayden, not surprised that he deflected her playful throw. He had been the perfectly attentive date. Jamie had been wowed by him. Hailey's heart was full of pride at sharing them with each other. How blessed was she that she got to have such a fun new friend like Jamie and a great date like Cayden?

"Hey, quit wasting our dinner," he ordered, but with a mischievous gleam in his eyes that warned he was already plotting his playful revenge.

From the time they'd arrived at the venue, he'd been

all smiles. Mostly he'd been that way since he'd gotten to her house other than a short moment where he'd been moody when they'd been discussing her playing pickleball. She'd guessed what had been bothering him. He didn't need to know every detail of her life, but she'd quickly enlightened him, anyway. The thought that he already knew so much, that she thought of him all the time, first and last thing each day, terrified her. Being so wrapped up in him, in spending time with him, was scary as she wondered how they'd proceed when things ended. That he was still friends with Leanna gave her hope that maybe they'd find a way to be friends, too, as she couldn't imagine her new life without him as a part of it. That was what was the scariest. How had he become such an integral part of her new life when she'd meant to never let any one man dominate her time?

"I think we have a few grains to spare," she assured him. She'd be skimping on the rice, anyway, and having more of the grilled vegetables. Amazingly, she'd dropped another five pounds over the past month. Each one had required a lot of work and discipline as she was dining out with Cayden so frequently.

"You say that as if I'm not a starving man." His words lacked conviction as he tossed a grain of rice back at her.

"Hey, the both of you quit that," Jamie warned from where she and Doug worked at the meal prep station next to Hailey and Cayden. "Act your age."

Hailey and Cayden exchanged looks, grinned, and simultaneously tossed rice grains at her friend. Snorting, Jamie rolled her eyes and started to join the fun, but their chef instructor cleared her throat, putting a stop to their shenanigans.

Not surprisingly, Cayden was an excellent slicer and dicer of their vegetables, which Hailey appreciated because he distracted her to the point that her wielding a knife while standing close enough she could feel his body heat wasn't smart. She'd never been a great cook. At least, not to hear John tell it. She'd worked long hours and still prepared their meals, but her best attempts had failed to impress him. Nothing she'd done had impressed him. She'd never had great self-confidence. After spending so much of her life with John it really was no wonder that she'd spiraled downward and believed she hadn't deserved better. Other than school and residency, he'd isolated her then consistently chipped away at her self-worth. Glancing over at the man working next to her, his gaze lifted to hers. Grinning, he winked, then went back to stirring the food mixture in the cooker, completely oblivious to how his simplest gesture set off an emotional tsunami.

Happiness bubbled. She was out on a double date with the most gorgeous, wonderful man and her new friend whom she adored and seemed to adore her back. All evening, she caught herself looking his way, shocked really by how quick his smile was, how desire *for her* shone in his eyes. Concern ebbed away her happiness.

She hadn't planned to date anytime soon after her move but meeting him had changed that. When things ended, how could any man ever measure up? She was spending more and more of her spare time with him. If she wasn't careful her new life was going to revolve completely around Cayden. That terrified her. She and Cayden weren't forever. Even if she wanted them to be, which she didn't, she wouldn't be able to maintain her shiny new facade indefinitely, and eventually her new life would collide with her old and he'd see the real her, the version that never would have caught his attention.

Fake it until you make it, right? With her hair and lash extensions, facial treatments, and so forth, she had the faking it down pat.

Or maybe not as she dreamed of kissing Cayden, of doing much more than kissing him but, other than quick pecks and lots of hand-holding, she had pulled away each time. Some things couldn't be faked. What if Cayden found her as lacking as John had? What if their becoming physically involved was the catalyst to revealing what no amount of makeup and self-help books could hide?

Yeah, she was getting way too attached to Cayden, was way too caught up in what he thought of her, and as lovely as their evening was, she needed to take control of her new life back and quit planning everything around him.

CHAPTER EIGHT

"GIRL, YOU'RE NOT looking so good."

Hailey hadn't needed Renee's assessment to know that. She'd gone to bed not feeling well and had awakened feeling worse. Still, she'd headed to the hospital. She'd only been on the job a couple of months. She wouldn't miss work unless she was literally unable to move. She was moving. Barely. So, she'd work and stay masked to keep from spreading germs to her patients and coworkers. "I'll be okay."

Maybe.

Cayden didn't have any direct admissions and wasn't on call so Hailey didn't see him that morning. Just as well as she didn't want him to see her so subpar. Makeup couldn't hide her putrid color. By lunch, she gave in to Renee's demand that she reach out to the hospital administrator to see if someone could cover the remainder of her shift. Not once during med school or residency had Hailey missed a single day, but she was miserable.

Fortunately, the hospitalist coming in for the evening shift was available, allowing Hailey to head home and to bed. By evening, she admitted defeat and called out for the following morning.

She slept, woke several times, forced fluids, then fell

back into fitful sleep. About dawn, she settled into a decent rest and didn't wake until almost noon. Unfortunately, she was still running a temperature and had body aches that rivaled being hit repeatedly by a baseball bat.

"Got. To. Drink." With the fever on top of her stomach issues, she was going to get dehydrated. She shuffled to the kitchen, opened her cabinets and saw nothing appetizing, then went to stand in front of her refrigerator. Nothing there appealed, either.

She got a glass of water, then headed onto the patio. Maybe just sitting there where she could see the sunshine and the lake would help. Maybe it did as she couldn't say she felt any worse. No better, but not worse. Feeling worse might be impossible, though.

"Quit feeling sorry for yourself."

Eventually, she went back to bed. She didn't recall falling asleep, but she must have as her phone ringing startled her awake. She reached for it and realized she'd missed several calls and texts from Cayden.

"You left work early yesterday and haven't responded to any of my texts. If you hadn't answered this call I was headed your way and not leaving until I put eyes on you," he told her. "Are you feeling better?"

She shook her head, grimacing as pain stabbed through her head.

"Hailey?"

Her lips stuck together as she tried talking. "Not better."

"You sound terrible."

"Thanks," she managed, opening and closing her dry mouth.

"Do you need anything?"

"To feel better. Going to sleep now." Except she needed to drink something with electrolytes, first.

After disconnecting the call, she opened a delivery app and placed an order. Drinks, crackers, soup. She had this sick thing down.

For fear she'd dose off and not wake up when her supplies arrived, she made her way into her living room, blanket, pillow, and all, and crashed onto her sofa.

Picking up the grocery bags and a package of sport drinks from Hailey's front porch, Cayden rang her doorbell again. After a minute or so, her deadbolt clicked, and the door opened.

She blinked, her long lashes sweeping across her cheeks. Dark circles and makeup rimmed her eyes. Her hair was disheveled. She wore an Ohio State sweatshirt and a pair of loose pajama pants and had a blanket wrapped around her shoulders.

"You look terrible." The moment the words escaped his mouth he longed to take them back because he'd swear her already pale skin blanched a few more shades.

"Sound terrible." She coughed, emphasizing her point. "Look terrible. Feel terrible." Her puffy eyes met his. "What are you doing here?"

He held out her groceries as if that somehow explained why he was there. "I came to check on you."

"I'm fine."

She didn't look fine. If it was flu season, he'd think she had the flu. "Is it okay if I carry these to the kitchen?"

She moved aside. "Enter at risk of catching whatever I have."

"I'll take my chances." He generally didn't get ill, but

he'd use caution, making sure not to touch his face and would wash his hands well.

"Okay." She looked lost for a moment, then appeared overcome with exhaustion. "I need to go to bed." With that, she turned, stumbled, and righted herself just as he reached her, groceries still in tow. "Just need sleep."

"Have you eaten today, Hailey?" He placed the groceries on the floor to free his hands and followed her, not touching but close enough he could catch her if she started going down.

She paused in her slow shuffle. "No."

"Once you're in bad, I'm going to cook you something." He wasn't leaving her side until she was safely in bed. Like the rest of her home, the room was done up in whites and turquoise. Throwing off the color theme was a shelf loaded down with books. She'd been telling the truth about self-help books. There were dozens of them. The thing he liked most was a painting of a young girl staring off into the blurred distance. Had she gone to one of the markets without mentioning it to him?

"I bought soup." He had to strain to hear her mumbled words.

"I'll get one of the sport drinks. You could use the electrolytes. Then, I'll heat the soup."

She didn't argue, just crawled into her bed and pulled the covers over her body. Eyes closed, she grunted something that sounded like thanks.

With one last worried glance, he left her room, grabbed the groceries, and proceeded to her kitchen. He should have come over when he hadn't heard back from her the previous night. He'd tried texting and calling but had just thought she'd gone to bed early. When she still wasn't responding by this evening, he'd had to know she was okay. She wasn't okay.

He found a metal straw, poured some of the sport drink into a cup, then brought it to her room.

"Hailey, let me help you sit up long enough for you to sip on your drink."

She roused, raising a little, and taking the smallest drink in history prior to her head returning to her pillow. He placed the cup on a painted mermaid coaster on her nightstand, then headed back to her kitchen.

He unpacked her groceries, putting them away, with the exception of the soup and saltine crackers. He heated up the chicken noodles, spooned out a small bowl, put a few crackers on her plate, then headed to her room. She'd gone back to sleep. Did he wake her or let her sleep? If not for the fact that she'd not eaten or drunk much, if anything, all day, he'd let her rest. But if he couldn't get liquids inside her orally, she would need an intravenous infusion.

"Hailey, wake up. You need to eat."

She mumbled.

"Hailey." He shook her shoulder. "It's time to eat and drink. If you can sit up, I'll feed you."

Her eyes opened and she peered at him. "Why are you in my bedroom?"

"Not for the many reasons I'd like to be. Actually, that's not true. With you ill, this is right where I want to be, taking care of you." His words stunned him, but he assured himself that's what friends did for each other. "Let's get you scooted into an upright position."

"May not stay down. Or in." She winced. "Not been a good twenty-four hours."

"Noted. You still need to eat and drink. If you can't keep anything in, you're going to Venice General for intravenous fluids."

"I—thank you." She attempted to push herself off the pillow but failed. Cayden helped her to sit with her back against her headboard.

"Take a drink." He held the cup for her while she sipped through the straw. "Can you feed yourself or do you need help?"

"I'll try." She took a few bites then seemed bored with her food.

"Try or I'm bringing you to the emergency department to get fluids." Seeing her so weak was wrecking him and he needed to be doing something, anything, to make her feel better.

"No ER." Grimacing, she took another drink, then let him feed her half of the soup, watching him with hooded eyes with each delivered bite. She held up her hand. "No more. Need to sleep."

"Okay, sleep. I'll wake you for more fluids after we see if you're going to keep this down."

He wasn't going anywhere until she was improved. A lot improved.

Hailey woke with a start, having heard a noise in her bedroom. There, in the low light streaking in through her windows, Cayden stretched out in the oversized reading chair. He'd pulled it next to the bed and didn't look nearly as comfy as she felt when curled up there.

Why was Cayden in her bedroom? Why was his hand holding her forearm as if he was afraid to let go? Then the former night's events came rushing back. Cayden had come to her rescue. She had vague memories of his waking her throughout the night to drink.

She glanced at the clock, then pulled free from Cayden's touch. Oh, no. She should be at work. She was new and had no-showed. Would they fi—?

"I called last night," Cayden interrupted her panic, "and let the hospital know you wouldn't be in today."

Part of her wanted to protest at his high-handedness, but gratitude filled her. How had he known to? Not that he wasn't aware of her work schedule, just that she was surprised he'd thought to call in for her. "Thank you."

"You may not be thanking me if word gets out that I called in sick for you. That might be difficult to explain to Renee."

Hailey rubbed her temple. Yeah, Renee getting wind wouldn't be good.

"How are you feeling this morning?"

"Alive," she mumbled. "Alive seems an improvement from yesterday."

"You were pretty rough when I got here."

She reached for the drink he had by her bed, took a sip, then nodded. "I'm embarrassed that you saw me like that." Grimacing, she touched her hair, then covered her face with her hands. "And like this."

"You're beautiful, Hailey. No makeup required."

Mortified that he'd seen her without makeup—no, that wasn't right. He was seeing her with two-day-old makeup she'd slept in. She probably looked like a clown. "You've obviously caught whatever I have. Delirium is setting in."

Looking much too serious, he shook his head. "No delirium, just good taste. Are you hungry?"

She nodded.

"Do you feel up for toast? When I was putting away your groceries, I noticed you had purchased bread and oatmeal, too. I'll gladly make you whatever sounds good."

Embarrassed that she was just lying there while he was offering to prepare food, she scooted up, meaning to rise, but dizziness hit.

"I can make it," she said anyway, hoping the room stopped spinning so she could stand.

"I'd rather you let me."

She pressed her fingers to her throbbing temples, thinking maybe it was her head spinning rather than the room. "Don't you have to be at work?"

"My office manager rescheduled my appointments."

Guilt hit. He was a busy man and had things to do other than nurse her back to health. He had stayed with her all night, had awakened her to drink, had helped her to the bathroom and held a washcloth to her forehead when she'd gotten ill.

"I don't want your appointments canceled because of me." She'd inconvenienced him enough.

"Already done, Hailey. I'm not going anywhere today other than staying right here so I can take care of you."

"I—okay. I'm going to go to the bathroom. Toast and a drink sound wonderful."

Having someone to take care of her was wonderful. She'd gotten sick when she'd been twelve. Her mother had held her most of the night. That had been the only night someone had held her while she was ill. Her mother, and now, Cayden.

Gratitude filled her. He truly was a kind man. And, hopefully that really was just gratitude she was feeling and not anything more because falling for Cayden would be all too easy. She couldn't do that.

Not if she didn't want to end up with a broken heart that no amount of nursing back to health would heal.

The following Saturday, Cayden eyed the sunscreen-coated woman from where she sat on the edge of the swimming pool. She swirled her toes in the pool water. Her nails were flamingo pink and her big toes each had a tiny palm tree with sparkly leaves. He wasn't a feet man, but Hailey's never failed to catch his attention. Probably because they were attached to her toned legs that were glistening in the sunlight.

"This is probably a waste of time as I've no plans to swim."

"Spending time with you is never a waste." He liked being with her. "Besides, we're focusing on floating, not swimming."

"Show me how floating is done again." She obviously stalled, making him question again if something had happened to make her so leery of learning. She wore the same black one-piece bathing suit with a pair of shorts that she'd worn to shark tooth hunt.

He moved closer to where she sat, placing his hands to either side of her hips on the pool edge. He looked directly into her eyes. "Are you afraid of the water, Hailey?"

She moistened her lips, then took a deep breath. "Yes."

"You're afraid because you can't swim? Be assured that we're going to change that. It may take us a few days or a few weeks, but you will learn to swim."

She eyed him, then stalled further by saying, "Maybe

I'm afraid because there are living things in the water that can hurt me."

"There are living things outside the water that can hurt you," he reminded her, not buying her excuse, especially as the pool water was crystal clear. "You obviously function just fine."

She feigned shock. "You're right. There are. I should go inside and cover myself in bubble wrap."

"Bubble wrap would make for an interesting swim lesson and might help you float."

Sighing, she ran her fingers along where she'd braided her hair. "You think I'm being silly, don't you?"

Silly wasn't one of the adjectives he'd use to describe her. Beautiful, brilliant, mesmerizing, frustrating, but not silly.

"What I think is that you aren't going to get past your water hang-ups until you are confident in your ability to swim. I'm sorry about what happened with Sasha, but that isn't something that happens often, Hailey. Nor does learning to swim mean that you have to go into the open sea if that's not your thing. Prior to what happened with Sasha, you wanted to learn."

"I do. It's embarrassing that I can't. It's just that…" She hesitated. "I tried to learn once before. It didn't go well."

"You didn't have me for a teacher." He'd taught numerous kids over the years he'd worked as a lifeguard. Teaching Hailey would be his pleasure.

"Maybe I'm not someone who is meant to swim."

Eyeing her, seeing the holes in her self-confidence, he yet again wanted to hurt her ex. "Work with me, Hailey. We will get you there."

She still looked hesitant. "I don't want to upset you if I'm not able to do the things you want me to do."

"I'd never be upset with you for not being able to do something, Hailey." Surely, they had spent enough time together that she realized that. "I'd be disappointed if you didn't try at all, but never upset that you tried and failed. It's the trying part that I count as the most important."

She stared into his eyes, her gaze holding fast as his hands went to her waist. Seeming to know what he wanted, she nodded and slid forward as he guided her into the water and against him. The water only came to his waist but, with their height difference, came in just beneath her breasts. Cayden gulped.

"See, this isn't so bad." Holding her felt good, just as it had when he'd lowered her into the water at the beach. Hailey against him felt right.

"Only because you're holding me," she pointed out with a self-deprecating smile. "If you hold me like this the entire time, I'll be fine."

Cayden wouldn't mind holding her the entire time. However, he wanted to help her overcome her fears and he especially wanted her able to safely navigate in water. "I won't let anything happen to you, Hailey."

He meant in the pool, and yet, with her in his arms, how protective he felt of her gave him pause. He wouldn't let anything happen to her. Anywhere. Not if he had any say in the matter.

Clinging to him, she seemed to sense that his mind had gone deeper than the surface of what he'd said. She squeezed where she held on to his arms. "Then, let's get this over with."

"Such an enthusiastic student," he teased.

"It's not that I'm not grateful that you're spending your Saturday trying to teach me. I am appreciative. It's just that," she hesitated, seeming to not know how to express her concerns as she shrugged.

Unable to resist, Cayden leaned in to kiss her temple. Once again, her citrusy scent assaulted his senses, making him deeply inhale. But it was how the feel of his lips pressed to her, how zings of awareness shot through him that had his legs threatening to buckle. He cleared his throat. "We'll stay where you can stand up at any time you feel you need to. Just relax and trust me to keep you safe."

Too bad he didn't trust his ability to keep himself safe from how his emotions were getting so tangled up with Hailey.

"I do trust you." Seeming surprised by her admission, she stared at him with eyes so blue they shamed the pool's bright color. After a moment, she tentatively smiled and loosened her death grip on his arms. "Tell me what to do."

Cayden told her, and as she attempted to do as he asked, he kept his hands at her midsection, keeping her afloat. "We're going to keep practicing this, Hailey. We'll go from one side of the pool to the other for as many times as needed."

"As many times as needed? I hope you have all day."

"I do." His hand beneath her abdomen, Cayden guided her through the water. They made the trip several times. "You did great," he praised, helping her to her feet.

"I didn't do anything except lie there."

"That's what floating is all about. Just lying on the water."

"Without sinking," she added.

"Not sinking is an important component of successful floating." Just as keeping his gaze locked with hers was an important component of keeping his mind off how her wet suit clung to her body.

"Maybe I'll eventually float without you having to hold me."

He had mixed feelings about that. As much as he wanted her success, he liked the excuse to touch her. "Practice makes perfect."

"It'll take a lot to convince me that you weren't born perfect."

Her comment surprised him. "You think I'm perfect?"

"As close as I've encountered." Sunshine reflected off the water and her eyes, creating a surreal, almost mystical look.

"I'm far from perfect, but you make me wish I was." She blinked. "Me?"

"It's no secret that I'm attracted to you, Hailey."

She hesitated, then, a small smile on her full lips, she placed her hands against his chest. "I'm attracted to you, too, Cayden." Her hands trembled. "How about we finish and get dried off?"

Cayden didn't need water to float. She was enough to have him soaring.

CHAPTER NINE

STARING AT HER reflection in her bathroom mirror, Hailey rubbed her plumped lips together, evenly spreading the shiny gloss. After they'd gotten back to her place, she'd showered to wash off the pool's chlorine, donned a sundress and sandals, and carefully reapplied her makeup. She'd applied lotion, styled her hair, and changed outfits twice. Butterflies danced in her belly as she stared back at her image, barely recognizing herself as the same woman she'd been just a few months ago. What would Cayden have thought of that woman? Would he have noticed her with her dull hair and her ineptitude with anything to do with beauty? Would he have looked at her the way he had while they'd been in the pool? Like he'd wanted to kiss her? To do much more than kiss her?

Hailey gulped. No doubt he had finished in her guest bathroom long ago and was waiting for her. She could hear where he'd turned on the television in the living area.

With one last look in the mirror, she left the reprieve of her bedroom's ensuite bath. Only, when she went into her living room, Cayden wasn't there. For a moment, she thought he'd tired of waiting and had left. The shade to the glass patio doorway was pulled back. He must be on the covered patio.

She was quite proud of the comfy outdoor area she'd created. She'd spent many an hour out there already and it was one of her favorite things about the house. That and looking out at the little man-made lake and watching birds come and go. Fortunately, she'd not seen any alligators, but was told that one occasionally sunned along the banks. She was no more a fan of alligators than she was of sharks or jellyfish so if she never spotted one, she'd be just fine.

His back to her, Cayden was sitting on the comfy oversized lounger with his feet propped up. Going around to join him, she realized he'd fallen asleep. How cliché that she'd taken so long getting ready that he'd dosed off? The irony of it had her smiling.

With the freedom granted by his closed eyes, she studied him, taking in each of his features. His dark hair was still lightly damp from his shower. His thick lashes spread out long over his cheekbones. His chest rose and fell rhythmically with each breath. He was so handsome that he made her question why he was really there, with her, saying things like that he was attracted to her. Had her drastic makeover really been that successful? That the new her could attract someone so wonderful?

He looked so peaceful that rather than wake him, she sat down beside him, snuggling close enough that she leaned against him and closed her own eyes. She wasn't one for naps and couldn't imagine falling asleep when she was near someone as dynamic as Cayden, but being next to him, letting herself relax against him, was nice.

Only, it didn't take long for his breathing pattern to change, hinting that if he'd been asleep, he no longer was. She shifted to glance at him and met his half-lidded hazel gaze. Had any man's eyes ever been more beautiful? More mesmerizing?

He didn't say anything, just brushed his fingers along her face, skimming her hairline, then gliding along her chin ever so gently. Goose bumps prickled her skin. Her heart quivered. All of her did. His touch was reverent, as if he couldn't believe he was there *with her*. Surreal. Maybe she had fallen asleep and was dreaming.

"Cold?" he asked.

Hailey shook her head. She wasn't cold. Quite the opposite. Her insides burned. Her gaze lowered to his mouth and temptation hit so strong that she longed to know what it would feel like to kiss him for real and not the light touches they'd been playing around with for weeks. Breathing was more and more difficult. Maybe that was why she scooted so close that his breath became hers.

He didn't move, just waited to see what she was going to do. Hailey wanted to know her next move, too. She was no seductress, no siren to lure men. Yet she'd have to be blind not to see that, for the moment, Cayden was under her spell, and his breathing was as ragged as her own at just her lightest touch. His reaction had her heart racing and her body aching, and made her crave him enough that resisting temptation was impossible.

She stretched the tiniest amount, pressing her lips to his tentatively with her eyes wide open. She didn't need to watch him, though. She could feel his response, could hear the low half growl, half moan that escaped him when she lingered, tasting his mouth.

"Hailey." The way he said her name emboldened her. She placed her palms against his cheeks, marveling that she touched him, that she threaded her fingers into his hair, then pulled him to her.

"Hmm?" she whispered against his mouth, so close she could feel the warmth of his breath. "Tell me what you want."

"You know what I want." His hands were on her now, her shoulders, her back, her bottom as he lifted her to lie upon him and molded her firmly against him to show her just how much he wanted her.

She'd never quite envisioned this moment when she'd bought the lounger, but she'd never be able to see it again without thinking of Cayden beneath her, his hands cupping her bottom as they kissed. Oh, how they kissed.

Hailey wasn't sure how long they kissed. An eternity could have passed, and it wouldn't have been enough to fully savor him. She wasn't sure how much time passed prior to her fingers sliding beneath his T-shirt, removing his T-shirt so she could run her hands over his chest and shoulders. She loved touching him, experiencing his responses. Soon, she couldn't think about his responses for her own, though. All she could do was feel.

"You're sure?" he asked.

Hailey wasn't sure of anything except that he best not stop the magic he was wielding over her body. She wasn't sure what words came out of her mouth, but they must have been the right ones because his smile was so beautifully perfect as he caressed her face.

"Hailey," he said, kissing her and forever changing her, winding her so tightly that she had no choice but to explode into tiny bits of colored confetti that floated back to earth from some heavenly place.

* * *

If there was really such a thing as grinning from ear to ear, Cayden imagined he was doing exactly that as he marveled at the woman he held close to his sweat-slickened body. Marveled because she was marvelous. As his coworker, his friend, and his lover.

His lover. Because he loved her? Right after the most amazing physical experience of his life was not the time to be contemplating his feelings for Hailey. Delirium had obviously set in, because when he looked at her he couldn't help but think that he wanted to hang on to this feeling forever.

Forever was a life sentence he'd not planned to endure.

So why did forever feel like it wouldn't be nearly long enough if Hailey was by his side?

"Anyone ever tell you that you're an amazing kisser, Hailey? An amazing everything."

"No. But then, until today, I'd only ever kissed one man."

Cayden's eyes widened. "You're kidding?"

Taking a deep breath, Hailey rolled so that she was lying next to him rather than on him. "I wish I was," she half mumbled, not looking at him. "John was my first and only boyfriend prior to, well, um, you."

"You'd never kissed anyone other than your first boyfriend?" He'd known she wasn't overly experienced. Had liked that, even. That innocent air about her had been one of the reasons he'd not rushed their physical relationship. Had he known the intensity of what they just shared, nothing would have held him back short of Hailey herself.

She shook her head.

"How is it that you've only kissed one man other than me?"

"Men weren't exactly beating down my door."

He scooted to partially sit up and stared at her in such shock that, had her skin not still been flushed from what they'd done, she'd have blushed. "Were the men in Ohio idiots?"

She snorted. "I've mentioned that I made a lot of life changes beginning just prior to and continuing after moving to Florida." She reached up and touched her hair. "My appearance was one of those major changes. New hair, new eyelashes—" she batted them "—corrective eye surgery to lose my glasses, eyebrows, extreme diet and exercise, facials, fillers, and makeup consults with how-to classes, manicures, pedicures, the list goes on." She grimaced, then reached for her shirt. "Honestly, it's exhausting and things I'd never bothered with before. I wouldn't have had time even if I'd wanted to, not with med school and residency and John. Trying to improve one's looks is time-consuming and expensive. I started in Ohio, and my first week here I was at appointments every day, some days two or three. Now I spend my Thursdays and some Fridays doing maintenance appointments."

"You don't need to improve your looks, Hailey. You're gorgeous."

"You didn't see me before," she reminded him, putting her shirt back on.

"Doesn't matter. I'd have still found you attractive." His attraction to her went way beyond her hair and nails.

Hailey laughed a hollow sound that held more pain than humor. "You say that, but that's because you're looking at the new me. The me that, short of going under the reconstructive knife, has maximized her looks. No one found me attractive. Just John and he—" She stopped. Her gaze lifted to his, seeming horrified at what she'd just told him.

Idiots, he thought. John and every man who'd ever made her see herself in any way other than beautiful.

"He what?" Cayden prompted from where he sat next to her on the lounger.

Not looking at him despite his willing her to, she shrugged. "I prefer to think he liked me in the beginning, but honestly, he may never have. I was his meal ticket and security blanket. To put it bluntly, I was basically his sugar mama."

Her confession shocked him. Little things she'd said and done that he'd put down to feminine independence now took on a new slant. He furrowed his brows. "As a resident?"

"My parents weren't wealthy, by any means, but they had done all right for themselves. I inherited a decent chunk when their house was auctioned off as it was on a nice piece of land in a popular area in Cincinnati. Fortunately, Dad had set up a trust with his life insurance policy and the trustee rolled most of the estate sale into that investment account that I couldn't access until recently. I got a monthly living expense payment from the trust but I couldn't access the bulk of it until finishing graduate school or my thirtieth birthday—whichever came first. Thank goodness he did that as otherwise, I'm not sure I'd have anything left because John spent every penny he could get his hands on."

Whatever amount her inheritance was, Hailey was the real treasure.

"I'm on record as saying the man was an idiot." How could the man have been in a long-term relationship with Hailey, have had her vying for his love, and been more interested in things?

"It could be argued that I'm the one who was foolish, because it was me who let him take advantage of me for so long."

"You obviously cared about him."

She nodded. "I thought I loved him and vice versa. Now, whether from time away from him or my therapy, I recognize that I was so desperate for love and attention that I was easy prey for him to swoop in and convince me that he was all I deserved."

"You deserve good things, Hailey." Everyone did. Cayden hugged her, not liking how she remained stiff in his embrace. "The best things."

"So my therapist keeps reminding me." Not seeming comfortable with his holding her, she reached for her underwear and sundress, putting them on prior to continuing. Once dressed, she walked over to stare out at the man-made lake that bordered her backyard. "I didn't date in high school. Not a single date. It wasn't because I didn't want to, but that no one asked."

The pain and embarrassment in her voice had Cayden's insides aching for her. That she'd felt the need to move away from him after what they'd just shared had his insides aching, too. Surely, she knew there was no reason to feel embarrassment with him?

"Apparently, you've been surrounded by idiots your whole life."

She turned, met his gaze with her sad blue eyes that ripped at his heart when they'd been so happy, so full of desire, just minutes before. "I was an introvert and wasn't involved in much during my school years. At first due to bouncing from one foster home to another, but then, after my parents adopted me, because I was happy to have a family and wanted to be with them. I met John early in my college freshman year around the time my mother died from breast cancer. My father died less than a year later from a broken heart. John was the only person in my life."

"I'm sorry, Hailey." He wanted to hold her, to wrap his arms around her until she felt so loved that loneliness could never take hold again, but when he stood to go to her, she shook her head. Sensing she needed to say whatever was in her heart, he grabbed his clothes and got dressed while she continued.

"Even after I acknowledged that our relationship was over, I went with the status quo rather than making the break." She took a deep breath. "Ending things meant being completely alone in the world. That scared me."

"You've obviously overcome that fear." At her look of doubt, he pointed out. "You moved to a state where you didn't know anyone. That takes guts."

Her expression remained dubious. "Or a really strong desire to start over where no one knew the old, boring me."

"You were never boring, Hailey." Unable to stay away a moment longer, he crossed the patio to where she stood and placed his fingertip against her temple. "What's up here is completely fascinating."

"I'm glad you think so." A tear slid down her cheek, gutting him.

"Don't you?"

She swiped at the tear, waving him off and taking a few steps away from him. "I'm working on that, too."

"As part of this big makeover you've done?"

She nodded. "I'm creating the life I want."

His brow lifted. "That sounds like a line from a self-help book."

"That's quite possible. There's a bunch of them on the shelf in my bedroom and I've read them all at least once." Glancing toward him, she didn't quite meet his eyes. "Now you realize I'm a messy work in progress and we shouldn't have done what we did a few minutes ago, not with the baggage I carry."

"Who doesn't have baggage, Hailey?"

Hailey's gaze lifted to his. "You."

He harrumphed. "You think I don't have baggage? I must put on a good show, then, because I've enough to fill an airport. We could start with the girlfriend I dated through high school and my first two years of college. I planned to marry her the summer prior to starting med school."

"What happened?"

"She got pregnant by some random guy she met on a girls' trip to Miami. I might have forgiven her, except apparently it wasn't the first time she'd cheated."

"I'm sorry."

"It gets better," he admitted, wondering how such an amazing day had turned into a confessional. "Hurt, I jumped into another relationship, which started off great. I was planning to propose, but that time it was my roommate who Cynthia cheated with. After that, I quit believing in love as I realized that when it came to women, I prefer being friends with benefits, like my relationship with Leanna was, rather than anything with promises of fidelity and forever."

Which had him circling back to his earlier thoughts about Hailey. Because no matter how much bringing up the past might make him want to recant those earlier thoughts, he couldn't. Hailey was unlike anyone he'd ever met. Beautiful in ways the eyes couldn't see, in addition to wowing him with her eyes and infectious smile. Smart, funny, trustworthy.

Fidelity and forever not only didn't feel impossible with Hailey, but rather, his heart's inevitable destiny.

Stunned by the women who had been in Cayden's life, Hailey stared at him, thinking she could toss his own words back at him. His exes had been idiots. How could any woman have had his love, have had him wanting to spend his life with her, and her to have treated his heart so callously?

Hailey just couldn't fathom it.

She also couldn't fathom how she was going to move past what they'd done earlier. They'd had sex. Good sex. Phenomenal sex. Sex that had blown her away. Sex that he'd enjoyed, too. He had been right there with her every touch and moan along the way. Not because she'd been worriedly trying to make sure he liked what they were doing. She'd been so caught up in what he was doing to her body that she hadn't been thinking, just feeling and touching and basking in such unexpected pleasure. He'd given that to her so selflessly, had made her feel so good.

Just looking at him, she wanted to grab hold and never let go. Which was foolish and why he'd just reminded her that he preferred being friends with benefits and didn't do commitment. No doubt he wanted to make sure that, in her inexperience, she didn't mistake what they'd done to mean anything more than what it had been. Sex.

Her heart squeezed in protest. What was wrong with her that despite all her big plans and goals she'd fallen for the first guy she'd become involved with? She'd not even planned to date, had known she needed to focus on herself and not a relationship. He'd been so deliciously tempting that she'd been unable to resist, had convinced herself that she was just dipping her toes into the dating world by spending time with him. Ha. How foolish was she? Would she never learn?

"I—you're right." She stood a little straighter, needing all her strength to do what needed to be done. Self-preservation demanded she take control of her life and fortify the miniscule barriers he'd blown through to reach her vulnerable heart in such a short time. No way could she recover from a heartbreak at Cayden's hands. Her heart was much too fragile from where she'd pieced it back together after John's crushing it. No way would she go back to the weak, clingy woman she'd been, begging for John's love and attention. "I'm glad we can discuss this like adults and that we're in agreement. Promises of forever and fidelity would ruin our friendship." She didn't want to hear fake promises. She wanted…no, she did not want that. She couldn't want that. To want that would bleed her heart dry. "I owe you the biggest thank-you for what happened between us, because sex was never like that with John. Now I'm curious as to what all I've been missing out on and look forward to fully jumping into the dating world."

That she'd shocked him was obvious. His eyes had

widened, then narrowed. "You plan to jump into the dating world?"

She nodded. "I haven't learned all the things I should have learned by this point in my life. Thank you for helping me realize how fun sex can be when it isn't bogged down by emotional entanglements. Is it always that good? I mean, with other people?" Realizing he could take what she'd said as her fishing for a compliment, she quickly added, "Oh, never mind. I'll find out for myself."

Nausea gripped her stomach at the thought of anyone touching her other than Cayden, but she kept her tone and expression light.

Cayden continued to stare at her in disbelief. Had his previous involvements been clingy afterward? She wouldn't cling. She knew doing so would be futile. Just look at how long she'd clung to John. She'd never do that again.

But if she continued seeing Cayden, would she remain as determined? Or would she fall into a lifetime of desperately wanting to be loved and end up devastated?

Look at how passionate she was about him after just a few months. She had to put herself first, to preserve her new life, and not let anything or anyone steal that from her. Not even herself.

"But I think what happened between us shouldn't happen again. With us being coworkers, continuing the benefits part of our friendship would be too complicated."

"You don't want to see me again?"

Only during every waking moment.

She hated herself for the thought, for her weakness, her foolishness.

"Not outside of work and Venice Has Heart."

He raked his fingers through his hair, paced across the patio, then turned to her. "Did I miss something, Hailey? Something I did wrong?"

She shook her head. He'd done everything right and that was the problem. "It's best if we don't do this again, and we need to see other people. I've spent so much time with you that I haven't gone on dates with anyone else. I want to experience all life has to offer that I've been missing out on."

A cold look settled onto his face, erasing the warmth he'd always looked at her with. "Fine, Hailey. You have fun experiencing all those things you've missed out on in life."

With that, Cayden left.

Crumbling with sobs that wracked her body, Hailey sank onto a chair, cradling her head in her palms. Just look at what a mess she'd made of her new life, falling for the first man to smile her way.

Fortunately, she'd stepped up to the plate and done what was right for her self-preservation.

Surely, her heart would forgive her when it realized how much pain she'd saved it down the road.

CHAPTER TEN

A MONTH HAD passed and a tired-from-tossing-and-turning Hailey arrived at the Venice Has Heart event's medical tent. She'd not seen Cayden yet that morning, but not doing so before the day ended was unavoidable.

Not seeing him made it easier to deceive herself about how tangled up she'd become in the fantasy of being the recipient of his attention.

Her heart had yet to forgive her. So had her body for depriving it of Cayden's magic. She missed him more than she could have imagined. Not that she didn't see him or that he wasn't polite. He was. But he didn't look at her the same. He never met her eyes. Never smiled at her. Never laughed with her. Never texted her funny memes or messages to have "sweet dreams" as she drifted to sleep. Never…never anything because whatever had been between them, they were now only coworkers.

It was what she'd needed to happen, but was still slowly killing her.

Which reinforced that their ending sooner rather than later had been the best thing that could have happened, even if only her logic and self-preservation instinct agreed. Even her friend Jamie had thought Hailey was nuts when she'd revealed that she couldn't be involved with Cayden. Her poor heart wouldn't have survived if she and Cayden had grown any closer. Whether it was going to currently was debatable.

Had anyone ever died from a broken heart? What was she asking? Her own father had died from his broken heart over grieving his wife. Having Hailey in his life hadn't been enough for his will to live to press on. How sad that even for her father she hadn't been enough?

After the change in their relationship, Hailey had briefly considered bailing on the Venice Has Heart event, but she wanted to volunteer and be involved in the community. That had nothing to do with Cayden. She met with the group the previous week, enjoying reconnecting with the Krandalls and Benny, but seeing Cayden smiling and laughing with Leanna had been pure torture. That he'd avoided speaking with Hailey completely had been for the best because she might have burst into tears at how hollow she felt without him in her life.

"Looks as if we've had a great turnout for the run." Having been rushing around helping check runners in and making sure everything was in order, Linda sat down in a folding chair and fanned her tanned face with the torn-off side of a cardboard box. She smiled at Hailey. "Bob and I ran the half marathon this morning before daylight. We didn't want to be slackers."

Hailey didn't think anyone would ever accuse the couple of that.

"How long have you been married?"

"Since I was sixteen and we eloped."

"Sixteen? Was that even legal?" Hailey stared at the women in astonishment. "That's so young."

Linda laughed. "Didn't feel too young and my daddy

probably could have forced the issue if he'd wanted. He didn't because he knew I'd been wanting to marry Bob since I was five." Linda's expression brightened with her memories. "He wrote me one of those check yes or no boxes letters asking me to being his girlfriend."

Hailey couldn't help but smile. "I take it you checked the yes box."

Bob stepped up behind his wife and grinned. "That would have been too simple for my Linda. She wrote back asking if I wanted babies and puppies. When I marked yes, she wrote back saying she was going to marry me." He gave his wife an indulgent look. "Who was I to argue with the prettiest girl in class?"

Hailey stared at the couple. "You only dated each other?" When they nodded, she added, "Didn't you ever wonder if you missed out by not dating anyone else?"

"There was no need to date anyone else when I met the best in kindergarten," Bob assured. "Linda's the only date I wanted. Still is."

Linda patted his cheek. "Ditto, darling."

Hailey watched them with more than a little envy. What would it have been like to have loved and been loved from such a young age? To have grown up knowing that your someone was always there?

They chatted for a few minutes then Bob left to check on where the vendors had set up their booths.

"Isn't he a sweetheart?" Linda asked, watching as he left the tent.

"I'll admit I'm a little jealous."

"He's definitely a keeper." Linda's gaze cut to Hailey. "Is there no one special in your life?"

Face aflame, Hailey fought picking up the cardboard

piece Linda had fanned herself with earlier. "I... There was, but we're not involved anymore. It was never going to work. I mean, I miss him, but—" What was she doing? Linda didn't want to hear her pathetic love story. "Yeah, it wouldn't have worked out."

"What makes you think it wouldn't have worked out? Bad temperament, bad finances, bad breath, or bad sex?"

Hailey's jaw dropped, then managed to say, "None of the above."

"Then, if you miss him as much as it sounds you do, you need to do something to make it work out. Flirt with him a little or something to let him know you're still interested."

"I've never been one of those girls who were natural-born flirters." Not that it would matter if she was. Cayden barely acknowledged she existed these days.

"Just smile and bat those pretty eyes. If it's meant to be, things will work out," Linda advised. "Now, let's double-check our supplies before heading to the main stage for the kickoff. You don't want to miss that."

Yeah, missing Cayden was more than enough.

They were just finishing their check when, clipboard in hand, Cayden walked into the tent.

Hailey's chest tightened. Linda's question echoed through her mind. How had Hailey known it wouldn't work? It just wouldn't have. He was him and she was her. To have continued would have just been delaying the painful inevitable. The only real question had been at what point had she wanted to accept her heartache and refocus on her self-healing and being the best her she could be.

Wearing navy shorts and a Venice Has Heart T-shirt

and baseball cap, Cayden was gorgeous. But then, he was
no matter what he wore. How could she readily argue his
inner beauty was his most stunning attribute when he
was so gorgeous on the outside?

*What if your best self had been the you who had been
with him?* her heart whispered before she could hush it.

His gaze went to Linda and didn't budge, almost as if
Hailey weren't there. "Anything you ladies need before
we officially get started?"

You. For a brief moment, she worried that she'd said
her thought out loud. Neither Cayden nor Linda were
gawking at her, so she must not have.

"We're good," Linda told him. "No one has needed
our services, yet, but that will change once the race gets
started. Do you recall last year when those men ran into
each other and the one was knocked out cold?"

Hailey was glad Linda continued to chat with Cayden,
because it allowed her to try to tamp down her silliness.
She did not *need* him. That the thought had entered her
head annoyed her. She missed him, a lot, but that didn't
mean she needed him.

"Isn't that right?"

Hailey blinked at Linda. Having no idea what she'd
just said, she took a cue from her self-help books and
smiled. That must have been an okay response. Linda
went right back to talking with Cayden until he took off
to head back to where Leanna was deejaying the event
live on the radio station where she worked.

"Maybe you should try your flirting skills on Dr. Wilton," Linda suggested, causing Hailey to choke on air and
have to cough to catch her breath. "He's a great catch."

He was a great catch, but he didn't want to be caught.

Hailey coughed again, searching for the right response. Fortunately, Linda laughed and nudged her arm. "Don't look so horrified. It was just a suggestion. Come on. They want us all there for the official kickoff and it's almost time."

Leanna introduced Cayden to the group of volunteers, participants, vendors, and spectators and as with everything, he gave a dynamic motivational pep talk to everyone there. Next, a heart transplant patient who was walking the event said a quick prayer. Cayden wished them all luck and to always have heart.

The official buzzer sounded and the runners were off.

Hailey and Linda made their way back to the medical tent, where Hailey would be most of the day. The first fifteen minutes were slow, but then Cayden arrived on a UTV with one of the runners sitting in the truck bed–type back. Another volunteer drove and, from where he rode beside her, a gloved-up Cayden pressed a bloody gauze pad against the injured woman's knee.

"This is Aimee. She fell and has a pretty nasty gash on her knee from where she hit the pavement," Cayden informed her as he helped the forty-something woman out of the golf cart. As Hailey gloved up, he helped Aimee get settled onto the exam table that had been set up in the tent.

Hailey expected him to leave, but he knelt next to where she had to examine the woman's wound. She pulled off the gauze and winced. "You took a nasty tumble."

"Oh, I'm one of those people who never does anything halfway." Aimee sighed. "I'm not sure what I tripped over. My own feet, I guess, as there was nothing on the pavement."

While Cayden swapped out his gloves, Linda asked questions to fill out a medical encounter form, then had Aimee sign a release.

Apparently planning to assist, he handed a squirt bottle of sterile solution to Hailey. "Saline?"

Did he know it was all she could do to keep her hands from shaking as she took the bottle? Could he hear the thundering of her heart at how near he was?

"Thanks." Taking the bottle, she rinsed the bleeding wound, clearing out a few stray bits of gravel and wishing she could clean out the wounds of her heart as easily. "The cut is deep and needs sutures to close it."

Aimee winced. "I figured. This isn't my first bout of clumsiness."

"I can send you to the emergency room or I can do the sutures. Your choice," Hailey offered, grateful she'd noted the suture kits in their supplies.

"If you can do it here, then please do." The woman looked relieved that she wasn't going to have to travel elsewhere. "My husband was running ahead of me and doesn't know I fell. He wouldn't complain, but I'd like him to finish the race."

"Gotcha." She glanced toward Cayden. She caught his eyes unexpectedly and her heart ached when her gaze met his and saw a glimmer of something before it disappeared. Her eyes stung with moisture. Not now, she scolded herself. Now was not the time to be dwelling on Cayden. Recalling why she'd glanced up, she asked, "Since Aimee told Linda that she's not allergic to anything, could you draw me up a couple of milliliters of lidocaine, please?"

Cayden did so and handed the syringe to her, taking

care for their hands not to touch. *No worries, Cayden*, she thought. *Our touching might have rendered me a heaping mess and you'd have had to sew Aimee's knee without me.*

Changing her gloves over to the ones in the suture kit, Hailey kept her gaze focused on Aimee. She injected the area to anesthetize the skin, activated the needle safety device, then handed the syringe back to him. "I'll close her with the Ethilon number four, please."

Cayden had already pulled out the suture material and dropped it onto the sterile field drape.

Once Aimee was numb, Hailey used the curved needle to put in nine sutures.

"Great job," Cayden praised when she was finished.

Instantly, her eyes prickled with tears again. He was the most positive, uplifting person she'd ever met. Not once had she gotten the impression that he wanted to take over. He was confidently content in her abilities, had been cool with assisting, and had vocalized his appreciation for her skills. He hadn't pointed out that she'd struggled to get that first knot in place because her hands had been shaking. Shaking that hadn't been from lack of belief in herself, but from his nearness. Cayden shook her whole world. He had from the moment she first noticed him from across the hospital cafeteria. If only she'd known then what she knew now, she could have avoided him completely and saved them both a lot of trouble. Only... only, her patient was eyeing her sutured knee.

"Unfortunately, no matter how great of a job, you're going to have a scar, Aimee," she warned the woman, then gave instructions on home care and the need to follow up with her primary care provider for a wound check and suture removal.

When finished, aware of where Cayden was talking with Linda, Hailey disposed of her gloves, then took the medical encounter form that Linda had started to record care provided. Before Hailey finished, the golf cart driver arrived with another runner. Hailey started to stand, thinking she'd finish the simple notation of what she'd done on Aimee's knee later, but Cayden stopped her.

"Linda and I will triage him while you finish your note."

So, willing her hand to be steady, she documented the basics of suturing Aimee's knee, stealing a few glances to where Cayden knelt next to the man sitting on the table Aimee had recently vacated and which Linda had wiped with disinfectant. Kind, gentle, caring, compassionate, all those descriptions and more ran through her mind as she watched Cayden interact with the newcomer, watched him laugh at something the man said when Linda placed a cooling towel on the back of his neck and handed him a sports drink.

Cayden glanced at his watch, then toward her, catching her watching him. His smile faded. He had no smile for her, instead quickly looking back toward the runner, then standing to say something to Linda. Having finished the chart, a wrecked but determined to trudge forward Hailey joined them.

"Roger, here, just needs to cool down. He started out too hard too fast and got overheated. I don't think he's going to need intravenous fluids, but you can keep an eye on him. Leanna messaged that she needs me to join her for the broadcast."

Leanna. Because although Hailey was an emotionally tangled mess, Cayden was used to moving from friends with benefits to just friends or whatever it was they currently were. Maybe eventually they'd be friends like he and Leanna were. Or were he and Leanna in the friends with benefits category? Maybe he'd even eventually prove right all those who believed that when he settled down, it would be with the beautiful deejay.

When he settled down? He had no plans to ever settle down. If he had—she'd what? His willingness to settle down didn't mean he'd have ever chosen Hailey, that he could have ever loved her.

Sighing, she met his gaze and her breath caught that he hadn't moved, but was looking at her with a sad longing that he failed to hide.

Oh, Cayden. Could you have ever grown to love me? Was that even possible, when she'd barely started loving herself and he'd said he no longer believed in love?

Was she truly so gullible, so desperate to be loved, that whatever had been in his eyes made her want to believe in the seemingly impossible?

Cayden had stayed late into the previous night working with his team leaders to make sure they had everything set for the event. With only a few snafus, everything seemed to have gone smoothly. Definitely, the day had been a success, raising needed funds and awareness of heart disease and ways of preventing it within their community. The official activities had ended, and the breakdown and cleanup process had started.

"Cayden?"

Recognizing Hailey's voice, Cayden braced himself. At the hospital he could compartmentalize his interactions with her, could draw upon his professionalism as a shield from the slaying being near her gave him. But, here, he'd lost that edge and had slipped more than once, asking himself over and over what had led to her pushing him away after they'd shared such an intimate connection. What they'd shared had been different, special, addicting. At least, to him. She'd shut him out almost immediately. *Why?*

Had she sensed his growing feelings for her? Sensed that he'd been leading up to telling her that she'd changed his mind—his heart—about so many things and so had pushed him away?

"I know it's been a long day, but are you busy after all this is done?"

Knowing he couldn't just keep standing with his back to her, he sucked in a deep breath and turned to face her. She looked as tired as he felt. He hadn't really anticipated her staying from start to finish, but she'd jumped in to help wherever needed all day. He shouldn't have expected less, not from Hailey.

Maybe she'd been trying to be kind by ending things, afraid she'd hurt him further if they continued. She didn't have to worry. Her reminder of why he didn't get emotionally involved had served its purpose. He'd keep his heart locked away for good this time.

He nodded. "I have plans."

For a moment he thought she was going to turn to leave, but instead, her gaze met his, full of a tumultuous mixture of resignation and forced courage. "With Leanna?"

He nodded. She'd asked him to go eat with her to go over the day's events and to make notes on what worked well and what they could do to improve for next year's event while it was fresh on their minds.

"I... Okay." Why was she looking at him that way? She was the one who'd insisted they end their relationship. "Have a good night then."

Disappointment on her face, Hailey turned to leave. The urge to stop her hit him hard. But he wouldn't. The past month had been difficult. How much harder would it be if he gave in to the urge to beg her to give them another chance? To let him continue with her in the new life she said she was creating for herself?

How crazy was that when she'd let them go so easily? When he'd been about to hand her his heart and she'd shoved the door closed before he could? Three times and he was out. Only, Hailey was nothing like his previous two heartbreaks. Even calling them that felt wrong when they barely registered in comparison to the world-shattering pain Hailey's cutting him out of her life had unleashed. He needed to just let her go.

"Was there something in particular you needed, Hailey?" he asked anyway, causing her to turn back.

She stared at him a moment, then shook her head. "Nothing. Have a good night and thanks again for involving me in today. It was truly a blessing to be here."

She'd been busy in the medical tent with Linda and then with doing heart health consults. She'd taken a few breaks for grabbing something to eat and he'd seen her strolling around to watch the kids playing in the bouncy house, a faraway smile on her face that made him wonder what she was thinking. He'd bet it hadn't been about the things seeing her watching those children had elicited within his bumfuzzled brain. He blamed lack of sleep.

Last night and for the whole of the last month. He was physically, mentally, and emotionally exhausted.

"Thank you for volunteering," he found the will to say, even adding, "We hope you'll be back next year."

Her lower lip disappeared into her mouth for a moment, drawing his gaze and eliciting self-disdain at how her tiny gesture twisted him into knots.

"I'll always be there if you need me, Cayden."

Her wording seemed strange and he continued to mull it over while he watched her leave, and he struggled to keep his mind on task during his and Leanna's dinner. She was quick to point that out to him, and when she asked him to her place for drinks, he was quick to say no.

He only wanted one woman and she no longer wanted him in her life.

Grateful for her shower to wash away the day's grime and the tears she'd given in to on her drive home, Hailey towel dried her hair, then put on shorts and a T-shirt to sleep in. It had been a long day, and one with extreme emotions. She'd loved volunteering but being with Cayden outside the hospital setting had highlighted her downward spiral ever since she'd ended their relationship.

Since she'd pushed him away. That was what she'd done. She even knew why. Because he scared her. The way he'd held her, kissed her, touched her, looked into her eyes as he'd made love to her, that had terrified her. Because he made her believe that he cared and she hadn't known how to deal with that. The only two people who had truly cared for her had been gone so long that she'd forgotten how wonderful it felt. It's what she'd craved with John, but never gotten. But Cayden, despite the words he'd said, hadn't held back. He'd nurtured every-thing good inside her.

Then.

Now he'd cut himself off from her emotionally and was unavailable to her in every way.

Calling herself every kind of fool, she headed to the kitchen, got herself a glass of water, and headed out to her patio. Her gaze immediately went to the lounger. She needed to get rid of the thing because she couldn't look at it and not recall how she'd boldly kissed Cayden, how he'd kissed her back, then made love to her. She'd set her fears aside that night, kissed him and made love to him with-out any past doubts getting into her head despite there being so many and Cayden had been why. He'd nurtured her confidence, lifted her up to discover the things she hadn't previously learned about herself and life.

She'd moved to Florida to start over from past mis-takes and had ended up making the biggest mistake of her life. Because she'd not trusted in what she'd seen happen-ing between them, not trusted in what she saw when he smiled at her, not trusted in her ability to decipher what was real and what she wanted to be real.

Too late she was seeing clearly what she'd had and lost. Question was, what was she going to do about it? Be-cause Florida Hailey refused to go down without a fight. Sure, that she thought she could compete with someone of Leanna's caliber might seem deluded to some, but Cayden hadn't loved Leanna. Not like he had with her. Because she was lovable.

She was. Whether it was months of being away from a man who'd emotionally abused her or doing her therapy and self-healing, she finally realized she was lovable beyond whether or not Cayden ever chose to risk his heart with her again. She was lovable.

Or maybe she was so exhausted that she was delusional. One or the other.

Either way, she had to find Cayden and tell him everything in her heart. He'd always been easy to talk to, but telling him how she'd let fear hurt them both wouldn't be easy. Could he ever forgive her?

Her doorbell rang. Heart racing, she walked into the house, then peered through the front door's peephole. Cayden! Without thought, she flung the door open and barely prevented herself from flinging herself into her arms.

"You're here." Did he think her strange that she was grinning at him? Why was she grinning? Just because she'd had an epiphany did not mean that he felt any different.

"Can I come in?"

She moved aside, allowing him into her house, watched him automatically start to go out to the patio area, but he changed his mind, stopping in the living area instead.

Mind racing, Hailey followed him there, sitting down on the sofa since he'd taken the chair. "Why are you here, Cayden? I thought you had other plans."

"Leanna had suggested we meet to discuss things we'd do differently or the same at next year's event while it was fresh on our minds. We finished early."

"It wasn't a date?" Happiness filled her. More than it should. Just because his plans with Leanna hadn't been a date didn't mean he was going to forgive and forget that Hailey had been too afraid to let him love her.

"I've not been on a date since with you. I have no interest in dating."

"Oh." Then, sucking in a deep breath and reminding herself that she would be okay no matter what happened, she bared her heart. "Me, either."

His brow lifted. "How are you going to experience all the things you've missed out on in life? The things you couldn't wait to experience?"

Hailey grimaced at the pain she'd caused him. If he'd give her the chance, she'd make it up to him. "I was wrong about what I had missed out on. Dating was never the life experience I was missing out on. Not really."

"No? You'll understand that I find that confusing since that was the reason you gave me for why we couldn't be together."

"Yes, I imagine you do find it confusing." But she was going to lower every wall around her heart and present it to him. Hopefully, since he'd came to her house, that meant all hope wasn't lost. "What I had been missing and never experienced was you, Cayden."

Shock registered on his face, and he swallowed. "Me?"

She nodded. "I gave a decade of my life to a man who was emotionally and mentally abusive. I allowed it to happen. I'd forgive him for doing me wrong, but it never stopped him from doing it again. Probably as a defensive mechanism, I convinced myself that I didn't want to be in a relationship again, that I wanted to be single and free. In reality, it was another relationship like the one I had with John that I didn't want."

"Understandably so." He stared directly into her eyes, making her feel very exposed.

"I know you didn't understand, probably could never

understand," she continued, "why I said the things I did on the night we made love." She refused to call it sex ever again. "How could you when you grew up in a loving home where you were always wanted? That wasn't my life. Between foster homes, John, and even with my adopted parents to some degree, I was never necessary." Sweat popped out on her skin and she walked to stand next to where he sat on the sofa. "I convinced myself that in my new life, I was enough, that I didn't need anyone to be complete."

His gaze didn't waver from hers. "You are enough, Hailey. You always were."

"I am," she agreed, kneeling beside him. "From the beginning, I recognized how different you were, Cayden. Just, everything about you. You were so handsome and wonderful that I never gave myself any confidence that you could truly be mine. I didn't think a makeover existed that would allow someone like you to fall for someone like me."

That's when it hit her that she'd washed away all the powders and creams, leaving her face as exposed as her heart. He'd seen her with smudged makeup that she'd replaced the moment she'd felt up to it when he'd taken care of her when she'd been sick. She fought the urge to cover her face with her hands as he studied her face. She needed to do this, to let him see her.

"You're beautiful, Hailey. With or without makeup."

His sincerity warmed her heart because, bless him, he meant what he'd said. She had to reveal everything to him, who she had been along with this new woman she had become and would continue to blossom as.

"You're seeing the makeup-less version that still has

lash and hair extensions and fillers. I'll be right back."
She went to her bedroom, got a box down from the top
of her closet. She carried it into the living room and set it
down on the coffee table. Her hands trembled as she lifted
the lid to reveal the contents of her former life. The last
photo she'd taken with her adoptive parents was on top
and her heart ached with missing them. They had loved
her and for that she'd forever be grateful. They'd given
her a home and family, even if it hadn't lasted nearly long
enough. She picked up the photo and handed it to Cayden.
"This is me. The real me who didn't believe you could
ever love her and so she convinced herself she didn't want
love or forever. The me who was so scared of what was
happening between us that I destroyed the most precious
gift I've ever known."

Still reeling that he'd driven to Hailey's rather than going
home, reeling at the things Hailey was saying when he'd
wondered if she'd even let him into her house, Cayden
took the photo, stared at the pretty young woman staring
back at him, and wondered what all the fuss was about.
Sure, Hailey's hair and lashes were different. Her lips
weren't as full, and her beautiful eyes were hidden behind
a thick pair of glasses. Reaching into the box, he pulled
out other photos, mostly school pictures which were never
the most flattering, but even with those, her beauty came
through. He glanced through the stack, coming across
only one that was of her and a man who must be her ex.

He tapped the photo. "How old are you here?"

Her gaze was glued to the photo. "Eighteen. I thought I
was the luckiest girl alive that John was interested in me.
I got rid of the other photos of us. There weren't many

considering how long we were together. I kept this one as a reminder that once upon a time, I thought he loved me and that I'd never be alone again. Clinging to that is what led to me staying in a bad relationship. I kept the picture to remind myself to never let anyone close enough to me for them to hurt me ever again."

He fought the urge to crumple the photo, but tossed it back into the box. "Maybe I should have kept pictures."

"It didn't work, anyway."

Knowing she meant him, Cayden flinched. "Hurting you in any way was never my intention."

She shook her head. "You didn't hurt me, Cayden. My holding on to the past that I came here to put behind me is what hurt me." She gave an ironic laugh and swiped at her watery eyes. "I changed my outer appearance because I wanted to be different. Sure, I was doing the therapy sessions, but I was still prisoner to the inner me who didn't feel lovable and so if I convinced myself I didn't want to be loved, then I could pretend my shiny new outer appearance was lovable."

He gestured to the photo. "You were never unlovable, Hailey. The woman in those photos is you and, of her, your lovability, I have no doubts."

Her smile was offset by her tears. "Thank you. You're the kindest person I know."

He snorted. "You think I'm being kind?" He shook his head and stood, bringing her up from where she'd knelt with him. He lifted her chin so he could look directly into her eyes. "Saying that you are lovable isn't me being kind. It's me telling you the truth."

More tears slid down her cheek and this time when she went to wipe them away, he caught her hand with his and laced their fingers. Bending, he kissed her wet cheek. "Don't cry, Hailey. I never want you to cry."

"I'm sorry, Cayden. About everything. I've messed everything up, haven't I?"

He shook his head. "The fake lashes and hair will eventually all fall out and you'll be back to yourself."

Confused, she stared at him. "That's not what I meant."

"Nor maybe what I should have said. I want you happy. I want you to look in the mirror and see the most beautiful, wonderful woman in the world. If those things help you to see what I see, then by all means, keep them. Do them for *you*, because they make you happy, but not because of your perception of anyone else's standards."

"I—okay. Now you sound like my therapist."

"What does your therapist say?"

"That I should use whatever tools necessary to rebuild my inner power and once I've rebuilt it, then I get to choose which tools I keep and which I toss aside."

"Smart therapist." He studied her, taking in every feature, every nuance of her face. "You embracing your inner power is going to a beautiful thing to behold, Hailey."

"I—when that happens, will you be a part of my life, Cayden? Not just at work, but in all of my life? I was wrong to push you away when all I really wanted was to hold you so tightly that you'd never leave. I've regretted doing so every moment since, no matter how much I tried to convince myself I'd done the right thing."

Hope had been building in Cayden from the moment she'd opened the front door and smiled at him. Hope that demolished the makeshift walls he'd put around his heart.

He could never defend his heart from her, not when she owned it.

"Haven't you figured it out yet, Hailey? I know how lovable you are because I love you. Completely, thoroughly, and to utter distraction. It's not anything about your outer appearance, but about what's in here." He lifted their laced hands to where he could press his finger to her heart, then grazed his knuckles across her temple. "And about what's in here. So much so that no matter how much I tried to keep my heart locked away, reminding myself of past betrayals, I fell for you anyway because you are unlike any person I have ever known. My heart knew that long before I acknowledged how I felt." He took a deep breath and looked straight into her eyes. "I love you, Hailey."

Hailey could barely believe what she was hearing. Was it even possible that he loved her?

"I didn't know." Staring at him in awe, she started over. "Maybe, I did know, Cayden. Because I felt safe with you, enough so that I told you things I'd never told anyone. Enough so that I showed you those photos and deep down, I knew it was okay to show you, that you wouldn't be repulsed."

"The only photo that did was the one with you next to the wrong man."

Happiness filling her, more than she'd once dreamed possible, she asked, "Are you the right man?"

"For you? You better believe it."

Wrapping her arms around him, Hailey hugged him, so grateful for the strong beat of his heart against her cheek. "I do."

"I should warn you that someday I'm going to want to hear you say those words to me again. We'll wait until you're ready, until you see forever in the way you've made me view it, but with you, Hailey, a lifetime will never be enough."

Hailey's heart might explode with joy from what she saw in his eyes. Love. Forever. That fidelity he'd mentioned. It was all there and more. She knew because all those things had to be shining back at him as he looked into her eyes. "Someday, I'd like to say those words to you again. You and you alone."

Then Cayden was kissing her, and all Hailey could think was that this must be what happy-ever-after felt like, because she was positive that was exactly what it was.

* * * * *

MEDICAL

Life and love in the world of modern medicine.

Available Next Month

Falling For The Single Mum Next Door Fiona McArthur
A Kiss Under The Northern Lights Susan Carlisle

....

Paramedic's Reunion In Paradise Alison Roberts
Healing The Baby Surgeon's Heart Tessa Scott

....

Hot Nights With The Arctic Doc Luana DaRosa
Nurse's Keralan Temptation Becky Wicks

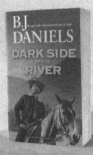

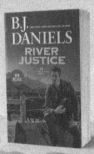

Subscribe and fall in love with a Mills & Boon series today!

You'll be among the first to read stories delivered to your door monthly and enjoy great savings.

WE SIMPLY LOVE ROMANCE

MILLS & BOON

JOIN US

Sign up to our newsletter to stay up to date with...

- Exclusive member discount codes
- Competitions
- New release book information
- All the latest news on your favourite authors

Plus...
get $10 off your first order.
What's not to love?

Sign up at **millsandboon.com.au/newsletter**